BOOK 1 OF THE LEGENDARY ARTIFACTS SERIES

# MAGI'S CURSE

## CHRISTOPHER J. HARRIS

# TABLE OF CONTENTS

# Prologue

As Fria, goddess of death, ice, and fate, waved her hand in front of the ice sculpture in her bedchamber, the mirrored surface clouded like frost on a window, then bled into a collage of reds, blues, purples, and blacks, before finally coalescing on the image of the burning city of Dalmarask. The god of lightning, Laevin, and his grandson, the god of fire and madness, Defurge, waged war over the city. Even though Laevin's bolts were focused on stopping Defurge, plenty of the citizens fell prey to errant discharges of electricity. Defurge's attacks were directed toward the city; as he beat his wings forward, waves of fire crashed against the city walls before he thrust his hands in the air and started to bring the very stars down upon the hapless capital.

This battle did not surprise Fria. With her ability to see the river of fate and the chance of any event occurring depending on any other event, she knew that eventually this would happen. Defurge would destroy one of the other gods' or goddesses' capital cities and cause so much devastation that it would force Laevin's hand. True, this was occurring several hundred years sooner than she had calculated, but that was always a possibility. A possibility that she had accounted for in her other plans.

After shielding himself from another of Defurge's attacks, Laevin finally closed enough distance to grab the smaller god by the collar and begin pummeling him with closed fists that sparked and cracked the air with each strike. Laevin would not kill Defurge. As Arbiter of the gods, Laevin had forbade such an action, but once subdued, Laevin would seal Defurge under the very city he destroyed, thinking that he would remain imprisoned for the rest of time. Of course, Fria knew that was foolish; in every branch of the river, Defurge eventually escaped. Normally that would have resulted in a small period of destruction, but after this battle, Laevin would see the folly in the gods and goddesses trying to shape humanity through direct intervention.

Fria wanted this. to finally leave mortals to their own devices and let them grow, live, and most importantly, to die for their own reasons. There was no other way to convince the dissenting members of the pantheon of the poetry in allowing mortals to choose their own paths. Although death was beautiful, a tear still rolled down Fria's frostbitten skin before freezing then sublimating into vapor.

Death was grand, the most unique part of life, because without death, life meant nothing. All of the other members of the pantheon focused on life and the varying aspects of it, but in the end, everything mortal learned of Fria's embrace. Only at death did their life mean anything. It gave finality and a conclusion to growth. Things that did not die, that just continued to grow, upset the delicate balance that life and death were required to entertain. Few of the pantheon could see that, and no one else besides herself really understood it. Even Chivas, her husband, tasked with cataloguing, judging, and sending souls into their next life, didn't really understand death. He understood that an end could lead to a new beginning, but he didn't feel the soul leaving the body, the confusion that everything was finally over, and the peace that came with knowing it was the end.

Still, death on this scale was not something that Fria enjoyed. There was no beauty in dying to a falling building or conflagration. These deaths, the meaningless haphazard products of destruction weren't worthy of mortals, and as long as the gods and goddesses continued to meddle in human affairs, deaths like these would be numerable. Fria had seen in the river of fate that if the pantheon were to leave the mortal realm, then these collateral deaths would decrease in frequency, and that was gorgeous. So, she put this plan into motion. A plan that sadly culminated in meaningless loss of life but would be only one of the handfuls of destructions that her plan would cause. Still, less poor deaths would result from her actions, than if she were to do nothing.

As Laevin finally subdued Defurge, punching him until the younger god lost consciousness, Fria snapped her hand closed, causing the image on the sculpture to dissipate. With another wave of her hand, the mirrored surface frosted over again, then swirled with blacks and blues before finally focusing on the image of Chivas' workshop. Chivas, god of souls and subterfuge, clad in a black suit with lacquered hair that made it look like the black foot of a crow was perched atop his head, sat at his work desk furiously writing in a ledger with a quill pen. Behind Chivas stood a multitude of cages with Ywaigwai—emissaries of the gods—caged within. Chivas had the largest collection of Ywaigwai, a chimera that growled in protest, a steel-scaled hydra that sat placidly, coiled in a ball, and many more, but there was one, his strongest creation, that circled its cage, frustrated.

Raithe paced, flying left and right, up and down. His long whiskers trailed down his serpentine body. He was truly something else, a creation that Chivas had never been able to replicate. Raithe's short, almost vestigial, arms and legs were tucked against his side. He was half-dragon and able to pass between the mortal realm and the realm of the souls at will. He eyed Fria mistrustingly. He was so dangerous; Chivas had never once used Raithe as anything other than a pretty bauble to be contained and admired.

"Husband," Fria addressed Chivas.

"I'm a little busy, Fria. There are thousands of souls dying up there. I have so many to sort that even I am having trouble keeping up." Chivas' hand blurred as he wrote furiously, categorizing the souls, judging them, and choosing how they would be resurrected in their new life.

"Defurge and Laevin are fighting in the city of Dalmarask," Fria replied.

With his other hand, the one that wasn't writing with, Chivas removed a pocket watch, flipped it open, then glanced at it. "This is way ahead of schedule, Fria."

"I know it is sooner than we expected, but our plans remain unchanged," Fria said.

"You told me we still had hundreds of years before Defurge and Laevin's final confrontation," Chivas said, absent-mindedly.

"I told you the probability of it happening in hundreds of years. There is no certainty in the river of fate. Every little obstacle causes the river to bend and change course."

"You don't need to tell me how fate works."

"Yet you still seem unable to grasp the concept of probability."

Chivas sighed and put down his quill; the deaths in Dalmarask must have been slowing. Maybe all the people were dead already. He did not shut his ledger, only put his quill back into a pot of midnight-black ink. "And what does the river of fate say now? Are our plans still in motion, or have we doomed the mortal world? Will our champions have time to release the god and then destroy him?"

"A little ahead of schedule, but nothing we can't recover from. I have already laid the groundwork and will make the final adjustments before Laevin decides we all must leave the mortal realm. And what about your part in this?"

Chivas sighed again, looked back at Raithe's cage and buried his head in his hands. "Tell me there's another way."

"I can't. All the paths require the same action on your part. Raithe must be freed so that he can create your champion."

"I should have never created him. He will wreak havoc on the world, maybe even more than Defurge. The number of mortals Raithe kills and tortures will be astronomical."

"But when he is done, when all the pieces are in place, the mortals will be free of our intervention. They will finally have the will to lead their own lives, make their own plans, prosper into something greater than they would be if the pantheon still remained and guided their hands."

"Please Fria, don't make me do this. Look again at the river, find another way."

Fria's voice grew fierce and sharp. "You will do this!" Chivas' shoulders slumped as he took his hands away and he looked instantly ragged and aged. "Release Raithe and tell him how to imbue sorcerers with the ability to cast all magics in exchange for their souls, so the Ywaigwai will be able to live absent the presence of the gods. Then release the other Ywaigwai and tell them the same. Give Raithe as much of a head start as you can muster. His magi need to be the strongest. I will sacrifice my eye and the ability to see fate to create the soul we will require for my champion. Once all the pieces are in place, we will bring them together."

# CHAPTER 1

## *399 Post Cataclysm*

*The following is a summary of my research into the gods, their history, and the events that led to the cataclysm. I have left out conjecture as much as possible, but since most information was written by human scholars, some questions remain ambiguous.*

*I will be using the current standardized dating system of Before Cataclysm (B.C.) and Post Cataclysm (P.C.), but it should be noted that the Cataclysm occurred in the third era of Marianna, Year 235.*

*—Issaroh, The History of Divinity, Part 1, 147 P.C.*

Captain Bronwyn Amyna stared down the three disrespectful recruits who had arrived that morning from the war over the Iron Bridge to the south—a three-day ride if the soldiers came directly. Their injuries—a limp, two amputated fingers, and partial blindness—were enough to see those of privileged birth could retire from the front line. Now it was up to her to make sure they were still of some use to her country in the guard corps of Emestria. Not a single one had risen to attention. They idly talked despite her presence. Captain Amyna cleared her throat but received no response.

"Ey, I thought they said the captain was supposed to come greet us?" asked a man with a bandage wrapped tightly over his left eye. He smiled wryly as he stared at Captain Amyna. Her icy blue eyes locked with his unbandaged one.

The morning's sun glinted off last night's snowfall and the assortment of armaments lining the perimeter of the training area. Arranged in orderly rows were mostly spears, shields, and halberds, but some swords and two heavy crossbows as well. The guard didn't use rifles, so none were provided for practice—black powder was much too expensive. Saltpeter mines had yet to be discovered in Emestria, if there were any. All of the mines discovered so far were in Tara, a nation far to the east.

Captain Amyna wasn't in the mood for defending her title today. As both the youngest and first female captain of the guard, her identity should be no mystery to these men. She turned and walked over to one of the shields leaning against a rack. She lifted a bulky tower shield and dragged it over to the chatty man. This particular shield's leather straps were purposefully loose, making it more difficult to hold. It was normally used as an example of why properly maintaining your equipment was so important. In addition, the curvature of the steel had been a prototype for a new shield configuration, but proved difficult to hold because of the vibrations being focused on the wielder rather than dispersed around them.

"Three strikes," Captain Amyna said, holding the shield toward him.

"What?" he asked.

"What, *Captain*," she corrected, then dropped the shield at his feet. "If you can withstand three strikes, then I will yield my position to you."

He laughed and a wide grin crossed his face. At six foot two, he was a good four inches taller than his new captain and outweighed her by at least fifty pounds. Using two hands the man raised the seven-foot sheet of steel and brought it down, sinking the three-inch spikes into the sandy ground to stabilize it. The other two recruits widened their distance.

Captain Amyna untied her hair from her ponytail. The straight golden tresses waited patiently on her pauldrons. She loved to feel the locks follow in her wake as she fought. With a single hand, she hefted her massive greatsword from its scabbard on her back and leveled the four-foot straight steel blade at the man, calling her shot. He leaned his body into the curvature of the shield and braced his feet against its weight.

Amyna took two steps forward, pivoted on her third and twisted, spurring the sword into its trajectory. The muscles of her arm and shoulder tightened, controlling the strike. The wind whistled behind it as it cut through the air. At the last second, Amyna curved the strike up, bringing the six-inch flat of her sword against the shield, not wanting to waste a honed edge on a lesson. She struck right above the shield's center, leveraging the shield's weight against the man.

The resounding clap of steel on steel echoed in the arena, startling some guards performing mid-morning training. The recruit's smile turned to shock as the shield's purchase in the ground gave way and the vibration shook his hold of the leather straps free. He faltered and stumbled backward, while trying to regain his grip.

Captain Amyna pushed forward, bringing more weight to bear, and brought her weapon back for a second strike. It wasn't needed. The recruit had lost his grip completely and stepped free of the massive steel slab, which now fell to the ground with such force that it provided more danger to him than protection. Her blade's point now hovered inches from his throat. Captain Amyna's steady grip prevented it from wavering or showing any sign of weakness.

"I yield," the recruit said under his breath.

"What was that?" Captain Amyna asked, not moving her sword.

"I yield," he repeated a little louder. "Captain," he added before she sheathed her weapon.

The demonstration had caught the attention of one of her lieutenants, who was training a half-dozen men on defensive stances. The woman now approached. Few of the women in the guard kept their hair long like their captain, and the lieutenant's closely cropped hair was completely hidden in her helmet. Only her frame and lack of a beard betrayed her gender.

"Lieutenant Jakul, put these three through basic. They need to relearn how to behave in front of their superiors."

"Wha … No!" the recruit interrupted, forgetting his lesson already. "I know magic. I shouldn't even be here. I should be in the noble guard's employ."

Captain Amyna turned. "Must not be from that great of a house if your father could not buy your way out of the war." The man's face turned beet red from anger, embarrassment, or most likely a combination of the two. "If the noble guard wanted you, they would have hired you, and you wouldn't be in front of me today."

"Captain?" The concern in Lieutenant Jakul's voice helped calm Captain Amyna's ire.

Squaring her shoulders, Captain Amyna addressed all three of the former soldiers, "This is not the army. Some of your skills will be transferable, but your job in the guard is to protect the people of this city. Tensions are high; the people are scared, cold, and hungry. If you march about town brandishing your weapons, acting like soldiers, you will only increase their misery. You are lucky to be chosen for the guard. Don't forget that. I expect all of you to treat the people with respect and dignity.

"Basic training for all three." The captain headed in the direction of the great hall as Jakul started to issue orders.

Bringing up the recruit's financial situation wasn't something Captain Amyna was proud of. She had let him anger her with his comment about magic. When she was awarded the position of captain of the guard, she was also afforded the right to study magic; a right normally only bestowed upon those of noble blood. After two years of rigorous study, she had failed to cast even the most basic of spells. Her failure was well known, and the implication in the man's comment didn't go unnoticed.

There was little food left when she arrived in the great hall. A half-dozen long wooden tables—able to accommodate up to twenty men each, but now empty—were neatly arranged in the middle of the building. Like most common buildings in Emestria, the walls were of thick wood, and the few windows were now shuttered to conserve heat. Mid-morning daylight seeped into the gap between the window and shutter. A large fireplace at the end of the hall provided the majority of the light, but several candles were still set up to illuminate the tables further from the fire.

As Captain Amyna approached the cauldron, still lingering next to the door of the kitchen, the pungent aroma of cabbage increased. The stew was utterly devoid of meat, and only a few vegetables were scattered at the bottom of the cauldron. She scooped up as much of the broth as possible. At least that would have some protein. Grabbing one of the stale pieces of bread that remained, she sat in the now-empty hall. Most of the guard would have eaten before morning practice. Despite her regimented lifestyle, Captain Amyna still indulged her habit of sleeping in whenever possible. She wasn't lazy, but handled her paperwork in the late evenings, when fewer interruptions would be expected.

"You know, if you came earlier, you wouldn't always be eating scraps," the surly old cook said as he carted the cauldron back to the kitchen.

"Well, you'd think the captain would be afforded the courtesy to have her meal set aside," she replied.

"Can't play favorites," he said, disappearing behind a door.

*Damn that man.* Previous captains had their meals served in their chambers, and she was well aware the practice only stopped when she achieved the rank. If he were one of the guards, she could have beaten him into submission. Of course, he was not, and she had yet to figure out a way to obtain leverage over him and have her meals set aside.

She had experienced other, similar insults that her predecessors never dealt with. Amyna had to pick her battles. There was a fine line between forcing compliance and fostering discontent.

After her meal, she decided to stroll down to the markets to search for more sustenance. Perhaps some fishers had stumbled upon a catch. Despite hating fish, she knew protein was protein. Her knee-high black leather boots echoed on the cobblestones as she walked through some of the poorer sections of Solstice, the capital of Emestria. Like the hall, the buildings were unpainted wood with clay-shingled roofs. Some of them lay in disarray, their doors either broken completely, or left ajar. It was a grim reminder of how many were dying in the war with Rouke, now approaching its second month.

Yellowed snow in one of the drainage ditches to the side of the road where someone had emptied a chamber pot this morning caught her attention. Thankfully, the snow that still lingered in the ditches covered up most of the offending odors. During renewal and planting season, ice melting from the mountains would help keep these ditches clear. Citizens were supposed to use the outhouses, situated far from wells, but at night and in the glacial season they often resorted to the centuries-old habit of chamber pots.

Fewer doors were broken as she approached the market district, and a few women tended their front-steps, brushing away the light dusting of snowfall received last night. Most of the buildings were domiciles with stalls outside to sell their wares, mostly produce. Some were shops which supported tradesmen: cobblers, blacksmiths, leatherworkers, and the like. Without their usual trade, the market merchants had shut down one storefront right after the other—the streets were barren of relief. The ground had frozen solid and there was no produce. Nothing was open. No one was staffing any stalls. She would go hungry this morning.

Some kids played in an alley, but upon closer inspection, it was not a game. They chased after rats, trying to swat them with pieces of wood. Captain Amyna told herself that they were helping their parents keep the vermin under control or letting off steam, taking their frustrations out on the pests. She had heard the stories, though. Her people resorted to eating rats and mice to stay alive. If the kids were lucky enough to catch one, they would at least have some food in their bellies today. She shuddered at the thought.

Home to hard winters and long nights, Emestria bred people who were tougher than most, their strength and speed unrivaled. This advantage was part of the reason they weren't well-liked in the continent, Primerra. Emestria included the northern most landmass of the continent, and Solstice and Porton were located on an island only connected to the rest of Primerra by a large iron bridge. Emestrians mostly kept to themselves; they bothered little with what the rest of the world thought of them. However, this year that toughness was being pushed to the breaking point. No stranger to conflict, Emestria had embroiled itself in a war against its neighbor, the country of Rouke.

In previous years, even during the glacial season, the capital did not want for food. A stockpile of grain, root vegetables, and fish would have been prepared to feed them through the long nights. But their enemy had strategically planned an offensive right before the harvest. Rouke formed a blockade on the Iron Bridge's southern gate and seized the farmland and villages, now cut off from Solstice. Without access to the Iron Bridge, there was no way to replenish supplies. During this time of year, the waters surrounding Emestria became infested with ice floes that threatened to demolish any boat foolhardy enough to brave them.

This wasn't the first time Emestria found itself fighting Rouke. Fifteen years ago, Rouke and Tara had tried to claim one of Emestria's territories, Lynnfield. The two nations were allied at the time, but relations between Tara and Rouke had soured since then. Tara had signed non-aggression pacts with both Rouke and Emestria after the war and dissolved their treaty with Rouke. The war only ended when Rouke deployed an apocalyptic weapon, some sort of ultimate magic, that not only wiped out most of Emestria's army at the time, but made the entire region of Lynnfield inhospitable to life. Rouke must have deployed the weapon early, or not understood it's power when they did, because many of their soldiers, along with Tara's, had been killed. Which was probably why Rouke never used the weapon again.

The citizens of Emestria were on half rations, hoping to last until the renewal season when they would be able to resume normal trade or maybe enlist the help of friendly nations. Corinth could still be considered an ally, and the non-aggression pact with Tara meant they would still trade if they could get around the Roukian blockade of the Iron Bridge. If not for the Emestrian's tenacity, they would have surrendered long ago. Instead, they would slowly starve through a bitter glacial season rather than submit to their aggressors.

Emestria had nowhere near the wealth of Tara—who exported precious gems, metals, and saltpeter from their mines, but the emperor of Tara had a fondness for the iron mined in Emestria. Only that iron could be forged into Emestrian steel, a feat the Taran smiths had yet to replicate. King Bryant had gifted the emperor four hundred pounds of Emestrian steel in the negotiation of the non-aggression pact between the two countries five years ago. The steel wasn't required for rifles or cannons, but it allowed a more accurate shot.

Amyna's hate for Rouke filled her belly, and she had forgotten about food by the time she returned to her chambers. A hundred years ago, Rouke was nothing more than city-states that spent most of their time fighting amongst each other. But then they created a centralized confederacy and turned their sights on the lands held by other nations. Emestria had tried to negotiate a non-aggression pact with Rouke after they destroyed Lynnfield, but Rouke refused to take responsibility and actually expected Emestria to surrender more land to the burgeoning nation of Rouke in exchange for the pact.

A large stone building next to the training arena served as the barracks, but Captain Amyna instead headed to a smaller offshoot of the building. As captain, she was afforded a private room instead of group housing. The room was small, a few feet between the bed and the walls on all sides, with a small table in one corner that served as a makeshift desk since her meals weren't served in her quarters. But it did have a washroom with a tub. Water could be heated in the fireplace, which Amyna now stoked with an iron rod. She kept the fire burning throughout the colder months, and the room smelled of burnt maple and smoke.

Captain Amyna removed her armor, the pauldrons and breastplate affixed via straps to her padded leathers. Previous captains wore full plate, but she needed her armor light and supple so she could move with ease, dodging in and out of combat. She had to be lithe, nimble, and clever since she didn't command the magics others did. After every humiliating defeat, she had trained harder, until it didn't matter how many spells her opponent cast because she would close the distance before the first rune of her adversary's magic materialized. If she struck before the runes were complete, the spell would be interrupted.

Captain Amyna's shoulders slumped as she saw the new papers on her desk. A report of the war, along with what she dreaded most, requests for more of the guards she commanded to join the conflict. The guard corps had run out of volunteers long ago, and although she did her best to select men without families, she would likely have to start sending those with older children to serve in the war. With a sigh, the captain sat at her desk and started to review the papers. The general, who commanded the army, was requesting twenty-four men. She would not only lose those men, but would also need to increase the number of guards that served double shifts to replace the army conscripts.

The captain took her files of the men currently serving in the guard corps and started to put check marks next to those that she would consider conscripting into the war. She rubbed her temple with each new mark as she went through the list. Thirty men were identified to serve, and she went through the list a second time, circling those that she thought had the best chance of surviving or wouldn't leave too many fatherless children.

A tap at her door startled Amyna. The benefits to living in the captain's chambers could occasionally be outweighed by annoyances. Three hot meals a day versus cold stone floors. Privacy in a room barely big enough to maneuver in. A warm crackling fire and chambermaids knocking on your door to put more firewood in, even though you damn well know how to.

"Go away," Amyna said.

"But miss," the chambermaid replied.

"I can feed my lousy fire, and it's Captain."

"Yes, miss ... Captain, but you have a summons from the castle."

"Leave it at the door," Amyna groaned.

"It's important."

"So is my bloody privacy." Captain Amyna stormed the scant few feet to the door and opened it with a heavy hand. The maid proffered a single page of paper to her. She averted her eyes, unwilling to meet the captain's gaze. Captain Amyna snatched the note and read it.

"Oh, bloody Chivas, lord of lies." Amyna walked back to the fire and tossed the paper in along with a couple of logs. The maid didn't leave but remained standing in the doorway, perhaps waiting for a reply.

"You've delivered your note. I'll leave when I'm ready." Captain Amyna stoked the fire again.

"Yes, Captain." The maid pulled the door closed slowly. It did not make much of a sound when the latch reengaged.

"General Tiernan," Amyna grumbled. She began the process of re-donning her armor, latching the straps back on the padded leathers that lay over her white shirt. *Any real general would not be summoning me to his war room. He would be on the front lines, with his men, risking his life. Instead, he's calling on me to likely to request even more men from the guard to the army. To discuss a war that I'm not even allowed to fight in because I'm a woman.*

General Tiernan had protested her appointment as captain, despite her winning the tournament affording her the rank. It was only when King Bryant himself had supported her claim that the general acquiesced. The king's involvement did little to quiet the rumors nobles spread that she achieved her rank by whispering sweet words into the right ears.

Despite having no personal relationship with her king, she did love him—as all loyal subjects should. The invincible hero King Bryant was one of the few survivors of the catastrophe at Lynnfield. Her father had fought and died in that war, and she now carried a sword similar to his as a remembrance.

When King Bryant's brother had passed, the people secretly rejoiced that such a noble man would now lead their nation to greatness. That goodwill was squandered through the bickering and money lending of the nobles. The mighty nation of Emestria now stood on the precipice of disaster.

Captain Amyna grabbed a thick green cloak for warmth and wrapped it around her body as she left her room. The quickest way to the castle from here was through the nobles' quarters. She debated going around. What would be more depressing: seeing the poverty her people struggled with or the luxury those with means enjoyed? Despite the war, the nobles still hoarded their wealth, entertaining delusions of buying their way into the good graces of Rouke when the country fell. *Their houses will be the first to be pillaged, and all their machinations will be for naught.*

Private guards were stationed at the gates of the nobles' quarters. One of the liberties of captain—yet to be stripped away—was the privilege of taking the shortcut through this part of Solstice. She stood in front of the guards, and they made no movement to unbar the gate until she parted her cloak, displaying the stamped insignia of claws and horns on her breastplate. She quickly covered the steel back up, ashamed of how it shone, having never seen war.

Even the streets of the nobles' quarters seemed devoid of life. Expansive mansions of brick and glass windows were set apart from the paved street with wrought iron fences and gates. Plumes of gray smoke puffed skyward from their chimneys. During the renewal season, fragrant flowers blossomed in their well-manicured garden. The monarchy did not hold balls to curry the nobles' favor any longer, being too poor to do so.

There was little for the nobles to do aside from reading their books, acting out their plays, and lounging about indulging in gluttony.

Captain Amyna revealed her armor again to be allowed admittance to the castle, but once inside, she was able to travel unhindered. The carpets that once adorned the stairs had been sold long ago, along with the rugs that covered the cold stone in the great halls. The barren fortress was pitiful. It was dark as well; to conserve oil and wax, only a portion of the lamps were lit. Before the ports froze shut, the monarchy was obliged to spend most of its money trying to purchase food.

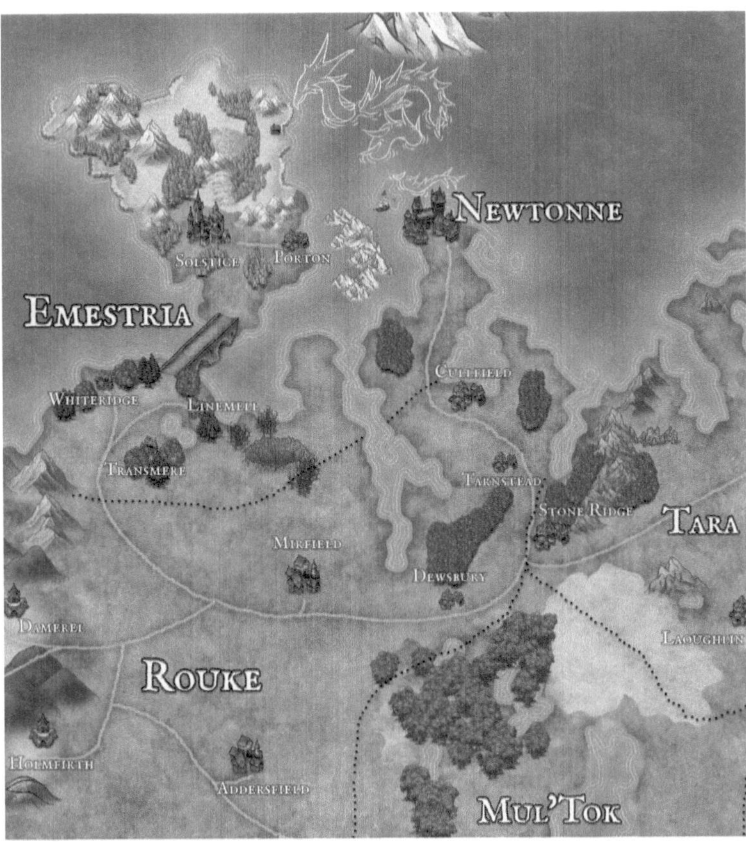


As she approached the war room, the guards barring entry allowed her passage. Golden light illuminated the hallway as the doors opened.

The scent of lavender, linseed oil, and a slight hint of mold wafted from the room. A large ornate table carved with the topography of Northern Primerra dominated the space. Bookcases along the walls were littered with maps, scrolls, treatises on war, and tomes about military strategy. Inside the room she saw the leathery face of the general, the frail features of the advisor, and, to Amyna's surprise, the king. She knelt with such force her knee slammed into the floor.

"Your Majesty," she greeted him, averting her gaze, putting a closed right fist over her chest, and bowing her head as low as she could in a kneeling position.

"Please stand. You can't guard your king if you're always on your knees." King Bryant said before widening his eyes in surprise, likely now aware of the implication. This caused the general to guffaw and the gold-spectacled advisor to snicker. They were quickly silenced as the king frowned, narrowed his eyes, and shot them a disapproving glare. He cleared his throat and Captain Amyna rose.

King Bryant, the youngest of the heads of state in Primerra at the age of forty-two, was only seventeen years the captain's senior, but his hair had grayed after assuming rule, and now his face was wrinkled and leathery with the stress of the current war with Rouke.

The doors behind Captain Amyna closed, and she noticed two soldiers in the corner. A woman stood between them—bloodied and bruised. Her wavy, light-red hair came down to her jawline. It was damp with sweat and clung to her round face. Her lip was split, and the skin of her face yellowed from not-yet-healed bruises. She was exceptionally short, maybe only four and a half feet tall.

"With a heavy heart I lay bare the state of our nation," King Bryant said. "Our coffers are nearly empty, the people are starving, and our rations are running out. We will be lucky to survive the winter at this rate, even if we hold our ground at the Iron Bridge. These are not secrets. The citizens have been whispering them for months. Morale is starting to falter and I'm afraid if things don't change soon, this war will be lost."

"Yes, milord," Captain Amyna agreed quietly.

"But we have been blessed with a chance at our salvation. Do you know of the Legendary Artifacts, Captain Amyna?"

"Old wives' tales and myths, from what I understand," Captain Amyna responded with disdain. *This is not the time to be entertaining such whims.*

"Yes, so I thought as well; items of such immeasurable power that whoever possessed them would inspire armies and conquer the world." The king paused and took a book the advisor had been holding. Two scraps of leather sandwiched irregularly sized cotton pages. The book looked out of place compared to the weighty tomes against the far wall.

"There is a scholar." King Bryant placed the book on the table. *An End to War* was written in sloppy cursive on the cover. "He has been researching them for some time. He believes that if one ruler could obtain enough artifacts, that country could stop all conflict between nations. With artifacts like these, no enemy would dare oppose Emestria.

"He has cataloged where he thinks they now reside, lost to time," the king continued. "I thought it was merely a naïve dream, but if you found one, that would be proof that the others likely exist. Please, General Tiernan, fill her in on the rest. I'm needed elsewhere." The king walked past Captain Amyna and out of the room.

"Bronwyn—" General Tiernan started.

"Captain Amyna," she replied, correcting him.

"Captain, most of these items are rumored to be scattered across the globe, hidden in various tombs, ruins, and hoarded by powerful beasts. However, we recently intercepted a spy—"

"I'm not a spy," the woman in the back of the room interrupted before one of the soldiers bludgeoned her, and she fell to her knees. Captain Amyna gripped her sword hilt and turned to face the soldier, a private in the army—not one of her men. Still, he shrank under her stare. Only the lanterns dared a hiss as they waited to see what she would do. She couldn't stand them hitting a defenseless prisoner, even if she were a spy. Captain Amyna, satisfied that her point had been made, removed her hand from her weapon and looked back to the general. The men breathed a collective sigh.

General Tiernan continued, "We intercepted a spy that revealed information: one of these relics resides within our borders. In exchange for her life, she agreed to guide us to it. We have formed a small expedition. You're to lead them into the White North to collect this *scholar*," he said with disdain, "and retrieve the artifact. This spy refused to impart the location, despite our best efforts at convincing her. It's in the mountains to the northwest, but finding the way into the tomb requires navigating a maze of tunnels that this spy claims to be able to do. We have assembled supplies and horses, and they're awaiting your presence before departure. Gather what you need, but be quick. Time is of the essence."

"Sir, why am I being selected for this command? Surely there is a more suitable candidate."

The general massaged his temples and sighed. "Captain, despite our differences, your men respect you and will follow your lead. You have always put the best interest of the nation above your own, and I trust you will continue to do this."

Tiernan turned his attention to the soldiers with their prisoner. "Take this filth out of my sight. Bind her and deliver her to the expedition."

The men started to roughly escort the prisoner from the room. The woman winced and hobbled, and the soldiers had to practically carry her out.

As the doors shut, the general resumed speaking: "This spy and the scholar you are recruiting are enemies of the kingdom. If at any time you believe they are acting against the best interests of Emestria, cut them down and leave them to freeze in the cold. You're dismissed." The general turned his attention back to the table and began discussing battle plans with the king's advisor.

Before exiting the castle, Captain Amyna heard a meek, "Excuse me." She turned to see a maid quickly running up to her. It was curious that she would be addressed by one of the king's attendants. "Our liege asked me to deliver this to you." The maid handed her a folded parchment with the royal seal; Captain Amyna's name was written in elegant calligraphy. She waited until she exited the castle to open and read what it said.

*Captain Amyna, I have personally chosen you for this task because you are one of the last people who genuinely believes in me and this nation. It is not an easy one and I did not decide on asking you to do this lightly. The man you're seeking is in exile on the North Shore, beyond the tundra. He goes by the name Miro Krestel, but it would not surprise me if he did not go by that name any longer. He will be reluctant to help, but he saved my life in Lynnfield. Hopefully, he'll agree to assist you.*

The captain tucked the piece of paper between her leathers and breastplate. Krestel was the name of an influential, noble family. They commanded most of the logging rights in northern Emestria, even some north of Solstice, but to Amyna's knowledge logging on those lands stopped after the Battle of Lynnfield. It was odd that they would still have a member of their house residing north of Solstice, and she had never heard of an estate, let alone any type of lodgings in the White North. *With a spy and a spoiled noble, this will not be a pleasant expedition.*

Captain Amyna always believed in traveling light and did not need to gather anything for the expedition, aside from what she took with her that morning. But she stopped by her room to collect the papers dictating which men were to be sent to the war, and delivered them to Lieutenant Jakul, who would most likely assume the captain's duties in Amyna's absence.

She made her way to the northern gate, where the troops were stationed. There were eight horses, two of them lashed to a single wagon. A half dozen men lazed about, making jokes and otherwise commiserating. They were some of the worst men she commanded. Capable fighters, but cocky, headstrong, and prone to insubordination. She wondered what they had been promised to accompany her on what she was now thinking was a suicide mission. If King Bryant himself had not asked her to do this, she would swear it was a ploy to send her to her death.

The White North was inhabited by all sorts of perils that were waiting to snap one up. Wolves as big as horses, leopards hell-bent on destruction, and sudden snowstorms were all things she worried she would have to contend with. The expedition would head to the northeast and follow the coast up. The air was colder, but they could avoid most of the forests that were so thick it was easy to lose yourself in them.

Captain Amyna mounted the best-looking horse and then called back at the men, "Mount up, we ride." They milled about for a minute or two before finally climbing atop their steeds. One of them commanded the wagon and it lurched forward. Captain Amyna peered into the back to inventory what they had been provided: tents, rations, weapons, and a single rifle. Enough gunpowder for two shots. Not extravagant, but it would serve them well. Curled on the wagon's floor, on a blanket was the spy—gagged, bound, and looking to be unconscious. *Good,* she thought. *I will not have to worry about her running for a while.*

# Chapter 2

*I have classified the gods into three different waves of divinity. First, the greater gods, being those that came into existence and shaped the world: Laevin, Marianna, Chivas, and Kyrie. Second, the full-god siblings: Fria and Seraph, born of Laevin and Kyrie. It was at this point in time that civilization became more structured under the pantheon's guidance. Third, the lesser gods, were those born after written records of civilization: Lau'O'Penake, Defurge, and Ramun.*

*—Issaroh, The History of Divinity, Part II*

The covered wagon started to move, or it had been moving. Clara wasn't sure. The bustle of a crowded town was replaced by the hum of the northern winds, which snaked their way under the canvas, chilling Clara as she tried to huddle under the blanket. Fresh pine needles helped block out the stench that her body exuded for the last couple of unwashed weeks.

As Clara's body ached with every little rock they rolled over, she reminisced on how she had gotten into this particular predicament. A gods-damned whale had knocked her, her men, and passengers out of their boat. Whales had no business being north this time of year. The fish migration had happened over two months ago, traveling south to warmer waters, and the Emestrian fisherfolk were enjoying their well-deserved time off.

She had managed to get herself atop a nearby ice floe, saving herself from the fate her crew and passengers succumbed to, freezing in the water or becoming a late-night snack for something dwelling beneath the waves.

She thought her luck had continued when she had been spotted by a patrol boat—Emestrian's defending their borders from possible Rouke incursions. She was surprised to be taken prisoner. It was only after noticing the squid-ink she religiously applied to her hair had washed off in the water that she understood what was happening. Emestrians either had trouble—or didn't care—that her light-rose hair wasn't the same as the fiery locks of Rouke. The torture started almost immediately. They tried to get her to admit to being a spy.

Which of course, she wasn't. She was a smuggler. Smuggling used to be a gray crime, punished by a stay in the dungeons, seizure of the goods transported, and eventual deportation. Since the war, that had changed. Emestrians' normal xenophobia was even worse now that they were at war, and she had paid the price for that.

She had endured the punches and snapping of her fingers before they finally broke her ankle. It became evident to her then there was no way out of the situation; they would break her body until she died of infection or internal blood loss, so she told them she was a spy. It was a lie, but at that point she wanted a quick death. It wasn't her first time undergoing enhanced interrogation, just her first time in an Emestrian dungeon. Emestrian torturers were unique in that they didn't heal the bones after they broke them. They wanted her to know that she would never be able to walk or hold anything properly again.

Her last gambit, of telling them about the Legendary Artifact within their borders—Alcide's Mantle—managed to save her life. She didn't really know how to find it, just its rough location, in the mountains to the northwest. Now she would probably die anyway. Even if they managed to recover it, there was no guarantee that she wouldn't end up dangling from a rope by her neck. She had to take the chance so she could see Scarlette, her daughter, again.

"Did you see her hair?" a guard asked outside of the wagon.

"Yes, they say she's a Roukian spy," a second voice responded.

"Supposed to know where we're going," the first guard said. "Although, I heard she's keeping our final destination secret."

"Give me thirty minutes with her; I'll find out what she knows, among other things," the second said. Both men uttered low, guttural, cruel laughs. The implication wasn't lost on Clara, and the knot in her stomach began to grow.

"Shut your traps before I come back there and break your jaws." The voice of the woman from that bright room cut through the banter. Clara breathed a tentative sigh of relief as the men stopped talking after their admonishment. The rhythmic thumping of the horses and the squeaking of the wagon wheels permeated the quiet stillness for the next couple of miles.

Another guard rode up to the front of the wagon and asked the driver, "Hey, what do you say I give you half my bonus and you look the other way tonight?" His voice was low but still loud enough for Clara to overhear.

"Bron…um, Captain Amyna will kill you if she hears you talk like that," the first guard warned.

"Even she has to sleep."

"A little two-for-one special?" the wagoner asked.

"Sure, why the Chivas not. I'll give you half too," the first guard agreed.

Clara sobbed. She endured so much pain and humiliation. All she wanted was to survive, but now she wanted to die. If death came seeking her, she would not beg this time. Hopefully in the next life, Scarlette would understand.

Clara dug her nails hard into her palms. The decades-old habit helped to push back the emotional pain and concentrate on the physical. She had developed the habit when Scarlette first got sick with blood poisoning. The habit was cemented after she had lost her daughter.

"Hold up." The woman's voice interrupted the conversation from far away. The wagon stopped moving, and the sound of the horse's hooves diminished. A single horse approached the wagon and the back panel opened. The blonde woman held her hand down to Clara.

"Untie her," she commanded. The wagoner went into the back where Clara was and tugged on her gag and bindings until they came loose.

"Get up," she said to Clara. Clara did her best to stand. One of the men dismounted and the driver of the wagon roughly pulled her to her feet. After the wagoner lowered the gated back, both men forced her out. With the help of the two men, the woman practically lifted Clara with one hand. She winced as she maneuvered her arms around the woman and legs around the horse, coming to rest uncomfortably behind the saddle.

"Hand me my wrap," the woman told the wagoner.

He dug around for a bit and tossed her a thick fur. She positioned the blanket over Clara, wrapping it around her. Clara blinked, the white snow reflecting the afternoon sunlight. It had been so long since she had been outside. She spent weeks, maybe more, in the dungeons of Emestria.

"I will personally be seeing to the health and well-being of this prisoner," the captain seethed at the surrounding men. "Our journey is entirely dependent on her arriving at the mountain healthy. She has been guaranteed her life by the king himself, if we find what we're looking for. I don't need her to be desperate for escape and freezing in the cold." The woman got the horse moving again and Clara almost lost her balance.

"Hold the saddle or you're going to tumble," she said to Clara. Her voice was commanding, but not laced with hate like the others. It was a small consolation, but a least this woman seemed to understand Clara was integral to this mission.

"I can't." Clara held out her hands, which resembled deformed claws at this point. The woman looked down at Clara's broken fingers.

The golden-haired woman grumbled a little but she grabbed Clara's hands and put them around her lightly armored waist. "Can you hold on like that?"

"I think so," Clara replied. The woman, these mens' commanding officer, spurred her horse; she and Clara moved to the front of the formation.

"Move!" the woman called out and the caravan continued on its way. "If you cooperate, then no harm will come to you," she said as Clara forced a sniffle.

Clara wished and hoped it would be true with every fiber of her being. Trusting an Emestrian again was not a liberty she could afford. But her captor's hair was blonde. Perhaps she wasn't Emestrian. Blonde hair was common in Corinth, and Clara had never met an Emestrian with hair the color of the sun. Whether she was or not, Clara's survival now hinged on this woman. There had to be a way to guarantee that protection.

They traveled along a sparse forest. Signs of logging were present; Emestria was rife with large coniferous trees, one of their few exports. Faint birdsong pierced the stillness, but next to the noise of the men and horses, the surrounding landscape was eerily silent. Only when a clop of melting snow slid off a branch did their environment seem to make any noise. Clara preferred the way the ocean smelled, like salt, fish, and seaweed.

The discomfort on the horse's back paled in comparison to the agony Clara felt inside the wagon. At least the animal knew well enough to avoid the stones jutting from the snow. Still, every bounce of the horse sent searing pain up her leg. She debated stifling a wince, but figured that it would be better to be seen as injured and helpless. But she was warm; it had been so long since she was warm. Clara had thought her blood had been replaced by ice after that night on the ocean. The numbing cold made the pain in her frozen hands wane.

She buried her body inside the fur and against this woman who she would convince to protect her. She had been in the room when they called Clara a spy and hit her. Would the captain keep Clara safe now? When she was hit, the captain hadn't intervened.

"Thank you," Clara said in a soft, timid voice. She spoke so gently she thought her voice was inaudible.

"It's my responsibility."

Clara was surprised that this woman heard the meek gratitude through the sounds of the horses, men, and wind.

"Your name's Bron?" Clara asked in the same faint whisper.

"Captain Amyna." The woman nudged the horse into a faster pace. "Make haste men, there is a clearing in the distance. I want to make camp before nightfall."

Clara gritted her teeth as a sharp stab of pain radiated up her thigh from the horse's canter, but the thought of being able to rest made the pain bearable. She made a mental note to always refer to this woman as Captain or Captain Amyna.

Once they reached the location of the camp, Captain Amyna began issuing orders, causing the men to hustle about. "Dirk, Claude, I want you collecting wood. We need to keep the fire burning. Rustle up some game while you're out there. Chauvin, Lance, start pitching my tent. Cormac, sort out the wagon and prepare supplies for dinner. We need something hot to keep our spirits up. I also want some pine needles for tea. Gilbert, pitch the other tents. Chauvin and Lance will help you when they're done with mine. By the book, people—I want this campsite cozy and homelike by the time I return."

Clara had never seen a woman command the way Captain Amyna did. Sure, Clara led her own smuggling operations, but jobs were agreed upon by all the crew, not given with absolute authority. This captain had the liberty of issuing orders and getting instant compliance, which would have been nice when Clara proposed dangerous operations. However, based on the conversation the other guards had, even Captain Amyna's leadership had its limits.

The captain rode the horse around the camp in ever-increasing circles, winding through the trees that now started to grow thicker. Now and then the captain would stop, dismount, examine something she saw here or there, and remount. When the light of day started to slip behind the mountains, they headed back to the other men.

What had been a flat blanket of snow was now completely transformed. Four tents were erected in a small circle, one bigger than all the others, but not by much. A large fire blazed in the middle. Steam and the pungent aroma of boiled meat came from a pot suspended over the fire.

The horses had been tied to some trees outside the camp, with blankets draped over their backsides. The captain led her horse to the rest.

Captain Amyna dismounted. "Lance, remove my saddle and secure my steed." She turned to the still-mounted Clara.

"We walk from here, your ladyship," the captain said.

*Is she trying to make a joke? Can't she see I'm in no mood for a joke?* Clara debated laughing to appease her but decided otherwise. It was more important to foster the persona of the scared woman in captivity. Laughing would ruin the illusion.

"I can't." Clara had not tried putting her full weight down on her foot yet, but she was sure from the pain she would collapse the minute she did.

The captain walked back up to the horse. "Which one? Both?"

"My right." Clara cast a glance toward the injured leg. The captain helped support her as she got down. She picked Clara up and cradled her like one would carry a bride across the threshold.

"You'll be fed and allowed to rest. With your injuries I doubt running will be possible, so bindings may not be necessary. You understand that even if you were to run you would not get far in this weather. Alone you'd be easy prey for the wolves that hunt these lands. The White North is not a place you should underestimate.

"Make some room, men," Amyna barked as she approached the fire. She set Clara down and started to remove her right boot.

The pain Clara experienced when the boot was put on was almost as bad as the captain now undoing the laces. Clara previously avoided looking at her misshapen limb, but in the light, she saw the deep blue and purple markings around the protrusion on her ankle.

"By Laevin's beard, If I don't do something, you risk further injury," Amyna said, her face turning white. "I need a splint, some seapo root, and someone make her a walking stick. And get me some gods-dammned alcohol. I know one of you lot smuggled some on this trip. The last thing I need is hungover guardsmen if trouble comes looking." The camp erupted in a flurry of activity. Amyna lightly put Clara's boot back on to support the break and hoisted her up. "Open my tent."

Once inside, Amyna laid Clara down among some furs. One of the men came by a short while later with a wineskin. Captain Amyna took a swig before pouring some into a cup. "Drink this, then we'll set your leg."

"I used to be a smuggler," Clara replied. "It's going to take a lot more than this," as she drank the unfamiliar alcohol. She used to be a smuggler. If she survived, she would be a penniless vagrant, spending her nights drunk in a ditch. Was this more or less booze than she would receive as a beggar?

"Drink the whole thing then. You'll want it for the pain." Captain Amyna tossed Clara the wineskin.

Clara sat up and first drank the alcohol in the cup before starting to guzzle from the sheep leather. It burned and she coughed from the strong vapors. She'd never had a bone re-set before, but she was sure the pain would be greater than when it broke.

"I'd hope that my men would never torture someone like that," the captain lamented as she peered out at the gathered guards. "But desperate times make for desperate people."

"It sounded like your men would be willing to do a lot worse," Clara said angrily, the alcohol already loosening her tongue. It was the good stuff.

"I heard. I do not know what this country is coming to. We used to be good people." One of the men came over and handed the captain a couple of bowls of stew before scurrying off.

"They ended up catching a rabbit, so there should be some good meat in there." Amyna handed Clara one of the bowls along with a spoon.

Clara attempted to pick the wooden utensil up. It was like balancing a hammer on her finger. Every overcorrection sent the soup sloshing onto the furs. Cradling the bowl between her misshapen fingers, she slurped at the food like an animal. Her lips still stung from when the torturer's had punched her face. Amyna looked back at her with a mix of disdain and pity.

It was one of the few solid meals Clara had eaten in the last couple of weeks. She cared little for the captain's approval of how she ate. *Her* people did this to her, made her an animal. The captain came over, knelt beside her, and started to feed Clara the stew with the spoon. Clara paused but forced another sniffle as she swallowed the nourishing mouthfuls.

After Clara finished eating, one of the other men brought a couple of pieces of wood and a branch fashioned into a walking stick. Captain Amyna set the walking stick next to Clara and lowered herself to the leg. The captain removed the boot and ripped two strips of fabric from Clara's oversized tunic.

"This is going to hurt," Captain Amyna said, handing Clara the spoon. "If I do this, you might never be able to walk without a crutch. But you'll never be able to walk if I don't. Are you ready?" She waited for Clara to nod. "Bite down."

Clara bit down on the spoon and closed her eyes. Captain Amyna placed the wood pieces against Clara's skin, one branch on each side of the leg, the fabric draped over the shin, and then came the pull. Bone crunched and her eyes watered as the captain tied the splint tighter. Clara tried not to, but she cried. But she would not break, not again, not like in the dungeons. There had been no hope of freedom in the dark stone confines, but now she at least had a chance. She closed her eyes, squeezing tears out. Clara thought, *I'm ruined, cursed to the gutter for the rest of my existence.*

The captain sighed and went back to her post at the opening of the tent. A little while later they brought her a steaming mug. She blew on it and knelt beside Clara. Supporting Clara's back, she helped her sit up.

"Drink this. It will help with the pain." She saved Clara the embarrassment of fumbling the cup between her defective hands. As Clara lowered her bottom jaw, Amyna tipped the mug, allowing her to sip the tea brewed from seapo root. It was sour, but warm. After Clara finished the last of it, the captain helped her lie back down.

"Is the artifact real? Or is this a ploy to buy yourself more time?" Captain Amyna asked after a quarter hour.

"Honestly, I don't know. I was told it is real, but I have no idea how to find it. My mother always said the mountain will show you the way." The less information the captain knew, the longer she would need to protect Clara. She held her hands in front of her face. The alcohol blurred the edges and obscured the unnatural twists. They didn't look horrible any longer. "Do we have more booze?"

"I think you've had enough. What's your name?" Amyna took off her armor.

"Clara."

"Are you a spy?" Amyna asked.

Clara concentrated so her words wouldn't slur. "Just a smuggler with some dumb luck. Your military found me after my ship was disabled. They spent weeks trying to get me to admit to being a spy. It wasn't until they broke my ankle that I gave in." She blinked as Captain Amyna became two blurry versions of herself. The bitter, acrid root tea numbed her tongue. The sudden onslaught of dizziness caused the room to slowly tilt. It wasn't just the alcohol that was causing the change in perception. Whenever she shifted her head, it took the room an extra second to stop moving.

Amyna paused, and looked at Clara, her demeanor softening. "You don't have a Roukian accent. Where are you from?"

Clara replied, "Newtonne." Although that wasn't where she was born or raised, Newtonne was still home to Clara. Newtonne was a trading hub to the East. Clara had originally traveled there to participate in legitimate trading, but found herself involved in piracy and smuggling. They were more profitable than regular trade operations.

Amyna nodded. "A pirate and a smuggler … still doesn't make you a spy." She paused, likely debating her next words. "What were you smuggling?"

"Food in, money and people out."

"I've heard rumors of some of the guard stationed in Porton ignoring, and even helping, those in your … line of work. I don't approve of their actions, but I understand their motivations. The people of Emestria that wish to leave should be allowed an avenue to do so, and for that you have my gratitude. However, the food you bring should be given to the people, not sold to the nobles who can afford your high prices." Amyna stared at the others gathered around the campfire before tying the opening of the tent closed. Double knots, very tight, so they could not be undone from the outside.

When they had money, Clara had helped some escape, but the captain didn't need to know that. "How about, return some of that gratitude and help me get out of here? If you can help me get to Porton, I have money and connections to travel home," Clara said under her breath, so only the captain would hear. Amyna slightly shook her head as she looked at Clara. Clara sighed softly and added, "I can get you out too; you don't belong here."

"I'm sorry, but this is my home and if there is an opportunity to save it—regardless of how slim—I'm going to take that chance. Help us find this artifact and then you can go home."

Clara silently cursed herself. It was too soon to try, but the debt of gratitude gave her false hope. "And what if we don't find it?" Clara asked. Amyna did not reply. "What if something happens to you? You've heard what three of your men were willing to do while your back was turned. What if you're not around at all?"

Before Captain Amyna could answer, a voice from beside the fire said, "So, I guess the captain decided to keep her for herself."

Clara could tell they were trying to be quiet, but the voice carried anyway. Clara never understood why people didn't realize that if voices could travel through thin walls why a tent's canvas would muffle the sound. Clara's eyes pleaded with her captor.

"Hold your tongues or I'll cut them out and you'll never be able to please your wives again," Amyna shouted at the huddled shadows on the tent's canvas.

"That won't happen," Captain Amyna told Clara with confidence. Emestrians were so headstrong, they believed themselves invincible and infallible. *It might be for the best if they lose this war*, Clara thought. Rouke or Emestria, what did it really matter who controlled what lands? The nations that had at one point in time claimed to have patron gods or goddesses were so headstrong about where their borders extended.

That's what happened to Lynnfield. Emestria claimed it was part of their original kingdom. The people of Lynnfield, where Clara was born, didn't want to be part of Emestria, or Tara, or Rouke. They should have been left to their own devices.

Captain Amyna pulled the furs out from under herself and laid them atop Clara. "You need these more than me," she said before curling herself up in her cloak.

Clara quietly sobbed, overcome by the danger, pain, and compassion.

"If anyone opens that tent beside me, you scream as loud as you can." It was the last thing Captain Amyna said to her that night.

# CHAPTER 3

*Fria, goddess of ice, death, and fate, was the first born of the two full-god siblings. Also called The Vigilant Eye, she was able to see the river of fate and determine the probability for any given event to happen.*

*—Issaroh, The History of Divinity, Part VII*

Captain Amyna woke to Clara's panicked screams. She whipped her body around, grabbing her greatsword, snarling in a feral stance. Someone was at the tent's entrance. They fumbled with the toggles of the tie.

"Captain, Captain, you must come quick," Claude called from outside.

"Quiet," Captain Amyna said to the scared Clara. Captain Amyna's muscles were stiff and sore from sleeping on the frozen ground.

"It's one of the horses, it's gone," Claude cried.

Captain Amyna rose and shouted, "Back off, I'll untie it."

She started to undo the knots she had made the night before on the tent flap cords. To the trained eye they were easy enough, but from the outside one would not know how she had tied them. Wearing only her leathers and cloak, she stepped outside. The cold air blew in with an intense hatred of the tent's heat.

"Nobody in or out until I come back, you hear!" she commanded Claude at the tent's entrance. "In or out!" she reiterated.

Captain Amyna glanced back at Clara. The woman pulled the furs around her and was staring at Claude. He averted his gaze when Clara looked at him, turned his back, and held his spear at a slant in front of the open flap.

He wasn't one of the three who conspired yesterday. *Clara didn't care, they were all the same to her, but does that matter?* Captain Amyna thought, *The girl has a point: What if something does happen to me?* She rethought her plan to press forward. She would be publicly embarrassed to return and request replacement guards. She would be thought incompetent in her leadership. Would she let her ego and ambition put this prisoner in danger? Captain Amyna headed for the other men, unsure what she should do.

"What the Chivas is this bloody ruckus about?" Captain Amyna asked as she strode toward the men huddled about where the horses were tied. The camp was situated next to the forest proper—to the north— with some trees bordering the other three cardinal directions. The forest wasn't so thick that vision was obscured immediately to the north, and the other directions were so sparse that one could easily see for hundreds of yards. Something she noted that she hadn't seen the day before was some of the trees had been damaged during the night. It was too regular to be from last night's storm.

All guards were accounted for. Next, she searched for tracks. A slew of red drops stained the nearby snow—too big to be a cut. She kicked some snow over the spot, obscuring the evidence. Panicked men would be too much trouble.

"Back off," she said, clearing a way through them.

"The binding snapped in two. Didn't even make a sound," Chauvin said.

"The Great White Beast," Lance exclaimed.

Captain Amyna took stock of the scene. One of the ropes was broken and the horse was nowhere to be found. Judging by the bloodied snow, something had attacked. She gratefully assumed last night's heavy snowfall was obscuring any tracks. She did not need a bunch of scared men telling ghost stories.

"Did anyone see or hear anything?" Amyna yelled. *How was a horse attacked and even I didn't wake?*

"No, Captain," Chauvin replied.

"Any footprints, any blood, anything?" Amyna pressed. These guardsmen hadn't been in the employ of the corps long enough to learn to properly assess a scene. They spent their days guarding ration carts, doing little but looking official.

"No, ma'am."

For once, the captain was glad they had missed something. Normally she would have berated them for missing a detail such as blood, but they were probably scared enough as it was. "Well, someone must have not inspected the ropes when they tied up their horse. Who was on shift when this happened?"

After a pause, when no one else provided confirmation or refutation, Dirk spoke up. "I don't know, she was here when we last checked and was gone in the morning."

"So, you're telling me none of you men bothered to check the horses during the night?" Captain Amyna yelled back at them.

They were quiet.

"This is why we double-check the ropes and the animals, gods damn it. So that one of them doesn't bolt at night. Now some poor guard at the castle is going to lose sleep when our horse returns with no rider." *Yell more. Scare them into being more scared of you than what could be out there.* "Next time one of you scabs messes up, I'll beat you within an inch of your life and you'll be pulling the wagon instead of the horses," their captain threatened, whipping around to look at the men. Stories about the horrors of the White North were well known.

"Pack this camp up; we're heading to the coast," the captain shouted. "We've lost enough time with all your lollygagging." The coast would be half-day's ride to the east. It wasn't the shortest route. She had hoped to skirt the forest longer, but she needed them away from whatever attacked. If they lost a horse every night, they'd lose the wagon and have to travel on foot.

While backtracking to her tent, she surveyed the area again to confirm what she saw that the others had missed. Two trees eight feet apart, all their branches under fifteen feet snapped in the same direction.

She ordered her subordinates back at camp, telling them to pick this up faster, to pack those tents correctly. Keep their eyes off the young lass. After a while they began joking, laughing off their jitters. At one point, Lance mentioned the White Beast again.

"White Beast? More like the great dumb idiot that can't tie a knot," Captain Amyna roared in false laughter. "Someone was dropped on their head as a babe." This of course caused all the other men to mimic her sentiments about Lance, and relax into a more jovial mood. *Now they will not just have to put up with my taunts but all their comrades if they spread ghost stories about giant cats.*

Clara sat by the dwindling campfire as the others packed. Captain Amyna got her horse and rode up next to Clara. She extended a hand, helping Clara back onto the horse. She dropped her walking stick and Claude picked it up, securing it to the horse's saddle bag. Wrapping her arms around the captain, Clara leaned against Amyna's back. Captain Amyna motioned for Claude to bring a fur over.

"Now I'm going to try to find that damn mare. You lot finish packing up camp and head northeast. I want to make it to the coast by nightfall. We'll travel north along the cliffs and breathe some good sea air. Maybe we'll even catch a fish or two when we rest tonight. Lance, you ride in the wagon. You're the scrawniest of the bunch so it shouldn't slow us down."

Hopefully, these men weren't aware of how much she hated fish; her real motivation was to get away from the forest to get a better view of their surroundings.

Captain Amyna led the horse away from camp and headed for the damaged trees, with their snapped branches. She made sure she was far enough away before dismounting to search for signs of what caused the broken branches. Hopefully her captive was smart enough or too scared to try anything stupid, but Captain Amyna held on to the reins just in case.

Clara leaned over and threw up. She wiped her mouth before saying to her jailor and protector, "I'm sorry, I guess I'm hungover. Usually, I can handle my liquor."

"Root tea numbs the pain but comes back up in the morning. You'll feel better after a couple of hours." *In addition to loosening the tongue.*

Captain Amyna knelt and examined the snow underneath one of the evergreens. The top branches of the tree were intact, but anything below fifteen or twenty feet was broken. She pushed some felled boughs on the ground aside to see if they were concealing any tracks. *Nothing, so that rules out something that walked or ran. More damaged trees in the distance, and the branches are all broken at the same height. So, if it was a bird, it could have descended into the forest, flown perpendicular to the underbrush, then grabbed the horse and swooped up? Are there birds large enough to lift a horse in Emestria? Rocs—large hawks rumored to live in the desert—were able to hoist an elephant, but nothing like that up here. A giant owl? An owl would have flown silently. I don't know of anything like that, and its wings would have blown the tents and put out the fire.* Bronwyn hated mysteries; she was never good at solving them.

"We're not looking for the horse, are we?" Clara asked.

"If we make the coast before nightfall, the lost horse shouldn't slow us too much." *Outside of the trees, we'll have a better line of sight. That will give us time to prepare a defense. If we're lucky it won't hunt us once we're out of its territory. I don't think we're in any danger, it seems content to pick off a horse. It will just slow us down.* Captain Amyna turned and remounted. "Let's head back to the others, make sure we're keeping a steady pace."

Captain Amyna snapped the reins, but the horse refused to move; the animal snorting and stomping its hooves. She snapped them again and it reluctantly trotted forward. The low bellowing chortle that followed shook the ground and startled them and their horse. Captain Amyna and Clara almost lost their balance when the mount broke into a gallop. Then a deafening roar caused the snow to shake from the laden pines. Captain Amyna snapped the reins again, pushing her steed as fast as possible. Behind her, thick branches in the distance noisily cracked as the lumbering monster charged.

# CHAPTER 4

*Seraph was the goddess of life and love. She took the most mortal lovers—the only other god that came close was Laevin—but she only sired two progeny, the twins Defurge and Lau'O'Penake. Seraph was able to change her appearance but seemed to be restricted to human forms. It is believed that a similar ability was passed on to her child Defurge.*

*—Issaroh, The History of Divinity, Part VIII*

The trees crashed as the giant snow leopard charged them—there were ear-shattering roars and snapping pines, but the creature's footsteps did not make a sound. The beast was at least twenty-five feet long with a ten-foot tail that waved deftly behind it, allowing the feline to change direction almost instantly. It disappeared into the forest as it ran, its white pelt and black spots blending well with the snow and dappled shadows, reappearing right behind them. Trees and branches crashed as it leaped alongside.

Captain Amyna snapped the reins again, but the horse was starting to tire. The tree line ended to their left, revealing a barren plain ahead. It would make a good place to stage a defense. She spied her men in the distance. Perhaps together they would stand a chance. The animal disappeared into the forest again.

Captain Amyna yelled at her men. "Form a line, it's com—"

The leopard crashed through the trees, cutting her off. The horse faltered, throwing her and Clara to the ground. Captain Amyna sprang to her feet and ran toward the ferocious beast, snow flinging into the air with each step. Her feet struggled for traction against the layer of ice underneath last night's snowstorm, but her momentum kept her moving forward.

The leopard lunged at a couple of horses and pawed at Claude, sending him into a thick pine, and crushed Lance underneath its massive furry forelimb. Chauvin dashed for the trees, but the leopard bit into him, mangling mount and rider. His body fell to the ground when it reopened its jaws. Dirk hid behind the wagon and was crushed underneath it as the leopard pounced, knocking it over and splintering it.

More than half the men were dead in minutes. If Amyna got close enough to subdue the beast, they would have a chance at survival. Once in range, she dropped to her knees, sliding along the ice underneath the gargantuan animal. She swiped up with her greatsword, ripping into the flesh of its underbelly. Blood seeped from the wound. Her remaining men stopped in their tracks, frozen in fear.

"It bleeds," she yelled, skating to the other side of the massive thing. "If it bleeds, it can die."

The leopard swiped at her, and she jumped back, slicing at its paw as she did. The sword raked against the eight-inch claws.

***

Clara tried to hobble away as fast as she could. The direction did not matter, as long as she put as much distance between herself and the monster as possible. Her splint helped with the first dozen steps, but she then collapsed under the weight of her body. Then she scrabbled along the ground, the ice slicing into her hands as she went.

So this is how she would die, as a snack to some giant cat. She should have jumped in the water and let the serpents eat her. She would end up in the belly of something anyway. Clara gave up hope and lay down in the snow. The pain was too much to move any longer. Closing her eyes, she waited for the monster to finish her off.

She whispered, "I'm sorry, Scarlette." Clara had endured so much, with the hope that she could escape, to visit her estranged daughter for her birthday, like she had done every year. She wasn't supposed to; Clara had surrendered Scarlette to her father. The cruelest bargain she was ever forced to make—give up your rights as mother so your child can live.

She balled her right fist, fingernails finding the cuts from the ice, but it didn't hurt, not really. All she could feel was pressure. Everything was numb. She knew that numbness wouldn't continue as the giant cat bit her in half.

Screams of men and the sound of battle assaulted Clara's ears. Something lifted her into the air, and she thought, *This is the end. The leopard has me.*

She was surprised when she was flung onto the back of something. Captain Amyna. She came back for her. They were going to escape.

Clara opened her eyes to see the antlers of a reindeer. How did Amyna find a reindeer?

She wrapped her arms around the captain so she would not fall, but the familiar cold metal of the breastplate was absent. And the cloak was a different color, a bright royal blue. This was someone else. The hood from his cloak was down. He had shoulder-length brown hair and a thick, wooly beard with snow and ice clinging to the wiry whiskers. They were heading in the wrong direction, toward the monster.

"You're going the wrong way," Clara shrieked.

"I make this bargain with Fria, goddess of ice, death and fate, the Vigilant Eye, Fragma Frios!" he screamed as he traced runes with his right hand. Two light-blue circles punctuated with unintelligible markings appeared before his outstretched arm, then faded away. The ground groaned before a powerful crack echoed off the landscape. Sheets of ice forced themselves from the ground and scraped against each other, forming a thick, semitranslucent barrier between Amyna and the leopard.

***

As a wall of ice formed between the captain and the leopard, the cat slammed headfirst into the giant barrier. Another sharp, ear-splitting snap as a fissure ran up the frozen surface; however, the wall did not break. Magic? Amyna took her opportunity and began running to the edge of the structure, hopeful that the impact dulled some of the animal's senses.

As she ran, she could make out a blurry brownish and blue shape obscured and distorted by the frozen water. Had this been the person to cast the magic? Did one of her men know how to cast? How? She saw them all die. Did Clara know magic? The beast bellowed at the advancing shape. Whomever it was would soon learn the limits of magic.

"You have to stop, Naani; you can't do this!" she heard an unfamiliar voice yell.

The leopard yowled and growled in protest. Amyna was almost to the edge of the wall.

"I can help her, Naani," he insisted. "You have to stop!"

Amyna took stock of her surroundings as she rounded the corner. She breathed a tentative sigh of relief. Her prisoner was alive, on a reindeer. Now there was a man walking toward the creature, yelling at it. But it seemed distracted. She could use his folly and sacrifice to her advantage. Running as fast as her boots allowed her in the snow and ice, she held her sword to her side, lining it up for a strike on the creature's flank. As she readied for the swing, the monster darted its head in her direction and swiped hard with its paw against her breastplate. The steel groaned as the edges dug into her chest and she found herself airborne, landing several feet away with a thud on the powdery ground.

Amyna tried to get back on her feet, but she could hardly breathe. The air had been knocked from her body. She tried forcing air in, so she could at least defend herself after the creature killed this man. But it didn't attack—it continued growling at the stranger loudly, but did not advance.

"Because you're yelling at me!" he shouted, and the leopard's body relaxed. Then he approached the creature, calmly, without fear.

Her body ached for oxygen. Her heart thumped loudly in her ears, her limbs weakening. But her eyes were transfixed on the man and beast.

The cat roared and the stranger didn't even flinch. "I'm sorry, Naani. Let me see what I can do," he said as the leopard held out its paw like a dog would to shake. The fur was wet with the blood Captain Amyna had drawn.

"Seraph, Goddess of Life and Love, lend me your blessings, Ligos Medus."

A single green circle bordered with runes descended onto the creature's paw as the man put his hands on top of it. The runes snaked away from the circle and seeped into the wound, the green light staining both its sides. Tendrils of energy reached across the wound and pulled the skin back together. Then, the magic faded, and the man turned his back on the creature and walked back to the reindeer.

Captain Amyna looked about for the second magic user. The ability to form a wall of ice and heal wounds were from different schools of magic. She saw no one else, and found herself having difficulty concentrating. Her vision was narrowing from the adrenaline her body was forcing through her system to keep her conscious.

"Does that woman mean you any harm?" he asked Clara, pointing at Captain Amyna.

"No," Clara answered, but then stopped abruptly and didn't explain further.

"Okay, let's sort this all out. I'm Miro." He surveyed the battlefield. The bodies of Captain Amyna's men were strewn about, the red blood that used to sustain them now freezing against the ice and snow. Their horses fared no better.

"Naani, go fetch my sleigh," he called out to the leopard.

It growled lowly in response before leaving in the direction Miro had come from.

Miro walked toward the captain, who was kneeling in the snow. She tried to forcefully push the cold air in and out of her lungs. As he knelt beside her, she gripped her sword tightly and raised her hand, keeping it between this stranger and herself. He gently pushed the hand to the side.

"I need to examine the damage that has been done," he said, ignoring the defensive stance and detaching the breastplate from her tunic.

She tried to keep his hands away from her, but her labored breathing sapped her strength. Her eyes had trouble focusing; she might be concussed as well. He reached under her shirt, touching her stomach. She attempted to lift her greatsword to defend herself, but her arms failed her again.

Miro whispered some quiet words and traced lines above her chest with his other hand. The faint green circle moved over her body, wrapping around her. She breathed deeply, finally able to easily suck in the frozen air. Rising to her feet, she stepped back, a snarl on her lips. She leveled her sword at Miro.

"You have internal bleeding," he told her sternly. "Some of your ribs are broken. I need to bring you back to my cabin where I have some herbs, so I can cast proper healing magic. If you kill me now, you'll die out here. Why don't you wait until after I've healed you to decide whether to kill me?"

"My men," she said as soon as she could manage the words. "Help them."

He looked down and slightly shook his head. "I'm sorry, they're already gone." He sighed. The corners of his mouth turned down and he averted his gaze. "No magic is strong enough to bring them back once they've left."

"It's because of you and that beast," Captain Amyna hissed between her teeth as he put an arm under her, preventing her from falling back to her knees.

"Yes, it is," he responded, his voice flat.

Miro helped her limp back to the reindeer where Clara was still mounted. He was slightly shorter than Captain Amyna and struggled to support her adequately. If he was Emestrian, he wasn't full blooded. He lacked the girth of an Emestrian man. But she still sensed some of the Emestrian strength in his arms. Captain Amyna leaned against the reindeer, still unable to keep her footing without assistance.

Miro gathered the bodies, pulling them through the snow and lining them up neatly in a row. Six people's families were one member shorter because she failed.

Soon the great cat came galloping back, pulling a sleigh with its teeth, the sleigh teetering and twisting, spilling items as it did.

"Naani, carefully," Miro said as he continued to arrange the men. The leopard slowed to a graceful stroll and dropped the sleigh's reins when it approached the reindeer. While the reindeer didn't flinch or startle in the presence of the leopard that dwarfed it, Bronwyn's knuckles whitened as she gripped her sword's hilt.

"Naani, come over here and help me." The leopard traipsed over to Miro, seemingly carefree and unbothered by the carnage. "I need six holes. Make them big enough for these people."

The giant cat started to dig into the ice and snow, flinging the frozen earth at Clara and Captain Amyna. "The other way, Naani," Miro said.

The beast dug the graves two at a time. Once completed, Miro maneuvered the bodies into the depressions. He tried to be dignified and did not roll them in, but he had trouble lifting the men and they ended up being roughly lowered into their final resting places. He had not bothered removing their chain shirts, helmets, or leather breeches. After depositing the bodies, the leopard pushed dirt over, filling the holes. Miro placed a single stone over each mound of fresh earth and approached the reindeer.

"I'm sorry I had to take care of that now," he said. "If we left them out, they would have been scavenged."

He turned his attention back to the leopard. "Naani, you can have the horses as your offering. Take your time but come see me when you're done so I can heal the rest of your wounds."

To Captain Amyna's dismay, the leopard immediately started to feast on the carcasses of their mounts. Miro helped Clara off the reindeer. The splint was gone, and she seemed in worse pain than when she had the leg set. With Miro providing support, she hopped on one foot over to the sleigh. Captain Amyna walked slowly after them.

Clara sat up front and started pestering Miro with questions as soon as he put the reindeer into its harness. "You talk to animals?"

"Sure, you can't?" he asked, finishing hitching the reindeer to the sleigh. A peculiar reply. Clara and Amyna raised their eyebrows at each other.

"No. What does he say?" Clara asked.

"She said she's protecting you." Miro hopped up into the sleigh himself, sitting in the front, next to Clara.

"Protecting us?" Amyna snapped. She gestured around her. The battlefield was littered with broken weapons, graves were the only hint her men had been here aside from their bloodstains, the wagon was shattered and their supplies likely destroyed, and a giant cat was feasting on their dead mounts. "She attacked us, unprovoked."

"She wasn't trying to protect *you*, just this one," he said to Amyna, pointing to Clara. "She thinks you were hurting her."

"I'm Clara. Why was she trying to protect me?"

"She had a special relationship with the priests of Lynnfield. She was their guardian," Miro said, his voice trailing off.

"I'm not a priest," Clara replied.

"One of your parents then?"

"My father," she gasped. "How did you know?"

"The gift of light rose-colored hair is given only to the priests—and their descendants. After they came of age, they in turn would be trained in the priesthood. But I guess that tradition doesn't exist anymore."

"I was young when my father left. That was before the war. My mother and I went to stay with an aunt." Clara's sudden ease around him bothered Amyna.

"I'm sorry about your father and Lynnfield," Miro said as he hitched the reindeer to the sleigh.

"Thanks, I guess. I don't really remember it."

"Lynnfield was a beautiful town. Filled with wonderful people. In the spring, blanketed in flowers. Harvest time was especially pleasant. They grew these juicy red apples. I've never tasted any as sweet as the ones grown in Lynnfield."

"You've been there?" Clara asked as her eyes widened. "Before the war?"

"I was. I stationed in Lynnfield after my training at the academy. Every year the priests would make their pilgrimage to the mountain. They would bring bushels of apples and other foods as an offering to Naani, and in return she would protect them; the White North is no place for people."

Captain Amyna interjected, "Well, there are no more pilgrimages, so that thing should be put down. It murdered six of my men in less than a minute."

"You may be right, but she's the last of the spirit cats that I know of. I couldn't be the one that ended their tenure in our world. If, however, you want to go back to Emestria and organize an army to hunt her, I won't stand in your way. But know this: she will fight back, and many more will lose their lives. From my understanding, Emestria can't afford a war on two fronts." Miro pressed his hand against his chest, massaging it. "It would be better to let her time come and for her to pass in peace. I don't know how old she is or how old a spirit leopard can live, but I sense her aura is draining."

"How does she move without making a sound?" Captain Amyna asked, dismissing his comment about Emestria's military.

"As a spirit leopard, she has many tricks, like moving while making no sounds, or putting people to sleep with her purr. Her furry paws do well in concealing her tracks. All the spirit animals had abilities. Although I don't know if any besides Naani even reside in our world now."

"Can we hurry this up?" Captain Amyna complained, her breathing strained. "I don't want to be out here come nightfall, or if that cat decides it's still hungry after the horses."

"Have it your way," Miro said as he snapped the reins, causing the reindeer to strain against the weight of the extra passengers as it started to pull the sleigh along the snow.

# CHAPTER 5

*In discussing divinity, it is important to acknowledge the three other divine beings, the spirit guardians, Ywaigwai, and demigods. Demigods were simply the product of gods mating with mortals, and not necessarily always humans. An island in Selunia with very large and broad children lays claim that Marianna once mated with a sea giant and that their people can trace their lineage back to them. A similar claim is made in Emestria in regard to their patron goddess, Fria.*

*—Issaroh, The History of Divinity, Part XII*

They traveled all day until they came upon a log house. The square building had at least two shuttered windows, one barely visible on the east-facing wall. A narrow porch wrapped around the entrance to the eastern side. Large pine trees—too thick put to one's arms around—bordered the house on the north and west. To the east, a cliff abruptly dropped off. Judging by the diminishing sounds of crashing waves and ice jostling together, they had been increasing in elevation the further north they traveled, and the distance between the coastline and the water below had gradually increased. Signs of animal life were more present here, Amyna catching glimpses of rabbits, foxes, and squirrels in increasing frequency. Miro got out of the sleigh first and helped Captain Amyna to her feet.

"I'll be back for you in a bit, Clara," he said as he swung one of Captain Amyna's arms over his shoulder.

Captain Bronwyn Amyna hated having to rely on someone else, but she was too tired, and her breathing had become labored again. Miro got her inside his cottage and headed back out for Clara.

Captain Amyna scowled as she looked about his home. The quaint cottage's air was thick with dust and mildew from old tomes. Hundreds of books littered the abode, at least a dozen or two opened. Dishes were haphazardly stacked in a washing basin. A few half-charred logs occupied the fireplace and thick layers of dust caked most surfaces.

Clara came in soon afterward and Miro helped her into a seat near the table. He cleared the books off the table roughly with a sweep of his hand, and they flopped to the floor, causing clouds of detritus to inundate the stale air. Captain Amyna waved a hand in front of her face, trying to dismiss the dust.

"Now hop up, so I can examine your wounds." Miro took Amyna's hand, helped her onto the table, and motioned for her to lie down. He started to roll her tunic up.

"Unhand me." She pushed him away with considerable force, knocking him to the ground.

Undeterred, he stood back up. "I only want to take a look at your ribs, determine which ones are broken. Don't worry, I'll leave your dignity intact."

Captain Amyna liked him less now because of the condescending way he talked to her and his reference to her dignity. She acquiesced, but only because she had little choice this far away from Emestria, and let him roll her tunic up below her breasts.

"Does this hurt?" he said, tenderly pushing down on one of her ribs. Captain Amyna winced. "You suffered two fractures to your left rib cage."

"Really? I could have told you they were broken," Amyna said, sitting up.

Miro frowned. "Lie back down. I'm going to make a poultice." He went to the corner of the room that served as a kitchen, only a few steps away from the table. He picked up several jars and inspected the contents, putting some back down and placing contents from others in his mortar. Lastly, he poured some type of viscous liquid in and started to grind everything together with a pestle. Once he had sufficiently pulverized the ingredients, he brought the concoction over to Captain Amyna. He rubbed it on her ribs as gently as possible. This made Amyna quite uncomfortable—she rarely got seriously hurt and was never treated by men.

Captain Amyna expected the poultice to reek; they usually did. Instead, it smelled of lavender. *Does lavender grow this far north? How does he find lavender? Does he trade wood or fish with traveling merchants? Would a merchant even sail this far north?* It made little sense. Nothing in this place made any sense. How did one get so many books being so far away from civilization?

"I'm trying to be gentle, but it needs to be over the break." Miro began massaging the compound into her skin. She steadied her breathing, ignoring the ache. She had broken bones in her arm and foot previously, but that did not require rubbing plant matter over the fracture. They were set and allowed to heal naturally. Amyna had heard of magic that could mend broken bones, but was under the impression it was rather costly. When Miro stopped kneading, he held both hands above her rib cage and chanted.

"Seraph, Goddess of Life and Love, lend us your hand, mend what was shattered, and make it new, Lagos Medus." He traced small circles in the air as he did this.

At first, the runes were barely visible to Bronwyn's eye. They glowed bright green before dimming. As she looked at her ribs, the poultice now briefly glowed with the same color the runes held. She gasped as the pressure in her torso disappeared. She breathed in without pain, and tried sitting up.

"Hold on," Miro said, firmly pushing her back down to the table. "You'll need to let the herbs work for a half hour or so. When you can put your hand on the area without discomfort, they've done their job.

"Now let's see that leg," Miro said, addressing Clara. "Go ahead and take your boot off." Clara shrugged and presented her traumatized hands. Miro gazed sadly upon them.

"How old are those breaks?" he said, concern in his voice.

"Maybe a week, probably two, hard to tell." Miro's face soured more at Clara's words.

"Did you spend some time in the Emestrian dungeons?" Miro asked and Clara nodded in reply, causing Miro to shake his head. "I stayed there for a while as well. I guess old habits die hard. When will they learn? I might be able to do something about those, but moderate your expectations. Once the bones start to heal, I can't mend them properly."

"What about breaking them again, first?" Clara asked.

A smuggler's livelihood depended on her hands. Captain Amyna didn't know if Clara would want to return to that work. This experience might have demonstrated all too well the dangers of the trade.

"Possibly, but let's try without breaking them first."

Miro came over to Clara and undid the boot, then rolled her pant leg up. The leg was purple and bruised from the ankle to her upper thigh. It resembled something that had floated in the sea for a couple of days, something dead, bloated, and gory. He spread the poultice on the ankle first. Clara drew in sharp breaths between clenched teeth. After her leg, he moved to her hands, rubbing the gloppy mixture over her palms and fingers. Captain Amyna noticed the way Clara stared at her fingers hopefully and felt a weight in her chest more painful than the broken bones. Then Clara shot Amyna an excited glance. The fingers didn't look any different to Amyna, but she was across the room; maybe they changed a little. Or possibly, Clara's hope was so desperate she wanted them to look different.

"I'm going to put a pot of stew on," Miro said, turning to the kitchen to start making the meal. "It's salty—nothing out here except sea serpents and the occasional eel, but meaty and high in calcium if you eat the bones. Perhaps you two would like to tell me what you're doing this far north?"

"We're looking for someone," Clara blurted out. Captain Amyna glared at her, dismayed that Clara would share so much information with a stranger so quickly.

"I'm sorry," he said glumly. "If they are out here, they're likely gone by now. Even if they had stayed on Naani's good side, there are worse things in the tundra. In the morning I'll take you as close as I can to the capital. You'll have to walk the rest of the way." He paused. "If you can tell me what they look like, I can let you know if I found them. That's what I do most days. Luckily for you, I go looking to see if anyone has decided to try and venture north. When I find them, I bury them to give them dignity in the next life."

"He's supposed to have been living out here for years," Amyna said. "Perchance, the other with you?"

"There was no one out there with me—"

"The one that cast the ice wall," Bronwyn said, cutting him off.

"Oh, that was me," he said, flashing a less-than-charming smile.

"Don't lie," Captain Amyna challenged. "You used healing arcana, so someone else must have used the Frian discipline." After the battle, she was still recovering from hitting her head in the snow. It wasn't until now that she remembered about the use of two different types of magic. The fight with Naani was clear in her head, but the details afterwards were a bit fuzzy, and she still felt a little dazed from Naani's strike. She had been overwhelmed by her pain and the failed state of her expedition. So much so that her initial thoughts about two sorcerers had been forgotten.

Even though she never learned how to use magic, she studied extensively. She had to know what her opponents were casting, so she could rush in or dodge before they finished the spell. Each sorcerer practiced a single school of magic, and someone couldn't learn the spells of a second. Some spells even had identical runes, and which school you were proficient in dictated the nature of the spell. To Amyna's advantage, the glowing light of each school was different, otherwise trying to read the magic during a spell would be impossible.

"He did," Clara interjected, still staring at her hands. "I saw him cast it from the reindeer."

"How is that possible?" Amyna wondered aloud.

"Some of us can cast magic from multiple schools," Miro explained.

Captain Amyna could not believe what he said. This man was probably younger than her, but he spoke with this air of authority that belied his age.

"Who is us?" Clara asked.

"The magi," Miro replied offhandedly.

"Are you acquainted with King Bryant?" Amyna asked.

"You mean Bryant the betrayer?" he snapped, before regaining his composure. "Yes, I knew him."

"He sent us up here, to find Miro Krestel, I think ... " Amyna said. This man was at least fifteen years Bryant's junior. How could the king owe his life to a child? How dare he call her king the betrayer? He was one of the few noble people left in this world, but she did not press the point. She would need Miro's help in finding these artifacts if they did exist.

"I am not a Krestel. Return to Emestria and tell him I won't fight in his damned war, and I don't appreciate his tricks." Miro slammed the pot shut as he shouted his refusal.

"People are dying," Amyna shouted back. "Children eat rats because they have nothing else to fill their bellies, and you won't lift a finger to help." This was not why she ventured north, but she could not imagine someone turning a blind eye to the suffering of children. His outright refusal and jumping to conclusions had her blood boiling.

"And many more people will die if I involve myself." His words were sharp and quick. "More children will grow up without fathers and more fathers will be burying their sons. Why must the answer always be war?" There was sadness in his voice. *Real honest-to-gods sadness.*

Captain Amyna composed herself, trying to hide her anger. "And how would you end this?"

"Diplomacy or trade. Surely Rouke wants something, or they wouldn't be marching to the frigid north. Instead, the wealthy cling to their riches, and the poor end up dying or being bred into soldiers. And then the cycle, the never-ending cycle, repeats."

"That's not why he sent us," Clara interrupted, stopping the two from barking at each other like rabid hounds on leashes. "We're here to recover an artifact."

Miro's frown disappeared. "What type of artifact?" he asked, some trepidation in his voice.

"The Mantle of Alcides," Clara said.

"The mantle was destroyed during the war in Lynnfield," Miro said, before returning to his cooking.

"No, the priests moved it. Before ... before it happened. I was young, but it was to keep it safe, to stop Emestria from getting it. My father moved it back to his tomb. My mother told me how to find it," she said, her voice finding confidence at the end.

"Tell me," Miro said, turning back to Clara. His eyes were alive in a way they weren't moments ago. "These woods are no place for the inexperienced."

Captain Amyna prepared to enter into another heated debate with him. But she held her tongue, tempering her anger.

"I think ... I think only I can find it," Clara explained. "Or someone like me. My mother said the way is hidden to any outside of our people. The mountain will show us the way." It was cryptic and effusive, but she had yet to offer any other explanation. Amyna knew how much Clara wanted out of this country, so surely, she must not know much else beside that.

Miro looked Clara up and down before saying, "Maybe you can find the way. How much training do you have?"

"Training in what?"

"Geomancy, of course." Here was Miro nonchalantly saying another phrase Amyna was neither familiar with nor believed existed. There was something slightly off about this hermit.

"None," Clara groaned. "I don't know what that is." Miro said strange things with no explanation of their meaning, exasperating Captain Amyna. Why did he expect them to know what he was babbling about?

"Well, tomorrow I'll try and train you a bit, to see if you can harness the power of the land. If not, there's no point in us trying. That mountain is a maze; we'd be stranded for years if you didn't know the way. Some say the mountain moves to keep you lost."

Captain Amyna looked at him dismissively. "And what does this artifact do?"

"The mantle is supposed to be impenetrable," Miro said. "Able to shrug off an arrow as well as fire, lightning, or any other manner of spells."

"What help will that be in a war?" Amyna asked. A cloak would do little to protect a soldier's front. When the soldier was downed, an enemy could recover the artifact, thus giving the hard-sought relic to the enemy.

"Probably not much, but there are others." Miro spoke so quickly that words almost jumbled together. "Others with fewer military strengths. A sword that can tell you if someone is lying, a goblet that never runs empty, a cornucopia able to create food, and many more. Finding one would be proof enough to go after the others."

"Why do we need to waste time with this cape, then?" Amyna asked. "We go and find the one that makes food." Emestria was starving, cut off from supply routes. An infinite source of food would negate the point of Rouke's offensive. Emestria could concentrate on holding the line at the Iron Bridge and not need to risk soldiers in trying to push Rouke back. Eventually Rouke's own supply lines would be strained.

"I have no idea where that one resides. Aside from the mantle, no one has seen or proven their existence since the cataclysm. Most think they're just tales and others believe that the objects are fakes used for ceremonial purposes."

"The mantle isn't fake," Clara said. "My father brought it to the mountain because it was so important."

"I agree that they most likely exist, but who's to say the mantle will still be there when we arrive, or that it can do what it was claimed to do?" Miro explained. "Bryant won't agree to a greater expedition without some proof."

Captain Amyna sighed; he was infuriating to be around. Clara also displayed some reticence around the strange man, but not in the same way as her. If Amyna didn't know better, she would think that Clara was trying to endear herself to him.

Miro finished making the meager stew. The meal consisted mostly of some type of fish and a few root vegetables. Amyna stared at the food and crinkled her nose. It was salty and reeked of the sea, but it was food—the only nourishment left after the beast smashed their wagon.

Suddenly, Clara screamed at the top of her lungs. Outside the kitchen window, a large vibrant blue eye glared at them. Amyna recognized the eye from that death dealer of a leopard. Miro turned and went to close the curtains.

"She's curious," he said, dismissing Clara's alarm.

"Is that thing your pet?" Clara asked, her voice regaining its natural tone.

"What, Naani? No. I guess she gets lonely and comes to hang around sometimes. When I first came here and tried to build this cabin, we'd work all day, and she'd come by during the night and knock the whole thing down. I finally figured out she was mad because we hadn't made her an offering. She is inflexible about receiving her offerings. After a couple of sea serpents, she calmed down and let us build.

"Back in those days, there were lots of leopards, so she didn't come round here often. But now, so few—if any other than her—exist, she comes by a lot.

"If you'll excuse me, ladies, I need to make good on my word and tend to Naani's injuries." Miro rose from the table and headed outside, grabbing his cloak as he exited.

After he left the room Clara asked, "Do you think he can really talk to the cat?"

"I think he's rather mad in the head."

"But she stopped when he told her to and dug the holes for the men..." Captain Amyna recognized the look of guilt on Clara's face. She had been doing her best to dismiss the feeling and keep the same look off hers.

"Perhaps it's a command spell or something. I still think there's another person. Did you notice how he kept saying 'we' without any explanation?" Amyna didn't trust Miro. A man living out in the vast White North all by himself: he would be on the cusp of insanity if that were the case. If he had a compatriot, that would be enough to keep him sane. He slipped up and said "we" when talking about building the cabin.

"But I saw him cast the magic," Clara argued.

Captain Amyna sighed. "Yes, it appeared as if he cast the magic. He made it look that way to conceal a partner." Another damnably annoying mystery for Amyna to figure out.

"What partner?" Clara asked, her tone reeking of frustration.

"I'm guessing that it's the real scholar. King Bryant told me the man saved his life during the war. Miro couldn't have been more than nine or eleven then. How does a child save the life of a king? My guess is the real scholar is scouting us and using him as the bait. He's probably his son; he did bring up fathers and sons when he talked about wars."

"What do you think he's doing with the leopard?" Clara asked abruptly.

"I don't bloody know. If you're so curious, investigate." Amyna was being facetious, but Clara was off the chair and hobbling out the door before Amyna could tell her to stay put. She sighed and picked away at the disgusting fish goop she was forced to shovel down.

# Chapter 6

*Many of the gods took mortal lovers and gave birth to demigods, people of extreme strength and speed. Alcide's was the most famous of those demigods, but there are conflicting stories about his ultimate demise or lack thereof. The two most reliable tales indicate he was either poisoned by his wife and succumbed to that poison, or that he was allowed to leave with the gods because he proved himself worthy. It is difficult to parse which stories are true and quite possible that stories of other demigods are being conflated with stories of Alcides.*

*—Issaroh, The History of Divinity, Part XV*

Clara stepped outside into the cold night with Miro. A faint green light appeared to originate from the side of the house and faded. As the door closed, Naani practically crushed Miro as she rose to greet Clara, yowling and purring. Clara flinched and retreated to the door.

Miro finally unwedged himself from between the massive leopard and his house. "She says she wants to talk, and she doesn't understand why you won't listen."

"Tell her she's scaring me and to stop growling."

Naani stopped almost instantly.

"Tell her yourself; she understands." Miro came to stand by Clara.

"Why were you surprised earlier that I couldn't talk to her?"

"The type of magic practiced in Lynnfield, the Penakian discipline, could be used to talk with animals. I assumed because of your hair you knew it. Naani was very fond of the people of Lynnfield."

"Hi, Naani. I'm Clara, nice to meet you," she said.

Naani bellowed back and Miro translated. "She said she's so happy to see a flower-haired person. She thought she would never see one again."

"My name is Clara," she said trying to get Naani to use her name.

"Oh, don't bother with names. Naani refuses to learn the names of anyone younger than two centuries. I used to try to teach her mine, but she doesn't even listen."

"Then what does she call us?"

"Well, she calls me 'nice man,' not even 'the nice man.' She keeps calling you the 'flower-haired one' and your compatriot the 'sun-haired one.'"

"Can I touch her?" Clara asked.

"Sure, if she doesn't mind."

"Should I be careful?" Clara held her hand out to Naani but pulled it closer. "Will she hurt me?"

"No, she won't. She was trying to protect you after all."

"She sure has a funny way of protecting people," Clara said, putting her hand out to Naani's nose. It was cold and wet. Frozen patches of dark red around Naani's mouth and on her chin still lingered, causing Clara to grimace. She walked away from the house toward Naani's paw. Clara reached out and grabbed the big cat's forelimb. Naani tilted her head and let out a soft purr.

"She's kind of like a huge house cat," Clara remarked before putting both her arms around the massive forelimb. She could almost reach, and then Naani lifted the limb, and Clara was suddenly airborne. She let out a surprised, but excited laugh.

"Be gentle, Naani," Miro said as he walked around to meet Clara on the other side. Clara's muscles tensed and her vision darted between Miro and the door. She was out here alone, with him; Captain Amyna was inside. And now he had put himself in between Clara and the door. Naani stopped purring and flopped her other paw between the two. A low growl echoed in Naani's throat, directed at Miro. And Clara did feel like the spirit guardian was protecting the 'flower-haired one'.

"How did she become a spirit guardian?" Clara asked.

"I don't really know. From what she's told me, and what I've read of them, she was just another ordinary leopard in the beginning. Then, she was blessed by the gods, given intelligence, and the tasks of protecting the forests of Emestria and escorting the people of Lynnfield."

"Does that mean the gods are still around?" Clara asked, curious since she had always been taught otherwise even though her parents had still prayed to Lau'O'Penake, Goddess of Nature and Rebirth.

"Some think they still watch over us, but I don't think that's true. If Lau'O'Penake was still around, how could she let anything like the catastrophe at Lynnfield happen?"

"You said you were there?" Clara asked. "Were you part of the Emestrian occupying force?"

Miro hung his head before replying, "I was. I'm sorry. I thought I could make a difference because I knew the healing arcana at the time. I was a fool."

"And that's why you refuse to fight now? But couldn't you just work as a healer instead of spending your time out here, where your help is limited?"

"What if the person I heal goes on to kill twelve more? What if they burn down a building with children inside? I refuse to be a party to death any longer."

Clara nodded stifling her disagreement with the claim. He had healed her and the captain. What guarantee did Miro have that Captain Amyna or herself would not go on to cause more harm? Clara's daughter, Scarlette, had done no wrong. If he was avoiding the world, keeping his gifts for himself, wasn't he just dooming those like her to a painful death?

"Can I see your hands?" Miro asked.

Clara looked at him strangely but then abruptly pulled her hands up to the pale light of the moon. She flexed the fingers and balled them into little fists. Ten perfectly jointed fingers caused her eyes to water and a giddy smile to cross her lips.

"Looks like it worked. Glad they didn't need to be rebroken. I hate doing that kind of stuff. I am quite sure your friend in there would have though. She might enjoy dealing in roughness." Miro looked back at the cabin with animosity.

"She's not a bad person," Clara responded.

Miro ignored the comment and changed the subject. "What were you in the dungeons for?"

"I'm a smuggler. My boat capsized and a patrol discovered me. They took one look at my hair and declared me a spy."

"That sounds like Emestria." A frustrated breath forced its way from his throat.

"What about you? You said you were in the dungeons."

"War crimes," Miro said, then flashed a false, ridiculous smile.

"You shouldn't joke about those types of things." Clara positioned herself between him and the door as he sat down on a tree stump. "Can you really use two types of magic?"

"You saw it with your own eyes, didn't you?"

"Captain Amyna thinks there might be someone else out there," Clara said, the suspicion in her voice obvious.

"Well, you've seen ice and healing. How about some fire and lightning?" Miro traced two rune circles in the air, one with each hand. A dexterous feat even without casting magic. His eyes glowed. Purplish-blue energy crackled around one of his hands, weaving and flitting between his fingers. A red-orange ball twisted in the palm of his other hand, a wisp of flame tickling the air right above it. The flame didn't emit any smoke, but the frosty night shimmered with heat.

"So according to her theory, that means there are three people out here now." Clara took a step back, looking to her left and right. She didn't know what was a scarier thought, that one man somehow could control multiple schools of magic, or that there might be other sorcerers lurking in the shadows.

"It's just me, and I mean you no harm," he added. "Can I ask you a question?" Miro snuffed out the fire in one hand and the lightning dissipated from his other.

"Sure, I guess. As long as I can ask one in turn."

"Are you in any danger? Why were you traveling with her and those men?"

Clara shook her head but then froze. "I am. They were going to execute me as a spy. I kept telling them I was a smuggler, but they wouldn't listen. I said anything I could to stay alive. Then I remembered the cloak, and Emestria was desperate for coin, so I thought I could buy my freedom. Now I'm afraid if I don't return with it, they'll hang me, and even if I do, they still might. I need to hope, though."

She paused for a bit and her tone became more reflective, and her voice heavy with insinuation. "I could try to escape. You fixed my leg. But where could I go? We're a two-day ride from the nearest town and I doubt I would survive in this cold. Maybe with the help of someone that knew the area, I could make it to Porton. If I could make it there, I'd be safe."

"I have my reasons for seeking the Mantle of Alcides." Miro straightened himself out and flashed a reassuring smile. "I'll make sure they stay true to their word."

"And if we don't find it?" Clara asked.

"We'll return here until it is safe to get you to Porton," Miro offered. "No one will come looking for you this far north."

"What about Captain Amyna?" Clara asked.

"I don't know. I'd hope that if we tried, but couldn't recover the mantle, she would have no animosity toward you. It would become more complicated if she insisted on returning you to the capital. I'm sure they wouldn't look too fondly upon failure, hers or yours."

Miro rose from the stump and started to go inside. "Interesting that the great treasure of Lynnfield is going to be surrendered to Emestria because a smuggler tipped over in her boat. Life never works out the way you want."

Clara took a step back as he walked past her. "Wait, you said I could ask you a question."

"You did, a lot of them."

"Not the one I wanted though. My father was a priest, which meant he could cast some magic, but what if I don't want to learn the Penakian discipline? What if you taught me the healing arcana instead. Could I still find the tomb?"

Miro frowned. "Unfortunately, it doesn't work like that. We're each attuned to one of the gods more than we are to the others. We don't get a choice in our abilities; they're innate. Even if they weren't, there is a reason why they call it the healing arcana and not the Seraphim discipline. It is much harder to learn to cast healing magic. We could spend months training even if you were gifted."

"So what was the first school you learned?"

"The healing arcana; you see I'm a bit of a prodigy." Clara cocked her eyebrow and Miro let out a soft chuckle. "It also works a little differently than the other magics as well. All magic takes a toll on the user, but it's temporary and a good night's sleep is enough to shake off the effects. You're altering the landscape or people's perceptions or emotions with the disciplines. But with healing arcana…" Miro grew oddly quiet and didn't explain anymore.

"How exactly are you going to teach me?" Clara asked.

Miro smiled before replying, "You ask a lot of good questions."

Clara returned the smile, pleasant, not a devious one.

"To cast, you'll have to learn to form the runes for a spell, call upon Lau'O'Penake to assist you, and have a firm grasp of what you intend to do. Then you use the spell's name and hopefully something happens."

"I have to call upon the goddess' favor? But what about what you just did with the lightning and fire."

"Magi don't have to obey all the rules. Those with decades of experience can learn to tap into the raw nature of magic. I met one that could cast magic by just uttering the name of the spell. I've heard of others that don't even need to do that."

"Were you born a magus? Can anyone become one?"

Miro's shook his head, his smile turned sour, and his eyes seemed hollow. "As far as I know, yes. You just have to be willing to make sacrifices."

"What type of sacrifices?" Clara asked, hoping that more questions would improve his mood. He seemed to want to share what he knew, but she could tell he was holding back on this information.

"Only everything you love about the world, yourself, and those you care for." Miro turned back around and disappeared into the cottage. Clara wasn't quite sure if she could believe the comment. He seemed serious, but even in the short conversation they shared, he wobbled between pleasantries and morose comments with every other question. She didn't think it was all an act, but one of the moods was forced; though she couldn't tell which one. She hoped it wasn't the pleasantries.

Clara sat down on the stump Miro previously had. She had to hop up onto it, her legs hanging awkwardly over the edge. Naani inclined her head and stared at her in an intelligent way.

"So, you're supposed to be some type of guardian to my people?"

Naani let out an excited chuff.

"I still can't understand you, but you know what I'm saying. You'd think my father would have told me he was escorted by a giant cat in the pilgrimage. I mean, that's the type of story a little girl would eat up. I know my own will love it when I tell her about you."

Clara smiled thinking about the story she would tell Scarlette on her next birthday. Her daughter would love this type of story. The smile was brief as she unconsciously sunk her now straightened fingers into her palm. The pain reminded her that happiness wasn't in her cards.

Clara couldn't quite tell what Naani's reaction was to the idea of telling others about her. "Of course, maybe you are supposed to be some type of secret. That would explain why my father was so fervent in his beliefs. How else could you let some heel of a goddess that doesn't stop suffering dictate your life?" Clara sighed, and then groaned. "I guess I shouldn't say things like that anymore if I'm going to be begging for her power to cast magic."

Naani stood, then walked behind Clara. Clara turned to watch as the cat curled its body around the stump and Clara. Clara leaned back into the soft, thick fur.

"You know, the people of Lynnfield, the flower-haired people, are still around. We just don't live there anymore. A lot resettled in Corinth, but there are others. If one of your duties was really to protect us, shouldn't you be there with us? Why remain in Emestria? It will be destroyed in months anyway.

"You could come with me, back to Newtonne, or see more of my people in Corinth. A lot of people would pay good money to see something like you."

Naani let out a soft growl, closer to a grumble than anything else.

"Well don't be like that. It's not like I'd try to sell you. My daughter has the same hair as me, and she's sick. I'd use the money to treat her, which means you'd be protecting the people of Lynnfield once again." Clara turned contemplative, trying to think of the best way to display a giant cat so people would have to pay to see it. Would Naani allow people to ride her? That would be the best way to profit off Naani.

"Of course, I'd need to find a way to get you across the ocean. You might be too big to sneak across the Iron Bridge, even with the putting people to sleep thing. There's no way I can get a boat big enough through the ice floes to house you. But then we'd have to wait until Rouke had conquered Emestria. Can you swim? Tigers are good swimmers."

Miro opened the door, and a gust of freezing air permeated the cabin. Captain Amyna was still picking through her stew, pushing the stringy meat to one side and scooping the vegetables up with her spoon.

"I'll help you find what you're looking for," Miro said, as he walked over and pushed books from a couch. They thumped against the floor as they fell, some of them toppling over and opening, straining their spines. Amyna sighed, looking at the discarded books. "But you made a promise to that woman out there. Emestria agreed to give her freedom in exchange for that cloak. I don't like deal breakers. I want to find the mantle. If we are unable to retrieve the artifact, Clara won't be returning to the capital."

Captain Amyna opened her mouth to disagree but then stopped. He was right; even she couldn't deny what their fate would be if they failed. Clara would face execution. If Miro was foolhardy enough to follow them back, his fate wouldn't be much better. The general would believe failure was an act of sabotage. Amyna wondered if she would have to face any consequences. A demotion?

"I never caught your name," Miro said.

"Captain Amyna."

"I won't call you that. What is your first name?"

"I've earned the right to be addressed by my honorific."

"I'm sure you have. I have a title too, but titles mean nothing out here. I saved your life, could have left you with broken bones, and I agreed to help you in your quest. I think that awards me the privilege of knowing your name. I'm not one of your soldiers."

"Then I will use your honorific, Lord Krestel," Amyna said.

Miro's eyes widened and his jaw tensed. His upper lip curled as he snapped, "Never call me that." Even he seemed shocked by his outburst.

The Krestels were one of the more powerful noble families, with their lineage going back hundreds of years. Amyna knew that five years ago their patriarch had passed, and his land was divided among his children, a common Emestrian practice. However, the eldest had eventually re-consolidated their holdings. Their families were full-blooded Emestrian, which meant Miro was probably a bastard. That would explain his disdain for the name.

Miro looked at her again and said in a more even tone. "If you never say that name again, I will address you by your rank, but I deserve to know your full name for my assistance."

Captain Amyna hesitated before replying, "Captain Bronwyn Amyna." Miro nodded his approval. "As a captain, I was allowed to study magic, and I've never heard of a magus."

"There are very few. I've only met one other."

"And exactly what is a magus? You can cast multiple schools of magic, but is that from some type of magic I've never heard of?" Miro sighed and Amyna continued, "I gave you my full name because you wanted to know who you were traveling with. I deserve the same respect."

"It's not a specific type of magic per se. Are you familiar with the Ywaigwai?"

Captain Amyna wasn't pious. Many in Emestria still prayed to the gods, but they were gone now. They left after the cataclysm, which was almost four hundred years ago; something about a city being destroyed. She was slightly familiar with the Ywaigwai. "Weren't they emissaries of the gods? I thought all the Ywaigwai left with the gods?"

"Some of them might have, but they still exist. They're as elusive as the magi that they grant power to."

"So, you what? Prey to Ywaigwai and they give you power?"

"Not quite. I have no guest room, but you two can take the bed in the loft," Miro said, changing the subject. Something that didn't escape Amyna's notice.

"Thanks."

The loft was not a separate room, just a bed tucked away on top of the living room, cramped but manageable. It would be a cozy fit. Amyna stood and stared out the window at Clara, turning away from the window quickly as Clara re-entered. She cursed herself. Clara would think she was just staring outside at the leopard, or the falling snow. Retreating from the window signaled more distrust than remaining there.

Captain Amyna waited a while before heading up to the loft. The air was cold, despite the fire. She took her armor off, but for additional warmth she bundled up in her cloak. Miro had furs, and she wrapped herself in them. The bed was small, especially for two people. But Clara was rather diminutive, so when she finally headed off to bed as well, there was enough room for the two of them.

Captain Amyna woke in the middle of the night to muffled screams. She reached for her greatsword and pulled it from the scabbard. Her eyes took a moment to adjust to the low light of the fireplace's glowing embers. She thought someone had grabbed Clara; put their hand over her mouth. But Clara was fine, still comfortably asleep. They were a man's cries. She leaned over the loft railing to see their host tossing and turn-ing uncomfortably in sleep, followed by occasional howls muffled by the pillows. At first, she thought he must be awake, the movements were so violent. But after softly calling his name and receiving no reply, he did not stop what he was doing or acknowledge her presence. Night terrors.

What can you expect living by yourself, alone for years? Between talking to animals, isolation, and claiming to be able to cast multiple schools of magic, Amyna was starting to seriously doubt this man's mental competence.

*Perhaps it would be better if we return to the castle after he teaches Clara the necessary magic and request more men to go to the mountain without this crazy hermit. He seems genuinely nice though,* Amyna found herself thinking before she banished the thought. *This is a wolf-eat-wolf world; everybody has a motive. You must find out what it is and use that to your advantage.* Shaking her head, Amyna returned to bed. She lay for another ten to fifteen minutes listening to his wails and screams until, finally, they subsided, and she was able to return to sleep.

# CHAPTER 7

*Lau'O'Penake, goddess of nature and rebirth, was unique among the gods, in that it seemed instead of both children inheriting divinity, it was split between her and her twin brother, Defurge. Lau'O'Penake was not immortal and passed after each millennia. The gods circumvented this limitation through the creation of a Legendary Artifact able to resurrect Lau'O'Penake.*

*—Issaroh, The History of Divinity, Part IX*

Captain Amyna's nose crinkled in disgust as she awoke to the sound of frying fish, the pungent, salty aroma making her gag. Clara had already left the bed. Donning her armor and boots, Amyna took her sword with her as she climbed down the loft ladder.

She found Clara downstairs at the table, waiting for her meal and talking to their host while swinging her feet underneath the table like a small child. She gazed up at Miro and peppered him with questions, her voice lighter than Amyna had previously heard. Clara's hand was balled around her fork as she pulled fish into her mouth. It seemed that Miro was making the meals as people woke. Amyna folded her arms and stared down at Clara. Noticing the disappointed look, Clara held the fork properly and stopped swinging her legs. A knowing smile passed between the two of them. Clara was laying it on rather thick.

Captain Amyna was both shocked and disgusted. Fried fish for breakfast was odd, but now there were pickled eggs, *disgusting*. What was most shocking, however, was that Miro had washed and shaved the scruffy beard that haunted his face yesterday. He looked even younger, almost handsome. Before, she had trouble believing he was in the war with King Bryant, but now she doubted that he was as old as her. She sat next to Clara, trying to catch up with the conversation.

"I don't know much of the Penakian discipline, but I should be able to teach you a little," Miro said as he flipped the fish on the skillet. "Your aura is dim, but strong."

"My aura?" Clara asked.

"Every living thing has an aura." For some reason, he turned to Amyna after saying that, staring at her strangely. "We magi can see them, one of our gifts other sorcerers lack. That is a person's magical affinity. If it is weak, you'll never use magic. If you possess a strong aura, you can learn. As you progress, it becomes brighter."

Miro put two more plates of fish down with a small mound of pickled eggs on the side. Amyna examined the cup in front of her. Thankfully, the water wasn't brine extracted from the ocean or some such nonsense. She took a sip, apologizing to her taste buds about the coming meal and swearing to consume as little as possible.

"I guess I have a weak aura then," Amyna said. She had not meant to say anything. Not complaining about this horrible slop she would be forced to eat took all her energy. The words just spilled out.

"You don't have any. I've never seen anything like it before," Miro said. "Perhaps I'll have to study and research you to figure out why."

Clara roared with laughter.

Bronwyn Amyna gritted her teeth as the tension in her shoulders intensified. Instead of the rage, all she could muster was a bitter defeat.

*It is strange how you can be the strongest person in the room, but some things still make you feel so little.*

She had always hated her magical ineptitude. Sure, she compensated with her fast and fierce fighting style, but she still wondered if she did master spell casting, how deadly she could truly have been? Dancing through combat with one arm swinging her massive sword, flinging spells with the other...

Miro said, "In Lynnfield, they practiced nature magic. Controlling the earth, talking to animals, and manipulating plants. That's why Lynnfield was so great at growing crops. I don't know, but if I teach you, that might be enough when we're in the mountain. It's a four-day ride."

Captain Amyna said, "Yes, I figure we start midmorning, travel until evening, and make camp. We don't have any horses, but perhaps your sleigh won't slow us down too much."

Miro stiffly exhaled from his nostrils and his voice raised an octave higher. "I *was* telling Clara that there is no point making the trip unless she can use some magic. Probably how she's supposed to navigate the mountain. The land would react to the people of Lynnfield in a way it didn't for other sorcerers. A magic where they tied the land to those of their heritage. There might be some signs, or messages left on the rock, that only she can perceive. I think it's a spell cast long ago, but I don't think Clara will need to cast it. It's more like the spell recognizes someone of the correct lineage and ability to command magic. I was going to start teaching her after breakfast."

"Can't you teach her on the way?" Amyna asked, letting her fork drop to her plate noisily.

"And then after four days, if she hasn't learned, we just wait at the mountain hoping she can learn before we become prey for wolves or wendigos?"

His tone made Captain Amyna's teeth grind. "Fine, but we need to be quick about this. Time is of the essence." She shoveled the fish into her mouth. She decided to force it down, just ignore the taste long enough to swallow it.

"Wow, you're hungry," Miro remarked.

Captain Amyna glared at him. Comments about her eating habits were not appreciated. Once she had forced down enough nutrition to get her to her next meal, she began to grill Miro. "So, King Bryant said that you saved his life. How?"

"That's a subject I prefer not to discuss. After I saved him, though, Arty made me a deal, a promise, and failed to honor it."

Captain Amyna could not believe what she heard. It would be blasphemy to call King Bryant by his first name, Artorius, but to use a nickname was sacrilege of the highest order. "In my presence, you will refer to him by his honorific or King Bryant."

"Sorry, I will not be calling him anything other than Arty, and if you continue to insist I use his honorific, I'll find a nickname for you as well. What do you think of Wynnie?"

"Lord Kres—"

"Captain Amyna," Miro said, interrupting her. "I will not refer to him as anything other than Arty. He hasn't earned my respect."

Captain Amyna said, "Don't you two have some training to do?" Clara gave Amyna a nervous glance, then gave the same to Miro. Amyna's blood boiled at this simpleton's words. She stood as calmly as possible and put her dishes in a pile with the others. *Such a messy house.* "I'm going to make some tea and then see if I can find us something sensible to eat."

Miro and Clara went outside to begin their training and Amyna poked around the kitchen searching for a kettle, finally finding one obscured by dirty dishes. It had not been used in years; a thick layer of dust caked the lid. At least the inside looked to be clean. Wiping away the grime that had settled on top, she went about making tea. First, she packed the teapot with snow, then took a handful of pine needles and shoved them in. She added more snow periodically as it melted.

While she waited for the tea to boil, she set about the house looking for a bow and arrow or something similar to catch game. All she found was a set of fishing poles. Her nose wrinkled at the idea of more fish. She would make some snares and go hunting with her sling. Luckily, she carried those things around with her in one of her pouches.

Outside the window, Miro and Clara stood not far from the house. He was trying to teach her how to throw rocks with magic. As he held out his palm, swirling particles of dirt and small rocks formed. A push caused the projectiles to fly forward like grapeshot. *Not a highly effective spell.* However, there was no doubt about it—he was casting. Stone projectiles weren't part of the healing arcana or the Frian discipline.

Once the tea was ready, Bronwyn poured herself a cup. Clara was not getting the hang of casting, and Miro kept having to show her how to trace the runes. Occasionally, she got a rune or two right, but the whole circle would dissipate when she failed at the next.

Captain Amyna did not know why he was teaching Clara such an insignificant cantrip. The spell would be useless in battle, except to annoy an adversary. It could be used as a distraction, but that would be all. Bronwyn thought about this self-proclaimed magus. Like all practitioners of magic, he was overly confident. The Magic Knights she met in Emestria were all power-hungry and only concerned themselves with learning more spells. Having access to more schools of magic, Miro would be eight times worse. However, the spells he had cast so far were rather unimpressive. The most complicated had been the ice wall, but that was only of slightly moderate difficulty.

Every year before the war, Emestria held a competition for the nobles to display their spell proficiency. Bronwyn had seen truly devastating exhibitions: sorcerers conjuring storms and flinging razor-sharp icicles to eviscerate their opponents. Once, she saw someone freeze a dummy in ice in a matter of seconds. Nothing Miro cast was close to the level of skill the knights wielded. *Jack of all trades, master of none.*

Bronwyn finished her tea, anxious to catch something to eat besides fish. When she went outside, she startled at the sight of the leopard. She had gotten used to it being around, forgetting the beast was there until it moved or made a noise. Seeing that thing brought back the horrors of watching her men butchered so quickly. She wanted to put the menace down, but was unsure if she would be able to survive a fight with it. Especially now, since Clara and Miro treated the leopard as a pet.

Sure, she could take Miro without the monster, or Naani without Miro, but together would be difficult. Clara would be no help, and might possibly side with Naani and Miro. Captain Amyna's time would be spent focusing on the beast while Miro pestered her with his insignificant magics. Eventually, his annoyances would cause Amyna to slip up, and then in a blink of an eye, the devil cat would latch onto her—ending her. She shook her head, dismissing the idea.

Naani continued to ignore Captain Amyna, grotesquely chomping down on a serpent. *How does a cat catch a sea serpent? Aren't they more of a deep-sea creature?* The dark-blue scales were dusted with a slight frost. As Naani bit off another portion, little chips of ice sloughed off. *Must not be fresh; stored in some underground larder before given to the creature.*

*Miro's fishing poles would not be sturdy enough to reel in something that size,* Bronwyn thought. With magic, though, one never knew. Perhaps he froze the leviathan and reeled it in when it bobbed to the surface. Or did he use lightning and shock the water, stunning the thing? Either way, the leopard bit into it, and the noise made her nauseous. The sound reminded her of the way her men's armor had crunched beneath the leopard's claws and teeth. They weren't the brightest that the guard offered, but they were still her men, men with families. Parents, brothers, sisters, maybe wives or husbands, and children of their own. And they had died, under her leadership, and now she was playing guest to their murderer's master.

Captain Amyna got back to the house in the early afternoon. She went about cleaning and plucking the grouse she had managed to down with her sling. She had also happened upon some spice leaf while hunting and gladly took that with her. In the root cellar, she took some of Miro's gold potatoes, celery, and onions to make a hearty soup. Once the bird was prepared, she put a large cauldron on to boil, filled with meat, vegetables, herbs, and snow. The heavenly fragrance of a harvest dinner permeated the small cabin. She drank another cup of pine tea, warming her hands on the cup as she did.

She peered outside again. Clara was starting to grasp the concept of rock throwing. Every other time she successfully hurled a small clump of dirt.

Captain Amyna allowed her prize to cook for a couple of hours before removing it. She cut the meat away from the bones and tossed it back into the soup. If she simmered the bones overnight, they would have a hearty stock for their trek. Miro and Clara came back in while she was cleaning the bones. Clara appeared famished, but Miro had a disapproving look on his face.

"What, don't you like fowl?" Amyna quipped.

"No, you didn't need to. I could have made a stew or fried something up," he offered.

"I've had quite enough fish, thank you," Amyna said. "Now let's get some real meat in our bellies." The thought of not forcing down salty, flakey meat for dinner, to eat some hardy sustenance, brought a smile to her lips. She poured some pine tea for Miro and Clara and stirred the soup. Satisfied with the consistency, she procured three clean bowls and ladled out dinner for them all.

Clara was ecstatic, but that seemed to be her general demeanor lately. Miro was less eager, but after a stern look from Amyna, he also began to heartily eat the food, almost making a show of it. Captain Amyna finished off three helpings by herself. She couldn't remember the last time she had such a rich meal while sitting indoors next to a fire.

"I'm going to go check my snares," Amyna announced after her final bowl. "I hope I had some luck, and we'll have some meaty game on our trip."

"I wish you hadn't," Miro opined. "I don't like consuming animals from the land."

Captain Amyna had heard of certain cultures where the eating of any animal was frowned upon, but never one that only allowed sea creatures. "I don't see what the difference is between a fish and a bird."

"Fish don't talk" was his only reply.

Captain Amyna left, thinking about his statement. That implied he spent his time talking to more animals than the leopard. To think that the grouse she served for dinner was possibly his friend. She tried to clear her mind of the thought, but her snare had caught a rabbit. What if this hare came to him every morning, and he gave it a piece of carrot? She broke its neck. There was one more hare and a fox. With a twinge of guilt, she broke theirs as well. Hopefully, these were not his pets. She took the animals back to the cabin.

Normally Amyna would skin and clean them inside, but out of consideration she did this outdoors. The entrails were tossed in the snow, a meal for another predator. After cleaning the prey, she stored them in the larder. The cold would freeze them, and the trio could eat the meat at their leisure. Rather than wash her hands inside, she gathered snow and rubbed it between them. As it melted, the water dripped off, carrying the fresh blood of her kills with it.

Her hands were frozen and raw when she went back in, so she poured herself a cup of tea to hold between them. Clara had already retired to bed and Miro was sitting at the table reading one of his books. Amyna sat across from him. At first, they did not say anything.

"I'm sorry, I didn't think ..." She started, attempting to put words to the way she was feeling, but they escaped her.

"Don't worry." His voice was hostile and cold. "You're within your right to eat the type of meat you want."

"Do you talk with them?"

"No, most animals are too afraid of humans, even if they can communicate." He sighed. "Did you catch anything?"

"Two hares and a fox."

"That should be enough for the journey." He forced a smile. "I would offer to bring some fish as well, but you seem opposed to the idea."

"I'm going to boil the bones overnight," she said about the grouse. "We should get some nourishing stock."

He nodded. "It's good tea. Thank you." His head was firmly in his book. Possibly avoiding her gaze.

"It's easy to make. Just some pine needles and water. I'm surprised you don't know how."

"I do, it's just been a while since I've had some."

"Will we be able to leave tomorrow? I saw she learned that spell."

"I think we will. I don't know what she needs to find the tomb, but hopefully fostering her link with the land will suffice. You should get some rest. I'll tend the pot because I need to study more."

Captain Amyna nodded before ascending the ladder to the loft. She stripped off her boots and armor and made herself comfortable. Normally, she fell asleep easily, but for some reason it eluded her. The soft sound of the pages turning every couple of minutes kept her awake. She dozed intermittently, but it was not until he put out the candles and laid down himself that she closed her eyes for the night. He did not scream in his sleep, so Amyna slept well, without interruption, but her reluctance to rise early the next morning suggested otherwise.

As they prepared for the trip in the morning, Clara and Amyna finished off the soup, while Miro fried himself up more fish. The stock was loaded into several wineskins and the sleigh packed with their provisions: the hares and fox, the stock, a kettle and pot, wood for kindling, and bedrolls. They were limited in what they could bring and would be forced to cram into one tent. Someone would always be on watch, so it would not be too cramped with just two sleeping. After loading the sleigh, Miro went round the back to his stables. He returned with four reindeer; one he lashed to the sleigh. Two of them had saddles.

"What is the other reindeer for?" Amyna asked, perplexed.

"Once we enter the western forest, we'll need to all go on the sleigh. I'll let all but one reindeer go. They'll keep the wolves occupied long enough for us to reach the mountain."

Captain Amyna smiled in agreement at the shrewd nature of the plan. Maybe he didn't treat all animals like pets after all.

Miro approached Naani, waking her from her midmorning nap. "Naani. We're going to the mountain."

The leopard growled in response.

"No, you can't come. You know the wolves up there are out of control."

More growls from Naani.

"I'll keep her safe." Naani stood, facing Miro and her lips curled. "Look, I have a plan. I'm going to have them chasing reindeer."

The great feline yowled open-mouthed at Miro.

"You can't come. You need to stay here and guard the eastern forest. That's the end of it, Naani. If I see you following, I'll run us right into the wolves."

Despite Miro's insistence, Amyna glimpsed Naani tracking them, now and then. Miro would yell at her to go home, which caused the leopard to keep its distance, but she never left.

The first three days were uneventful. When they had entered the western forest—which Captain Amyna could only tell by an expansive, barren tundra between the east and west—on the second day, Miro released the reindeer, sending them off in opposite directions. They talked little as they traveled. Captain Amyna and Miro kept scanning the trees for movement. Clara, who had been quite talkative at the cabin, was cognizant of the danger and spoke rarely.

It wasn't until the third night that they started to hear the distant howls.

# Chapter 8

*Kyrie, goddess of wind, battle, and motherhood, and Laevin found themselves joined in an informal union. There is debate on whether it was a loving union or not, but the full-god siblings Fria and Seraph were born of that union.*

*—Issaroh, The History of Divinity, Part VI*

Miro's voice was quiet but urgent when he woke Amyna up on the fourth night. "We have to move, now."

As she grabbed her greatsword and breastplate, Captain Amyna exited the tent. Miro had already thrown snow over the fire and the burnt pine was now overwhelmed by the bitterness of smoke. Outside of the still hissing fire, the night was deathly quiet, until the howl pierced the air. Knowing what it meant, she ducked back inside the tent to don the rest of her armor.

"What's wrong?" Clara asked, sleepy eyed. This only warranted a finger to her lips from Amyna. Clara followed her advice and remained quiet.

A second howl echoed off the mountains. Illuminated by the lone lantern Miro had prepared and the dying embers of the campfire, the three compatriots' shadows danced against the trunks that surrounded the camp as they hurriedly grabbed what they could and loaded it haphazardly into the sleigh. They left the tent and Captain Amyna found herself trying to stare past the gaps in the trees, now resembling prison bars, except they would not keep their jailers at bay. Few clouds were in the night sky, and the full moon illuminated some of the surrounding woods. Dark silhouettes rushed through the forest, and Captain Amyna hoped they were reindeer trying to flee the ravenous hunters that would soon be upon them. But in her heart, she knew those were the beasts already beginning to surround them.

Miro lashed the reindeer, which snorted nervously and beat its hooves in demand that they would escape. Only taking the bare essentials, Miro, Clara, and Captain Amyna piled into the sled and Miro called for the reindeer to run. However, they had not been quick enough. Shortly after they got the reindeer moving, the shapes dashing by started to slow and turn toward them. Miro snapped the reins harder in a futile attempt to outrun their pursuers. The sleigh barreled through the forest as fast as the reindeer's legs could carry them.

They reached a clearing to find a wolf a mere forty feet in front of them. *It is not the wolf you see that gets you*, Amyna thought, remembering the story the one-armed hunter had told her in the tavern so long ago. So she was prepared when one of the giant beasts came out from the forest and sank its fangs into the reindeer, toppling the sled. Clara was clumsy on her feet, but Miro and Amyna were quick to take up a defensive for-mation.

So far, she counted four, but she knew there were likely more. Large timber wolves, five feet high, eight feet long, with three-inch fangs. They tore the reindeer from its bindings and two more wolves materialized from the woods.

"Stay together," Miro shouted amid the snarling and snapping. "We need to take down the pack leader!"

One of the creatures lunged at them and Amyna met its bite, her sword crashing into its maw eliciting a whimper.

"Stay together!" Miro yelled again. "I conjure this pact with Kyrie, goddess of wind, battle, and motherhood, bar my enemies, Fragma Kyros."

The rune circle expanded, and white sigils interlaced, forming a semi-translucent barrier around them. Their voices echoed off the shimmering white energy, and the wolves' snarls reflected back at them. The next couple of lunges bounced the wolves off the invisible shield, but the third almost made it through. Bronwyn attempted to cut the beast with her sword, but the animal retreated before she made contact.

"Can't you talk to them?" Clara cried. "Tell them to leave us alone."

"Have you ever tried talking to a wolf?" Miro responded. "They're stubborn and only care about the pack."

"What's the plan?" Amyna asked.

"Wait for the leader," he repeated.

Terrified, Clara wedged herself in between Miro and Amyna.

"I don't think we have time to wait." Amyna gripped her sword with both hands.

A wolf lunged and the barrier fizzled, falling around them as small shrinking white runes. Amyna sliced the wolf's forelimb with her sword. It recoiled and held its paw off the ground, but did not retreat.

"I make this pact with Fria, goddess of ice, death, and fate, the Vigilant Eye, Fragma Frios," Miro chanted.

The snow at their backside piled up and glowed blue. A frozen barrier came between them and a couple of wolves. The barred canines made short work of the wall, pushing through and crumpling the haphazard snowbank.

Another wolf materialized through the trees. She was larger than the others.

"You better do something!" Amyna said to Miro, readying her blade to fend off another lunge.

Both Miro and Clara were becoming more agitated. Amyna never thought she would be happy to hear the bellowing growl of Naani, but now the spirit guardian came charging through the trees, catching one wolf in its jaws and tossing it at another.

The confusion gave Amyna the opening she was looking for. She rushed toward the larger wolf. Another lunged at her, but she slipped through the attack by rolling forward. There was nothing between her and the den mother now. She raised her sword and barreled forward. An eighth beast ambushed her from the shadows, clasping her arm in its jaws, wrenching her to the ground.

"Inflagrata!" she heard Miro yell as a fiery red-and-orange sphere contacted the wolf that had downed her. "Slatara!" he called again.

Shards of ice rained down from the trees, trying to stop the advance of the next two wolves, but the third was undeterred and bit into her right leg. Even Naani was unable to scare the wolves as they bore down on Amyna. Another bit into her left leg and they wrenched her limbs, trying to pull her in different directions.

"No, Serra!" Miro yelled.

The sky turned red as a beam of sickly white light connected with the wolf on her right leg. One moment, it was there, and then it floated off in the breeze like ash off a cigar. The wolf still latched on her left leg paused before meeting the same fate.

Amyna scrambled as best she could to stand. She turned to see Miro levitating off the ground, his arms outstretched, lightning crackling between his fingertips, and his eyes glowing white. With Miro exposed in the air, a wolf made a lunge for him, but the electricity jumped from his fingertips, engulfing the creature, leaving it a smoldering hump of burnt fur and flesh.

"Useless, unworthy," Miro chanted in a low, deep voice. "Everything comes from nothing, and to nothing it shall return." Lightning gyrated along the ground until it contacted yet another beast. "Life, love, family, it all means nothing." Arcs of electricity danced around him, forming a barrier.

Clara crawled away in fear, several bolts of lightning almost hitting her.

"We live, we die, we eat, we're eaten," he continued to chant.

Naani now turned her attention from the wolves and started bearing down on Miro. He continued, undeterred. As she charged, lightning arced from Miro's fingers and ricocheted off the leopard's side. Naani bore the brunt of two more strikes before rearing up and smashing Miro under the weight of her body.

The wolves seemed unsure of what to do next, but when the leader lunged, sinking her teeth into the leopard, the others fell in line.

Amyna, bloodied but still able to move, got to her feet and thrust her sword into the she-wolf's hide. It howled in pain. Amyna steadied her greatsword, ready to strike again if it lunged at her, but the she-wolf took stock of the situation and limped away, giving off a yowl to signal a retreat to the others.

Clara ran up to Naani. "Get off him! Get off." She tried to push the leopard, but it refused to budge.

Amyna saw the deep-red blood pooling underneath Naani, where the she-wolf had bitten. It had struck the femoral artery. Naani's eyes were blinking slowly, and her breath was labored. Amyna walked to her head. She looked down at the once-great leopard and all she could see was an animal in pain.

She knelt beside her. "You did well. You protected us. If I can ask just one thing, can you roll over, so we can say goodbye?"

Naani breathed a heavy sigh and rolled on her side, the blood gushed from her severed artery. Miro was there, unconscious in the snow. Naani's underside was scored with burns from the lightning. Amyna placed a hand on the side of Miro's neck. His pulse was slow, but strong. Some residual electricity stung her fingertips.

"Is she okay? Is Naani okay?" Clara struggled to steady herself, her voice high pitched and frantic. She tightly clenched her fists.

Amyna slung one of Miro's arms over her shoulder. "He's alive ..." She paused before saying, "Naani's not going to make it. They severed an artery. There's nothing else we can do."

"Oh, Naani." Clara knelt beside the leopard. Each breath became increasingly labored. Clara softly stroked the animal's muzzle, red with wolf blood. "You did good. You protected me."

Amyna wanted to tell her they did not have time for this. They had to move before the wolves decided to come back, but she could not. Naani should have this comfort in her last bitter moments. She eased Miro to the ground before kneeling beside Naani and gently stroking the fur along her face. There was no death rattle; Naani took one last big breath and let it out slowly and silently before closing her eye for a final time. Clara cried, and Amyna did her best to not be caught up in the moment. She sat quietly as Clara buried her head in the fur of Naani's face and wept.

Amyna put a gentle hand on Clara's back. "Miro's unconscious, and we don't have the reindeer or sled anymore. We need to gather what we can carry and leave this area before they come back."

Clara stared at her with tearstained eyes and nodded.

Amyna wanted to issue orders, like she did with her men, but held back and let Clara move at her own pace. They carried what they could, and Bronwyn hoisted Miro's arm back over hers as they started to head farther west.

Amyna only made it about a half mile. Her left leg was not that bad, but her right bled profusely. Her shoulder had fared the best: only a couple of the wolf's teeth had managed to leave superficial cuts. No major vessels were injured, but she was still losing a lot of blood. She collapsed under the weight of Miro. The cold helped with the pain, but her fingers were numb. The blood loss would only cause the hypothermia to set in faster. She attempted to stand but immediately fell to her knees from the excruciating pain in her leg.

"Maybe we can stop for a bit," Clara offered. "We're probably far enough."

Amyna dropped Miro and rolled him onto his back. "Did he teach you any of that healing magic?"

"No, that's the wrong school."

Amyna knew it was, but she hoped that some of his ability would rub off on Clara and she would be able to learn multiple schools. Magi didn't seem to obey the rules of magic she was familiar with.

"We need to wake him up," Amyna said.

Clara shook his shoulder, calling, "Wake up, wake up." When that did not work, she shook him harder.

"Let me do this." Amyna slapped him across the face. Still no response. She slapped him again harder. He stirred with the second assault. She hit him one more time for good measure.

"What the Chivas," he said, touching the red welt on his cheek.

"I'm losing blood. I need your help." Amyna's voice was steady despite her worsening condition.

"I've expended a lot of magic. I'm not sure how much I'll be able to heal, but I'll try my best."

His fingers traced runes, and he laid his hands on her leg. The wound started to stitch itself together and the pain dissipated. He looked at her blue fingertips and lips. "You're hypothermic," he said, with noticeable worry in his voice.

"I know," she said sternly. "Now do the other leg."

He repeated the process, closing that wound as well. She still bled from the bite in her shoulder from when the other wolf took her down. Her pauldrons had mitigated most of the damage, so she opted to not ask Miro to heal that one as well. The previous spells seem to have taken a lot out of him. Rivulets of sweat flowed freely from his temples.

He began to volley questions at them. "Where are we? How far away are we? Where's Naani?"

Clara said, "Naani's gone ..."

"What? How?" he asked.

Amyna slapped him again. "What the Chivas was that!"

"What are you talking about?" Miro replied.

"The floating and lightning and then Naani attacking you," Amyna said. The color had started to return to her lips with her fury.

"I ... I ... I remember the wolves." Miro shook his head and put a hand to it. He struggled with his words. "They bit you ... and then you were down on the ground. And then I can't remember anything besides that."

"You started floating off the ground, speaking in this low, weird voice. Lightning was everywhere. You almost electrocuted Clara. What was that!" Amyna demanded again.

"And you were casting spells without forming runes or asking for the gods' power" Clara added.

A look of realization came across Miro's face. "The magi's curse. In times of great emotional strife or physical harm, we are overtaken by the spirits that lent us their powers, to ensure their investment is protected."

"What do you mean, a curse?" Amyna asked.

"It's difficult to explain. When it happens, you don't have any control over it. Then once you've exhausted the power, you die, so the Ywaigwai can come and claim your soul."

Amyna shook her head, waiting for more of an explanation, but Miro just stared at her in a daze. "You called me Serra," Amyna said.

"That's someone I knew a long time ago. I guess I got confused." Miro held her hand strangely out of the blue. He looked her straight in the eye. She had never really seen his eyes until now: one green, one blue.

"If that ever happens again, run, run as fast as you can." His tone was so serious. She could hear the fear in his voice. "Get as far away from me as possible."

Amyna remembered the warning of the general. *They are enemies of Emestria. If they should pose a threat, cut them down.* She gripped her sword. One quick slice, take his head off now. It would be so fast he would not know what happened. She mulled it in her mind for a minute. *We need the mantle first. Then I will decide.*

Worried about her fingers, Miro removed his cloak and wrapped it around Amyna. Now he supported her as they continued to trudge through the night.

"Do you think they'll come after us?" Clara asked.

"No, I think Naani will be enough to satisfy them for a while," he said, his voice void of emotion.

"Why did she attack you?" Amyna asked.

"Because she sensed I wasn't myself anymore. Or Clara was in danger? Naani would have valued Clara's life more than mine."

"But she didn't kill you." Why had the leopard spared his life but murdered her men so quickly? "She could have killed you. Why didn't she kill you?"

"I don't know. Maybe she thought incapacitating me would be enough. Maybe she tried. By the gods, did I kill Naani?"

Amyna said, "More or less."

Miro didn't press the issue. Amyna let him support her, but she also looked at him suspiciously. *How did he do that? What does he mean? Run? Taking his head will be a much swifter solution if I find myself in that position again.*

It was quiet as they continued walking through the snowy night. When day broke, they made camp, and Clara and Amyna got a couple of hours of sleep, but Miro was jittery and shook, his face colorless. When Amyna woke, they made some pine tea and reheated some of the grouse stock. It warmed their bodies. The color had already started to return to Amyna's fingertips. After eating and drinking, she addressed Miro. "You should get some sleep, then we'll continue."

"I'm not tired," he said. "I don't need to sleep." Beads of sweat still decorated his brow. His face was white, and his breathing was quick. Amyna shrugged, not willing to argue with him.

"Serra?" Amyna asked now that it was just her and Miro.

"Someone I cared about. She helped me build the cabin."

"And did the wolves?" If he called out Serra instead of Amyna's name when the wolves were about to get her, that meant Serra might have died in that way, ripped apart in front of Miro.

"No, something worse. You look a little bit like her." His voice shook and he averted his eyes, so Amyna didn't ask anything more.

# CHAPTER 9

*Defurge, god of fire and madness, inherited much of the power of the twins, but it came at a price. Often called the mad god, Defurge sought a singular purpose, to find his sister, whom the gods tried to keep away from him.*

*He was able to change shape between all manner of creatures: humans, beasts, or more fantastical beings. One description is consistent throughout Derfurge's many forms: all of them possessed an immunity and control over fire, and had a red gem embedded somewhere on their body.*

*—Issaroh, The History of Divinity, Part X*

Clara was glad that the wolves had only caught up to them when they were close to the mountain. They were able to make the rest of the trek in two days through the dense forest. It would have been a few hours with the reindeer, but they did not have that option anymore. They had only brought enough food for four days, and lost most of that when the wolf overturned the sled. Clara had grabbed one of the hares, some of the grouse stock in wineskins, the pot, and kettle. Any more than that would have been too much to carry. Everything else was lost in the snow or would be consumed by the wolves.

Captain Amyna talked little, and startled on several occasions when there was a sudden noise or shadow in the trees. Clara had never seen this behavior from her. Captain Amyna avoided conversation, especially when Naani was mentioned.

Amyna scared up a little game, so the three of them kept their bellies full until they made it to the mountain. Elevation gradually increased on the second day, and the trees grew sparser and thinner. The depth of the snow decreased and hard rocks, hidden underneath the white blanket of cold powder, threatened to twist Clara's ankle several times. Pine scent grew weaker with each step and they soon found themselves looking up at a well-formed path up the side of a medium-sized mountain. The path seemed to be cut into the rock, negating the need for climbing gear, and crisscrossed up the face of the brown behemoth before them. Judging by the crushed trinkets—ceramic jars, painted tiles, and small wooden and marble idols—this was no ordinary path, but was rather one carved by the people that once came here on pilgrimages. Her people, the people of Lynnfield.

"Now we see if the magic you learned will be enough, Clara," Miro said.

Clara walked up to a boulder on the side of the path. There were no signs she could see. "I don't know what to do," she responded. "I thought I would know when I got here, but I don't. Should we start walking?"

"No. Listen to the earth, feel it beneath your feet. Listen to the mountain, feel it with your hands."

Amyna snorted at the comment.

Clara knelt and put her hand to the ground, wiping away snow so she could touch the cold earth. She closed her eyes and waited a minute before admitting, "I don't hear anything." Then she placed her hand on the mountain and closed her eyes, listening for something, anything. Amyna gasped and Clara opened her eyes. At first, she didn't know what elicited the noise from Amyna, but then Clara felt it. A pebble rolled uphill, around her foot. Looking down, tiny rocks moved in the same direction.

"Did I make them move?" Clara asked. She removed her hand from the mountainside and noticed a brown glow to the rock where she had been touching. "But what does it mean?"

"I think we follow the rocks," Miro said.

They started on the path the stones had shown them. Every time they came to a fork in the road, Clara placed her hands back on the mountain and the pebbles moved to show them the way. The number of paths and forks were probably done by the priests of Lynnfield, to confuse anyone from finding the tomb. Clara wondered if what Miro said about the mountain changing paths to keep you lost was true. Naani's death still weighed on her, but the act of leading the group through the mountain helped calm her. She was doing this; decoding this cryptic message her mother left, following in her forebearers' footsteps.

They walked for a whole day through the labyrinth of the mountain. Caverns—some natural, others too regularly shaped to be—honeycombed the topography occasionally. Clara started to worry she was not doing the magic correctly, that she was not making the rocks move in the right direction. She dreaded the idea that the three of them were going in circles. But Miro seemed confident, and Amyna did not betray any hesitation. Clara found herself trying to juggle the versions of herself that appeased either Amyna or Miro. The excitement of using magic appealed to Miro. Amyna got quiet whenever Clara expressed that excitement. *If I have any hope of getting out of Emestria, I'll need Captain Amyna when I return to the capital.*

"Best camp here for the night." Miro pointed at an overhang that created a little cave. In the center, a fire pit—decades old with soot barely visible—lay with a half-dozen good-sized flat-like rock benches stood.

Perhaps they had been worn away by wind and time, but the shape was too regular. It had to be created by man.

It wasn't quite a cave, too shallow to be that, but pillars of rock made a makeshift doorway, and the far wall protected them from a hundred-foot drop. The other exposed section had a half wall, almost like a stone banister. The winds blew around the structure, convincing Clara the whole formation was made by the people of Lynnfield. Clara wondered if other priests had hollowed the stone to make the firepit and shaped the mountain face. Would she ever be able to warp stone like that? All she could manage was to throw a rock and make pebbles roll. She was more capable with her axe than with the magic she was being taught. *It takes time,* she consoled herself. *Probably less when I get Miro to teach me how to be a magus.*

They made camp and cooked up the hare Clara brought. The meal had been saved for when they were starving; they had not stopped to eat today, and the morning's breakfast was only what remained of the grouse stock. Without sustenance, they had stopped every half hour to give their aching muscles a break or catch their breath. There were no complaints from Miro this time. Empty bellies rarely complain about food.

Captain Amyna stepped away to look down the cliff face, leaving Clara and Miro alone for a bit. Clara took the opportunity to say, "If I had been able to cast healing magic, maybe I could have helped with the wolves. I could have saved Naani."

Miro gave her a pointed look and Clara rephrased her comments to seem less like she was fishing for answers. "I just felt so useless, having to watch her die and knowing I couldn't do anything to help her."

"Even if you knew healing arcana, it would have been dangerous." Miro sighed and buried his head in his palm. Clara couldn't tell if it was frustration or sadness. "Healing isn't like the other magics. With the magic I taught you, you're making a small change in the world that disappears the second your rock has been projected. When you heal, you don't get to just cast the magic and have the effect disappear. You draw upon your lifeforce and need to maintain the magic long enough for the body to support the healing necessary. The only reason I could bind Captain Amyna's wounds is because I no longer had to maintain the magic supporting Naani. You might have killed yourself trying to heal Naani, and she wouldn't have wanted that."

"Do you want to talk about her? I only knew her for a bit but would have liked to know her better."

"I'll try. Naani was given a purpose by the gods, to protect your people, to protect you on this journey to the mountains. She achieved her goal. She died doing what she was meant to do."

Clara understood the sentiment a little bit. She couldn't have sacrificed her life to save Naani, even if she was a magus. Miro's display of power and assurances that it was a death sentence seemed real. But Miro didn't have a daughter with a blood disease that required regular expensive healing magic. Clara clasped her hands together and let her right nails dig into her left palm. A daughter that didn't even know Clara was her mother because she had to relinquish Scarlette to her father, someone that could afford the treatments. Even if it cost Clara her own life, she would gladly give it to cure Scarlette permanently and maybe that's why the healers could only treat her illness, not cure it; the healers weren't willing to make the necessary sacrifice.

Miro still seemed shaken by Naani's death, so she didn't ask any more about healing arcana or magi. Clara believed that if she stuck with Miro, he would eventually let her know the secret to becoming a magus.

In the morning, they set out again.

"Am I doing this right?" Clara asked Miro. "I think we're lost."

"No, it's a big mountain. It's a long way," Miro told her.

They reached what Clara assumed was the tomb by midday. Her mother had only mentioned the one tomb, so this had to be the final resting place of Alcides. Two massive granite doors capped a cave on the side of the mountain. Each door was three feet wide and nine feet tall. Their stone façades were carved with casting circles and runes. Clara recognized some of the runes for the spell that she learned to throw rocks, the ones Miro had taught her at his cabin. She had no idea what the others were. Miro was staring at them, similarly perplexed.

Clara tried pushing and pulling on the door, but it would not budge. She placed her hand on it, on the boulders near it, thinking it was a trick like with the rocks. Nothing worked on these stubborn slabs of granite.

Looking at the carvings one more time, Clara thought of something else to try. "Lau'O'Penake, goddess of nature and rebirth, grant me passage, Petravolis," Clara chanted as she formed the spell. Instead of the swirling dirt it had previously created, the runes faded from view. Then the matching symbols on the door began to glow a bright yellow. One of the doors began to open. It scraped and groaned from the years of accumulated dirt and disuse.

The tomb stretched endlessly into the dark. Like many of the catacombs, it was cut through the rock, but unlike them, it was squared off, with cracked tile for floor. Clara stared into the inky void. Along the walls, there were sconces holding unlit torches. There was a tarry substance in a nearby brazier, which was most likely oil at some point. Captain Amyna wrapped the handle of a spent torch with a cloth and lit it with her flint and steel. The quiet lick of the flames beckoned them forward. With each step, the cold mountain breeze mixed with the stagnant air of the tomb. The smell of earth was strong in this place, a musty yet pleasant aroma.

This was holy ground to the people of Lynnfield, her people. Thus, the yearly pilgrimages. Despite her own misgivings about how much Lau'O'Penake had looked out for Scarlette's interests, Clara's father had traveled here to return this mantle, which had to mean something. Maybe the goddess did have some plan that took Clara and Scarlette into account. Why else would this journey take Clara to meet a magus, someone capable of teaching her how to become like him and heal?

As they walked down the corridor, Clara marveled at the images of what she assumed was Alcides etched into the walls. In the natural stone, depressions had been formed depicting a heroic figure in many battles, with people bowing to him, monsters crushed under his feet, and gods twice his size bestowing blessings. One stood out, and Clara found herself drawn to it. Alcides held a lapidary hammer while sitting in front of an anvil. Broken weapons, instruments, and household items lay at his feet. *How did he use such a small hammer to break all these things?*

Miro said, "Alcides was half-god. To join the gods in the afterlife he had to prove himself worthy. So, he traveled around the world to complete acts of heroism and prove his worth. The first was slaying a rogue spirit guardian that had gone rabid, a ferocious bear with an impenetrable hide. That did not stop Alcides, though. He picked up a club and bludgeoned the beast. He may not have been able to pierce its skin, but he did damage to everything inside. He then had the animal flayed and made into a cloak. Proof of his deed—that he was worthy.

"The bludgeoning or the death of the spirit guardian caused the hide to lose some of its invulnerability. But the cloak was still remarkably resilient, saving Alcides a handful of times throughout his quests. It was rumored he uncovered countless artifacts through his trials and tribulations. The mantle is the only one I corroborated. And here I thought it was destroyed at Lynnfield."

They continued to move along the corridor until the trio came upon a ten-foot statue of Alcides. Perched atop the marble sculpture was his brown furred mantle. The bear's head was over Alcides, and the pelt from the arms draped over his shoulders. Despite its age—Alcides lived over five centuries ago—the bear looked as if the skinning happened only yesterday.

Beyond Alcides, the tomb continued further, and Clara wondered if they traveled all the way back, would they come upon his sarcophagus or would there be bones laid upon some type of raised dais?

Clara wanted to reach out and grab the mantle, but part of her wanted to leave it there. To walk away. Her family and ancestors had done so much to protect it. And she was doing what, trading it for her life? How many other people had given up their own to make sure this artifact remained hidden? Was it even right, her desire to live? To sacrifice this for herself?

But, it was not just her life she was trying to protect.

Was this the test that Lau'O'Penake could have set in motion, the one that would lead her to being able to cure Scarlette? No, she needed Miro to teach her the healing arcana, and the only way to do that and leave this country would be to surrender the mantle.

Miro seemed similarly awestruck. He stared at the garment wide eyed. His hands trembled as he looked on. Captain Amyna snatched the cloak with little fanfare or reverence. She gave it a couple of hardy slaps and clouds of dust from fifteen untouched years—shortly before the destruction of Lynnfield—filled the tomb. Then a vibration sounded from the darkness, familiar, yet muted—like an anchor's chain dragging across the edge of a ship's deck. "I don't think we're alone," she said.

Just out of torchlight, something undulated. Captain Amyna drew her greatsword and prepared, the mantle sliding to the floor as she did.

She was much too fast for the creature's feeble lunge. The head was severed in one fell swoop. A huge snake; the detached jaw still mawed at the air, the arrow shape atop of its skull indicating it was venomous. Bronwyn picked the mantle back up and tossed it over her shoulder again. Triumphantly, she hoisted her sword onto her back. The beast's body heaved and twisted. The movements seemed to be more than the last twitches of death.

"It's not dead," Clara bemoaned.

Captain Amyna turned around. The body still writhed painfully. Two membranous sacs spilled out of its neck. As the tissue parted, there were two heads where she had severed the first. The scales were light and almost translucent, but quickly hardened.

"Great, a hydra," Miro said, putting words to what Clara was thinking.

Undeterred Captain Amyna tossed Miro the mantle, grabbed her sword, and dodged as one of the heads made a lunge at her, and like the first, she severed it with ease. Predictably, this led to a three-headed hydra.

"Stop cutting them off!" Miro complained. "You've got to burn them after you sever them. Hold out your sword."

Captain Amyna seemed deterred at the prospect of not being able to eliminate as many heads as possible. She displayed no fear toward the creature, not that she had displayed any against the wolves or Naani. In fact, she seemed to be immune to fear, at least from what Clara had seen.

"I call upon the blood of Defurge, god of fire and madness, bless thy weapon with flame, Inflagrata Implementis." Miro's runes circled and surrounded the blade. The runes disappeared with the circle, and the symbols reappeared on Amyna's sword. They glowed bright orange and the tip now sported a small flame. She took one look at it and continued her dance with the hydra.

Clara was entranced watching Captain Amyna fight. She ducked and dodged with ease, causing the creature's advances to be ineffective. She was like a mongoose. Her innate understanding of the creature's reach allowed her to goad and taunt it into useless strikes. She jumped and twisted in the air as the thing tired itself out trying to catch a piece of her. It was much different than when she fought the leopard or wolves, monstrosities that came charging with little worry of physical harm. They lacked strategy and relied on brute force. This thing, however, tried to back Amyna into a corner. She read its movements and deftly deflected blows or sidestepped, keeping the monster exasperated.

Two of the heads attempted to corner her at once. Amyna used her sword to knock the first set of fangs away from her flank, then spun and did the same to the second. The third head lunged forward, and Amyna hopped backwards, just out of the venomous bite's range. The jaws snapped and Amyna seemingly playfully batted the stone scaled beast's jaw away with her sword.

With each movement, Captain Amyna was drawing further toward the edge of the darkness of the tomb, separating her from Miro and Clara. When another strike threatened to push her completely out of torchlight, Amyna dashed to the side, around the statue of Alcides.

The hydra swung its tail away from the statue in an attempt to trip the captain, but she leapt over it once, then twice as it swung back, almost like she was jumping rope. The heads swooped back around the statue, forcing her back toward the wall again and despite the thought of being backed into a corner, Amyna smirked.

As the hydra went to try and surround her with two of its heads again, she ducked under the head coming from one side, using it as an obstacle to slow the other. Slowly she backed away behind the statue one more time.

Finally, it had enough of trying to catch Amyna and turned the attention of one of its heads toward Clara. The wide grin now painted across Amyna's face indicated this was exactly what she wanted. The first slice was so fast Clara had not even noticed it until the head tilted off its neck.

Captain Amyna dipped as the second head, now furious, tried to strike her, and with an upward swing she severed that one as well. The third head tried to escape in a futile bid for survival. With a powerful downward strike, she sliced the last neck in two. Captain Amyna smiled confidently.

And Clara now understood why Amyna was sent on this mission. Up until that point, her considerable prowess had been wasted, but this creature allowed Amyna to display the skill she had trained for.

"That was amazing, Captain" Clara said in awe.

"That was very reckless," Miro rebuked Amyna. "One scratch from a hydra's fang and there would have been no way to save you. If you had backed off a little, I could have helped with magic."

"I was never in any danger," Amyna said with a satisfied smile. She watched as her greatsword cooled. Once the orange runes faded and the flaming tip dissipated, she slid the weapon into the scabbard at her back.

"It was young," Miro continued to admonish her. "If you had kept cutting off necks without the flame, we would have had a twelve-headed hydra in no time."

"Well, lucky for us, you used your little fire spell, O great and powerful magus," Amyna teased, waving the fingers of one hand dismissively, eliciting a sigh from Miro.

Clara walked up to one of the heads with trepidation. The jaws opened and gasped for air.

"Be careful, Clara, they can still bite even if they're dead," Miro warned. "Their poison is very potent."

Clara took several steps back.

"That's actually how Alcides died," Miro added, the confident tone in which he told the story earlier returned. "His wife, jealous that he might have taken a lover, put a drop of hydra poison on his shirt. The next time she thought he was going to see his mistress; she gave him that shirt to wear. Even contact with the skin is enough to kill."

Clara nodded and Amyna rolled her eyes.

"It goes to show you that even a demigod is still vulnerable to the human condition," Miro said.

"It goes to show you that you shouldn't betray your loved ones," Amyna corrected.

"Yes, yes," Miro agreed in contemplation.

"How do you propose we travel back to Emestria?" Captain Amyna asked as she started to walk from the tomb, taking the mantle back from Miro and tossing it over her shoulder once again.

"I can use the rocks, and we follow them backward," Clara declared, happy to be of some use again.

"No, I mean once we're off the mountain. It will take us weeks to walk back to Solstice. We don't have horses, our reindeer is dead, the sleigh is wrecked. The wolves will probably have had their fill …." She stopped momentarily and rephrased, "They'll come hunt us again." Amyna listed the failures of this expedition. There were still many compared to their lone triumph of a bear's hide.

"I saw some goats on the mountain," Miro offered. "They're generally hard to work with, but if we can make a deal with them, they might be willing to take us." The goats, like everything else in the north, were exceptionally large. The extra mass aided in maintaining body temperature in the cold.

"What don't you talk to?" Amyna chided.

"Wolves," Miro muttered under his breath.

Captain Amyna looked to a wide-eyed Clara and reassured her, "They'll be plenty big enough for you, just hold on tight. It might be a little difficult for Miro and me, but we'll try some of the larger members of a herd."

As they started down the mountain, Miro kept an eye out for goats. Captain Amyna held the mantle over her shoulder, almost like a draped towel. She seemed to have little regard for it, and Clara worried Amyna would drop it again.

"Captain Amyna, do you think I could hold it?" Clara asked.

"Sure, but don't strain yourself. If it's too much to carry it, just give it back."

The two of them treating her as a child had worn her patience thin. She was older than Captain Amyna. Clara's eyes and mouth sported faint wrinkles, while Amyna's skin was still young and taut. But she allowed it. She needed them to underestimate her, to be protective of her. Amyna tossed Clara the mantle.

Clara almost dropped it but was glad she had not. The artifact looked so common, but she had this newfound reverence for the relic that Amyna lacked. Was it some new connection she had gained praying to Lau'O'Penake, or a tiny hope that there was a grand plan in all of this that took her into account.

She wondered what the mantle's ultimate fate would be. Would the king wear it as some proof his rule was the gods' will? Maybe a general or soldier would wear it into battle. Blood and dirt would stain the pristine hide. Perhaps the kingdom would sell it to some collector of noble birth, or it would sit in some dusty corner, forgotten. It felt so wrong having to turn this artifact over to the Emestrians.

Clara debated running back to the tomb. Replacing it and leaving Miro and Amyna lost on the mountain. That's why her father brought this here, why he never returned, to keep it out of the hands of Emestria. But then of course, if she ran with the mantle, she would also be lost. She was at home on the seas, able to fish for her food and find a safe harbor when she needed to sleep. Here, though, she was out of her element. She did not have the skill to hunt and was unsure what plants were edible. She had been relying on Amyna for all that knowledge.

She also wanted to learn more about magic. Had she reached the extent of her powers, or would she be able to learn more? Could she one day cause the very earth to shake and swallow up her enemies? She had heard of people able to cast that type of spell. Or would Miro teach her how to be a magus? Able to learn healing magic and return to Corinth, far to the east where her mother, aunt, and daughter now lived? She could make a good living as a healer, better than smuggling. So much so that even if she couldn't learn the spell to treat Scarlette's affliction, she could afford the treatments. She was sure that her two compatriots couldn't see her nervous tick as she tucked a hand behind the mantle and pressed the fingernails firmly into the meatiest portion of her palm.

She was also growing accustomed to Miro and Amyna. They always argued, which had been annoying at first, but now and then she would chuckle at their fighting, which earned her looks of derision from them both. That made her want to laugh more, but she would put on an air of seriousness, causing them to return to their quibbling.

The goats were not hard to find. There were plenty on the mountain, however, every herd seemed unwilling to talk, much less descend from their lofty perch. Finally, they caught a group grazing on a plateau, eating some of the hardy weeds that thrived in the cold weather. Miro approached by himself, under the guise of having a pleasant conversation. He sat among them and laughed and joked. It was different than when he talked to Naani. They always shouted at each other.

Clara wondered if all animals talked differently? Leopards like to shout, goats like jokes. Would Miro teach her that magic? Could she one day have a conversation with a horse or cat? How would cats like to be talked to? She thought they would enjoy whispering.

Captain Amyna was less amused by the situation. She tapped her foot anxiously, staring at Miro.

A sudden sense of dread gripped Clara. What if she returned the mantle and the Emestrians did not keep their bargain? She had always been aware of this possibility in the back of her mind, but frankly, she worried they wouldn't survive. Especially after the run-in with Naani. She took a little confidence from Miro's word that he would make them honor their deal. He went berserk with the wolves. Was he able to control that power if he was calm—and wanted to? If he could, the king would be forced to honor their deal. This made her feel a little more at ease.

Miro finally got the goats to agree to take them as far as Solstice, or at least a day's walk. The goats worried that if they got any closer, they would end up being someone's lunch. In Emestria's despair, its citizens had been hunting everything they could, and Clara knew without a doubt they would happily eat a wild goat. They bargained for four bushels of onions in exchange for passage; a deal if Clara had ever heard one. *These goats like onions; who would have guessed?*

Riding a goat was a lot more difficult than riding a horse or reindeer; they had no saddles. Amyna tried to hang onto the horns of one of the goats, causing it to bleat in protest and refuse to move. So instead, they each laid down on their goat's back and lightly gripped it around the neck or chest. To make matters worse, the goats went up over the mountains.

Clara tried to open her eyes as little as possible. The goats scaled enormous cliffs or bounced down steep slopes of loose rocks. The goats did not think this was dangerous or scary to their passengers. Even Amyna was perturbed by the situation. The few times Clara opened her eyes, she saw Amyna's were squeezed shut. Miro, however, relished the experience. Every time Clara looked over, he would be trying to balance himself atop the goat to get a better view. Clara wondered if there was some spell able to negate fear that he employed.

# Chapter 10

*Laevin, lord of lightning and scrying, was not originally the head of the pantheon. As civilization expanded, many of the gods' patron nations started to buttress against each other. Rather than risk all-out war and annihilation, an arbiter, Laevin, was chosen to decide when a conflict had played out and the spoils of victory for each civilization and god.*

*—Issaroh, The history of Divinity, Part III*

It took three days to reach Emestria. They had discarded most of their supplies; the goats were big but refused to carry extra weight because that had not been agreed upon in their deal. Captain Amyna, Miro, and Clara had no food the first night. The second and third were more of the same, except now it was even harder to hang on, given their fatigue from the lack of nutrition.

The goats, true to their word, tried to drop them off one day's walk from Emestria. However, they chose a one-day walk for a goat and wanted to leave them in the mountains, surrounded by unscalable cliffs. This was probably all part of their plan, and changing the destination required Miro to agree to an extra bushel of onions.

When they finally dismounted the goats—close to Solstice—the goats expected to receive their reward immediately. Miro explained to them that he did not have the onions. Amyna marveled at the goats' skill in negotiating, but utter lack of sense when it came to whether Miro had the promised foodstuffs. Miro promised that in two days, the onions would be brought back to this location by midafternoon, and he used some sticks, stones, and branches to mark off the area. *The goats trust too easily.* Amyna would have reneged on their bushels of onions if it were up to her.

For the fourth night, they went hungry. Amyna dreamed of the lavish feast that awaited her when she returned triumphantly. She rose early the next morning, a rarity for her, and prodded and cajoled her comrades into leaving right then. If they hurried, they could make it back to Solstice by dinner. She might even make it in time to get some actual meat in her stew in the great hall that evening.

She entertained the idea of dining at the palace, but banished the thought. To her, that was too great an honor and luxury. Luckily, the woods were devoid of life this close to Solstice. They were able to walk in relative solitude. Amyna still kept a keen eye and ready ear scanning for signs or sounds of trouble. However, it was uneventful, and for the best; she was exhausted.

When they reached Solstice, the sun had started to dip down below the western mountains. The guards at the north gate were surprised to see Captain Amyna. She hoped that was because few people ever entered via this side of town. Maybe they were shocked to see only her return, without her men.

*Families are bereft of loved ones. They are not coming back. The men died under my leadership, and I'll personally visit their houses to make the announcements. This evening will be filled with teary-eyed children and weeping widows and widowers.*

Clara and Miro seemed uneasy being in the capital, but Amyna walked with confidence. This was her home, where she felt most comfortable. No surprises in store for her. She made for the castle first to report on her expedition, which Clara and Miro were less enthusiastic about. Miro had spent time in the dungeon as well. Perhaps the proximity to a location of torment for them made them wary. Only with her sincere word that she personally, as head of the guard, guaranteed their safety did they agree.

"I've returned with the Mantle of Alcides," Amyna announced to one of the castle guards.

He gave her a perplexed look.

"King Bryant himself tasked me with retrieving it. Inform him of my success."

Despite this man being her subordinate, he seemed unwilling to grant her request. However, when she gripped her greatsword's hilt, he acquiesced. Her troops were well aware of the wallops she dished out to those that chose to ignore her orders.

The guard tracked down a chambermaid and delivered the news. Amyna expected her to dash off, but instead she strolled to the king's chambers leisurely. *What has this castle come to in the short time I have been gone?*

Her worries were quelled as she saw none other than King Bryant himself striding toward them, absent the general and his advisor. She kneeled briefly, placing her hand over her chest, before rising, remembering their conversation in the war room.

"Captain Amyna. Welcome back. May I see it?" King Bryant requested—as if he would be denied anything he wanted.

Clara held out the mantle reluctantly.

"I expected ... something more ... I don't know, regal?" King Bryant said.

"Arty." Miro spoke up, seemingly annoyed that King Bryant had yet to acknowledge his presence.

"Sir Krestel," King Bryant replied, "I would prefer it if you didn't call me that."

"It's just Miro." The corner of Miro's upper lip twitched at the correction. "And I would prefer it if you kept your word, but we can't always get what we want, as you so eloquently put it one time." The king hung his head, avoiding eye contact with Miro, directing his gaze toward Amyna and Clara instead.

*It is odd, this man chastising someone so much his senior,* Amyna thought.

"You made a deal with this woman." Miro gestured toward Clara. "I trust at least this pact will be honored. Or do you wish to break that as well?"

Captain Amyna wasn't sure, but it sounded like Miro just threatened her king. It was more than a threat though. He looked at King Bryant as if he were his equal, and the king finally met Miro's gaze with some semblance of respect. They squared off like rivals or old lovers, rather than a bastard with a nobleman's surname and his liege.

"She's not a spy, just a smuggler," Amyna added, hoping this information would placate any worries the king harbored. She did not like the way Miro talked to him, and the hairs on the back of her neck were beginning to stand on end.

"In exchange for the Mantle of Alcides, you shall receive a writ of passage, allowing you to leave the kingdom at your leisure. However, if you do return, I request that you seek an audience prior to doing any business. For your safety, of course." King Bryant's regal tone returned. "Now, how am I supposed to know if this is the Mantle of Alcides?"

He was holding the mantle aloft when Miro started chanting. "I implore you Laevin, god of lightning and scrying, Bolta Levos." The circle appeared much faster than any spell Miro had cast at this point, except for when he was levitating. The bluish-purple runes coalesced into a bolt of lightning, shooting toward King Bryant. The lightning blunted and dissipated when it made contact with the mantle, as effective as a torch thrown into a lake. Amyna was quick to move, but not quick enough. She had been caught unawares by Miro's sudden betrayal. Forcing him against the wall, she held her sword to his throat, but she had not been fast enough to prevent the spell from shooting toward the king. The other two guards grabbed Clara.

"That's quite all right," the startled king replied. He still held the mantle aloft. The king seemed pleasantly amused at the display. "You may release them."

Captain Amyna relaxed her grip before pressing the sword a little harder against Miro's neck. She leaned in close, her lips inches from his ear. With fierce conviction she whispered, "If you try anything like that again, I will end you. It will be quick and quiet and there will be nothing you can do."

Miro didn't react, only leveled a half smile toward her. Usually, men cowered at her threats. When she finally released him, he smoothed out his robe before saying, "He wouldn't believe it was real unless he saw its power firsthand."

"Fascinating." The king checked the hide for any sign of damage from the reckless spell. "Is it just lightning? Or does it repel all spells? What about weapons?"

"I don't know; we hadn't tried anything till now," Miro said, chuckling.

Amyna brandished her greatsword at him again. "You didn't know it was going to stop the magic?"

"I had very good reason to believe it would," he said while shrugging and scratching his head.

"Very well," King Bryant continued, undeterred. "Tonight you, the … smuggler …"

"Clara," Amyna corrected as the king struggled with what to call her.

"Yes, Clara. You, Clara, and your men are invited to dine with me at the castle. Tomorrow we will make an announcement. Miro, I'm afraid you're still not welcome." King Bryant grinned.

"So, my usual room then?" Miro asked.

"Yes, I assume you know the way and won't need to be escorted?" King Bryant replied.

"Of course not, wouldn't want you to go out of your way to show your guest some common courtesy," Miro said before turning and walking down one of the hallways. He opened a door and descended some stairs and then was out of sight.

"Now, I'm sure your men are anxious to spend time with their loved ones, but I graciously request their presence," King Bryant said.

"I'm sorry, my liege." Amyna raised her right fist over her heart. "We were the only ones to return. We buried them in the north. I plan to inform their families."

"I'm disappointed to hear that. We will try to make compensation when the kingdom is in better straits. In the meantime, we can increase their rations to double. Hopefully, that small gesture will convey our gratitude and condolences."

"I shall inform them that King Bryant himself made this offer," Amyna said while slightly bowing.

"While Captain Amyna is informing the next of kin, Clara, perhaps you would like to retire to our library? I would entertain you, but we have war planning and outside of myself, the advisor, and General Tiernan, others aren't privy to that information. Not that I doubt you aren't a spy.

"Please show her the way," the king told a chambermaid.

"I could go with Miro," Clara said while being led away.

"I'm sorry; he'll be otherwise occupied." King Bryant headed up the stairs to his war room.

***

Two of the men did not have families to speak of, but only some friends and acquaintances, as they were orphans brought up in the employ of the guard. One other man was survived by his elderly father, who wept bitterly at the news. Another's young wife screamed, wailed, and clawed as Amyna held her, trying to provide comfort. There was an older matron with three young boys that seemed more appreciative of the extra rations than distraught at the loss of her husband. However, the last family was the worst.

His wife had a simple beauty about her. When she found out the news, she became somber and sullen. Her children wailed and kept asking when he would be back. She explained to them multiple times that he would not return. Each time they seemed shocked by the information only to ask again a couple of minutes later. Captain Amyna stayed with this widow the longest. The third time the mother informed the children, she started to sob openly. Amyna embraced the widow and cradled her head as she laid it onto Amyna's shoulder.

"Your husband was a great man. He may have saved the entire kingdom with his sacrifice." Amyna did not have the heart to tell the mother, *You are most likely better off. He threatened to do unspeakable things to my prisoner, and if he had not died, he would be facing disciplinary hearings.* The point was moot. At least some good could come of this, and her children would not be forced to wither on half rations.

It took longer than Captain Amyna thought. She was famished and ashamed that all she could think about was going back to the castle and possibly arriving in time for dinner. Fortunately, they had waited for her to return. The king sat at the table making pleasant conversation with Clara. The advisor and General Tiernan sat to either side of the king and a couple of servants waited at the edges of the room.

"Captain Amyna! Now we can eat," Clara exclaimed when Amyna finally arrived. Clara's excited attitude seemed out of place with the events of the last couple of weeks.

"My apologies; I didn't want to rush my duties." Amyna was both pleased and dismayed to see the humble spread before them. She had pictured a suckling pig, fruits from all over the world, cheeses she had never heard of, and a dozen different types of bread with butter. Instead, what greeted her was a modest bird, some soup, stale rolls, and several small casks of wine.

Emestrians were quite fond of drinking to withstand the cold winters. Nobility drank wine, but the commoners usually partook in spirits fermented from root vegetables. It was a little disappointing, but she would have felt guilty taking part in a more extravagant meal.

"Yes, thank you for doing that." General Tiernan feigned interest as he began to impatiently grab his soup from a servant. "I would have offered, but I knew you'd attend to your responsibilities personally."

The false claim didn't even deserve a reply from Amyna.

"Captain Amyna, we are grateful," King Bryant said. "The families may not appreciate it now. But in the future, the fact that their commanding officer delivered the news will mean something."

"Thank you. You are too kind." Amyna felt like she was playacting. The fatigue, hunger, and emotional toll of informing the families made her want to be alone. However, in the castle she felt she needed to act a certain way. Maybe that is all living in the castle and dining with the king was, playacting. She resigned herself to be a pleasant dinner guest.

"Your first Legendary Artifact," the king started. "That must be an exciting story. Care to regale us with your adventures?"

Amyna was about to start droning on about it, but Clara smiled knowingly and began to retell the tale. "Well, first there was this giant leopard. She was as big as a house. She attacked us, but it was a misunderstanding ..."

Amyna didn't pay attention to the content of Clara's story. Rather she noticed how Clara had switched back into speaking excitably like when she was talking to Miro at the cabin. It was almost imperceptible the way the men's attitude changed toward her when she acted bubbly.

"And that's when we met Miro. He healed my leg, and he could also cast Frian magic, which Captain Amyna thought was impossible ..."

Amyna tensed as Clara came to this section in her meandering, unintelligible retelling. With the general here, he might request Miro's execution if he heard about how Miro lost control during the wolves' attack. Amyna stared intently at the general, waiting for him to say something about Miro. But Tiernan was too engrossed in his meal to pay attention to Clara's story. Amyna bored of it as well, having already experienced everything. Only King Bryant followed with pleasure.

"... and so Miro got the goats to agree to take us back," Clara said. "Oh, and we owe them five bushels of onions. In two days, midafternoon. It's only a couple of hours ride. Goats are excellent dealmakers because at first, it was four bushels, but they tricked us, and we had to give them five. From there we walked back to the castle and now we're having dinner."

Captain Amyna was glad Clara left out certain details. Perhaps she was more tactful than she let on.

"What adventure," the king remarked.

"What are you going to do with it?" Clara now asked, her air of cheeriness dissipating.

"Well, it would be of little value on the battlefield," King Bryant admitted. "Sure, it might shield a soldier from an attack, but if we then lost a soldier, we would lose the relic. Tomorrow we will make an announcement. Tell the people that help is coming: we've found one artifact and there are others that we will uncover. After that, it will be kept in the royal vault. When the war is concluded, we'll have a statue of Alcides commissioned and display it there. Clara, this relic is a symbol of hope for my people, and we will treat it with care and reverence," he said, trying to put her mind at ease.

"Captain Amyna, do you think that you would like to continue this hunt for artifacts? With Miro."

"I would do anything for my king," she replied, snapping to attention. "However, I must talk with Miro and learn his reason for seeking the artifacts before I take him along. May I ask where his room is, so I can discuss the matter after dinner?"

The general bellowed a loud guffaw. "His room? Why, he is in the dungeon, my dear captain. Can't let a man like that loose in the capital.

It is dangerous, you see. Speaking of which, during your travels, did you ever feel that he was a threat to our kingdom?"

Captain Amyna tensed at the question she hoped to avoid. She saw King Bryant wince as well. His eyes seemed to plead with her, there was definitely something more to his relationship with Miro than either let on. Amyna answered quickly before Clara could say anything. "He is well versed in history and has studied these artifacts, although one could learn this information from his writing. His peculiar knowledge of magic allowed him to cast spells from multiple schools, which I thought impossible till traveling with him."

"What type of magic?" General Tiernan's asked suspiciously.

"Nothing major. I saw him cast healing spells, summon a lightning bolt and wall of ice, and various other cantrips and minor castings," Amyna lied outright. Although the general was not her commanding officer, the guard corps being separate from the military proper, this would still be grounds for court-martial. She looked about the table to see if anyone would contradict her statement. She didn't know if the general, advisor, or king was even aware what a magus was. No one seemed to use the word, and in all her training she had never come across a description of someone that could use magic like Miro did.

"And did he ever cast without rune circles, or without saying prayer?" The advisor finally added something to the conversation. Amyna thought it a peculiar question and perhaps her judgment that the king didn't know about magi was premature. The advisor seemed to have some inkling of what Miro was capable of.

"No." Captain Amyna paused. "I found him to be a jack of all trades, not having mastery over any one school, but dabbling in all of them." No one bothered to correct her on that account either.

"Very well," General Tiernan grumbled.

"Your Majesty," Amyna redirected, "how are we to search out more of these Legendary Artifacts? I read through his book about them during our journey, but there was no mention of any within Emestria's borders."

"Yes, our people have never been one to rely on anything but the strength of their arms and the wits in their heads. I am working on plans for an offensive at the Iron Bridge. It should buy you two enough time to successfully escape the siege. We secured Roukian uniforms. I figure we make a charge and you two could slip through in all the confusion."

Clara spoke up. "Actually, if you were to give me a small boat, I could smuggle them both out to Newtonne. If we were given proper provisions and compensation that is." She took a bite of the meat on her plate and smiled coyly.

"Well, bless our luck." The king returned her smile. "We will provide you with a small vessel, food for the journey, and generous compensation for your time. However, I would like to make you a proposition. Rather than us paying you once for your smuggling expertise, how about I offer you a job?"

"I'm afraid I don't work cheap," Clara replied. "What do you have in mind?"

"I enjoyed the retelling of your adventure. In exchange for providing me with more of your colorful commentary, I am prepared to hire you as the official chronicler for this expedition. I can provide a monthly salary. It won't be as lucrative as smuggling, but it might be safer."

"Sire, are we really in a position for such frivolity?" the advisor asked.

"I'm sure we have some things of value left we can offer. Perhaps ... Yes. I will give you my prize messenger falcon, Ferdinand. With a homing stone, you will be able to provide regular updates. Consider it your down payment for the first couple of months."

Captain Amyna was shocked. Messenger falcons were exceptionally rare. Even the emperor of Tara only employed a dozen. Amyna didn't even know King Bryant owned one.

"I'll take the bird as payment for the first couple of months," Clara said. "By the third month, I will be expecting monetary compensation."

*Clara makes a good goat,* Captain Amyna thought while taking a bite of her roll.

"Very well, then," the king laughed.

"Sire," the advisor said, trying to intervene again.

"There is nothing to worry about." He turned his attention to Clara. "It's a secret, but I'm affianced to a princess of Tara. She has a sizable dowry, so once you and your friends see us through the winter, I will be able to afford your services. Until then, I can find some assets to liquidate."

He turned his attention back to his advisor. "How much do you think one of those nobles will buy my crown for, Edward?"

"Sire, please don't joke about such things." His admonishments elicited laughter from the king.

The convivial tone started to make Amyna uncomfortable. "Your Majesty, if I may, how do you know Miro? He provided little information about your association."

The king, advisor, and general shot each other suspicious looks. The room was suddenly silent. "Oh yes, well, we served together at the Battle of Lynnfield. He was part of my regiment, our support mage."

"Was there a lack of suitable candidates?" Amyna resumed her questioning, undeterred about how nervous it made everyone. "He would have been so young."

"Yes, he does appear young, but he is only one or two years my junior," King Bryant explained. "I guess ruling diminished my once-handsome looks."

"That's only because he's been playing house in the north with no worries," the general spat between mouthfuls of meat.

The conversation returned to Clara and her chronicling, which concerned Amyna. No one wanted to ever discuss the Battle of Lynnfield. Her father died there, and she had never been able to get a straight answer from anyone on what happened. An apocalyptic weapon of Roukian design, she was told. If that were the case, why hadn't Rouke deployed the weapon again? They could destroy the Iron Bridge, as well as wipe out the Emestrian army. She tried to keep her composure about this latest round of avoidance.

After ten more minutes the conversation lulled again. "Sire, if I may, I wish to take my leave and determine what motives Miro has for assisting in obtaining these artifacts."

"Very well." The king called to one of the serving maids. "Marielle?"

She approached and offered a slight curtsy. "Your Majesty."

"Please bring our guest some food and show Captain Amyna the way."

The servant gathered a portion of the banquet and started to guide Amyna. They went out into the main hall, along the corridor, and down the same flight of stairs where she had seen Miro disappear. The dungeon was this way. A knot festered in Captain Amyna's stomach. Not from the idea of him being locked up, but from the carefree nature he marched toward imprisonment. He acted as if it was no small thing to be confined in a five-by-five cell. As the maid continued to walk through the halls, Amyna avoided staring through the bars into the meager cells lining either side. Thankfully, there were few prisoners, but she still had difficulty meeting their gaze, knowing what happened down here. After seeing Clara's battered body, it made everything more real. She knew about the torture techniques to extract information, but never witnessed it firsthand.

Little light was kept in the dungeons and the smell of unwashed bodies and bodily excretions overpowered the faint hint of blood. Each cell contained a cot, but most of them bore holes and tears in the fabric. A lone straw pillow—evident by the sharp yellow protrusions—was supplied for each cot, and aside from that and a chamber pot, nothing else was present in the cells, not even a stool.

The military handled interrogations, but the guard corps kept one man stationed down here. Of course, they did not participate in army affairs like torture. She always hated assigning dungeon duty, but one man, Kaleb, volunteered for it despite the lower pay because of the security afforded by the position. Unless there was a violent escape, the dungeon was far away from any real danger. It always bothered her—the man that volunteered. She worried that Kaleb enjoyed seeing the broken bodies of the abused. His voice echoed along the stone walls.

"No, she's sixteen now. Even has some noblemen looking to become her suitor, but I'm old fashioned. No courting until after she comes of age."

"Ah, but young love never waits. If you don't start entertaining some of them, she might do something drastic and elope." Amyna recognized Miro's nonchalant attitude.

"Hey, that's my little girl." Kaleb's demeanor was also jovial.

"All I'm saying is they all grow up sometime," Miro said.

"Everyone except you, of course. You haven't aged a day since the last time you were here, more than a decade ago."

"Well, Kaleb, my good man, it's the cold air up north. It freezes your blood, so you always look young." Miro laughed.

"Someday you'll tell me for real. My wife is starting to notice every little gray hair that pops up."

Captain Amyna and the servant were now within sight and the guard snapped to attention, resuming the post that he so blatantly ignored up till now. As Amyna approached the cell, looking through the bars, she noticed it was different than the others. Along the walls, ceiling, and floor were runes etched in the stonework and colored white. She had never seen these symbols before and wondered if it was something Miro did during his time in the dungeon.

"The king provided a special meal for the prisoner today," the maid said, setting the tray down on a table Kaleb had been leaning against and taking her leave.

"Oh jeez, look at this." Kaleb admired the spread. "They even brought you some wine. You'll eat what the king eats tonight. See, he's not all bad."

Miro glanced at the dinner and narrowed his eyes. "Hey, does your wife still make those cheese sandwiches?"

"Of course, every day, that's my dinner."

"Well, I've eaten nothing but grouse for the last two days and ate a huge meal for lunch. It is such a waste of all this food. I'll tell you what, I'll trade you meals."

Kaleb looked at the food, then back at Miro. "Are you serious?"

"I'm stuffed, but man, do I miss your wife's cheese sandwiches," Miro lied. Captain Amyna had spent the four days with him starving together.

She wondered why he would refuse the food the king offered. Was it due to his aversion to eating animals from the land, or some grudge toward King Bryant?

"Okay." Kaleb fished around in his knapsack and handed Miro a meager piece of bread folded around the thinnest slice of cheese Amyna had ever seen. Kaleb looked toward his captain. "But I can't take the wine. I'm on duty and all."

"Save it for after work. I've got such a hangover already," Miro lied for a second time.

"I think that should be all right." Kaleb looked at Amyna. "Captain?"

"Yes, that should be all right," she said, remembering that she was the superior officer to this man. Over the last week, she had grown accustomed to not being in charge of others. She was out of practice at telling people what was and was not allowed.

"I would like to question the prisoner in private," she said.

"I don't know what you did, but now I truly feel sorry for you," Kaleb said, his stance relaxing before he looked back at Amyna and snapped to attention. "Yes, Captain. I shall go check the other cells."

Captain Amyna ignored the lapse in duty. She thought it a product of his casual nature around Miro rather than insubordination. "Remember to take your food," Amyna said.

Kaleb grabbed the plate, but left the cup of wine on the table.

"Captain, thank you for coming to see my new place. Let me show you around. This is the door." Miro shook the cell door slightly. "It's made of the finest steel. This is my bed and that, of course, is my only window."

Captain Amyna could not tell if he was complaining or joking. "Old friends?" Amyna motioned at Kaleb walking away. She waited until he was out of earshot. "Never quite trusted why he always volunteered for this post."

"What, Kaleb? No, he's the greatest. He checked on us after the military finished, made sure we were all right, helped us back to our cells, even shared some food when he had extra. So, what brings you by?" Miro flopped down on the bed. He put his hands behind his head, cushioning it from the hard stone.

"What is this?" Amyna pointed to the scrawlings on the wall.

"Confinement spells, so I can't cast while I'm in here. I taught the torturers how to do them, of course."

Clara had been traumatized by her stay in the dungeon. Miro acted like it was the best inn in town. Captain Amyna got close to the cell bars, so she could be sure no one else heard her. "The general asked me if you displayed any unique abilities or cast complex spells," she said in a low, steady voice.

"Oh." Miro suddenly became quite melancholy. "What did you tell them?"

"Nothing, but I can march back up there and tell them everything I saw. Unless you can give me some answers."

Miro got off the bed and approached the bars as well. "I told you what I know. I can't explain it, and I don't have any real control over it."

Miro was referring to his curse most likely, not what Amyna was interested in. "Not that. I want to know about the Battle of Lynnfield." Amyna burned her stare into his eyes, anxious for something, anything—one small detail about that battle. "You served with King Bryant; you must have seen what happened. No one will give me a straight answer."

"You don't want to know about the Battle of Lynnfield," Miro said, turning away.

Captain Amyna grabbed his arm through the bars. It was not forceful like every other time she had manhandled him. It was either the wine or the fatigue. She had not planned on saying the next part, but she did. "My father… he died at the Battle of Lynnfield." She spoke slowly, trying to camouflage any emotion in her voice. "I need to know what happened. Why I lost him."

Miro sighed and looked at her. He looked like he was going to deny her again and wrench his arm from hers. Her gentle hand must have convinced him otherwise. The sudden vulnerability disarmed his normal "laugh so you do not cry" attitude.

"I'm so sorry." He placed his other hand over hers on the bars. He was genuine, for once. "Only three people survived the battle of Lynnfield. Me, Bryant, and another."

"What happened?" she asked, trying to conceal the plea.

"There was a creature there. It's hard to explain … half dragon, half demon, ethereal. Only I saw it. It leveled Lynnfield and the surrounding area with one blast."

Captain Amyna's general combative demeanor returned. *Is this another one of his lies?* "*If* there is something like that out there, why isn't anybody talking about it?"

"Can you imagine the panic if you told people that not only this horrible monster exists, but it can literally kill everything: men, animals, plants, the very land, in the blink of an eye?"

Captain Amyna understood his point. She had wrestled with trying to calm her men's nerves about a leopard in the woods. She could not imagine what this knowledge would do, especially since Lynnfield had been so close to Emestria.

"But look," Miro started. "I'm going to kill that thing. I am going to find the artifacts and put an end to it with them. That's what I want, to make sure it can never do something like it did during the Battle of Lynnfield, ever again."

"King Bryant has sanctioned your expedition for the artifacts. He requested that Clara come too." Miro raised an eyebrow. "But if we're going to do this ... you need to be honest with me. You can keep up your careless jester act around Clara, but when it's you and me, you need to be real."

Miro averted his gaze. "Yes, I can do that," he whispered before starting to turn again.

Captain Amyna tugged on his arm. "One more thing. You said that Clara had a dim but strong aura. Were you joking when you told me what mine looked like?"

She could not believe she made herself so vulnerable like this. The wine must have gone to her head. But she had to know. She studied magic for years trying to master a single spell, but Clara learned more in one day than Captain Amyna did in years.

"No, it's quite perplexing."

"Oh," Amyna responded, her shoulders tensing again. She hoped he was trying to get under her skin.

"No, you don't understand; you don't have any aura. Everything has a magical aura. Even dead things have an aura sometimes, but you have no magical aura at all. I've never met anyone or read anything about something similar."

"Thanks for rubbing it in." Her shoulders slumped as she thought, *I've wrestled with this for so long, and he can't even show an ounce of compassion.*

"You're not getting it. Here, watch. Chivas, lord of souls and sub-terfuge, I call upon your guidance, Somna." Miro cast the spell to cause his target to fall asleep. Two minuscule circles the size of a fist bordered by black runes shrank and encircled Amyna's irises. The circles bounced off her eyes and popped out of existence. Miro went to cradle her in his hands, but the spell was ineffective.

"Get off me." Amyna pushed his hands away. *What a creep.*

"Listen. That magic didn't affect you."

"You're in a cell that blocks spells, that's why it didn't work." She waved her hands at the runes about his current domicile.

"Those aren't real. I just told them that to make them feel better. You have no magical aura because you repel some magic. That is why the sleep spell didn't work. That's your power."

"So, you can't make me sleep. That's not much of a power. Fire still burns, ice still freezes. I've been hit with plenty of spells. How did you even know I resisted it? Were you casting magic on me that I was un-aware of?"

"No, but when I healed you, I could feel something was different. It was like your body was pushing back on me, trying to reject the magic. I don't know what it all means yet, but I hope that in this play of life we all have a part. Maybe that's yours."

"Are you being real, or are you back to the fool?"

"I think I'm being sincere." Miro moved toward his bed and then turned around again. "Captain Amyna? I'm glad it's you that will be leading this. You're a great fighter, you're smart, most importantly you're a good person. Not many of those left anymore. Not everyone would have protected her from those men."

"How did you …"

"She told me while training," Miro replied before returning to his cot to eat his sole slice of cheese and bread.

"I'm the captain of the Emestrian guard; protecting her is my duty. Why is your opinion so low of Emestrians?"

Miro gestured to his cell. "Things look a little different on this side of the bars."

Captain Amyna hesitated at the comment and changed the subject. "We're going to be traveling incognito. It will be suspicious if you and Clara continue to refer to me as my rank. You should probably call me Bronwyn from here on out."

Miro nodded, "Bronwyn, it's a nice name, I like it better."

Bronwyn was unsure what to say: goodbye, goodnight, or see you tomorrow. Kaleb's footsteps approached, affording her the perfect opportunity to leave.

"As you were, guardsman," she said as she passed Kaleb.

Not long after she left, the two were joking and catching up again.

# Chapter 11



*Emestrian's have a saying: "Our bones are hard as rock, and our muscles as thick as the tundra." Anyone that has had the misfortune of getting in a bar fight with an Emestrian can attest to the veracity of the claim. It is believed this unnatural strength comes from the many demigods Fria sired and the fact that the isolationist nature led to a more concentrated bloodline. On a more personal note, in my youth, I did have the misfortune of picking a fight with an Emestrian. He barely flinched when I hit him with a bar stool.*

*—Issaroh, The History of Divinity, Part XXII*

Bronwyn stared at the passing landscape as they traveled by carriage to Porton. Some houses dotted the massive, flat landscape, broken up by trees and land to graze sheep and cattle. There were no sheep or cattle grazing, though. Some land was fertile enough for crops, but no crops grew in the winter. Many of these houses would have been empty for months, their occupants either being called to the front line or retreating to Solstice for greater protection.

From Porton, they would travel out of Emestria to the independent city-state Newtonne. This would be the first time she left the country of her birth. Her position would be filled by an acting captain. *When I return, will I have to prove myself all over again?*

Clara, on the other hand, was in a rather pleasant mood. Last night, she had been treated as a guest of the king and given a chamber room to stay in. Amyna found out from a chambermaid that it was the very same one the princess of Tara, Emerald Tiberius, would be residing in when she visited next spring. There was a warm fire, a comfy bed, and best of all, a bath. It was probably a hot bath, attended by one of the chambermaids. Clara probably had soap as well, and not the coarse stuff commoners bathed with but luxuriously smooth soap. From prisoner to honored guest. Amyna wondered if Clara had been treated so well because King Bryant was trying to persuade her of the mission's importance, on top of the generous sums she was promised.

Clara wore a falconer's glove, her new messenger falcon perched resolutely on her hand. Bluish-gray wings and tail feathers decorated the bird's body. A leather hood hid a white head, and Ferdinand fluffed the shorter feathers on his white and brown speckled belly from time to time. He cocked his head back and forth and occasionally let out high-pitched screeches that caused Amyna and Miro to flinch.

A messenger falcon was no small gift. A properly trained falcon and pair of stones could cost more than a captain would make in five years. And that was using Amyna's old pay, before the king started decreasing wages.

Miro was napping, slumped over on the same bench seat as Amyna. He had either stayed up late talking to his friend the jailor or he slept poorly on the prison cot. Occasionally, he would slide his feet against her boots, and she nudged them back onto his side. When she did, he woke and readjusted. Now Clara nudged Miro's shin until she roused him from his slumber. "Do you think you can teach me to talk to him?" Clara motioned toward the bird.

"Talking with animals is within your school of magic, but it's not a simple spell," Miro replied. "I'm also not a great teacher."

"Oh, probably for the best. Wouldn't want to listen to him complain about how I make him fly back and forth all the time." Clara tried to sound upbeat about the news.

"After we reach Newtonne, we'll head south." Miro gave a somewhat reassuring smile. "To the swamps of Mul'tok. There we can hopefully meet with my mentor. He used to be a teacher; he could—"

"I knew it," Amyna interrupted. The first words she had spoken on the trip. "I knew it. You're not the scholar. There's someone else."

"Issaroh and Arty never met, so I doubt he sent you up north to find him. But you're right, in a way. Issaroh is knowledgeable, and he's been researching an artifact for me. The last time we spoke, he was close, but we haven't been able to see each other since the war started. Too dangerous for foreigners to travel to Emestria."

Miro stared out the window with a forlorn look at her homeland. "What happened to this country?" Miro said, shaking his head. "Arty said he wanted to make it a better place, and now Emestria is worse off than when I left."

Amyna was happy to deliver the lecture this time around. "After we lost Lynnfield and the food shortages started, the wealthier class put more pressure on the monarchy to relinquish power. By the time King Bryant ascended—after his brother died—the country was already in dire straits.

"Once the war started, everything just got worse. I used to travel around town on my days off without my armor, but I was accosted on a few occasions, told to go home, that I wasn't welcome here, that I was the problem. So, I wore my uniform everywhere I went, to show everyone I was right where I was supposed to be."

After a short lull, Clara brought the conversation back to her travel plans. "Captain Amyna—"

"Just Bronwyn from here on out. We'll be traveling incognito and I don't want my last name or rank to draw attention."

"Bronwyn, if the king provides a suitable vessel, we won't need any connections until we make it to Newtonne. I will need to make one quick stop to pick up some things once we get going. It's not an easy trek; the ice floes are difficult to navigate. Lucky for you two, I'm probably the best person for the job.

"Once we're in Newtonne, we're going to have to lay low and keep quiet until we can leave the city. Rouke doesn't have an official military presence, but a lot more gangs of men with bright red hair have been hanging around. We'll be fine in port, but walking through the city proper, we'll need to avoid making a scene. Nothing will happen to us, but we might pick up a tail if they catch wind we came from Emestria." Clara went back to fawning over her new bird, chuckling slightly, and shaking her head.

Bronwyn engaged Clara with more stories of their experiences of the events that led up to the war, directing Clara's attention away from the bird. Miro had been quiet during this conversation, but now he suddenly jumped in. "Lynnfield was never Emestria's to begin with."

Bronwyn glared at him.

"It's true," Clara said. "I was only eleven or twelve when we left, but my mother and aunt talked about the war a lot. I didn't listen much; I was too interested in being a young woman to pay much attention to politics."

Miro said, "Lynnfield was an independent city-state located in the fertile region between Southern Emestria and Tara." He spoke slowly and gravely, like the conflict weighed heavily on his mind. "It refused Emestria's protection, and Emestria sent an occupying force. The people had no hope but to turn to Tara and Rouke.

"The nobles didn't jockey for power with Arty's brother; they bought it. Although well-liked by the people, Cassius Bryant III was a booze-hound and womanizer. He was more concerned with telling people he was king than acting like it. From what I understand, a lot of deals were signed in back rooms of bars and brothels, and that's how the nobles increased their political influence in Emestria."

Bronwyn wanted to argue with him. This was not the Emestria she grew up believing in. But she knew that Bryant's brother did have a reputation, and some say that is what led to his early death. It made sense that the rich capitalized on his vices. Emestria was a nation of succession by birth order, so it would matter little if he were unfit to be regent when his father passed. Growing up, Bronwyn had been taught Lynnfield was part of Emestria, and Tara invaded, but she realized it was in Emestria's interest to tell the story that way.

"Still, though," Bronwyn began, "King Artorius Bryant is trying to do good for this country. He has been selling the royal assets to feed the people and sustain the war effort. It's not *his* fault his brother sold all the political capital away during his reign. I think the artifacts are integral to that plan. If King Bryant can make life better for the everyday people, then they'll stop supporting the nobles, and order will be restored."

Miro chuckled. "I wonder how his speech with the cloak is going. Most likely not as he planned."

"I hope it's going well," Clara said. "I gave up something very important to my people; it has to mean something."

"You gave up something very important to your people so you wouldn't be executed," Miro said.

Bronwyn thrust a stiff elbow into his side causing him to double over in pain. Clara stared at him with daggers in her eyes.

"You're right, that was out of line," Miro apologized, after regaining his composure. "I didn't mean offense. I was just trying to say that you were put in an impossible position, and you didn't have a choice. When we find more artifacts, we can convince Arty to return the mantle and you can decide what to do with it. I hear several people from Lynnfield settled in Corinth. Perhaps bringing it there would be better."

"My mother and aunt live there now, in Angelis, the capital," Clara said. The apology calmed her little, and her voice still carried the sting.

The rest of the ride was spent in idle conversation, catnaps, and occasional stops to stretch their legs and partake in some water or crackers.

***

The trip to Porton had taken all day. King Bryant had arranged a room for them at an inn, along with food and drink. It was a modest lodging, with only three rooms available, a small kitchen, hearth, and one long table. A crackling fire provided much of the illumination, and whispers among the staff were the only noise that interrupted that crackle. The table and chairs were utilitarian, with no carving or finish outside of a thorough sanding, but the wood was good and didn't have any signs of splintering.

Miro had retired to his room as soon as they arrived. He spoke little after Bronwyn had reminded him of his manners with her elbow. Hopefully the comment about the cloak was born from spending a night in the dungeon as opposed to any real malice he held for Clara. Bronwyn could excuse him venting his frustrations on the captain of the guard—after all, she was a legal extension of Emestria. Picking on Clara was way out of line.

Bronwyn and Clara partook in the provided meal, a modest one: stew, bread, and some distilled spirits. It was a typical winter dinner in Emestria; one grew accustomed to eating this for five months of the year.

There wasn't a trace of fish in the stew. Bronwyn worried that Porton would share Miro's proclivity to put seafood in everything. However, fishing in the winter was fruitless, so her worries were unfounded. Clara and she were the only ones in the dining area, and the waitstaff looked at them sternly.

*That's right, although I am used to this type of food, most people will be on rations and have to eat protein bread during these times,* Bronwyn thought. *The king probably sent these ingredients or paid a high price for them to be served.* She was unsure what to do. She had already taken a few spoonfuls of the stew and she didn't want to seem like she was leaving her dinner for the waitstaff to eat because she was too good for it. When Clara picked up a roll to take a bite, Bronwyn put her hand over Clara's.

"Leave the bread and spirits," Bronwyn said under her breath.

Clara looked confused until she followed Bronwyn's eyeline to the staff waiting at the door. Clara hesitated but then nodded in agreement. The two of them continued to eat in silence.

When they finished their stew, Bronwyn stood. "Thank you for the meal, we are incredibly grateful." Bronwyn then placed five pieces of silver on the table, a whole week's wages for her. Once they were out of Newtonne, she could hunt and forage for anything they needed, so it would be better spent here. "We won't be needing the bread, and if the crown prepared anything for us in the morning, please divvy it up among the staff. We don't usually partake in breakfast and will be on the water, so it might all go to waste anyway."

Bronwyn and Clara made their way up the creaky wooden steps to their room. Clara and she were in one and Miro in the other. The third was occupied by another tenant that arrived earlier in the day. As Clara walked to their room, Bronwyn knocked on Miro's door. He took a minute to answer, but once he turned the handle, Bronwyn pushed, forcing it open, and knocking him to the floor. Miro blinked his eyes in surprise as she squatted in front of him.

"What was that about?" she asked.

"You knocked me over," he defended himself, matching her tone.

"This entire mission is dependent on Clara not deciding to rat us out to Rouke's forces the minute we're outside of Emestria," she said between her teeth. It was true, but it was more than that. She knew how hurtful it was to have someone you respect deride you.

"I know, it was stupid. I didn't get much sleep and I was hungry."

The meal on the carriage ride had been paltry and Bronwyn had completely forgotten he traded away the previous night's dinner for a measly cheese sandwich in the jail. She should have thought of him before giving the rest of their food away.

"Well, supper has been served and the leftovers given to the staff," she said in a surprisingly wicked singsong voice. "There will be no breakfast, so hopefully, you have some magic to fill your belly."

As Bronwyn turned to leave, Miro groaned. "You're so cruel. They treated me better in the dungeon."

Bronwyn shut the door and approached her room. She opened it slowly in case Clara was undressing. The room was plain: two small beds, each covered with a white sheet and a thin fur; two stools by basins of water; a single dresser. A nightdress was folded neatly on each bed. Judging by the thickness of the fabric, it would not provide much warmth. The fire in the main hall of the inn would allow a bit of that heat to make its way to their room. There were no windows, and the room wasn't drafty; the dress and fur would be enough. If not, Bronwyn could always don her cloak for added comfort.

Clara was in her small clothes, washing with a cloth at one of the basins. The opening of the door did not faze her, and she continued bathing with little regard for Bronwyn's entrance. Bronwyn followed suit and began to wash away the dust from the carriage ride. The water wasn't hot, about room temperature, cool against her skin.

"In the morning, I have to make a stop at the lieutenant's post," Bronwyn said. "I'll leave before you're up and meet you at the docks. Is that okay?"

"Mmhmm," Clara said as she continued to scrub with the cloth. She removed her small clothes to wash the rest of her body. Bronwyn averted her eyes, but Clara didn't so much as glance to see if Bronwyn was watching.

"Can I ask something?" Bronwyn asked. Clara nodded and she continued. "Why are you coming? I thought you wouldn't want to help Emestria after what happened in the dungeons."

"You and Miro didn't cause that. It might be fun to learn a little more magic, and I enjoy your company. Besides, the king said he'll pay. I don't know if I want to go back to smuggling, and maybe this will be a good way to make money."

Bronwyn nodded at the shrewd nature of the statement. "And the way you've been acting, I..."

"What do you mean?"

"With King Bryant and Miro..."

"Hmph, Emestrian men prefer their women docile and demure. I'm surprised you've managed to rise so far, behaving as you do," Clara replied.

Bronwyn breathed heavily, gritting her teeth.

"Oh, don't be like that," Clara chided. "When you're on the open water, you're not always afforded the liberty to be yourself. Sometimes you're stuck on board for months with people you can't stand. You learn to tolerate their behavior and act like them to avoid friction."

"You don't have to act like that around me. Like someone else," Bronwyn said.

Clara nodded. After Clara lay down, Bronwyn removed her own undergarments and washed. Although she had frequently bathed with the other women in the corps, ever since she had become captain, Bronwyn was afforded a private bath. The only time she bathed with others since then was when they were romantically involved. It would take a little getting used to bathing with others again.

Once she finished, she folded her uniform and set it beside her bed. She saw Clara's clothes lumped on the floor and Bronwyn shook her head, smiling. Despite their differences and the circumstances of their meeting, the two of them got along. In the wilderness, she had spent a lot of time feeling sorry for Clara but not sympathizing with her. Now, at least for a time, they shared similar goals. But Bronwyn worried that tonight's revelation meant they never got along at all. It only increased her hesitation about this trip. Would Clara seek some sort of revenge and turn them over to Rouke? Bronwyn might have to fight her way out of the city against a bunch of Roukian bruisers. That might be fun.

She hoped that when they got to Newtonne, they could continue to cooperate. She was not sure Clara was sold on the importance of their mission. Deserved resentments about her treatment in Emestria were more than warranted. But she seemed fascinated by this world that Miro surrounded himself with. She couldn't be faking that. Perhaps that and the prospect of learning more magic would be enough to keep her with them.

Bronwyn was sure that—at the very least—Clara would stay until she received her boat. Would she try to push them overboard and leave Emestria without them? Maybe she'd rid herself of the captain of the guard, a strong symbol of the Emestrian establishment, and she and Miro would sail off into the distance having quit the shores of Emestria that they harbored so much hatred for. *At least I know how to swim,* Bronwyn thought as she tucked herself into bed. Tomorrow, she would ask the lieutenant to set some extra patrols looking for overboard passengers.

***

As Bronwyn approached the port, she saw Miro standing idly with Ferdinand's perch, a piece of metal shaped like an upside-down U with stabilizing crossbars and leather wrapped over the middle, loosely gripped in his hand. Only a third of a dozen ships were docked on the two piers, all of those besides one with their sails neatly stowed. All but one were small fishing vessels. Along the boardwalk several shops were shuttered, and Bronwyn was unsure whether that was permanent because of the war or if it was just too early for them to open. They were probably all involved in the fishing and shipping trade and were likely seasonal.

It looked as if their cargo was heaped about Miro's feet. Nearby a handful of sailors looked at him, perplexed. A good-sized boat with ornately carved railings stood vacant with a gangplank leading up. It must have been new—the varnish reflected the morning sun. Clara was deep into a heated conversation with what Bronwyn guessed was the harbormaster. Despite towering over Clara by at least two feet, he leaned away from her as they exchanged words. Was there some problem with the voyage?

"Is this our ship?" Bronwyn asked Miro, coming up from behind him. She placed a small, wrapped package into his free hand.

"I guess it's too big," he replied, his eyes glued to Clara. Miro set the perch down and held the gift in front of himself, examining it. A green handkerchief neatly and carefully encased the rather light box.

"It's some salted fish and bread," Bronwyn said before he asked. "You didn't get to eat much in the dungeon, and I gave away your food last night without asking."

Miro wasted no time unwrapping and eating the salty meat while they both watched in amusement as Clara continued arguing. From the snippets Bronwyn caught they seemed to be haggling over the sale of the ship. Miro ate quickly, but Clara returned before he could finish the bread.

"He'll give us twenty-eight silver and the small boat for the king's," Clara said triumphantly. "I would have liked a lot more, but with the boat being useless until the end of winter he doubted he'd even get to sell it, given the state of the kingdom. Even then he has to redo the exterior, so it doesn't look the same."

"But Miss, we won't all fit on the smaller craft," one of the sailors said.

"Of course you won't," Clara replied. "You're not coming."

"But we've been paid in advance for the voyage," a second sailor argued.

"Look, I'm sure you're all worthy seafarers, but none of you have sailed the ice floes. It's not like sailing the open ocean. I need a small boat to do it well, and it will only fit the three of us, plus our gear, comfortably. I suggest you take the money you were given, go drinking in the taverns for a couple of weeks and then report the vessel floundered on your way back."

The men all stared at Clara, blinking at her suggestion. They were hired sailors, but they likely took some pride in sailing on a royal mission.

"But what if they don't believe us?" the first sailor asked.

"I'm sure if you give the nice harbormaster a couple of silver, he'll be happy to say that this new boat he just bought wasn't owned by the king." Clara smiled and all the sailors nodded and dispersed.

"Now you lot," Clara said, addressing Miro and Bronwyn, "load the gear and we'll start heading out before high tide."

Their supplies consisted of bedrolls, tents, rations, two lanterns, ropes, a spade, and a few other odds and ends. However, they apparently loaded it incorrectly, and Clara had them unpack and repack everything according to her explicit directions. Bronwyn was unsteady getting on and off the boat, so eventually, Miro just had her hand him everything from the dock as he stacked it. The second time Clara examined the loaded gear with scrutiny before finally giving it her approval and casting off, officially starting their journey.

"Well, hopefully there's still time to make my stop before we head to the ice floes. It needs to be low tide to get in and out." Clara pointed toward the shore. Revealed by the low tide, a small alcove was nestled between outcroppings in the cliff. "Otherwise, we might have to wait until tomorrow."

"We would have been farther along if you just kept the other ship," Bronwyn said.

"Bigger boat would have a harder time traversing the ice floes. Besides, it would have never survived the cave," Clara said, looking at the waves. She directed them toward the cave, telling Miro and Bronwyn when to row more or less.

"Still, a crew would have been nice, so we weren't doing all the rowing," Miro said, breaking a sweat.

"Oh, quit complaining," Clara responded, sharp and quick.

As they approached the alcove, they saw that it was more than a break in the rocks. Bronwyn nervously surveyed the cave. The walls were wet with water, and she realized that if they remained inside during high tide, they would be stranded or forced against the stalactites. It was only ten feet wide but seemed deep enough for their vessel, judging by the fact Bronwyn couldn't see the cave's bottom as they entered.

Clara had them stow the oars and she used one of three long poles to move them forward. "Give us a light," she said. Miro traced some runes in the air and whispered before producing a small flame in his hand. Clara and Bronwyn rolled their eyes as Bronwyn picked up one of the lanterns and lit a match. Sheepishly, Miro doused his magic.

The steady drip of water and dark interior made the cave feel ominous. The path was fairly straight, with a few slight bends, and wasn't much wider than the boat. The larger ship would have never fit through the entrance, let alone been able to maneuver inside. The ceiling was only a foot or two above their heads. Luckily, the mast on this vessel collapsed down. If it hadn't, Bronwyn doubted they could make it through even in a craft this small.

After a couple of minutes of gliding along the dark water, they saw a light ahead. The cave opened. The ceiling rose suddenly thirty feet into the air and almost as wide. A torch flickered at the top of a large rocky outcrop. Barnacles and rust coated the bottom five feet of a ladder affixed to the side of the wall.

Clara pulled the boat flush against the cavern and tied a mooring rope. She ascended wordlessly, making Bronwyn wonder if they were meant to follow. Bronwyn waited for Clara to look back expectantly, and when she did not, Bronwyn instead opted to stand next to the ladder, placing one hand on the rusty rungs. Miro continued holding the lantern aloft.

The ladder was about fifteen to twenty feet tall, and Clara ascended effortlessly. Once she crested the rocky outcrop, she disappeared over it. Bronwyn waited; her ears strained for the slightest sound.

"Who goes there?" a man's voice echoed. "Oh, Cap'n Clara," he added after a couple of seconds.

"Ahoy there, Rochet. How're things?" Clara and the unseen man were not speaking loudly but the words funneled to the water below.

"Shift's almost done," he said with a tone that suggested familiarity. "You're cutting it close. What can I do ya for?"

"Here to make a withdrawal."

"How much you need?"

"I'm cashing out. Got a little side venture that's going to keep me away for a spell. I'll need my extra gear as well."

"Probably for the best. Military is starting to increase patrols off the coast. Water's getting too hot for most folks."

The screech of metal grinding against rock filled the cavern chamber.

"Aye, got pinched myself." Clara's speech patterns were different than when she talked to Bronwyn or Miro. Her voice sounded lower and more gravely. Her sentences were curt.

"You got caught?" The voice sounded genuinely surprised.

"Happens to the best of us. Ended up receiving an official writ of passage out of the whole affair."

The voice whistled sarcastically in response. "All right, here you go. You give my regards to the East."

"Will do. You take care now."

The metal grated against the rock again, reverberating through the chamber. Footsteps followed and Clara reappeared at the top of the outcrop. An axe was secured to her back and a bag at her waist jingled with the sound of coin.

Clara slid down the ladder, gripping the sides with her feet and hands as she went, controlling her speed. When she got to the last five feet, she slowed and went back to using each rung one by one. It was obvious she had done this numerous times, had a sixth sense of when the barnacles and rust began, and stopped herself before reaching that section. Bronwyn gazed at Clara in surprise as she tossed a tied bag of coins on top of the rest of the supplies they had secured in the middle of the small craft. Clara took the pole to the other side of the boat and pressed it against the bottom, pushing them forward and out of the cavern.

Taut muscles in Clara's arms flexed as she moved the pole through the water. It was becoming increasingly apparent that her entire personality so far had not been genuine. It was a scary realization, that someone Bronwyn thought she knew might be a different person entirely.

Miro apparently did not share Bronwyn's awe as he began questioning Clara. "I always figured you for a dagger or short-sword-from-the-shadows type," he said, admiring the axe affixed to her back. It wasn't a standard boarding hatchet; it was larger than most sailors would carry. Next to Clara, it looked even bigger. The blade was plain but in the shape of a crescent moon. The pry bar on the opposite side was curved and exceptionally sharp.

"Where's the fun in that?" Clara asked. "Axes are better for sea travel. If you are knocked overboard, if the boat is low enough, you can use the weapon to hook the railing and hoist yourself back aboard."

Miro nodded at the cleverness of the solution.

"Good for cutting rigging, or prying open stuck doors or chests," Clara continued. "'Sides, someone my size charging you with an axe?

A dagger in the shadows can't hold a candle to the surprise that causes. Good to keep your opponent off guard."

"Makes me want to see you wield it in battle," Miro said.

"Keep yapping and you'll get to see me use it now," Clara said, silencing him and his annoying false bravado. Miro and Bronwyn exchanged glances, unsure if they were more impressed or intimidated. Bronwyn looked at the far horizon, hoping that would settle her stomach.

"Use the bail bucket," Clara said, turning around to see Bronwyn.

"I'll be—" Bronwyn couldn't finish before she leaned over the gunwale, spilling last night's stew. As she retched again, she yelped in surprise as gleaming white teeth appeared from the dark water. She flung her upper torso back into the boat.

"Just ice eels," Clara said with a chuckle. "That's why I told you to use the bucket. Count yourself lucky the serpents don't like chum."

Bronwyn grabbed the bucket and cradled it in her arms.

# CHAPTER 12


*Marianna, goddess of oceans, tides, and loyalty, often played the part of peacemaker between Chivas and Laevin in the beginning. In the initial vote on arbiter she supported neither. However, in the second vote, she supported Laevin over Chivas. Circa 300 P.C., Marianna served as Laevin's lieutenant rather than peacemaker. This was due to Chivas' actions in the events that would eventually lead to the cataclysm.*

*—Issaroh, The History of Divinity, Part IV*

The ice floes off the coast of Emestria were due to a combination of several processes. Every summer, sheets of ice from large glaciers to the north broke free and traveled south. By winter, they made it far enough to block traffic from Emestria's port to the rest of the world. The portions of the bergs below the surface would catch on a shelf where the sea shallowed near the coast. There, they jostled together, until they started to freeze during the glacial season. A strong undertow kept part of the sea's surface from freezing over completely, but also led many green sailors to strand themselves.

As they approached, the small boat started to be pulled by the current that ran through the ice floes. Bronwyn curled around the bucket. She had emptied the contents of her stomach long ago, but her body still felt the need to retch incessantly. She closed her eyes and tried to sleep. If she managed to, napping would make the voyage go much faster. A gentle hand slowly rubbed her back. Opening her eyes momentarily, she saw Miro with a look of concern on his face. *Isn't there magic that can help with this?*

Clara sat at the back of the boat, steering it. "Eyes on me, not her," Clara barked at him. "We're approaching the ice sheets. Grab that pole. It's going to be a little harder with only two of us, but we'll manage."

"I can burn through with my fire, cut us a clear path," Miro said, starting to make his way to the front of the boat.

"Really? You're gonna melt sixty feet of ice in frozen waters? How long ya think you can keep that up?" Clara admonished him. "Now you need to understand something. You're dumb. You don't know what you're doing. You're going to see paths that you think are shortcuts or safer, but that's because your head is up your arse. If you pay attention to me and do what I say, we'll make it through this fine."

Miro looked back at Bronwyn as she spilled more of her guts into the bucket.

"But if you are too busy looking at the pretty lass or think yourself a hotshot sailor on your first outing, you're gonna strand us and we'll freeze out here. Eyes on me," Clara admonished him again, but he nodded in understanding.

"Listen to her, you dolt," Bronwyn said before spitting bile into the bucket.

Miro did not look back, grabbed his pole, and kept his eyes glued to Clara. Ferdinand screeched, uncomfortable from the increased movement of the boat. His cage was covered, secured to the rest of the cargo, and his hood was on, but even a blind bird knew the seas were getting rough.

"When I say 'right,' you push your pole hard against the ice on my right," Clara said, keeping her eyes on the ice. "When I say 'left' you push on my left. Other than that, your pole is out of the water. Now stow the sail. We'll be using the currents from here on out."

Miro struggled with the canvas, the sense of urgency causing his fingers to fumble with the knots. He messily stowed it and resumed his post, pole in hand.

Bronwyn squeezed her eyes shut. The seas must have decided to take pity on her because she remembered little of the ice floes. Clara would shout "left" or "right" at Miro—and after she did, the boat moved in either direction or jostled violently against the ice. Sometimes there was a good thirty minutes between commands, and other times the orders came one right after the other.

Bronwyn assumed the worst of it was over when Clara told Miro to unfurl the sail and then tucked in behind Bronwyn. They must have taken shifts, one sleeping beside her then switching places. Bronwyn appreciated the added warmth. Her cloak was doing little to keep out the cold.

***

Bronwyn knew they were close to Newtonne when Clara began explaining the history of the city. "Newtonne has a vibrant city life, with many from Emestria settling there to get away from the stringent rules and culture of their home nations. Although smuggling is encouraged, we've developed a culture around subterfuge and it's become a sort of competition. We'll stop at Smuggler's Rock where we'll transfer to a fishing boat."

"I thought fishing these waters was pointless this time of year," Miro said.

"It is. Sometimes a boat will come on a good catch or two, but they mostly come out to facilitate the smuggling routes. During the winter, the ships will leave the docks with wooden fish and return with their catch plus an extra passenger or two. The harbormasters, of course, know what's going on and they take bets on who will have the most realistic fish on board."

"What's the point?" Miro asked. "If everyone knows what's happening, why all the complications?"

"It's fun," Clara replied. "Plus, the people came here to be away from the rules and regulations of the bigger nations. We all know there is a possibility that Tara or one of the other nations will try and lay claim to Newtonne eventually, so we keep our skills sharp to stay under the radar. Can never be too careful. Lately Rouke has more and more men watching the docks, not that the harbormasters would be dumb enough to allow them access. Rouke doesn't have a military presence in Newtonne, but everyone knows what they're doing here, trying to monitor who is smuggling what to Emestria."

Bronwyn paid little attention; her nausea still required considerable effort to ignore. Clara then started to tell Miro about the history of the town. The only tidbit Bronwyn picked up was the town was originally named New Town, but later generations changed the name to Newtonne to hide the founders' lack of imagination.

They stopped at a small outcropping of rocks and unloaded the gear. Bronwyn was overjoyed, until Clara explained this was merely a point to transfer to a larger ship, to avoid suspicion. Bronwyn groaned. She had a few precious moments to try to settle her stomach , but now off the ship, her body reacted to the lack of movement.

They waited for a couple of hours, just long enough for Bronwyn to adjust to being on land again, and Clara flagged down a passing fishing vessel. This one moved differently on the waves, or the water was different, and Bronwyn was forced to pray to the bail bucket once again.

She didn't even have the strength to stand, and her body ached. Miro supported her as she slumped against the gunwale of the ship. It only took an hour or two to reach the port. Thankfully, Bronwyn was allowed to disembark first.

The plan was to stay the night in a port inn. But they couldn't proceed right away, the reason being more of the faux subterfuge the people of Newtonne practiced. If they appeared to leave as dock workers it would bring less scrutiny to their gear and they wouldn't need to explain what ship they boarded. Clara and Miro helped unload cargo, for their ship and also others. Bronwyn rested on some crates next to one of the dock warehouses. Their boat was one of the last ones to arrive for the day, and there were few boats left that needed to be unloaded. They finished handling cargo after an hour. Miro put his arm around Bronwyn, underneath her arm, supporting her as they headed to the inn.

They rented two rooms, one for Miro and one for the women. Clara took Bronwyn's boots, armor, and cloak off before she collapsed into the bed, still dressed. Miro and Clara decided to let her sleep rather than try to wrangle the rest off her.

# CHAPTER 13

*The spirit guardians are perhaps the most curious of the divine. They were not immortal like the Ywaigwai or born of immortal loins like the demigods. Rather, they were animals here in the mortal world that were shaped by the gods' influence. With the gods' blessings they grew to unusual size, gained intelligence, and other supernatural gifts. They are rumored to have long lives but were still mortal.*

—Issaroh, *The History of Divinity, Part XIV*

The Speckled Crow put the inn of Porton to shame. Not because of the quality, but instead the lively nature of the clientele. It was not only a place for weary travelers but also the first stopping point on any sailor's long night of drinking ashore. The main hall was easily three times as large as the inn in Porton. Small tables that sat three to five patrons were interspersed around the hall, with a hardwood bar dominating most of the left wall. The top of the bar was smooth marble and a door to the right led to the small kitchen. Another door on the far wall led down to the cask room, where many a patron would enjoy a short fling that would barely be remembered come morning.

The shelves behind the bar carried a variety of unlabeled and unidentified multicolored bottles, and only the bartender knew what the colors represented. It was mostly rum—good rum, bad rum, spiced rum—it made little difference to those that called the Speckled Crow home, The Blue Cranes, pirates Clara used to sail with. At this point in the night, a multitude of discarded tins, steins, and broken glasses were heaped around the edge of the establishment. The servers would be much too busy to bother cleaning until the early hours of the morning, and instead swept the forgotten dishes to the side when they had a chance.

Oil lanterns hung above most of the tables provided dim illumination, except for those that had been cracked by an overly boisterous celebration or poorly flung swing. It was a miracle this place hadn't burned down decades ago. A beautiful cacophony of curses, jokes, and threats blessed the ear, drowning out the poor lute player sitting next to the fire. Piss, oil, sweat, and vomit competed with the faint hint of the sea brought in on the clientele's boots, a smell that Clara had dearly missed. Many of the Cranes were already here for the night, and most of the former Cranes as well.

After Clara had sat with Miro, she nodded to a barmaid that quickly came over. "What can I get ya?" she asked after a rough slapping on the buttocks from another patron.

"Two bowls of chowder and rum," Clara ordered. "Hope you don't mind," she told Miro as the woman walked away.

"Chowder sounds appetizing, and I could use a stiff drink after that voyage," Miro replied.

"Good for you, not succumbing to sea sickness," Clara said. "You might make a competent sailor yet."

The barmaid returned with the drinks. She had brought a bottle of rum and two cups that Clara filled to the brim. It had been far too long since she had tasted the warm embrace of rum.

"Bottoms up." Clara took several large swallows of the alcohol while Miro sipped gingerly. Clara put her hand beneath his cup, tipping it up, causing some to spill and Miro to swallow more. "Drink up, you got your ice wings today!" Clara shouted to the room, which led to cheers from the other patrons.

"Ice wings?" Miro asked, wiping the spilled rum from his chin.

Clara pulled down her shirt, revealing a tattoo above her left breast; a bird surrounded by shards of ice forming a small circle. "Your ice wings. Don't worry, we can get yours tomorrow," Clara teased.

"I think I'll pass."

Clara stood and addressed the room. "You hear this, boys? He traversed the ice floes—at night no less—and he doesn't want his tattoo."

This caused the room to burst into laughter, and a drunk, snaggle-toothed man walked over and draped his arm over Miro. "Oooh, he doesn't want to mar that smooth skin he's wearing," Henrie spewed, his breath reeking of booze. The gathered patrons booed in response. Calls of "fop" and "landlubber" were issued through the raucous crowd.

"Ooh, Henrie, you'll enjoy this one. He talks to goats," Clara said with derision.

Miro looked at her incredulously, but she continued nonetheless. The patrons laughed despite not knowing what she meant. When the barmaid returned with their chowder, Miro looked relieved.

"Excuse me, do you have anything for seasickness?" Miro asked.

"Everyone knows ginger tea and green apples are the best cure," the server said.

"Could I order some of that, please?"

"Sure, do you want me to bottle your momma's milk as well, or do you prefer suckling from the teat?" the barmaid asked loudly, causing the room to explode in more laughter.

She walked away before Miro managed to give a reply. He held his cup of rum and took a bigger swig. *More rum is the only way to deal with this crowd,* Clara thought.

"Eh, Clara, where you been?" a man sitting at a table toward the back of the room inquired. Atien was wearing his long red coat with ivory toggles going down the right side. His black boots were freshly shined, and he was sporting a leather tricorn hat. He had long, wavy black hair and deep-blue eyes. Clara smiled. It had been far too long since she had seen Atien. She must have missed him when they came in.

"Can you believe it? I got pinched by those bloody Emestrians. Damn hair dye washed off in the water and they got me." The crowd grew quiet. "And those Emestrian jails are no joke." Clara paused. "They've got the best water—must be taking it right off the glacier!"

The gathered men cheered and laughed at her comment while Miro shoveled chowder into his mouth. Clara approached Atien and hopped into his lap, avoiding spilling her drink. In addition to being pleasing to the eye, Atien had an undeniable charisma about him. Even Miro's eyes were glued to his sharp features.

"Man, that Emestria is one crazy place," Clara said, the room now focusing their attention solely on her. "I found this cat up there that killed a bunch of people just because of my hair color. Can you imagine that? What if I had dyed my hair that day?"

This was met with more exuberant laughter. She continued to recount her exploits, and Miro anxiously jostled his legs.

When the barmaid returned with a cup of tea and an apple, Miro seemed more than happy to take his leave. She put the food and tea down and sneered at him. Miro took the apple and ginger tea and began heading upstairs.

"Eh, you best take the rum if you want to have any chance with Bronwyn!" Clara called from the lap of Atien. Miro continued to walk but the crowd began to jeer and throw things at him, one of which was a full bottle. To appease them, he grabbed the alcohol and ascended the stairs. The upper floor was open to the tavern below, with a railed hallway that led to the few rooms. Clara watched from the main tavern floor as Miro passed the door of his room and instead went to Bronwyn's.

***

Bronwyn had collapsed on her bed, but the noise from the dining hall was too loud for her to sleep. She turned over as the door slowly creaked open. Miro sheepishly entered, holding something green and round wedged between his arm and body. He also had a white cup on a saucer, and something squirreled behind his back.

"I'm sorry, I didn't know if you were asleep, but they said downstairs that these might help with seasickness," he said, proffering the apple and a cup of liquid.

Bronwyn rose from the sheets. "What do you have there?"

"It's ginger tea, I'm told. It's supposed to settle the stomach."

She motioned for him to come forward and took the cup of tea and apple. The bedside table was close enough to set both upon it and still have them within reach. Any fruit during the winter was a rarity in Emestria. Still, she felt her belly turn at the idea of food. She thrust the apple back at him.

"I can't eat," she proclaimed before burying her head in the pillows.

"Try some of the tea," he offered. "Maybe that will help."

Bronwyn picked up the cup and sipped. She could not taste much. It tasted mostly like hot water with a sprinkle of earth. No where near as strong as the pine tea she consumed regularly in the colder months. But she took another sip after seeing his expectant expression.

"Now, what else do you have?" she asked, spying the bottle he had been hiding away behind his back.

"Rum, but I don't think you should be drinking."

"Nope, that's exactly what I need to feel better. Hand it here." Bronwyn extended her arm, her hand open, waiting for the alcohol.

He hesitated before handing the bottle over. Bronwyn held it to her lips and took a couple of swigs before lowering it again. Miro extended his hand, and she eventually handed the rum back. He took a small drink and set the bottle on the table beside the bed, across from her.

"I think we unleashed a monster," he said, kicking his boots off and letting them fall to the floor.

"How so?" she asked, trying a bite of the apple before swearing off it.

"You hear that laughter? She is telling jokes about us."

"Oh, can't take it, can you?" Bronwyn teased, the color starting to return to her cheeks.

"It's all good and fun, but can we not do this now?" Miro replied.

"Sorry." Bronwyn sat up and tried another sip of tea. "What's going on down there that has you in such a foul mood?"

Miro rolled his eyes and shrugged.

"Perhaps your little pupil isn't as innocent as you thought?"

Miro leveled his gaze with hers. "We all have different masks we wear. I will not begrudge anyone their choice on what they show me." He tried to hide it, but she could see the hurt on his face.

"No, I'm being serious, what is upsetting you?" she asked, with some compassion.

"Nothing," Miro replied. After a pause and Bronwyn's baited look, he relented. "Okay, she called Naani 'some cat.' I just thought she had some appreciation of what Naani was." He took a healthy drink of the rum.

"Naani was your friend, and she died protecting us."

"Naani was a spirit guardian and served an important purpose in the world," Miro said, trying to correct her.

"No, Naani was your friend first," Bronwyn replied, driving the point forward. "To me, Naani was an animal that murdered my men."

Miro recoiled at the comment.

"But Naani, like everyone in this world, was different things to different people. You can't let how Clara saw her change the way you saw her."

"How do you reconcile that—your men?" Miro asked.

Bronwyn motioned for him to give her another swig of rum before she would continue. "I saw blood in the snow after Naani took the first horse. I could have turned my men back right then and might have avoided the bloodshed, but I decided that the mission was more important. Maybe if we turned back, I might have saved them from the carnage, or maybe my men would have befallen the same fate and the journey would have ended."

She took another drink from the bottle before handing it back to Miro.

"Is that the first time?" She inclined her head at his words and he clarified. "Is that the first time that you've felt people lost their lives because of your actions?"

"In a way, whenever I transferred a guard to the army, and they died on the frontlines I've felt the responsibility of my actions. But that's the first time I lost people under my command."

"How do you deal with it? The guilt for what your decisions caused. How do you start to feel like you did what you thought was right at the time?"

"When I figure it out, I'll let you know," Bronwyn replied before motioning for the bottle back. Miro freely handed it over and she took another hearty swig. "What matters is what you were trying to accomplish when you made the choice. If you have the right intentions and act in good faith, you can't blame yourself." Bronwyn sighed. "Do you know what I could go for? Some pheasant."

"Your appetite has returned already?" Miro asked with ruby cheeks.

"Don't deny a woman food on her deathbed," she joked.

"I wouldn't dare," he said before standing to go to the door. He stopped abruptly. "I don't think it does. I think even if you meant to do the right thing, it is the end result that is important. It doesn't matter if you were trying to save someone if you end up getting them killed by your actions anyway."

"Ooh, or some boar. Get some ribs if they have them," Bronwyn called out as he closed the door.

# Chapter 14

*Chivas, god of souls and subterfuge, opposed Laevin's rule and arbitrations many times, arguing for civilization to have more autonomy over their actions. His eventual wife, Fria, goddess of ice and death, supported Chivas' arguments, but not as fervently as him. There is no question about the lack of affection in Chivas and Fria's union. They fathered no children together, although they both created many demigods.*

*—Issaroh, The History of Divinity, Part V*

Bronwyn awoke the next morning, blinking her eyes, trying to take in her surroundings. Her head felt fuzzy—that made sense, she remembered drinking some rum. On her bedside table were a teacup and a half-eaten apple. She remembered Miro bringing them to her, along with the alcohol. Turning over to ask Clara how the night had progressed, Bronwyn moved the sheets and uncovered her own bare breast. *Well, that is odd. I rarely sleep naked.*

Next to the other bed was some half-eaten cooked bird and ribs. She looked past them to see if Clara had already awoken, but in Clara's bed was Miro. She clutched the covers to her body, reached down, grabbed one of her boots, and threw it at him. He woke up with a start and stumbled to the floor.

"What are you doing in my room!" she cried out. "Why am I naked?" She held the sheet closer.

"I uh ... I came up to bring you some tea," Miro said, still fully clothed. "You had me grab you some food, but you were asleep when I came back. I tried to return to my room, but Clara and a gentleman were already there. So, I came back here and slept."

"Did you undress me?" she asked in horror.

"You were dressed when I fell asleep," he reassured her.

She grabbed the second boot and lobbed it at him. "Out!"

He scrambled to his feet and retrieved his boots before making a hasty retreat.

***

Clara heard the commotion upstairs and turned to see an exasperated and surprised Miro close a door a second too late, ducking as an apple sailed past him. It thunked against the floor. He sighed. Seeing Clara, he descended the staircase warily. His eyes darted across the room, checking the patrons as he went.

"The sailors are gone," Clara said. "Off to the docks or the sea for the day. Nothing to worry about." Clara sat at the table, penning a missive to give to her new falcon. "So, if I let this bird go, it's going to come back, right?"

"Wouldn't be much of a messenger falcon if it didn't." Miro tried to get the attention of a server. "As long as you have the homing stone, he will find you. What are you writing?"

"Eggs, sausage, and water for my friend," Clara called out, causing one of the servers to dash toward the kitchen. "Nothing much. Notifying him we crossed the sea fine, but his boat took heavy damage and floundered at the end. I secured passage back home for the sailors, but it might be a while before they can find a ship with room to take them.

"In truth, I want to send the bird away for a while. We're still in the port district so we're not under any scrutiny, but carrying a messenger falcon through town screams 'spy.'" Clara rolled up the sliver of paper and put it in a tiny holder to affix to the bird's leg. Miro glanced around, most likely trying to see where Ferdinand was. After spending some time with Atien last night, Clara had gone to Bronwyn's room to retrieve the bird. At that point, Miro was passed out in the bed and Bronwyn's attention was focused on her food.

By the time Miro's meal arrived, Bronwyn made her way downstairs, looking a bit disheveled. She shot a look at Clara and then at Miro.

"You're not allowed in my room. I don't care if you have to sleep in the street," Bronwyn hissed at him.

"That's not what it looked like last night," Clara teased. "You two were cuddled up on the bed like old lovers."

"We were not!" Bronwyn and Miro shouted in unison. This drew some looks from the breakfast crowd, but they quickly returned to their meals.

"Okay, he was passed out on the bed, and you were in the process of getting undressed with a near-empty bottle of rum in your hand. After undressing, you were deep in sleep. You should watch the drinking. The hangovers are worse after your twenties," Clara chided. "You want anything?"

"No, apparently I ate a lot last night," Bronwyn said, sitting down at the table. "What's the plan?"

"Well, we've got to buy some new threads," Clara said.

"What's wrong with my clothes?" Bronwyn asked. She looked down at her thick pants and shirt, both rumpled from being haphazardly tossed aside rather than folded, as was her normal habit.

"We're all dressed like Emestrians. Not the fashion of the city. Once we leave the port district, we've got to be wary of curious eyes. Don't want to have to shake a tail of Rouke brutes because they catch wind you're from Emestria. Your kind isn't exactly popular these days."

Clara rose from the table and headed upstairs. She returned a short time later with the falcon perched on her hand. She stepped outside and let it loose, hopefully to return. That last part still seemed dubious. Clutching the homing stone in her pocket, she hoped there wasn't some trick to the bird she was not aware of. It wouldn't do to send it off and find out she needed to issue some command word to guarantee the return.

***

The port district was a hub of activity, which surprised Bronwyn. Sailors walked to and fro, some of them in elaborate garb that included flowing jackets and overly decorated garments. Carts of fruits, nuts, and dried fish were being taken to the markets. Some of the alleys were full of groups of teenagers up to no good, while others contained overburdened stalls selling everything from carpets to jewelry. Grilled meat, freshly baked bread, and spices Bronwyn had only encountered on a couple of occasions—cumin, turmeric, sage—wafted from food carts set up along the main thoroughfare.

Clara caught a pickpocket trying to pilfer her coin and admonished him before threatening to separate his hand from his wrist if he tried it a second time. He was a child, and it seemed harsh to Bronwyn, but this city had a toughness about it different from Emestria.

In Emestria, men tall as mountains walked brandishing swords or axes and various armors. Here, your reputation afforded you respect. And that hinged solely on what clothes and jewelry you wore. Clara probably was similarly laden with jewelry prior to her capture in Emestria. In

Bronwyn's opinion, the gaudier the attire, the greater the berth was given to your stride.

Some of the men in long red captain's jackets had flintlocks at their sides. Emestria owned less than a dozen rifles, unable to afford more. These men had their *own* flintlocks, though they probably didn't have any more gunpowder than would be needed for a single shot. Gunpowder was the limiting factor when it came to firearms.

Bronwyn was thankful Clara talked her out of wearing her armor and carrying her greatsword. She realized now how out of place it would have been. Cloaks, a staple of any Emestrian outfit, caused eyes to linger in Newtonne.

They opted for inconspicuous clothing. Bronwyn refused to purchase a skirt, common attire for women in Newtonne. Instead, she chose a pair of black pants that were tighter than she preferred, paired with as modest of a plain white blouse she could find. Once out of the city she would either go back to her Emestrian garb or create some hybrid that would provide protection but not be too heavy. The clothes cost a fifth of what they would have in Emestria, even though they were made of nicer, but not as sturdy, fabric. Everything was cheaper in Newtonne; you could buy five pounds of flour, a pound of salt, or a quarter pound of sugar for fifty copper, one tenth of what they cost in Emestria. If Bronwyn had those prices in Emestria, she would be able to keep herself well-fed on her salary.

Clara and Miro opted for similarly light and simple clothing, although Miro seemed dead set on trying one of the privateer jackets the captains wore about town. Clara explained it would have been a faux pas for him to even try on a captain's jacket and convinced him instead to opt for a royal blue robe with yellow stitching along the hem. The garment was a stark contrast to his Emestrian robe. It parted down the middle, appearing more like a bath robe than the attire Bronwyn had seen sorcerers wear, but it still had a hood. She had yet to see a mage not wearing hooded clothing of some sort. Even the Magic Knights, Emestrian nobles trained in magic , wore hoods over their armor, although the cowl was usually down. Was this some agreed upon fashion they used to identify their own kind?

Magic Knight was an Emestrian term. Born from the fact that magic was a weapon of warfare and only nobles were taught it. Bronwyn looked to Miro, admiring his new robes, and chuckled to herself. Miro wasn't a Magic Knight. She really didn't know what to call him, which is why she always thought of him generically as a sorcerer. The idea of Miro in full armor seemed awkward. Bronwyn imagined him clad in steel trying to get on top of a horse and failing brilliantly.

Then what was he? In Selunia she knew they preferred shaman, Corinth called them priests, and Rouke preferred spellsword. She didn't know how every nation referred to their magic users, but Miro most definitely was not a Magic Knight. Apparently, Lynnfield called them priests, which lent a little credence to Miro and Clara's claim that Lynnfield was never a part of Emestria. Does this make Clara a priestess now? No, Clara as a priestess was just as absurd an idea as Miro being a knight. Heck, Bronwyn didn't even really consider Clara a sorceress at this point. Maybe apprentice sorceress?

Dismissing the arbitrary nomenclature, Bronwyn turned her attention back to the city. The port district was busy, but the city proper was packed. The streets were narrow and lined with stalls resulting in crowds so thick they needed to be forced through. Streams of people thronged about, moving like ice in a river, jostling against each other now and then or requiring one group of people to wind around the other. Even the smallest building was at least two stories tall, and despite the bright sun, the tall buildings shaded the streets. Even outside the port district, half the city was built over the water, supported by stone columns. The other half resided on the rocky land that buttressed the sea. The streets, if one could really call them that, were thick wooden planks, and you could still hear and smell the sea below. There were no outhouses or ditches for human refuse to be disposed in.

People from all around the world congregated here, and the crowds that choked Newtonne's streets presented all different shades and types of hair. In comparison, Emestria was depressingly monochromatic. Bronwyn stopped herself from staring at the people with the more vibrant hair colors and styles. She had never seen anyone like them before and was embarrassed this experience was new only to her. Emestria always seemed sizable—that the vast expanses of forests and tundra made it special. Now she realized how small it was. Perhaps the population of all Emestria could live in this one city. And there was still a whole world out there beyond this.

After a day of walking and running minor errands, they reached Newtonne's border. It was slow going because of the crowds, but as they approached the outskirts it became easier as the people dwindled. At the city's edge, they purchased some horses and a night at another inn—this one nowhere near as lively as the Speckled Crow, but still bigger and more crowded than the one in Porton—with plans to head out the next day.

Clara left early the next morning to purchase some dried fruit, nuts, cheese, and rolls with meat baked inside them. When she returned, Bronwyn was surprised; she was sure that Clara had finally abandoned them at the edge of the city, providing enough help to assuage any guilt.

# CHAPTER 15

*Mul'Tok was the most expansive of the pre-cataclysm civilizations, but after the cataclysm they found it hard to maintain their borders. Mul'Tok was the territory of Laevin, the arbiter, and was mostly protected by his judgment. After the cataclysm many of the cities of Mul'Tok were either abandoned, fell into ruin, or were subsumed by Tara, Rouke, or Corinth.*

*—Issaroh, The History of Divinity, Part XVIII*

The journey to the swamps of Mul'tok to find Miro's mentor would take about nine days. They skirted the border between Tara and Rouke; diplomatic relations between the countries were neutral and few troops were stationed at the borders. The trio avoided towns, which was for the best as Clara's bag of coin was noticeably less full after the purchase of the horses and provisions.

They ate Clara's food sparingly, as Bronwyn returned to her habit of trapping overnight and was amazed at how often she succeeded. She had never experienced a world so alive with animals. Miro fished in the morning when they camped near bodies of water and Clara would share in his catch, but Bronwyn abstained and instead ate leftover meat from their last successful snare. Freshwater fish was palatable compared to the mackerel common in Emestria, but fish was still fish. Some nights Clara ate both fish and meat. Bronwyn never felt so satiated, and her muscles relished the nourishment when she trained with her greatsword.

It was surprising to find a land so hospitable to life. The hills gently sloped and long, green grass blew in the wind. When they came upon thickets of trees, they were well-spaced and one would have trouble arguing they even constituted a forest. Streams, lakes, and ponds winded lazily along their path, despite Clara taking them off the roadway on most occasions.

The three towns they skirted were nowhere as large as Newtonne, but larger than Porton, from what Bronwyn could see in the distance. Were these towns independent like Clara claimed Newtonne was, or did they receive protection from either Tara or Rouke? Orchards, grazing land, and plowed fields were plentiful with large estates situated in the middle or on the border. When they did encounter people, they weren't met with hostility and were only given a cursory head nod, or a friendly but short wave. Was this what Lynnfield was like? If it were, Bronwyn could understand the forlorn looks she caught Miro giving the land from time to time.

Although Bronwyn had never been across the Iron Bridge, she imagined Southern Emestria was much the same. So why was Rouke pushing toward Southern Emesteria rather than pushing east toward Tara? Right, because Emestria was insulated, with few allies, and fewer financial resources. If Rouke tried to seize land from Tara, they would likely be crushed by Tara's overwhelming ability to field troops and mercenaries. Instead, Rouke picked off the little fish.

The trio got into a habit of Bronwyn covering the first watch so she could sleep in during the morning. Clara would do second, separating her night, and Miro would rise early, before first light, relieving Clara. Bronwyn could not express her joy that when she woke there was breakfast saved for her.

On the third night, much to Clara's delight, Ferdinand returned carrying a message from King Bryant. She read the note aloud.

*Glad you are safe. Update me when you have made progress in procuring the next artifact. We have displayed the mantle with a round-the-clock guard at the entrance to the castle. Everyday people flock to see the miracle and dream of salvation through your quest.*

It was short, but messenger missives left little room for elaborate prose. After a dinner of roast hare, Clara and Miro returned to their respective tents. They had ditched the third after the second night. Clara and Bronwyn had grown comfortable sharing a tent and it facilitated the changing of the guard.

Bronwyn made her usual rounds, setting up snares to catch the next day's dinner. After she set them, she sat by the fire to feed it and took her whetstone out to sharpen her sword. She was surprised, and a little chagrined, when Miro's tent flap opened. He had been a bit of a jerk as of late. He did not share in Bronwyn's wonderment about the wide world that awaited them, even though she knew he had seen little more of Primerra than she.

He came and sat by her at the fire. Picking up a small branch, he poked at the coals, even though she was managing fine before he arrived. "Do you remember anything of our conversation the first night in Newtonne?" he asked.

"Not much. I recall you bringing me rum, trying to get me drunk so I'd lower my guard." She was sure that was not his intention, but he needed some payback for his attitude of late. In fact, her opinion of the night had changed. After her hangover subsided and with the prodding of Clara's description of the night, she vaguely remembered Miro's nightmares waking her. She had been sweating and undressed herself underneath the covers after eating. The next morning, he was still in his own bed. Had her opinion of men fallen that low? The fact that she was vulnerable, and he still acted like a gentleman, was comforting.

Sighing, Miro said, "You said some nice things to me then."

"That doesn't sound like me," she continued. "The rum must have hit hard."

"About the responsibility for the death of others. How you were still grappling with the feelings yourself."

"And I'd tell you if I ever figured out how to reconcile them." A slight smile crossed her lips. This was their deal after all. He could keep up his false bravado around Clara, but he had to be real when they were alone, together.

"Have you?" He gazed into her eyes. His pleaded with her for an answer.

"Nothing more than that we make decisions in the moment. Life is messy. We can only do the best we can at the time. Sometimes people get hurt. As long as we make choices that we don't know will hurt people, we can take comfort in that."

"I still have trouble making peace with the idea. The responsibility haunts me every night."

"Is that why you have nightmares?" Bronwyn asked.

Miro's eyes widened and he jolted a little more upright. "What?"

"You toss and cry in your sleep." She tried to give a reassuring smile. "Most nights you're still studying before I go to bed, but I've seen it. I'm sure Clara has as well. I guess we don't talk about it because it seems like a very private matter."

"It is. I am stuck in my past and I don't know how to free myself."

"When you were in the ice floes with Clara, if we had run aground, do you think she would have let us freeze out there?" Bronwyn asked. Miro shook his head as she continued. "No, she would have pushed us back on the right track. She wouldn't focus on the mistake that led to our misfortune, but instead, she would concentrate on how to liberate us. I think that's all you can do. Recognize the mistakes of your past but move forward so you can free yourself of the ice. Isn't that why you're doing this? Hunting for the artifacts? So you can bring some measure of closure for us about what happened at the Battle of Lynnfield?"

Miro winced at the mention of the war. "I also want to help people. Despite my misgivings about Emestria, I do think we have a chance to usher the country—and maybe the world—into a place of prosperity. If Emestria were to retrieve enough artifacts, they could sign treaties with other nations from a place of power. Rouke would have to retreat and sue for peace, then Emestria could settle disputes between countries before war broke out."

"I don't think I would be traveling with you if this were only to satisfy your selfish desire for revenge." She used a branch to playfully knock his away and stoke the fire herself. "Nothing good ever comes of that. What brings on this sudden spell of vulnerability? You've been a hassle lately."

"I've felt a little useless," Miro admitted. "You've been keeping us fed and provide protection. Clara knows so much about the world in a way I thought I did, but obviously don't. I grasp at any bit of knowledge and flaunt it. I think I'm also nervous about seeing Issaroh. I don't think he'll be pleased with how I've spent my life since we last saw each other."

"Tell me more about Issaroh. Why does he live in the middle of a swamp?"

Miro perked up at the opportunity to recount his lore of times past. "Long ago, the god Laevin gifted his wife, Kyrie, a library that contained all the world's knowledge of the past and present. Immortal scribes recorded events as they happened in the world. When the gods left after the cataclysm, the structure sank from its heavenly location and descended to Primerra, landing in the region of Mul'tok. The weight of the books caused the library to sink into the ground and pushed the water up to the surface, creating the swamps of Mul'tok. Issaroh lives there, consuming all the knowledge about the world he can."

"That sounds like a pretty isolated existence," Bronwyn said after moments of being lost in contemplation.

"I guess we magi long to be alone."

"Ah, so you prefer magi, as opposed to magic knight or sorcerer? Tell me more about that. How exactly did you become a magus?"

"Well, you travel to the highest mountaintop and meditate for three days and three nights ..."

The look Bronwyn gave him stopped his fib midsentence. He had told various versions of the stories to Clara whenever she asked about becoming a magus, which was surprisingly quite frequent, almost every other day. She usually let the topic drop fairly quickly, but Bronwyn could tell Clara was a little more interested in it than Miro noticed. She had a look in her eye when asking about magi, a hunger for knowledge.

"I prefer not to talk about it." Miro looked intently at the fire, avoiding her gaze. "But it's not an easy choice to make and most everyone regrets it eventually."

"Do you regret it?" Bronwyn asked.

"Yes, the second after I made the decision. Issaroh had warned me, but the folly of youth—you think you know more than your mentors." Miro hung his head.

"Why did he warn you about being a magus? Isn't that a self-fulfilling prophecy?"

"He saw something in me that reminded him of his early life. He didn't want me to follow down his path, and I was determined not to, but in despair, we often make choices we regret." Miro was solemn and silent after he said this.

"How did you two meet?" Bronwyn tried to spur him into the conversation again.

"At the academy," he answered, not really engaging with the question. "He was one of my teachers."

"I thought the academy was only for nobles. No offense, but you don't strike me as one of privileged birth."

"Entrance was compulsory for nobles back then. If you didn't want your child to enter, and possibly go to war, you could pay for a substitute. I was an orphan and was purchased for that purpose. Because I had shown an affinity for magic."

"You were bought?" she asked, taken back by his cavalier attitude. That explained why he didn't appear full-blooded but was also a Krestel. Not a bastard, or at least not one of theirs.

"Not officially, but basically. The nobles paid an adoption fee, which was quite high. That's how the orphanages continued to run. The crown provided little funding for them."

"You never talk about your early life. How did you end up in an orphanage?" Bronwyn didn't know why she pressed him for so many details. Perhaps his lack of forthcomingness and how rare the opportunities were to question him caused her to yearn for more information.

"My mother died in childbirth. My father either blamed me or was overwhelmed at the prospect of having to raise a child by himself. I was dropped at the orphanage when I was still a babe." He sighed and Bronwyn could tell it was perhaps too much for him in one night.

"I enjoy talking to you, but I'm suddenly very tired. I think I'm going to go to sleep," he said, ending the conversation.

"Oh, okay. Try to sleep well," she offered apologetically for pushing him so far. "You'll feel better in the morning."

"Thanks." He rose to return to his tent.

Bronwyn replayed their talk in her head as she finished up her watch, and it was still on her mind when she woke Clara and headed to bed. It was honestly the most information she had gotten out of him at one time. To her surprise, she roused early the next morning and joined Miro before Clara woke, wanting to make sure the night's conversation had not weighed too heavily on him. His guard was back up, but Bronwyn decided to afford him the liberty and tolerated his brash nature, given it was probably rough for him to divulge so much at one time.

Talking late at night and early in the morning started to become their habit. Miro would spend the first hour of Bronwyn's watch with her. He was always wistful and contemplative, and she learned to pry details from him little by little. In the mornings, she would wake before Clara to check up on him. His mood alternated between chipper and downtrodden, and Bronwyn had trouble gauging which information would result in which temper. At least it prepared her for the day. When she woke to him being in positive spirits it would promise pleasant company, but his dour moods foretold a cocky attitude until nightfall. She usually ended up having to deliver a swift elbow or two to correct his behavior, but it was almost like he appreciated the reminder to be more considerate. More and more, though, she woke to see him smiling.

Of course, there were also evenings and mornings when she was not up to their conversation or tolerating his conduct during the day. He learned to gauge her moods as well and moderate his actions accordingly. On nights when she was having a rough time, he would bring her tea or some berries he had managed to forage.

One evening, he produced a handful of pine needles. She was surprised since she had not seen an evergreen for days. He explained he traded down feathers to a blue jay for the needles, and a goose had given up the feathers in exchange for half his morning's bread.

It was such a ridiculous tale; she didn't have the heart to tell him she only drank pine tea because of the cold and lack of alternatives. She was glad she hadn't. Once the drink was brewed and she sipped it, she was reminded bitterly of home.

# CHAPTER 16

*Ywaigwai were made with a sliver of the gods essence, just a fraction of their power. Since the Ywaigwai subsisted on the that power, it was thought that they left with the gods after the cataclysm, otherwise they would starve, being cut off from the gods, however the Ywaigwai that stayed found another source of energy to sustain themselves: souls.*

—Issaroh, *The History of Divinity,* Part XIII

The swamps of Mul'tok were not inherently dangerous—no more than any other swamp, at least. They were infested with the same creatures: snakes that would either poison or constrict, crocodiles waiting in the shallow water, jaguars stalking from the treetops, bats hunting for fresh blood, mosquitoes looking to infect with disease, and all manner of small critters that could deliver a noxious sting or bite. The moss-laden trees had knobby knees that protruded from the mud, ready to trip a careless walker. Dark green, thick grasses extended from ground to water with little distinction, causing wet boots and near falls into dank, foul-smelling muck. Many of these hazards were made all the worse by the canopy of trees that blocked out the sun for most hours of the day, making it feel more like traversing underground.

They were prepared for these dangers. Waterskins were filled as full as possible before entering. They proceeded cautiously and Miro finally relented and talked Ferdinand into operating as their keen-eyed scout.

Miro had refused up until that point, commenting that Ferdinand wasn't especially bright, even for a bird of prey. Clara and Bronwyn sliced and hacked at the vegetation barring their path and at anything that slithered in a way they disliked. If they happened to be poisoned, Miro had his magic.

A massive swarm of bugs annoyed them constantly, something Bronwyn had not expected. The capital of Emestria experienced few issues with insects. There were the cockroaches and flies that thrived on human existence, but except for summer gnats, residents suffered little from pests. The swamp was a different world altogether. All day they swatted and picked parasites from their skin. Then at night, it was difficult to sleep with bugs constantly crawling and chewing. In the morning when Bronwyn woke, her arms looked like gooseflesh with all the raised bites.

The second night, Miro attempted to thwart the problem by building a shelter off the ground between two trees for the three of them. It was haphazard at best, and in the morning, they realized the lifted bed did little to ward off the intruders. The third night, they slept around a fire stoked with wet vegetation, hoping the smoke would deter pests and predators alike. The trio coughed all night, breathing in the thick fumes, but it still did little to disperse the insects and arachnids. Toward the end of the fourth day, Bronwyn almost cried from exhaustion when Miro said he spotted the library.

The structure had completely sunk into the surrounding swamp, and if he hadn't known what they were looking for, the entrance would have been easy to miss. Surrounded by the fetid water, a fifteen-foot-wide circular dome covered in thick green algae ballooned six feet from the peaty surface. At Miro's behest, Clara called Ferdinand down and secured him in his cage.

Bronwyn hated the feeling of the mushy, semisolid swamp bed as they waded into the waist-deep murk. She practically felt the leeches crawling up her legs and sucking the blood from her. A considerable amount of time would need to be spent ensuring they were free of the critters before retiring for the evening. Crocodilians large enough to take down a human hadn't been seen yet, but that didn't stop her from unsheathing her greatsword as they waded through.

Miro attempted to summit the algae-covered mound first. There was a rope tied off for leverage, but the deep slick of vegetation in combination with the smooth glass underneath made it impossible to gain proper footing. He ended up having to crawl on his belly, his feet scrambling for traction. A trail of muck followed in his wake, and when he finally stood at the top, victorious, his entire front was covered in a slime of green and brown.

Bronwyn opted to go next. She regretted having worn the clothes from Newtonne. She had thought about switching to her Emestrian garb, which would have protected her more from bites, but the humidity and heat would be unbearable in the thicker clothing. Mud oozed down her blouse and stained the front as she climbed.

The footing at the top was no less precarious. The center, where a single glass frame would have stood, had been smashed, and another rope descended into the inky darkness. Bronwyn worried that with one wrong step, she would be sent tumbling into the unknown abyss.

Before Clara ascended, they tossed her some additional ropes to secure their supplies. Miro and Bronwyn worked together to haul them up, coating them in the same mess they were blanketed in themselves. Once they had their packs, Clara secured Ferdinand in his travel cage and had them bring him up as well. The bird screeched a ruckus into the air as muck invaded its home, and Miro rolled his eyes in response.

Finally, it was Clara's turn. They tossed her a second rope. Clara's many years on the sea ensured she was skilled in ascending rigging. She effortlessly braced her feet against one rope while pulling herself along the other they supplied. Bronwyn eyed Clara with envy as she crested the mound completely devoid of algae, except for her boots.

Next was the difficult task of descending into the library. The rope leading down faded from view after a short five feet. It swayed slightly back and forth absent any breeze. Bronwyn craned her neck to peer down into the bottomless hole but took a step back from the edge, worried about vertigo.

Miro got onto his hands and knees and crawled backward to the rope. He wrapped his hands around the hempen lifeline as he began to lean his torso back over the opening, and descended first. After the initial ten feet, the only indication that he hadn't fallen to his death was the lack of noise and the still-gentle tugging. After a tense five minutes, he called back up to them: "I'm in."

A small light emanated from deep within and Miro leaned back and looked up. Clara and Bronwyn went about tying ropes to the packs. They steadied the packs from above and then slowly lowered them through the broken skylight. Miro was standing to one side, and they had to swing them over in his direction. The bird and cage followed. Bronwyn was happy to have them go—Ferdinand had refused to shut up since the mud invaded his lodgings. *We all feel that way, but some of us have the decency to keep our opinions to ourselves,* she thought as they lowered him down. Thankfully, the incessant squawking diminished as the raptor traveled through the darkness. Clara was next, followed by Bronwyn.

After a tense descent in which Bronwyn was sure her hands would slip from all the algae that coated them, she expected to see a deserted skeleton of a building with decaying books and cobwebs. Instead, once

Miro and Clara had helped her to the ground, a monolith of a beast bore down upon them. The gray creature lumbered on two feet and had great big hands with three fingers each. It would have appeared human, except for the lack of a head. Bronwyn's hand shot to her blade's hilt, but Miro stayed it. The golem took no notice of them and continued to push a wooden carriage down the halls. It was ten feet tall, but made of rock or bricks stacked upon each other rather than flesh.

"They are the keepers of the library," Miro said as Bronwyn relaxed her grip on her hilt. "They won't bother us." The automaton blundered aimlessly along, unaware of their presence.

"Aren't they supposed to protect this place or something?" Bronwyn whispered.

"No need," Miro said, hoisting his pack over his back. "They were created when it resided in the realm of the gods. Issaroh!" His voice echoed in the void.

Despite reassurances, Bronwyn still winced and waited for danger to materialize from the dark corners and recesses. Unlike the swamp, the library smelled of leather, vellum, and a strange combination of spices that Bronwyn couldn't place.

Miro waved the torch he had lit in either direction, trying to find his bearings. "I think we should go this way." He motioned down one corridor.

"You think?" Bronwyn asked.

"I've never been here before," Miro said while scratching his head and offering a meek smile. They proceeded down one long hallway after another.

Bronwyn soon became acquainted with the second form of automaton that served the library: short—barely taller than Clara—dark-brown monkey-like creatures with wings. Unlike the golems, which lumbered through the halls, the smaller automatons ran erratically from place to place. They looked like old leather wrapped around some type of nebulous shape. Beady black eyes and mouths opened but led nowhere. Their teeth were sharp and white. Long, thin arms scraped the ground as they walked. Short feet caused them to hop as they ran, and in turn, their pointy tails bobbed and bounced behind. The wings seemed to have no use, except to help balance their awkward bodies. They crawled up the bookcases, replacing or removing tomes.

Bronwyn walked behind Miro to keep her bearings, but she scanned every empty aisle, every shadowed nook, and each one of the strange denizens that lumbered or skittered around. Her eyes alone seemed to dissect the room with delicate care. While Miro and Clara's boots thwacked loudly, Bronwyn rolled her step from heel to toe eliciting little more than a soft click as her heel touched the cold stone floor.

After the third or fourth hallway lined with stacks of books—Bronwyn lost track—they came upon a grand staircase that descended in a looping fashion to the floor below. A golem dragged a broom left to right across the carpeted stairs. If it weren't for the filth caking her shirt, it would be easy to forget the outside world was nothing but mud and bugs. The golem stopped sweeping and thudded up the stairs to begin cleaning the muddy boot impressions the trio left in their wake. Miro didn't even glance as the creature passed him.

Once down the stairs, they again found themselves in rows of scholarly-looking volumes. Miro continued to call out and was greeted with no response. Bronwyn began to doubt they would find his mentor at all. When they rounded another pair of bookcases, a light in a distant room silhouetted a humanoid figure unlike the golems or leathery imps.

Miro increased his pace, calling out "Issaroh," with greater frequency. The figure was seated at a desk and bent over, its head staring down at something on the desk. The shape looked deceptively human, but Bronwyn's hand hovered near her sword as Miro ran toward the doorway. Clara and Bronwyn picked up their pace, not far behind him.

"Issaroh!" he called to the figure, who glanced up. It was no clay or leather thrall.

"Hmm?" the old man said, squinting and readjusting his spectacles.

His hair was thin and stark white, with a long, braided beard matching in color. The dark skin of his wrinkled leather face was soft like freshly washed linen. A thin, light-brown robe, similar to the one Miro wore in Emestria, cloaked his figure. The hood was bunched up around his shoulders.

"Miro?" Issaroh readjusted his glasses again "Miro!" He rose from the table.

"Yes, it's me, you old coot," Miro said as he embraced his mentor warmly, burying his head in the old man's shoulder and exhaling.

"Let me see you." Issaroh placed his hands around Miro's face and examined him from multiple angles. "You haven't aged a day," he said with a bright smile.

"And you look fifty years older," Miro said, laughing, tears forming at the creases of his eyes.

"You wound me, young whippersnapper." Issaroh feigned offense before casting his glance toward Clara and Bronwyn in the doorway. "What's this? Did you bring us companions? Which one is mine?"

Bronwyn winced at the old man's gaze.

"Keep looking, grandpa, and you're liable to lose an eye," Clara said, stepping forward.

"Is she taken? I like that one," Issaroh said to Miro.

"Issaroh, stop being lecherous. These are my friends. I told them about how great of a teacher you are."

"Oh, so you've ruined it for me," Issaroh said. "Unless you ladies like an older, wiser man?"

"I'll cut you where the gods made you," Bronwyn threatened, revealing an inch of her steel greatsword.

"I changed my mind. Is she taken?"

"Stop, Issaroh, they're not used to you." Miro turned back to Clara and Bronwyn. "I'm sorry, he doesn't meet many people and his sense of humor is dated at best. He doesn't mean what he says."

"You wound me, good sir," Issaroh replied. "I'm as funny as I've ever been. What finally convinced you to leave your frozen exile and visit me?"

"We're searching for the artifacts," Miro said, his words jumbling together. "We already found one. This means they could all be real. I need to find information about the Soul Gem. I can trap the thing that destroyed Lynnfield."

Issaroh cast his eyes downward. "You can't change your fate. If you go after it, it will be the end of you. No matter how many artifacts you find."

Miro paused and stared at Issaroh. "You knew? You knew they were real, didn't you?"

"Yes. I've known." Issaroh continued to look away, unable to meet Miro's gaze.

"I can't believe this! You know what this means to me!" Miro paced in tiny circles, muttering to himself. He turned sharply and asked, "You haven't been looking for it, have you?"

"Miro, you need to understand. The artifacts are complicated." Issaroh held his hands in front of himself, slowly waving them up and down slowly in a calming gesture. "I've tried to—"

"I'll find the gem myself then!" Miro yelled and disappeared into the stacks, taking their lantern with him.

"Kids, am I right?" Issaroh joked to Clara and Bronwyn.

Bronwyn saw where Miro got his defensive humor.

"Well, ladies, it's nice to meet you. Don't worry, I'm not some old lech—I like to embarrass him."

Clara stepped forward. "I'm Clara, and this is Bronwyn."

"I should show you around. Knowing him, he won't give up until he finds what he's looking for. We could be here a while."

Issaroh walked past them and threw his hands up. "Welcome to the great Library of Laevin!" he shouted, his voice echoing off the walls. "The interior is a lot better with the lights on. I keep them off because I can't stand the hum from the generator."

"Generator?" Bronwyn asked, puzzled. She had never heard the word used in that way before.

"Oh, my dears, you're in for a treat. I'll have to introduce you to the wonders of electricity and indoor plumbing."

"What?" Bronwyn groaned, she didn't know what exactly he was referring to, but the idea of more water sent a shiver up her spine. Miro must have learned his trait of talking like everyone knew the same information as him from Issaroh. "That water is so full of leeches I would faint from blood loss."

"Oh no, it's pumped and filtered, as clean as a mountain spring," Issaroh reassured. "Similar to the outdoor pumps that draw from aquifers—like they use in Emestria. Except the water is kept pressurized and inside the building. A technology the gods employed, but didn't deem fit to pass onto man. And the lights don't use oil; they're powered by lightning that travels through wires. It's all perfectly safe, mind you."

Bronwyn wasn't sure if she liked the idea of being surrounded by lightning, but a clean bath sounded like a godsend. She looked at Clara with a deep smile. "The tour can wait. I need to wash. Point us to where we can bathe." She pulled at the old man's sleeve.

"Hold up, hold up. Let me grab a light." Issaroh retrieved two of the lit candles in his room and handed one to Bronwyn. He slowly started walking and they followed.

The overwhelming darkness had made navigation near impossible for Miro and the others, but Issaroh negotiated the building confidently, turning down one aisle, taking a left at the next junction. Bronwyn quickly lost track of the direction they headed.

Like Miro, Issaroh expounded upon his knowledge as he walked. "This place was built as more than a library. You saw my room—I had converted one of the private studies—but the wing we're headed to was more of a living quarters for the gods. Once they realized the potential of the golems and homunculi providing constant upkeep, they made additional chambers. The gods must have used it as a halfway point between their realm and ours, to acclimate to corporeal forms before they came to visit us. They were quite fond of their creation and would often walk among us—disguised sometimes, of course. They probably came here to remind them what it was like to be a human. To have to eat, bathe, and wear clothes. Perhaps they came here to experience what life was like and didn't descend to our realm at all on occasion."

They reached another circular staircase and started to climb. Issaroh was slower on the stairs, so Bronwyn offered him an arm to assist. He gently patted it in thanks and had her help him up.

"Wasn't this place built in the heavens?" Bronwyn asked. "How is it still functioning here?" A golem appeared out of the darkness and Bronwyn recoiled in shock, almost knocking Issaroh over.

"They are perfectly safe, my dear. The golems and homunculi were instilled with the powerful magics of the gods and given singular purposes. To pump water, to run the generator, to file books, to tend the gardens." Bronwyn cast Clara a disapproving look; Issaroh and Miro were way too similar. "When the library descended, they continued their tasks. The automatons must have redone the water supply somehow, and they dug out an entrance."

"You mean there was another way in?" Clara complained.

"Yes, quite inconspicuous," Issaroh said. "Inside a cavern at the edge of the swamp. It is rather secluded, and finding the right cave can be difficult for even me sometimes. It would be impossible for someone else to find, except by accident."

"Are they alive? The golems and homculees? Those are the small ones, right?" Clara asked.

"Yes, the *homunculi* are the little ones," Issaroh replied. "They're animated, but not living. They don't need to eat or drink and aren't capable of independent thought outside of their designated tasks. They seem to possess some sort of intelligence, though, to have figured out how to replumb the water pipes and obtain the materials to keep this place in good repair."

"How do they do that?" Bronwyn asked while looking out for more of the automatons.

"Well, the homunculi go out at night and forage. They bring the resources to the forge and manufactory in the basement. From there, they craft what they need. I've watched them to see how they work, but it is difficult to tell what they're doing most of the time."

The rows of books ended, and they started to pass statues and open doorways. Bronwyn had not seen a single door since she had entered. The gods must not have been fond of privacy.

"Ah, here we are," Issaroh said, spying a doorway and leading them toward it.

Thankfully, the bath was concealed by a wall that opened on both sides. The bathing house was made of black and white marble. Bronwyn held the candle against the stone and scanned for seams, but she had difficulty seeing any. Along the border, ornate hooks held towels and robes. They looked flawless, not moth-eaten like she expected. The middle of the floor housed a square recess and as she stared down, she saw the bath, six feet deep but lined with concentric steps two feet wide for every foot of height. To her dismay, there was no water. Around the rim were golden heads, draconic in nature. Their throats were each blocked by a metal plate, with the top of the plate extending out the top of the head. Eight dragons in total, two on each side, close together like pairs. One of each pair had eyes with blue gems and the other with red.

"Right now, it's empty," Issaroh said. "I had to stop bathing in it after a bad slip. Difficulty with slick surfaces at my age and whatnot." Issaroh walked over to one of the sets of dragons. He pointed to the plate bisecting the mouth. "When you lift them, the water will come out. Normally the red-eyes would have hot water, but not until I get the generator going. If you don't mind the cold, you can open all eight to fill it faster. Still going to take a while given its size."

Bronwyn stepped over to a dragon head and tugged at the stubborn heavy plate. Once she secured some leverage with her foot, the metal slab started to budge. Water trickled from the mouth, and she pulled as hard as she could, causing it to clang open. A forceful jet of clear water shot across and down into the bath. She turned and looked at Issaroh expectantly. He blanked, tilting his head from side to side.

"Oh right, I'll afford you ladies your privacy and try and start on some dinner," Issaroh said as he turned to leave. "If you need anything, call for me."

Bronwyn opened the other seven valves as quickly as she could, then removed her shirt, which slopped against the floor, splashing mud across the smooth marble. She shimmied off her pants to look down her legs. Small black flecks—leeches—stuck to her legs and slowly climbed toward her waist. She used the candle to burn them off one by one. After she removed and killed all the leaches she could by herself, she turned to ask Clara if she would burn the parasites clinging to Bronwyn's back. She gasped in surprise and guilt seeing the state of Clara's body. The pests had crawled up as far as her midsection. Clara waited expectantly for the candle.

"Here, let me help." Bronwyn walked forward and knelt, exposing the little buggers to the flame. They hissed then rolled up and fell off Clara's skin. Once Bronwyn had removed all the ones from Clara's front side, she started to do her back. After Bronwyn finished, Clara returned the favor.

The water had not filled the entire tub, but they were able to submerge themselves in the water that had risen to the tops of the lowest steps. The swamp melted off their bodies; their hair, however, was a different story. The women ran their fingers through while holding it underwater, trying to free the bits of detritus.

A slow hum began and a steady pale-yellow light came from sconces on the walls. The light increased until the entire room was bathed in the drab color. *This must be the lightning in the walls Issaroh was referring to. It does seem safe*, Bronwyn thought, *but there is no way I'm touching one of those glass bulbs.* Clear little bubbles of glass contained a bright orange wire that throbbed. Soon one of the homunculi came scuttling across the floor.

"God, they're worse than the stone ones," Bronwyn said to Clara.

"They're harmless, ignore them." Clara leaned her head back into the water. Her light-rose hair fanned out on the surface, and her body bobbed as she relaxed in the cool bath. A homunculus hopped up to the edge of the bath, tilting its small head back and forth at them.

"Go away," Bronwyn shouted, splashing some water at it.

The creature did not flinch. Then it turned and grabbed their clothes and dashed away.

"Hey!" Bronwyn yelled, clamoring up the steps.

"What?" Clara said, opening her eyes and sitting upright.

"It stole our clothes."

Bronwyn hoisted herself up over the edge and started running. The beastie was much too quick and escaped into the hall. Bronwyn skidded to a halt, mortified at the thought of jogging naked through the library.

"We've got our other outfits. Those were much too dirty to wear any-way." Clara resumed leaning her head back into the water.

Bronwyn returned to the tub, frustrated. "I'm gonna get them back. I'll hunt that little imp down. Let's see him skitter around once I cut him in two." One of the golems came through the door carrying a broom before she finished her sentence. "Oh great, now there's a rock one too. The little one already took our clothes!"

The golem paid her no mind as it swept the leeches and mud into a pile on the floor. It walked out and returned with a bucket, pan, and smaller broom. Bronwyn watched as it swept up the muck and emptied the pan into the bucket over and over.

"Can't you wait until we're done?" Bronwyn seethed.

"Bronwyn, would you relax?" Clara scolded. "You're ruining this for me."

Bronwyn sat back down, folding her arms across her chest. "I don't see what's so great about this place."

"This is where the gods bathed," Clara said. "Think about the decisions they made here. The fate of the world was determined in these halls. This may be the place they decided to quit the mortal realm forever. And look at it—this room is absolutely beautiful. Carved from a single piece of marble. And light that doesn't come from fire. How are you only concentrating on the staff, eager to wait on us hand and foot? Not even kings bask in this type of luxury."

Bronwyn gave up and decided to follow Clara's example. She leaned back against one of the steps, so her head was half in and half out of the pool. The gurgle of the cascading water took some of the frustration of the golems away. The water was cool but still warmer than anything she could pump in Emestria.

Bronwyn sighed heavily. "Can you imagine what this will be like once it's hot?"

"Oh, I'm coming back later when it is. I may decide to live in this room," Clara joked.

After an hour, the water reached the last step and Bronwyn got out to shut all the valves except for one head with red eyes. She hoped the bath would be hot by evening or the following morning. She breathed in heavily. then out, the tension in her body easing. For several minutes, they basked silently.

"Miro tells me you spent the night with a captain in Newtonne," Bronwyn said, trying to spur Clara into a conversation.

"I did."

"Someone you knew, or someone you met that night?"

"He's an old friend. I used to be his first mate but struck out on my own when I got my crew and started smuggling," Clara said, not opening her eyes.

"He wasn't a smuggler as well?"

"No, he ran a more traditional operation, sailing goods from port to port. At least that's what he does now. When I was his first mate, our business was a little less than aboveboard. A lot more lucrative as well."

"Really? Why'd he quit?" Bronwyn asked. She had a good idea Clara was saying he was a brigand in the nicest way possible.

"He wanted a safer life and a more reliable income, even if it meant earning less. I went into smuggling because I still wanted the big scores. I didn't care if it was a little dangerous. I needed to make as much money as quickly as possible," Clara said, before sighing.

"Why is that?"

"What about you?" Clara deflected "Do you have any friends back in Emestria?" *Friends* was heavy with insinuation.

"I was seeing someone a while ago, but it's difficult being the captain. Most everyone I meet is in the guard already, and fraternizing with subordinates can get messy. The last person I pursued left the guard so we could keep seeing each other, but then things didn't work out. I felt bad she gave up her position and there was extra pressure because of that," Bronwyn explained.

"That's why I never slept with crew members."

"But you had a thing with your captain."

"True, but I wasn't the superior officer. He was the one making the bad decision. I just got to profit from the favoritism," Clara joked.

They stayed in the bath until their fingers and toes wrinkled, and their skin plumped.

# CHAPTER 17

*After the gods' disappearance, many Ywaigwai remained on Primerra. In need of an alternate way to survive absent the god's power, Ywaigwai began making deals with sorcerers in exchange for that sorcerer's soul; thus did the magi come to be. I may be the first magus; I have never met one as old as me. I have also never met a magus that did not regret the deal they made.*

—Issaroh, *The History of Divinity, Part XVII*

"Dinner is ready," Issaroh shouted from the hallway.

Clara got out of the bath first, and Bronwyn was going to ask her about what they should do for clothing, but Clara walked over, toweled herself off, then put on one of the robes. Bronwyn followed her example; Clara was a lot better at relaxing than her. The towels were thick, pillowy cotton and wicked the moisture away from Bronwyn's legs and torso. Thin robes dangled from hooks set in the marble wall. As she caressed the smooth fabric it clung to the dampness of her hand. *Silk.*

Bronwyn turned as she counted the number of robes: eight, including the one Clara now wore and the one Bronwyn held in her hand. She pulled the white fabric with red flowers up her right arm and then her left and tied the sash around her waist. The robe barely covered her knees. Grabbing a towel, Bronwyn leaned her head forward and wrapped the thick cotton around her hair. Covered as best as possible, she left the bathhouse.

Issaroh waited patiently outside. The library was much grander in the light. It stretched endlessly in every direction. This part of the floor was filled with rows of bookshelves. Large crystalline chandeliers dotted with artificial lamps hung from the ceiling. A dozen golems and countless homunculi moved about, making it appear alive and busy.

Here on the second floor, across from them, expansive windows were obscured by dirt. Perhaps the space beyond the windows was once an elaborate veranda from which the gods would look down on the mortal realm. This side of the top story was lined with doorways, much like the one to the bath. Bronwyn marveled at what could be within those rooms—and what wonders awaited discovery. To the left and right, in front of winding staircases, were more rows of bookcases.

Issaroh led them toward a doorway at one end of the building. As they came closer, it opened into a lavish dining room with a long table that could easily fit twenty guests. Portraits of the gods that once resided here adorned the walls. Nestled in the far wall, a fireplace lay empty, as the current climate made it much too hot for a fire. At least below ground it was less humid. In the back corner, another doorway led to the kitchen.

Issaroh had placed plates on the end of the table, all close together so they wouldn't have to yell at each other for conversation. Miro held a book in his lap and had his boots perched on the table. He hadn't changed and was still covered in muck. Apparently, his interest in the books overwhelmed his need for basic hygiene. As Bronwyn walked by, she batted at his legs, knocking them down. "Keep your feet off the table, you jerk," she jested.

He did not respond, too engrossed in the tome.

Issaroh sat at the head, Clara to his left and Bronwyn to his right, next to Miro. In front of each of them was a plate of spinach with dark wrinkled fruit and a drizzle of oil. To its left was a small cup of almonds. To its right, a bowl of piping-hot red soup with shavings of green chives on top. Clara picked up the silver fork by her plate and said, "Wow, this is amazing."

"Yes, it's wonderful," Bronwyn complimented. She stared at Miro. "Have you thanked Issaroh for preparing us dinner?"

"Oh, thanks," he said, scooping up a handful of almonds and popping them all into his mouth without taking his gaze from the book.

Bronwyn rolled her eyes and turned her head toward Issaroh who shrugged.

"I see you found the robes," Issaroh said, glancing at Clara before returning to his dinner.

"Yes, one of those buggers stole our clothes." Bronwyn was about to launch into her diatribe about them but was silenced with a pointed look from Clara. This table only had room for one rude party guest and that role was taken. With one barely dressed woman to his side and another across the table, Miro hadn't even looked up or commented on them. *What is in that book that is more interesting than us?*

"Oh, usually they wait till you're asleep to do the wash." Issaroh blew on a spoonful of soup before swallowing. "Must have figured since your clothes were so dirty you wouldn't be wearing them. Don't worry, they'll be mended and folded in the morning at the foot of your bed."

"About that. Where should we sleep?" Clara asked.

"Take your pick, there are plenty of bedrooms. The gods did live here, after all. I situated myself in one of the studies because I'm old fashioned and wasn't comfortable taking any of the other rooms, but that shouldn't stop you."

"This place is amazing," Clara exclaimed, "but why haven't you shared it with the world?"

"If they found out now, they would pillage and strip it down to a shell of its former self. Now that I'm nearing the end of my life, I'll never see the day when the world matures enough to witness its splendor. But perhaps Miro would be willing to take over my vigil?"

Miro didn't respond and Bronwyn delivered a swift elbow to his side. It didn't elicit his normal whines of pain. "Uh, sure, whatever," Miro said without looking up from his book and turned a page.

Issaroh's shoulders slumped, and he glanced toward his bowl of soup while slightly shaking his head.

"It's rude to read at the table," Bronwyn said, trying to grab Miro's book, but he defensively cradled the tome against his body. "If you're not going to participate in the conversation, you should leave." *All that time traveling and all the effort he's made at being civil is gone in an afternoon. He can't keep his eyes off the books.*

"Hmm, okay," Miro said, standing up and turning to exit the room.

Bronwyn grabbed a couple of his almonds and chucked them at him. "And go take a bath. You stink like an outhouse."

"Okay, right." Miro waved his hand back at her.

Bronwyn turned back to the table fuming. Both Issaroh and Clara looked at her, concerned.

"I'm sorry. He knows how to strike Bronwyn's nerves," Clara said.

"No need, he used to do it to me all the time," Issaroh replied.

"How did you two meet?" Clara asked. Bronwyn had heard some of this tale from Miro but was now curious to determine how truthful he had been.

"I was his teacher at the academy when I was a younger man."

"What, when you were seventy-five? How long ago was that?" Clara joked, and Issaroh laughed in response.

"I'd say twenty years. I appeared much more youthful then. These last few years, my age is doing triple time to catch up with me," Issaroh said.

"So, how old was he when you started training him?" Bronwyn asked.

"Let me think. That was his last couple of years at the academy, so maybe nineteen or twenty?"

"Did you train him how to be a magus?" Clara asked. "Could you teach me how to be one?" The fingertips of Clara's hand turned white as she gripped her fork tightly.

Issaroh's smile disappeared. His forlorn eyes betrayed his displeasure at the question. "You must never wish that, ever." Issaroh's eyelids sagged, and the corners of his mouth turned down tightly. "To be one of the magi is to rob yourself of your soul and everything you hold dear—a fate worse than death itself."

"I don't understand," Bronwyn said in frustration. "I've asked him repeatedly about it, but he gives some silly answer every time. How does one become a magus? What must you sacrifice?"

Issaroh looked at both of them and sighed. Bronwyn's eyes, much like Clara's, begged for an explanation.

"You must promise me from the deepest part of your heart, that never, even in the depths of despair, would you consider it for a second."

The women nodded their heads slowly.

"When you're at your lowest moment, a being will appear to you. There are many different types of them; they're called Ywaigwai. They feed on souls. In exchange for your soul, the Ywaigwai will lend you its power and grant you your heart's desire. However, the wish is almost always contorted. It takes hundreds of years to forgive yourself, and many never do. Their hearts are always heavy with the mistakes they made."

"What did you wish for?" Clara asked quietly.

"Clara," Bronwyn scolded at the audacity of the question.

"No, it's fine. Let my story be an example of why it is no blessing. If I had told my tale to Miro those many years ago, he could have avoided the same fate. After the cataclysm, a plague ravaged the land. In the past, we would have prayed to the gods for salvation, however, that was no longer an option. I—along with many others—raced to find a cure. When my wife and young son were afflicted, I was devastated. I knew there was no way we could find a remedy in time to save them.

"So, in my lowest moment, a Ywaigwai appeared to me. He was a beautiful horse with a single horn sprouting from his head. He offered me the bargain, and I did not hesitate. I wished to find a way to end the plague. So, he brought me here, to where all the world's knowledge was contained. I pored over countless tomes day and night. After weeks, or maybe a month, I found the cure.

"I made haste to return home, but when I arrived, it was too late." Issaroh wiped a tear away before continuing. "My wife and son had perished. I missed my opportunity to say goodbye. Our house was pillaged—many thinking it vacant—and I lost any memento of them. I made a wish, trying to protect what I loved, only to lose much more. Such is the fate of all magi."

"I'm so sorry," Bronwyn said, shaking her head. "We shouldn't have asked."

"No, it's all right. I've told the story plenty of times to other sorcerers to warn them of the danger. In a way, it's cathartic to atone for my past. I wish I had shared that tale with Miro as well."

"Why didn't you?" the incessantly curious Clara asked.

"I saw what my son would have been in him." Issaroh sighed. "I started teaching him like a child instead of a pupil. When it came time to give him the speech, I balked. I couldn't tell him about the shame of my loss. I worried I'd lose his respect. Only later, after I found out he made the same mistake, did I tell him. He didn't take it well."

"Do you know what he wished for?" Bronwyn asked. This was the last piece of the puzzle. If she knew that, she'd be able to finally understand him.

"No, I do not. I searched for him after the war. When I asked him to tell me what happened, he broke down and cried." Issaroh removed his spectacles and massaged the bridge of his nose. "A week or two later, a friend of his from the war came and found us. They made plans to move away from Solstice, build a life together in the frozen wilderness. They seemed happy and she quieted his soul in a way I was incapable of. I thought it better to leave him be, give him a chance at happiness without me around, so I left them, promising to visit.

"A year later, when I returned, he told me she had traveled home, unable to stay with him. He thought himself a monster and had been acting like one. Eating raw fish and talking to that giant cat of his. That's when I told him what I did and how I became a magus. He cursed and yelled at me, throwing books. I stayed despite the treatment, knowing he needed someone. The next day he was sorrowful and depressed. He vacillated between emotional states every other week."

"Yes, I've been subject to his moods," Bronwyn consoled, although it had never been to that point. She hadn't pictured Miro as someone capable of such treatment.

"It's then that I told him what I thought being a magus meant. We were granted long lives to make peace with our past and to atone for our mistakes. I used my life to study disease and prevent plagues—like the one that cost me my family—from taking root. And I've succeeded: in four hundred years there hasn't been anything like it again."

"Wait, four hundred years?" Clara asked, leaning away from the table.

"Yes. I've been alive since before the cataclysm. I remember what it was like when the gods still roamed among us. My speech gave Miro some small solace, but he became obsessed with the idea of the legendary artifacts. To get revenge, to externalize his guilt. I've tried to temper that in him, but he hangs to the scheme like a zealot. It will be the death of him." Issaroh lowered his head and exhaled loudly.

"He's not doing it just for vengeance," Bronwyn reassured. "Emestria is going through a lot of internal strife and he's helping me find the artifacts to return the country to its former glory. He wants to help the people of Emestria. I wouldn't be here if it were only about his retribution."

"Well, maybe you can guide him where I couldn't." Issaroh smiled up at Bronwyn. "Now, I think I owe you two a tour."

Issaroh allowed them to finish their meal before guiding them through the facilities.

# CHAPTER 18

*Ramun, god of time and space, and traveler of the world, was the last god to come into existence and had features that appeared as a cross between a simian common in one of the islands of Selunia and a human. Originally a spirit guardian, Ramun fell in love with Lau'O'Penake and offered to give his life for hers upon her first death. His golden fur was skinned from his body and had regenerative powers; from it was created the Legendary Artifact to revive Lau'O'Penake.*

*—Issaroh, The History of Divinity, Part XI*

The tour had covered a dizzying array of strange contraptions and lore of the gods. Issaroh had shown them a garden with a miniature sun, the bedchambers of all the different gods, a room where golems spun wheels to generate electricity and pump water, curved metal pipes that heated water, and a manufactory the homunculi used to craft all the tools the library needed. The room with electricity, water, and manufactory were deep below the library, and they had to descend a long set of winding stairs that doubled back on themselves several times. Compared to the grandeur of the library, the lower levels were basic and utilitarian. Even the lights weren't set into sconces and jutted from the walls without protection.

Bronwyn remained a good sport until Issaroh mentioned the artifact that allowed the homunculi to write their books went missing over one hundred and fifty years ago. Then she lost her temper. Issaroh's indifference to the plight of Emestria forced her to leave them down in the basement with the machines. Issaroh lacked any compassion for Emestria, excusing his lack of care under the guise that nations had risen and fallen many times in his lifetime. Emestria wasn't just any nation, it was her home, and the home of most everyone she knew.

Bronwyn stomped up the stairs. *Why doesn't anyone understand or grasp the urgency of the situation or care what the ultimate fate of Emestria is?* Even Miro, who was born in Emestria, seemed to be more concerned with his mission of vengeance than delivering their homeland from ruin.

She made up her mind right then and there to find his smug face and set him straight. He had been taking advantage of her good faith. Quickening her pace, she went up the steps, taking them two at a time. It was much faster without having to help Issaroh and she quickly crested the staircase, returning to the library's main floor. She decided to collect her gear before tracking Miro down, backtracking and heading down another aisle that would bring her to the wall that led to Issaroh's study. However, there was a doorway that she hadn't seen. It was larger than the door to the studies where they found Issaroh. Cautiously, she approached.

The room was about twenty feet deep and fifteen feet wide. A long oaken table dominated the space and along the walls were stacks of paper and bindings for books. A dozen homunculi sat at the table, quills in their hands and dried inkpots at their sides. They stared motionlessly at blank pieces of paper. The sight sent shivers down her spine. Something was menacing about them sitting there, motionless, ready to start writing but frozen in time. Without the Eye of Sleepless Dreams—the artifact Issaroh said went missing—they would remain here motionless, unable to complete their task of chronicling history.

She backed out of the room and looked down the wall to see her pack and sword leaning against the doorway to Issaroh's room. Ferdinand cocked his head and screeched at her. Clara should keep his cage covered, so he wouldn't make that incessant noise all the time. After gathering her belongings, Bronwyn returned to the stacks to track down Miro.

After an hour of searching, she found him. Miro was slumped against one of the bookcases. Thinking one of the clay brutes must have knocked him unconscious while he was buried in a book, she ran up to him. At his feet were three opened books in a half circle around where he had been reading. One of the homunculi dazedly stared at him from the far-end of the bookcase and refused to move when Bronwyn tried to shoo it away.

When she got closer, she realized he had not heeded her advice to take a bath; he still smelled of the fetid swamp. Judging by his position, he had not been knocked unconscious by one of the golems but instead had fallen asleep while researching. She debated waking him and then laying into him about his lack of manners. However, the sight of him sleeping stayed her wrath. Perhaps they were all a little exhausted. That's why she had let a small comment from Issaroh tempt her into such a rage.

Curious if Issaroh had returned, she headed back to his room. She'd offer an apology, explain that she was overly tired, and then retire for the evening. As she approached, she saw that Issaroh was already in his study. He wasn't poring over the tome opened on his small desk, but instead rummaging around for something. She didn't wish to yell at him from across the library, and continued to advance.

When she got close, he still wasn't aware of her presence. He was intensely focused on looking for something. Not wanting to startle him, she didn't call out; instead, she waited for him to turn his attention to her. She was also curious to see what he was searching for.

He finally found what he sought. The bronze hexagonal tablet was about four inches wide and a quarter inch thick. Clutching it against his chest, he made for his bed and stuffed the trinket underneath the mattress. He was being so secretive, she now felt bad for having watched him without saying anything.

Bronwyn backed away from the doorway before he turned around. She waited for him to leave or say something. The lights flickered off immediately after a mechanical click. The soft rustle of sheets followed soon after, and then stillness. The apology could wait until tomorrow.

Miro's gear was still lumped against the side of the wall, but Clara's and Ferdinand were now gone.

Bronwyn went upstairs to the bath and gods' chambers. First, she stopped in the bath and slid the last plate down to close the remaining spigot she left open. During the tour she discovered her folly in thinking the water would heat magically. The water was still cool. They would need to let the water build up in the heating tank before it would provide a hot bath. In the morning, or perhaps tomorrow evening, she would have to drain and refill the pool with hot water.

After visiting the bath, she walked past the lines of rooms. One room was dark, and she peeked inside to see Clara asleep underneath the sheets. Issaroh had explained that this was the bed chamber of Lau'O'Penake, goddess of nature and rebirth, and her husband Ramun, god of time and space, and traveler of the world. Bronwyn decided to claim the room of Seraph, goddess of love and healing, for herself.

The room was decorated with dozens of portraits. It had taken her and Clara a while during the tour to piece together that in each portrait Seraph was with a lover. She sought out mortals that had lost their loved ones and became their new object of affection to ease their pain. It had been a little difficult to deduce when they first saw the room. Seraph changed her shape to meet the ideal of her lover's preferred partner. But the eyes and expression were the same in every picture, the eyes of someone that lost the love of her life and would never be consoled. In each portrait, the person she was with looked happy and content in comparison. Seraph had appeared as men, women, and sometimes neither, taking lovers of any gender. Bronwyn wondered if Seraph chose the task as penance for slaying her own mortal lover and father of her child, Lau'o'Penake, when tricked by the god Chivas, god of souls and subterfuge.

The bed was the most luxurious one Bronwyn had seen in the library. Large enough for her to lie down in any direction and still have her feet and head on the bed at the same time. The sheer white silk curtains hanging between the bedposts were finer than any fabric she had seen. The red sheets on the bed were of even greater quality. Bronwyn estimated that out of all the sleeping arrangements this would be the most pleasant in the humid climate.

It did not take her long to find the lever that Issaroh explained could stop the light. It was connected to a metal plate affixed to the wall. A metal lever attached to a hinge would stop the electricity to a particular room if pulled into the down position. After plotting out the course to the bed, she flipped the lever. A small amount of light bled in from the library and she was able to navigate her way to the bed without bumping into the walls. Bronwyn slid underneath the cool sheets and onto the comfortable mattress.

As her eyes adjusted to the darkness, she saw the vague outlines of the portraits, but not the paintings themselves. Clara had found this room sad. Bronwyn agreed the story was unfortunate, but she also found the idea of so many people being infatuated with you to be an appealing one. In the few relationships she had entertained before devoting herself fully to training for the guard, she had always been the one falling in love. As an adult, she realized her feelings were superficial and born of a desire to be loved and nothing more.

She slipped off to sleep quickly.

The next morning, she went to find Issaroh, to apologize for last night's outburst, but when she approached his room, she heard Miro's voice. Thinking them about to get into another argument she continued to approach cautiously.

Miro said, "Have you tried to look at Bronwyn's aura?"

"You know I don't use that ability around you," Issaroh replied. "It's too bright and hurts my eyes."

"The next time it's just the two of you, read her aura. There is none."

"So, it's very dim and not strong, she's not the only person to have no strong magical affinity."

"I've seen that before. There is no aura, Issaroh."

Bronwyn stood just outside the doorway, a little incensed that the two of them would choose to talk about this without her, but also curious as to what Issaroh had to say.

Miro continued, "And she can't even use magic."

"It doesn't come as easily to everyone else as it does to you."

"She studied for years and can't even cast the most basic of spells." Miro's voice, to Bronwyn's chagrin, was becoming increasingly excitable, like when he talked about the artifacts.

Issaroh started, "Miro—"

"And she resists it. Have you ever met anyone, or read of anything like that?"

"Miro, you're jumping to conclusions and getting upset."

"No, listen to me Issaroh. I'm not confused. I've healed her. You know how good of a healer I am. It was like I was trying to push through a barrier just to mend a bite."

Having tired of not being included in the conversation, Bronwyn cleared her throat and stepped into the doorway of Issaroh's bedroom and study. "It's not very nice to have these sorts of conversations behind my back, even if your intentions are good."

Miro threw his hands up. "See for yourself, Issaroh!"

Issaroh knitted his brows, lowered his head slightly, and gave Miro a disapproving look.

Miro shouted again, "Fine, I'll leave. But look." Miro turned abruptly and side-stepped Bronwyn before leaving the two of them.

Bronwyn turned to watch him disappear back into the stacks. "I wanted to come by and apologize for my rash behavior last night." She looked down at her feet. "But is there any truth to what he's saying?"

"Let's see," Issaroh said, removing his glasses and squinting in Bronwyn's direction. "Hmmm"

Bronwyn exaggeratedly raised her eyebrows.

"Yes, I can see what he's talking about, but you have to understand something about Miro. He gets overly excited and makes correlations where none exist. He's an extremely competent sorcerer, but a poor scholar."

"I heard that!" Miro yelled from somewhere behind the stacks.

"And he does things like use magic to eavesdrop, which is incredibly intrusive!" Issaroh shouted back.

Issaroh approached Bronwyn, who stepped to the side to allow him to leave. "Thank you for coming to apologize to an old man. I shouldn't have been as dismissive about Emestria's current strife. When you live a long time, sometimes the importance of events is lost on you. I'll look into what Miro is talking about." Issaroh put a gentle hand on Bronwyn's forearm and leaned in close to whisper, "But don't let it concern you. He really is a very poor scholar."

# CHAPTER 19

*Lynnfield was the only god's territory to be surrendered peacefully. Seraph, upon taking her pilgrimage to mend broken hearts, gifted the area of Lynnfield to her daughter, Lau'O'Penake. Around 200 P.C. there was a divide in the politics of Lynnfield. The priests of the theocracy were cast out, and the nation was renamed to Tara by their first emperor. The priests of Lynnfield managed to secure a city bordered by Tara, Rouke, and Emestria. During the Battle of Lynnfield in 384 P.C., Lynnfield was completely destroyed. Those that left before the events that led to the complete destruction resettled in Corinth, along with other nations.*

—Issaroh, *The History of Divinity,* Part XXIII

Expecting Issaroh to approach her about training, or Miro to let Issaroh know she needed to be trained, Clara hadn't broached the subject for a couple of days. But on the third day, Clara realized she would need to take matters into her own hands. Usually, Issaroh studied during the morning between breakfast and lunch, so this is when Clara chose to approach him. Issaroh had several books opened on his desk while writing in a thinner one. He didn't even notice Clara until she was almost standing right in front of his desk, but she wasn't even trying to be sneaky; he must have been so engrossed in his writing that he failed to notice. It's not like Clara was *that* quiet.

After clearing her throat, Issaroh readjusted his spectacles and turned his head upward with a smile. "Have you come to complain about Miro as well?"

A little taken back, Clara didn't answer until Issaroh flashed a mischievous smile. Realizing the previous statement was a joke or gentle jab at Bronwyn and Miro's tendency to butt heads, Clara resumed her planned avenue of conversation. "Has Miro told you that he trained me in some magic?"

"He's been rather occupied as of late…"

"Oh, well he trained me a little bit, taught me how to cast one spell, but he indicated that you might be able to teach me more." Clara was putting on her best "trying to get you to teach me something without revealing what my real motives are" act. If Miro was truthful about magi's ability to cast magic with greater proficiency, maybe someone as old as Issaroh might be able to permanently cure Scarlet's disease.

Issaroh's smile broadened. "Miro taught you? How much did he teach you?"

"Not much, just how to throw a stone, and there was something on the mountain, but it was a spell that was reacting to my presence or something rather than me casting anything."

"Hmm, Petravolis. That's a good place to start with Penakian magic. Only three runes…" Issaroh trailed off as he put the book he was currently writing in to one side, then shuffled through the others on the desk before sliding another book out. There was a rune on the cover, one Clara recognized from the spell Miro had taught her. Issaroh stood before telling Clara, "Come, sit down."

Clara did as told, feeling a little awkward considering she was an adult, and being told to sit and read a book was something that reminded her of school rather than learning magic. Upon opening the book, Clara was a little impressed by the neatness and care of Issaroh's writing. It wasn't just the common alphabet that the old men penned in, but a calligraphic version of it that seemed overly flowery. Was this how people wrote before the cataclysm, or just Issaroh's personal style? Either way, it probably took twice as long to write like this as opposed to using a more direct style—time wasn't really a factor when you lived forever.

Issaroh flipped past the first couple of pages, landing on a familiar looking illustration. He had very accurately drawn the circle and runes of the Petravolis spell in a soft brown ink. However, there were only two runes as opposed to three on the page, the one at the top and bottom right of the circle. Underneath the drawing were a handful of other runes, only one of which Clara recognized as belonging to the spell.

"What are all these?" Clara asked, pointing to the list of runes. Beside each rune was a single word: "Scattered," "Blunt," "Pointed," and "Diffuse."

"The modifier runes," Issaroh explained.

"Modifier runes?"

"Yes, the ones that tell the spell its intent."

"Miro just said you prayed to the goddess and tell her what you want to do."

A soft groan escaped Issaroh's lips. "Yes, but you also need a modifier rune in the casting of the spell." Issaroh pointed to the top of the circle. "That is the Lau rune, which you'll need for any spell in the Penakian discipline. This next one on the bottom-right is the Petravolis rune, which is specific for spells trying to alter solid substances or geography. The bottom-left is your modifier rune, in which you will trace a single one of these runes, shaping the spell. How did Miro teach you to cast without using a modifier rune?"

Clara quickly said, "He just made me use this one." Clara pointed to the rune with the "Scattered" description beside it. The last thing she wanted to do was cause Issaroh to be suspicious of her in any way.

"Oh… Well yes, that would work, but I'm surprised he didn't explain what the rune was."

"He didn't explain what any of them were. He just showed me how to trace the three runes. It was probably because we were pressed for time."

Issaroh shook his head slightly. "I wish I could believe that, but as far as I know, Miro hasn't tried to teach magic and was likely trying to teach from how he learned."

"What's wrong with that?" Clara asked.

"Well, for one he didn't teach you the modifying rune." Issaroh pointed to each of the runes in the list in descending order. "The scattered rune, Diotarta, will cause a number of semi-large particles to be flung at your enemy. With the blunt rune, Avtuv, the particulates are either grouped together or you draw a nearby rock of equivalent mass. There is no real shaping of the projectile, and it would be similar to throwing a rock. The next two runes get interesting. The pointed modifier, Koft, will cause the particulates to form in such a way to resemble a stone spearhead or spike, which is when the spell can cause significant damage to a target, especially if aimed correctly. Finally, the diffuse modifier, Cheo, will cause a cloud of fine particulates to be flung at the target. This is particularly effective for making an escape or blinding an opponent using ranged weapons. Don't think your skill with the magic will protect you from any blinding effects though. If you try to cast the spell in this way in an area with high winds, the cloud can just as easily blow your direction.

Magic can still be affected by natural forces, and once you've projected the spell, those same forces can impede your intentions."

"So, if I flung the Petravolis spell upward, it would eventually come down?"

"Yes, and that may be something you want to do, if an enemy was advancing with a shield protecting their front, or a shield wall was protecting another sorcerer in the rear."

Clara nodded in quiet contemplation. None of this was information Miro had even deigned to explain to her. Petravolis had seemed like a pretty worthless spell when he taught it to her, but with the modifiers, shaping the spell into a spearhead or an obscuring cloud seemed to be much better uses. Thinking there might have been a reason he taught her the most useless version of a spell first, she asked, "Are any of the runes harder to create than the others? The modifying runes that is."

"Outside of the physical dexterity of tracing the runes, no. They're just that, modifiers, no easier or more difficult than any other modifier. Almost all spells, and all of the elemental ones, have modifiers." Issaroh advanced the pages of the book a little, coming to another illustration. Clara noticed two circles of runes this time, an outer and inner circle.

"This would be the next ideal spell to teach you, after you've mastered Petravolis: Fragma Petravolis, the ability to construct a flat or tiered structure of the surrounding stone, earth, or sand. Most commonly it is used to construct a wall to protect from a forward-facing ranged assault."

Clara thought back to the fight with the wolves. Miro had cast a spell with Fragma in the name, but it definitely wasn't Petravolis. In fact, he had cast that particular spell twice. The first time it summoned a large sheet of ice to protect Bronwyn from Naani. The second time it had merely piled up snow behind them with the wolves. The sheet of ice made sense; it was thick and resisted Naani's charge. The snowbank made less sense, the wolves pressed through it easily. If Miro knew Fragma Pe-travolis, why would he rely on the other spell instead? Then again, trying to understand Miro was like cupping water in your hand; the longer you try to hold it, the more water slips through your fingers.

Admiring the illustration, and looking at the modifying runes writ-ten below, over a dozen, Clara began flipping through the book, looking at the increasingly complex arrays of circles and runes. The highest num-ber of circles she noticed was five, but the majority of the spells seemed to consist of three circles with nine to twelve runes written in the circles.

Issaroh looked on with a pleasant smile. "The more circles and runes, the more complex the spell and the more concentration and physical exhaustion it will cause to cast it."

Clara nodded before saying, "Except for the healing arcana; those are harder than regular magic."

"Not harder to form the runes or circles, but it is more taxing on the body."

"And you're probably much better at healing arcana than Miro."

"I'm afraid not. Something strange happened when the gods left; the mortals born after their departure seemed to have stronger magic. Even with me being a magus, you'd probably surpass me in your strength in the Penakian discipline given enough time and training. There is also the problem with the healing arcana that the older you are, the less vibrancy you have to lend the spell."

"I've heard of spells that can be used to cure a blood sickness; the inability for wounds to stop bleeding."

"Treat, but not cure."

"But if someone that was strong enough in the healing arcana, then they could cure it, right? Especially if they were a magus and healthy?"

"Not with the spell used to treat the illness. There might be magic that could cure it, but if a spell like that existed, I imagine it would be guarded by aristocracy or theocracy. I've heard tales that the church of Kyrie keeps a number of powerful spells under their watchful eyes, never letting others see them, and not even teaching their own disciples in their use."

"Like something that could have caused the destruction of Lynnfield?" Clara didn't know why she brought it up, it wasn't where she wanted this conversation to go, but it just seemed like an obvious jump in logic.

"Maybe, but I don't see why they would give that information to Rouke, especially when they were allied with Emestria at the time."

"Maybe Rouke stole it?" Issaroh shrugged and Clara started to get another idea. If there was magic that could cure Scarlet, and the church in Corinth had it, then perhaps she should be saving her money to hire a burglar rather than pay for treatments.

# CHAPTER 20

*Laevin is purported to have sired the most demigods, followed by Fria, Chivas, and Marianna. The demigods were stronger, tougher, and possessed more magical affinity than regular mortals. Often, they were gifted with legendary artifacts as a boon and proof of their divine origins.*

*—Issaroh, The History of Divinity, Part XVI*

They had been at the library for the better part of two weeks. At first, Bronwyn enjoyed the respite. She was able to take two hot baths a day, had plenty of variety in food from the expansive garden that the homunculi tended, and slept on the most comfortable bed she had ever experienced. The lavatories were indoors, with running water to wash away the waste. Only the most lavish of castles or nobles' mansions offered anything similar. However, in Emestria, maids or servants were required to fill the water tank. Here, that seemed to be done automatically.

On the fourth day, she had accompanied Clara and Issaroh out the entrance of the library. She had left them to do their training and deployed some of her snares. The following day when she went to check them, she found every snare had been set and snapped. Either she had caught animals too big to be held in place by the traps, or the animals she trapped were being carried away by larger creatures. So, she had started crafting a bow and some arrows.

Once she had them finished, she was able to hunt with ease. The swamp teemed with life. Miro didn't have any issues with eating reptiles, and although Clara was a little squeamish at first, it was a nice compromise. They ate mostly snakes, as she found rather sizable ones that constricted their prey. The smaller venomous vipers weren't worth the trouble; once cleaned there was little meat on them in comparison to the constrictors.

Bronwyn didn't even need to use the bow; the reptiles weren't afraid of people, and she was able to approach them with her sword. On one occasion she even caught a crocodile on land. She found their taste close to waterfowl with a mild, almost pleasant hint of fish.

Bronwyn avoided Miro as much as possible. What little progress he had made in tempering his less-than-desirable attributes was instantly erased now that he was around his mentor. He was noncommunicative and obsessed with the books. At least one homunculi was always hovering around him, waiting to reshelve the many books he took out, increasing her reticence. Their presence, and supposed interest in Miro, worried her. He spent little time around Issaroh, angry at his lack of help. Any time Miro chanced conversation with Bronwyn, his speech was rushed and difficult to understand.

It was easy enough not to see him. He spent all day in the stacks reading and tracking down tomes. Most nights he fell asleep among them, but sometimes he retired to a private study, his head laying against a desk. When Bronwyn happened upon Miro in this state, she would turn off the lights or drape a blanket or cloak over him, but that was the only time she could stomach being in his presence. After happening upon him in fitful slumber on a couple of occasions, she discovered that if she ran her fingers lightly through his hair he would stop and return to deep sleep.

Miro had a scary, manic energy in this place. Thankfully, he started taking baths, but even on those occasions, he did so while reading. But he smelled better, almost pleasant, with a faint hint of the spice she had yet to place that seemed to linger in the library. His obsession with finding this Soul Gem artifact obliterated any goodwill the return to hygiene might have provided. Bronwyn had tried to steer his research toward something to help Emestria. This only elicited a questionable promise to search for it after he found the Soul Gem. The people of Emestria needed help *now*. They might not last long enough for Miro's monster to ever be a worry.

Clara and Issaroh trained daily in the morning. He agreed to teach her more magic, and Clara remarked how much better he was at it than Miro. When she wasn't training, she was in her chosen room, flipping through books as well. Everybody was content to sit and read all day, frustrating Bronwyn. She wanted to be back out in the world and continue their quest. Maybe if Miro found and recovered this Soul Gem, they could go back to trying to find artifacts to help Emestria. For this reason alone, she tolerated his obsession.

On the afternoon of the twelfth day, as Clara was in her room reading, Bronwyn came to get Clara, hoping she could be convinced to go hunting. That might ease Bronwyn's own anxiety. At first, she had attributed her unease in this place to the golems and homunculi, but now they didn't bother her as much—except the ones hovering around Miro—but she still felt unnerved. She found herself investigating nonexistent noises, or her vision fixating on a blur of shadow; she also heard faint whispers that turned out to be nothing more than an overactive imagination—no one else had heard them.

Bronwyn walked to the room Clara had been staying in. This room exuded a sense of warmth and familiarity. Peculiarly, the bed wasn't situated against any wall but was in the center of the room. It was a canopy bed with posts going all the way up, almost to the ceiling, and connected by thin wood rods. Snaking up the posts and along the rails were flowers and vines.

When Bronwyn touched them, she realized they were artificial. The vines were carved into the woodwork and stained green. The flowers were circles of colored silk arranged and threaded through the wood. Against one wall, next to each other, were two wardrobes. Close by was a full-length mirror. Tapestries in aqua and tan, depicting animals, adorned the walls. Splayed out in the bed, Clara thumbed through the pages of a book.

"What are you reading?" Bronwyn asked.

"It's an account of Lau'o'Penake and Seraph," Clara said, turning to another page.

"Huh," Bronwyn replied. Her interest in the gods had waned after the first couple of days. "Do you want to go out and stretch your legs? Do some hunting?" Clara wasn't a hunter, but it gave Bronwyn an excuse to invite her outside the library.

"Apparently when Seraph tried to end her life, she spilled a single drop of blood." Clara didn't look up from her book as she talked. "That blood descended to earth and became Lau'o'Penake's twin brother Defurge, god of fire and madness. Where she had no anger, that is all Defurge was: raw, unfettered rage. He inherited all of Lau'O'Penake's immortality as well. I knew the stories about Ramun reviving Lau'o'Penake with a golden hide, but never the part about Defurge. He was always trying to find her, and the other gods had to protect her."

"That's fine, but don't you want to get outside, get some fresh air?"

"No, I'm good," Clara said, going back to her book.

Then Ferdinand screeched. Clara had set him in the corner, atop his cage.

"No, I don't want to," Clara said to the bird.

Issaroh had taught Clara the spell to speak with animals the second day they trained together, which at first delighted her. That pleasure dissipated when she started speaking to Ferdinand. Miro warned her the falcon wasn't very bright, but Clara didn't listen. He screeched again at her.

"Can she take you?" Clara said to the bird, which noisily protested. "Please, I need to read."

"What's it saying?" Bronwyn asked. She was the only one in the group incapable of talking to animals.

"He wants to go hunting as well, and refuses to go out with you," Clara replied, trying to turn back to her book.

Ferdinand continued creating a ruckus.

"He said all that?" Bronwyn asked, surprised the noise translated into actual sentences.

"Well, no," Clara said, turning over and closing the book. "He yelled 'hunt' and then when I asked if you could take him, he screamed 'Clara.' Now, he's alternating between the two words. I have to read between the lines with him."

*Well, at least she listens to the bird.*

Clara rose from the bed, walked to the cage, donned her leather glove, and picked up Ferdinand. "Shall we go?"

As they exited the room, they were almost bowled over by a frantic Miro. His steps were irregular, almost zigzagging as he lurched left and right. He raced down the hallway to the farthest room on this side of the library, the room of Laevin—god of lightning and scrying—and Kyrie—goddess of wind, battle, and motherhood. This was the first time Bronwyn had seen Miro without a book in his hand since coming to the library.

"I think I should check this out," Bronwyn said to a wide-eyed Clara.

Clara didn't reply as Bronwyn strode after Miro. As she rounded the corner, the sound of something small and metal clanging against the floor echoed in the expansive hall.

Every time Bronwyn entered this room—when she 'borrowed' clothes from Kyrie's wardrobe—she was shocked at the conflict the space evoked in her. In the middle was a larger-than-life bronze statue of a naked Laevin wielding a lightning bolt like a polearm, holding it like one would a battle standard. To say he was muscular would be the understatement of a lifetime.

Behind the sculpture was the marital bed, tackily decorated in gold and royal-purple sheets. Two wardrobes were on opposite sides of the room, stationed like soldiers ready for war. The left side was adorned with violet-and-blue tapestries with bright yellow lightning bolts and trim. On the right was a forty-five-by-fifteen-foot painting, depicting the goddess Kyrie in full battle regalia, ushering an army to follow her. She was the center of the mural, facing forward in a battle stance, looking like she was ready to jump from the painting and thwart her enemies. The two sides felt like they were constantly at odds with each other. It was not a surprise given the contentious nature of the gods' union.

"No, no, where is it?" Miro said, picking up individual pieces of jewelry before tossing them aside. Bronwyn didn't say anything at first. Frustrated with the lack of success in the chest, Miro made his way to a wardrobe and began tossing the pieces of clothing out one after the other. "Where is it?!"

Once the wardrobe was empty, he got on his knees and started running a hand along the bottom. Then he shuffled the clothes about on the floor, shaking them, hoping for something to be dislodged. He turned his attention toward the other wardrobe. Bronwyn pitied him and decided to try calming him down. As Miro got to his feet, she stepped forward, barring his path. He tried to go around her, but she stepped to the side, blocking him again. His eyes were wild in a frightening way.

"What are you looking for?" she asked.

"The seal, the seal," he muttered before pointing at a small hexagonal indentation in the base of the statue. Miro surprised her, grabbing her by her shoulders. His hands were shaking, and his erratic movements were being transferred to her. She pushed him back a little, not to hurt him, but to free herself from his grip.

"You took it!" he accused her. "You're always in this room. You must have it!"

Bronwyn gently but firmly gripped his forearms. With sadness in her voice, she said, "I haven't taken anything from this room. Whatever you're looking for, I don't have it." Bronwyn tried to use an even tone to soothe him. This was a new level of upsetting for her; he acted like an animal. This is probably the Miro that Issaroh had encountered outside Emestria after the war. Heartbreakingly, Miro cocked his head like Ferdinand or the homunculi often would.

"You don't have it," Miro said with clarity. He wrestled his forearms free from her. "Issaroh!" he yelled, making a break for the doorway. He dashed out of the room, almost knocking Clara over. Bronwyn followed after him with Clara closely behind.

Bronwyn could have run after him, pinned him to the ground, and tried to settle him down. But she didn't want to witness the wild look in Miro's eyes as he attempted to liberate himself, like so many of the rabbits she had caught in her snares. She followed but did not chase him as he bolted down the stairs yelling Issaroh's name. She didn't know what he would do when he found Issaroh, but she wanted to make sure Miro wouldn't touch Issaroh or hurt him.

This behavior was all new to Bronwyn and she felt responsible for having directed Miro's attention to Issaroh. *I should have said I don't know what he is talking about, or I hadn't seen it. Instead, I said I don't have it. Miro learned something from our fireside chats. How to read the subtext in what I say without me even meaning it.*

Issaroh exited his study as Miro approached. "What, what?" Issaroh yelled back at him. Miro went to grab Issaroh's shoulders, much in the same way as Miro had with Bronwyn, but she had followed him closely enough. She grabbed the back of his cloak and pulled him closer to her, so he couldn't reach Issaroh.

"You have it. I know you have it," Miro accused.

"I don't know what you're talking about," Issaroh replied, taken aback and looking to Bronwyn for assistance.

"The seal. Where did you hide the tablet?" Miro broke free from Bronwyn. She maneuvered herself in front of him, preventing him from laying hands on Issaroh. Miro ignored Issaroh and went into his study. Miro began picking up every book, holding them by the spine and shaking them, trying to knock something loose. Then he moved to the clothes, then the chest Bronwyn had seen Issaroh remove the seal from. Issaroh stared as he did. Tears formed in his eyes as he watched his pupil descend into madness.

Clara stood several feet away, staring at Miro.

Bronwyn pulled Issaroh aside. "I saw you hide the seal," she admitted quietly.

"He can't find it," Issaroh whispered in reply.

"Miro. I know where the tablet is," Bronwyn shouted.

Issaroh's eyes were full of terror.

"You do?" Miro turned to face her like an adder. "Where is it?"

"You'll never find it unless you listen to me," she said, her calming tone returning. "Breathe." He stopped, but his breath was rapid and forced. "Slowly," she added, and he listened to her, taking big breaths. "I need to talk with Issaroh and Clara."

"I can make ..."

She knew what he wanted to say—he can make her—but the icy glare she shot him prevented him from completing the thought. Good. If he completed that sentence, everything would be worse.

"You made a mess of that room up there. Clean it up while I talk with them. I'll come up and retrieve you when we've made a decision." She gauged his reaction. She could tell that he was still emotional, but the prospect of getting what he desired was great enough to temper his fervor. He walked past her, up the stairs. When he was out of their view, Issaroh entered, starting to pick up the belongings Miro had unceremoniously strewn about. This behavior shouldn't have been too much of a surprise for Bronwyn—Miro barely slept and hardly ate since coming to the library.

"At least he listens to you," Issaroh said, replacing his books.

"Why does he want that seal?" Bronwyn asked as she began to help him.

Clara stood guard at the door, probably waiting to warn them if Miro dashed back downstairs.

"He must have discovered where the Soul Gem is located, behind a door that can only be opened with Laevin's seal."

Bronwyn nodded in acknowledgment, noticing Issaroh's tearstained cheeks.

"If he finds it, he's going to try and fight his demon," Issaroh lamented. "It will kill him." Bronwyn felt like Issaroh wasn't telling her the whole story, but she had gotten used to dealing with the half-truths of these two.

"What if I tell him we can't go after the monster until I'm sure that we're ready," Bronwyn offered, betting on the fact she could temper Miro's erratic behavior. "You said he does listen to me."

"I can't take that risk," Issaroh replied, looking at her. "I can't lose him."

"I don't think he's going to stop." Bronwyn looked him in the eyes as she said this next part: "And I've seen how he's been these last couple of days. I don't know if I have the strength to watch him do this anymore. I know you want him to live a long life in this library, taking over for you, trying to make the world a better place. Maybe his way of atoning is confronting this monster, even if it means he might lose his life."

"I'm afraid he doesn't want to risk his life; he wants to sacrifice it," Issaroh said, averting his gaze, tears pooling in the wrinkles of his cheeks.

"Let me talk to him," Bronwyn requested. "Let me decide."

Issaroh nodded slowly in reply.

Bronwyn left Issaroh to his thoughts and walked past a silent Clara. She had gotten up to take her falcon hunting and now she was embroiled in all this drama. Bronwyn headed up the stairs to Laevin and Kyrie's room. She turned the corner; Miro had picked up the jewelry and clothes and now sat on the bed. His legs bounced up and down nervously.

Bronwyn came and joined him on the bed, sitting next to him. His hands were still shaking. She took his hands in hers, not out of a desire to hold them, but because she couldn't watch them shake like that. He breathed out heavily as she did.

"I don't think you're well," Bronwyn confessed. "When we met in the wilderness, I thought you untethered because you spent so much time alone. As we journeyed together, the three of us, you got better. But these days we've been in the library, I've been more concerned than ever that you aren't well. I've been thinking about how I can complete my mission without you."

"No, but I ..." Miro started. Bronwyn squeezed his hand to silence him.

"I don't want to. I think you could be a great help, but not like this." She turned to look at his eyes, but he averted his gaze. "You don't eat, you don't sleep. You're no use to me like this." She shook her head, unsure how to approach the subject. "Issaroh thinks you want to go against this monster to atone for your sins, to sacrifice yourself to get some closure. You don't talk about your past, and I've tired of asking. I wish you'd tell me, but you continue to punish yourself for something. Possibly part of that punishment is bearing the burden alone. I'm not going to continue this quest with someone that is looking for a way to sacrifice themself. That puts me, Clara, and Issaroh in danger."

"I'd never do anything that would hurt any of you," Miro replied, looking away, his words forced to be slower.

"I think I know that. However, with you like this, you're putting us in danger whether you realize it or not. I made you a promise, that I would help you defeat the monster you're after, but you made me a promise as well. You promised to help the people of Emestria."

Miro nodded, taking in Bronwyn's words.

"If we go after this Soul Gem." Miro's eyes lit up as Bronwyn spoke the words. "Then I need you to swear to me that before we confront this monster, you'll help my people. When we've delivered enough artifacts to secure their salvation, then we'll revisit your quest. But before we do any of that, I have to be sure that you're better."

"And how do we do that?" Miro hung his head again.

"To start with, you're going to sleep in a real bed tonight." Bronwyn motioned at the bed behind her. "And tomorrow you're going to go hunting with me."

He looked ready to object.

"You can fish, I'll hunt—but you need to leave the library. See the sun, look at the world outside of your books. And you need to eat meals, not handfuls of nuts and fruits when you have time. When you've done that—and after you're better—then we'll revisit the idea of the seal."

She stood and started to walk toward the door. He didn't say anything as she walked away. She found the switch next to the doorway and depressed the lever. The room went dark. Bronwyn waited until she heard him disrobing and sliding into the sheets and then she continued outside. She felt like his warden. *But that's what I signed up for, isn't it? I am supposed to be the one to put a stop to him if he ever becomes a danger to Emestria.* Lately, she had started to re-evaluate those orders. It no longer was about if he was dangerous, but instead whether he was able to complete the mission. He was a danger to Emestria if he didn't help them.

She canceled her hunting trip with Clara. Occasionally Bronwyn would walk by Miro's room, to listen for him breathing inside. Once she heard him tossing and turning, moaning, and crying out in his sleep. This had made her feel sorry for him in the past, but now hearing it pained her. After dinner, she checked again, and he still slept. She thought about waking him, but he had gone so long without resting, she calculated that's what he needed more than a meal.

# CHAPTER 21

*Selunia, the islands west of the main continent of Primerra, was the domain of Marianna. However, Dalmarask, the capital, was a trading hub located on the west coast of the main continent. It was an influential and prosperous city until its destruction during the cataclysm. The remaining lands of Selunia have been left untouched by other nations because of their extensive naval fleet.*

*—Issaroh, The History of Divinity, Part XX*

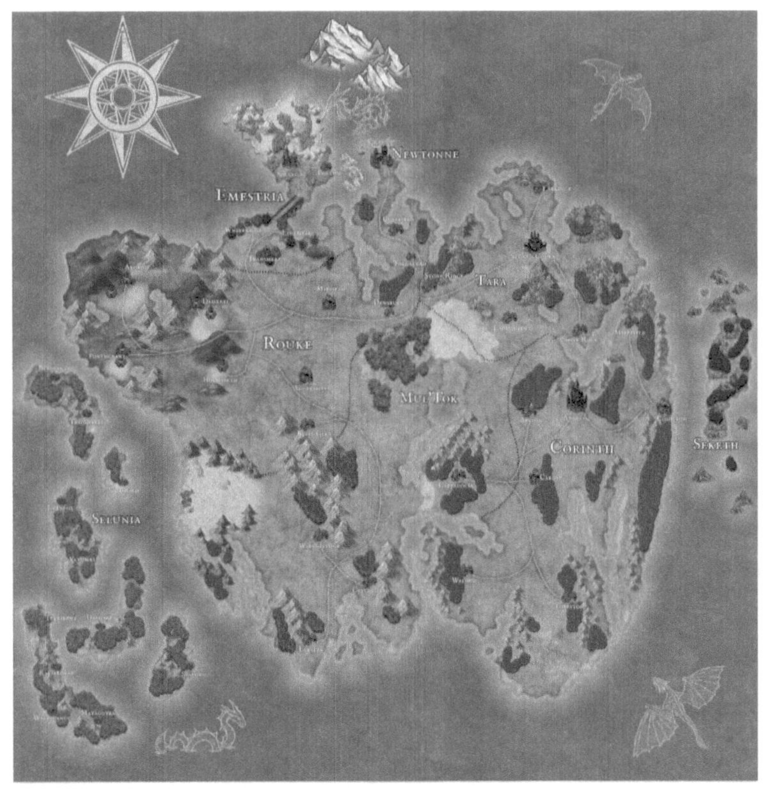

Clara was glad Bronwyn had put a stop to Miro's rampage. The two did fight from time to time and always argued, but Bronwyn could shut him down when she wanted, whether that was with a stern lecture, a quick elbow to the side, or a more heartfelt conversation like Clara overheard standing outside the doorway. Lately, Bronwyn hadn't resorted to elbows to moderate his behavior. Clara dashed from outside Laevin and Kyrie's room and retreated to hers before Bronwyn exited. Hopefully Bronwyn was unaware Clara had eavesdropped.

Bronwyn canceled their hunting trip, so Clara had to take Ferdinand out herself. It was quick. Despite the bird's lack of sense, it was an accomplished killer and usually caught its quarry on the first strike. This time it was a mallard. She gave some to Ferdinand and the rest to Bronwyn to clean for dinner.

Bronwyn excused herself to retrieve Miro but returned alone. "He's still sleeping," she said before sitting back down.

Perhaps for the best. Even though Clara had unlocked the spell to talk to animals, she did not share Miro's aversion to eating mammals and birds. She felt guilty knowing that his reason for abstaining was the ability she now possessed. Maybe it was Miro's time in isolation with only Naani and the animals to speak with that made him feel that way; she chose not to have conversations with animals before they became dinner.

Over the next couple of days, Miro followed Bronwyn around. Clara could tell that his heart wasn't really in it but that he was following the arbitrary guidelines Bronwyn had laid before him. His mood improved. It's not that he was happier following her, but more centered. He had the opposite effect on Bronwyn. She was more stubborn and less serious around him. He made her laugh through the absurdity of his actions. Seemingly, he enjoyed making a fool of himself for her amusement. It wasn't exactly an improvement on her character, but it was interesting to see their effects on each other. Both parties were oblivious to the change in their attitudes when they were together.

Clara enjoyed the time away from Bronwyn and Miro; it gave her more of an opportunity to do her own research on the Legendary Artifacts. Increasingly Clara felt that Issaroh and Miro were right in dissuading her in becoming a magus. If Issaroh's family had been taken from him, despite Clara's best intentions, something might happen to Scarlette. Instead, Clara was now focused on either finding an artifact that could permanently cure her estranged daughter's affliction, or enough artifacts that she could sell them and never have to worry about money again. Perhaps there was even an artifact that could create gems or gold. If there was one that could create food like Bronwyn thought, then there had to be one that could create gems or gold.

Issaroh and Clara practiced magic daily. He taught her a couple of spells but mostly focused on teaching her to read runes, so she could train herself one day. To her surprise, Issaroh confided in her that although Miro had a high aptitude for magic, he was a poor student. He took shortcuts too often and concentrated more on replicating spells he saw than learning the fundamentals. That is what made him such a bad teacher. She treasured Issaroh's encouragement and daydreamed of studying the basics so extensively that she would be able to surpass Miro in the mastery of nature magic.

It had been a couple of days since Bronwyn's heart-to-heart, and they were all seated at the table eating dinner. Issaroh, Bronwyn, and Clara made polite conversation, but Miro remained silent. He nodded along and smiled at their banter but didn't contribute. After quickly eating he excused himself to take a bath before retiring for the night.

Once he left, Clara said, "I guess you set him straight."

"What?" Bronwyn feigned shock.

Clara knew Bronwyn better than that but allowed her the liberty of naïveté. "He's eating meals, bathing regularly." Clara smiled and raised her glass of water. "Hasn't picked up a book in days. Someday you'll need to teach me your secrets to manipulate men."

"I've done nothing of the sort." Bronwyn frowned. "He's doing what I say so we'll give him the seal."

"Still, you have to admit ..." Issaroh smirked.

"I have to admit what?" Bronwyn asked defensively.

"He does whatever you tell him to," Clara said, finishing Issaroh's thought.

"Are you kidding?" Bronwyn countered. "He's as headstrong and stubborn as he always is."

"I'm saying that there is no way that Issaroh or I could have elicited such a change in his behavior," Clara said. Issaroh smiled and nodded in agreement.

"So, he listens to me. What are you implying?"

"Nothing," Issaroh replied, smiling at Clara.

"Right, nothing," Clara agreed. "But I have to wonder, why does he listen to you, but not Issaroh or me? It can't just be the seal."

"I led men for years in the guard corps. I know how to communicate my point and demand compliance."

"I led pirates and brigands, but he doesn't listen to me," Clara refuted. She was a little peeved about Bronwyn relying upon her experience in the corps, like she was the only one that ever held command.

"Yes, and I taught dozens of pupils through the years," Issaroh added. "Even Miro listened when I was his teacher."

"Whatever," Bronwyn said, brushing off their retorts. They sat in uncomfortable silence for a bit. The sound of their forks against their plates echoed through the room. "I think we should retrieve the Soul Gem." Bronwyn stared down at her meal, avoiding their gaze. Issaroh and Clara shot each other worried glances.

"Do you think that wise?" Issaroh hesitantly asked.

"No, this might all be an act," Bronwyn admitted. "But if it is, he will keep it up as long as he needs to. If he has taken my words to heart, then it is better to move now and see if he holds to his end of the bargain. Otherwise, we could spend the next couple of weeks waiting to see how long he's willing to keep it up. If it's all an act, then it's best if we part ways." Bronwyn averted her eyes. "If he is going to continue down this self-destructive path, then he isn't any use to me. It would be better to continue the search for additional artifacts without him."

"You're going to let him go if he doesn't help you?" Issaroh raised his voice.

"I don't see any other option," Bronwyn replied. "What other choice do I have?"

Her question was sincere. Clara sensed Bronwyn had been running these ideas through her head for the last couple of days.

"Well, if he had a deeper attachment to you, then he would be more inclined ..." The women dropped their forks and Issaroh was abruptly silenced.

"I hope you're not implying what I think you're implying." Bronwyn's intense glare caused Issaroh to shrink in his seat.

"No, I," Issaroh stammered. "He has a connection to you that neither Clara nor I have. If you give him more time ..."

"We've been traveling together for over a month now." Bronwyn rose from the table. "Despite his constant obfuscation of the truth, I've remained steadfast and true. If he's not willing to follow me, there is no hope for him." Bronwyn turned to walk from the room.

Clara shot a glance at Issaroh that elicited a shoulder shrug from him. "Wait, Bronwyn," Clara called, getting up from her seat to join Bronwyn in the hallway.

"What?" She spun around as Clara exited the dining room.

"All kidding aside. You know he … you know he will follow you. He looks up to you."

"Yes, and that's why it is time to put him to the test. Whether this is just an act, or he has truly decided to mend his behavior."

"It's only been a couple of days," Clara begged.

"No, it's been a couple of days this time." Bronwyn paused, her normal confident demeanor absent. "We've been together for weeks. He runs hot or cold day by day. I need him to tell me where his allegiance lies … I have to know now whether he's here to help or only to fulfill his desires."

"Don't you think you're trying to push him away?"

"No, I'm determining whether he's willing to assist us," Bronwyn replied, looking down at Clara.

Clara didn't like this defensive side of Bronwyn. Too often Miro displayed the same behavior, and Clara always excused it because of his immaturity, but he had started to rub off on Bronwyn. Clara stood tall and stepped forward. No one would bully her. "No, you're trying to test whether or not he will do whatever you want."

"I'm not. I don't know what you're talking about," Bronwyn stuttered and tried to leave.

"No, you don't." Clara positioned herself in front of Bronwyn. "Despite your denial, you know why he listens to you. You know how he acts differently around you. You may not feel the same way about him, but you want to test him."

Bronwyn tried to walk past Clara, but she blocked Bronwyn's retreat. "You want to force a confrontation, to make him show you whether he will bend to your will, or continue to pursue his desires, as selfish as they may be. You're playing a very risky game. If you'd give it a week or two—"

"In a week or two, how many more children will eat rats?" Bronwyn replied with spite. "How many other soldiers will die on the front lines? How many widows and widowers will be made with no way to feed their families? As much as you two would like to think I'm playing house, I'm not. My concern—my only concern—is for the people of my homeland."

"How many people would it take to cast me aside?"

"What?"

"How many people? Ten, twenty, a hundred? If you could save a thousand people by leaving me to die in this swamp, would you?" Clara asked.

"That's not a fair question."

"No, it's a real question. A thousand people saved if you cut me down right where I stand. Would you do it?"

"I might," Bronwyn said, pushing past her.

"Bronwyn," Clara said, exasperated. "Sleep on it. If in the morning you still want to go after the Soul Gem, I'll support you. Decide whether you're doing this for the people of Emestria, or yourself."

Bronwyn walked away without another word. Clara returned to the dining room where a curious Issaroh sat. Shaking her head, she said, "She's just as bad as Miro. Neither of them listens to reason."

Issaroh chuckled, and they continued their dinner without the drama those two brought everywhere they went.

Clara stopped by Miro's room before she headed to bed. The lights were off, so she figured he had gone to sleep. Next, she stood outside Bronwyn's. She wasn't sure if she would step inside to talk with her more, but she was relieved when she saw the room was dark as well. It was difficult for Clara to sleep when she retired herself. The night's conversation repeated over and over in her head. She knew that she and Issaroh were egging Bronwyn on, but Clara didn't expect the reaction she got. It hurt her when she asked if Bronwyn would cut her down to save a thousand people and Bronwyn hesitated. However, given the same question, Clara wasn't sure her answer would be different. It was an unfair question, and she sort of respected the fact that Bronwyn didn't placate Clara's feelings by pretending otherwise. She would do the same just to save one person: the right person, Scarlette.

Clara put a hand underneath her pillow and allowed herself to dig her fingernails into her palm. It wasn't as deep this time, because she had some hope that she could find a way to help her daughter. Finally, a little hope in the ridiculous path she had been forced to climb for the last ten years.

The next morning, Clara woke to Ferdinand's squawking. She was seriously thinking about sending the bird off with a blank missive to secure a couple of days away from him. She should have taken Miro's advice and never started conversing with the bird.

She decided to check in on Bronwyn. Perhaps the night would have cooled her emotions enough to have a somewhat rational conversation. However, she was not in her room. Next, Clara headed toward Miro's room, thinking Bronwyn might have told him something. As Clara walked, she heard voices. She slowed and crept forward on the balls of her feet. The fact that neither Miro nor Bronwyn were ever truthful with her assuaged the guilt of eavesdropping. She had heard the two's fireside chats on their way to the swamps. Eavesdropping was the only way to get any real indication of what was going on.

"I told Issaroh and Clara that I think we should go after the Soul Gem." It was Bronwyn. Clara was incensed that Bronwyn hadn't consulted with them after she had slept on it.

"Really? That's great," Miro replied cheerily. There was a pause after he said it.

Bronwyn's voice sank. "I don't know if it is."

"What? Why not?"

"Over the last couple of days, you've been better, but I think you're pretending, so that I'll think you're well."

"I'm not, I'm better." Miro's insistence sounded suspicious.

"I don't think you are." Clara frowned at Bronwyn's response.

"If you care for"—she paused—"the people of Emestria, even if it is an act, you'll keep to our agreement, won't you?" Bronwyn pleaded.

"I will. You made me a promise, and I made you one in return. I may not be a good person, but at least I honor my word." Miro's voice rang hollow in Clara's ears.

"Why do you say things like that? You may not be a good person? What should I think when you say something like that?"

There was a long pause as Miro didn't answer.

Bronwyn's tone softened as she asked, "What did you do?"

"I don't want to ..."

"Why not?" Bronwyn pleaded with him. "Why can't you tell me?"

Miro's lack of an immediate response increased the painful tension. "I want to help. I do," he consoled her.

"Then why do we need to go after this artifact first? What guarantee do I have that you're not going to take it and run? Live out some stupid fantasy of sacrificing yourself for the greater good?"

Clara started to regret her eavesdropping.

"I will just feel better," Miro tried to explain to the distraught voice. "I want to be more in control of my destiny."

"Your destiny? Do you not understand how frustrating this is for me? You won't tell me anything, but you expect me to bend over backward to accommodate your desires?"

"Are you going to? I mean, go after the gem?" Miro asked, his voice sounding unsure.

"Yes, we'll go after your stupid Soul Gem." Clara heard Bronwyn start to walk toward the doorway. "But you can't ... Don't make me regret it." Bronwyn's words had transformed from vulnerable to commanding. Clara took it as her cue to retreat as quickly as possible and dashed down the hallways to the baths. She stripped down in case Bronwyn decided to stop here next. Lowering herself into the lukewarm water, Clara lay back facing the ceiling. The approaching footsteps were followed by the grating sound of one of the plates being lifted, the rush of water, and the feeling of the bath warming. She couldn't hear Bronwyn enter the water but waited a while before opening her own eyes. Bronwyn had just settled into the pool and dipped her head underneath the water when Clara focused on her.

"Morning," Clara said, pretending she hadn't been listening in on their conversation.

"Morning." Bronwyn brought both her hands to her face and pressed them against the sides of her eyes before dipping her head beneath the water again. Her voice shuddered as she lay back. "I told him."

"And?" Clara asked.

"I don't know." Bronwyn dipped her head under the water and bubbles rose to the surface as she let out a muffled scream.

Clara waited until Bronwyn had resurfaced. "That bad?"

"I wish I could understand him." Bronwyn wiped the side of her face again. "It drives me crazy, not knowing what he's going to do."

"Hmph," Clara grunted. She was annoyed at being on this side of the conversation again. "There's nothing else to do besides see what's next, right?"

"I guess," Bronwyn replied, leaning back.

Clara was considering her part in this escapade. She now had plans on how she could get the artifacts to help Scarlette, which sounded like they would bear more fruit than any other of the plans she had thus concocted. Having a traveling circus where people paid to ride a giant leopard? What was she thinking? She still wasn't sure if she'd tell Scarlette she was her mother. She had a hard enough life already—and realizing that the woman she thought was her mother all her life wasn't, that might cause even more harm.

Clara dug her nails in as hard as she could. She didn't spare herself any of the pain this time. It was always hardest to block out the emotional hurt when thinking about the whole past instead of the little snippets she usually restricted herself to. Scarlette might want nothing to do with Clara after she had abandoned her own daughter. But it wasn't her fault; she was put in an impossible situation, having to choose between her daughter living or giving her up to the man she had despised.

Clara was just a stupid, naïve girl when she fell in love with Scarlette's father. When Clara became pregnant, the father wanted nothing to do with a commoner's daughter. He was already affianced to a noble woman—a fact he hid from Clara. But she was a strong, resilient woman with a loving—although poor—family. Her mother and aunt agreed to help raise Scarlette, but then after she was born, Clara became aware that something was wrong with her child—an incurable blood disorder that required regular expensive treatments.

Clara swallowed her pride and begged Scarlette's father for help with the treatments. He didn't even have to acknowledge the familial link. How can a father not care for his child? He only agreed to it on one condition, that Clara surrender all her parental rights so he could pretend the child was born out of his union with his fiancé. It was the hardest decision of Clara's life, something that she spent sleepless nights worrying over, but in the end a mother's love for her child is something that can't be denied. So Clara's daughter, now only ten, was being raised by the man that wanted nothing to do with her in the beginning. Clara would find a way to afford Scarlette's treatments again, a way to be part of her life again.

Scarlette likely loved her father dearly, and Clara was nothing more than a stranger that came by a couple times a year and gave Scarlette insignificant gifts. She would be more likely to believe whatever her father told her. Which would be that Clara abandoned her to live a life of adventure.

Now she was inundated with the problems that Bronwyn and Miro were either too bull-headed or immature to confront. Perhaps after this next chapter, she would quit the two of them and head back to Newtonne. She certainly had no love lost for that bird and would be happy to sell it on the black market. A return to smuggling and saving up enough money might be the only way.

Clara was thankful that Bronwyn did not want to go into more detail about her conversation, and she left Bronwyn alone in the bath after a short half hour. It was longer than she had wished to stay, but she didn't want to seem like she was avoiding chatting with Bronwyn. It would have been nice to talk about the previous night's misunderstandings, but Bronwyn's mind was otherwise occupied.

After drying and dressing, Clara made her way down to Issaroh. They departed as expected for their morning training. This man was four hundred years her senior, but she had more in common with him than with the other two. They both lost children, but Clara still had a chance to save hers. Although they didn't discuss it, Clara got the feeling he was equally exasperated with Bronwyn and Miro.

Today's lesson was about direction. Issaroh was trying to teach Clara how to use spells in novel ways to confuse and delay an opponent. Petravolis, the spell that tossed stones, could be used to distract, and a stone wall can trap an enemy if cast quickly and with the right geometric configuration.

Issaroh tired of their lesson quicker than he had on previous days, and they ended practice early. When they returned to the library, Bronwyn and Miro were standing in the doorway.

"I decided we should pursue the Soul Gem," Bronwyn said with faux confidence.

Issaroh physically recoiled at the suggestion. "If you think that best."

"Yes. If we secure the Soul Gem, I think we can rededicate ourselves to finding the other artifacts." Clara watched Miro as he said this. She was unable to determine if he was saying this for Bronwyn's sake or if he meant it. Clara cast her glance toward Bronwyn, who seemed hesitant and uneasy with the situation.

"Where is this Soul Gem?" Clara asked, uncomfortable with the silence.

"In the Desert of a Thousand Sands, on the coast where the city of Dalmarask used to lie," Miro said.

Clara and Issaroh looked at each other. Clara was unsure of what to do. Issaroh was obviously uncomfortable with the idea, and despite Bronwyn's uneasy demeanor, Clara knew Bronwyn wanted to pursue this course of action.

"How far away is that?" Clara asked. "We don't have horses any-more." Clara was searching for an excuse for Bronwyn to abandon the enterprise.

"We won't need horses. I can bring us within the ruins of that city," Issaroh said, letting out a shallow breath as he folded his arms across his chest. Clara glanced at Issaroh. His reluctance was equal to her own, but he was willing to wager on this course of action more than she.

"I can use my teleportation magic. I've been to Dalmarask before," Issaroh continued.

This was the first she had heard of teleportation magic. Miro likely knew of it, and probably knew Issaroh commanded it. Otherwise, why would he have brought it up? Clara looked back at the uneasy Bronwyn. This was a mistake, but Bronwyn was set on seeing this through, despite the pain it would cause.

"Let's prepare for the journey, then." Bronwyn's eyes followed Clara. She was unable to determine if the pleading eyes were meant to motivate her or support Bronwyn. Based on their previous conversations, Clara thought Bronwyn wanted her support.

"Yes, let's," Clara replied, a little confused.

"We'll need wraps to protect our faces from the sands and glass," Issaroh said, stepping toward Miro. "And something to keep our necks from the sun. Maybe a day or two's worth of food. I'm unsure how long it will take us to reach the cliffs and back. Come with me, Miro, I might have something that will suffice."

As Miro and Issaroh walked back into the library, Clara and Bronwyn were left outside. An uneasy silence permeated the air.

"So, we're doing this?" Clara asked after Miro and Issaroh disappeared.

"I guess we are," Bronwyn replied.

Clara sighed, unable to deter either party from this reckless gambit. She followed Bronwyn inside, wordlessly.

Bronwyn cut some fabric away from Seraph's clothing to provide face and head wraps for them. It was sheer, and although it would protect their eyes and nose, Clara wondered if less expensive fabrics would have sufficed. She worried that arguing with Bronwyn would upset her more than she already was.

By midafternoon, they had made their preparations. Clara decided to leave Ferdinand behind with a generous scrap of meat. They gathered in front of Issaroh's study. Miro and Issaroh wrapped their heads and faces in thin linen. It made Clara uneasy when she and Bronwyn had appeared with similar wraps in sheer purple fabric. Clara couldn't help but wonder if the choice of sheer fabric had something to do with Miro. Possibly Bronwyn felt that as long as he saw her face, he would keep to their bargain.

"Gather close," Issaroh said and they huddled around him. "Ramun, god of time and space and traveler of the world, bless our journey, Summa."

Around their feet, magic runes appeared within a circle. The runes bathed the room in a blue light that increased until Clara was forced to close her eyes or risk damaging them. And the world around them slipped away.

# CHAPTER 22

*In the third era of Marianna, 235, the cataclysm began. Rather than a singular event, it is instead considered by some to have lasted between fifty and one hundred years. I err toward the longer of the two in my recollection of events. The impedance of the cataclysm was Defurge and Laevin's fight at the capital of Marianna's empire, Dalmarask. The city was destroyed in their battle, and this is the last known appearance of any of the gods.*

*—Issaroh, The History of Divinity, Part XXIV*

Teleportation was a thousand times worse than traveling by boat. The minute the world came back into view, Bronwyn ripped her wrap from her mouth and doubled over, overcome by sickness. A gentle hand rubbed her back and held her hair away from her face. She wanted to snap back at Miro, to tell him not to touch her, but Issaroh's words rang in the back of her mind. *If he had a deeper attachment to you.* It tainted the idea of Miro touching her; she felt uncomfortable in a way that she hadn't felt when they were in the boat. *Normally I despise being touched while sick. Have I been allowing him to dote on me to manipulate him this entire time?* Bronwyn waited until her stomach settled before lightly brushing him off.

"Are you okay?" Miro asked as she stood back up.

"I'll be fine," she replied. She debated placing a gentle hand against his forearm as a thank-you but decided against it. Instead, she readjusted her covering and surveyed the surrounding landscape.

The sun was blistering white. The buildings that surrounded them had been laid to waste by intense fire. The sand turned to glass. This glass still blanketed many of the buildings, but sloughed off others and crashed to the ground. Thin shards crunched beneath their feet, punctuating every step. The sun's beams reflected off every surface and threatened to blind them. Bronwyn pulled the wrap farther up. It provided some protection against the sun's glare and only obscured the landscape a little.

"The city of Dalmarask," Issaroh proclaimed. "Razed in a single night by Defurge, god of fire and madness. He thought his twin sister was protected within its walls. After his assault on humanity, the gods decided to quit this world forever, convinced their presence brought more harm than good."

"Yes, but not before imprisoning Defurge within the Soul Gem and locking it away in the city's bowels, under the seal of Laevin," Miro added. "If we head for the coast, we should find a path down the cliffs. There should be a cave which will lead us to the area in which it is ensconced."

He motioned them forward. Bronwyn, although a little uneasy on her feet, followed him. Clara glanced at Issaroh, and they advanced behind Miro and Bronwyn.

Despite the knot in her stomach, Bronwyn found it hard not to admire the city—or the ruins of the city. Some buildings were completely razed to the ground, but others were perfectly preserved as glass sculptures.

"What were the buildings made of?" Bronwyn asked Miro as he advanced.

"A sort of mixture of water, sand, and clay," he replied. "It took generations to perfect the exact formulation that was able to support the structures, and that information is now lost to the ages."

Bronwyn shot a glance back at Issaroh.

"I don't know," Issaroh said.

If anyone knew, it would probably be Issaroh; he was alive when it still was a city, after all. They walked along, bracing themselves against the winds that whipped the sand and glass into the air. The empty city unnerved Bronwyn.

"Why did he think his sister was here?" Bronwyn asked, trying to raise her voice above the hiss of the sands.

"What?" Miro called, turning back.

"Why did he think his sister was here?" she repeated louder.

"She was," Miro replied. "The city was sheltering her. They knew he was coming, but they weren't prepared for this."

"Did he find her?" Bronwyn shouted over the wind.

"No. Marianna, the goddess of oceans, tides, and loyalty, spirited her away shortly after the assault began," Miro yelled back at her. "Lau'O'Penake's absence only enraged him further. He destroyed the entire city in response."

Bronwyn picked up her pace so she wouldn't have to yell at Miro to elicit an answer. "This was the cataclysm?"

"No, this was the start," Miro said. "After the gods left, it was a free-for-all. Without divine protection, the nations waged war with each other, confident the gods wouldn't intervene. Entire countries disappeared overnight. Legends tell of cities that just sank into the sea. It was chaos."

The winds intensified as they walked. Bronwyn strained to make out the silhouettes of Clara and Issaroh—everything was obscured by the swirling sand. Miro's hand reached down to Bronwyn's and she grasped it, thankful for the guidance.

The sand's shifting nature made every step that much harder. The ferocious winds buffeted them at every turn. Even Bronwyn's pants—that she had taken from Kyrie's wardrobe—were sliced into, exposing her bare skin. Her head wrap started to shred under the assault. Luckily, as they trudged toward the coast, the air was less full of glass and instead inundated with salt.

Bronwyn had given up trying to talk to Miro. The wind—more intense the closer they got to the shore—took the words from her mouth before she even spoke them. Her face wrap was in tatters, and she ceased looking where they were going, relying upon Miro's arm. Occasionally she glanced down at her feet but avoided looking forward. Without the protection, the wind flew biting shards against her face. Eventually, Miro stopped, and Bronwyn opened her eyes.

The wind was still as fierce as ever, but the sand was almost completely gone. Bronwyn stared down; the sea crashed against the cliffs. A thin path zigzagged down the side of the earth. She took the sheer fabric from her face but kept it wrapped around her head. The face covering was shredded and would offer no protection on their return home. This would teach her not to err on the side of fashion.

"That's where we're going," Miro called above the wind, pointing down toward the bottom where Bronwyn saw nothing but surf and waves crashing against the rocks at the bottom of the cliff face. She turned back around to see how far Issaroh and Clara were behind.

"We should wait for them," Bronwyn told Miro.

"They'll catch up."

He released her arm and began to descend. She waited for Clara to come into view. It was slow going down the cliffs, and Bronwyn was unsure of whether the other two knew where the trail began. Once Clara was within sight, Bronwyn indicated where she was going. A head nod from Clara convinced her to follow Miro.

The footpath down was narrow, but uncomplicated. The wind had blown away any stray sand that would cause one to slip. When the path got too steep, there were footholds, like someone had carved the cliff away. Bronwyn looked back often, trying to gauge Clara's progress versus Miro's. She didn't want to leave Clara behind, but letting Miro advance too far ahead was a worry.

Bronwyn had kept Laevin's seal on her—so Miro couldn't get the gem without her—but she still abhorred letting him out of her sight. Slowly, but eventually, she reached the bottom of the cliff. It opened into a maw of a cavern. Miro was anxious to proceed inside, but she made him wait until Clara and Issaroh arrived.

When Clara finally descended, she tossed her face covering to the side. It was just as shredded as Bronwyn's. She shrugged in apology and Clara returned the gesture. The cavern extended into the darkness. Miro retrieved and lit a torch.

Now that they had regrouped, they proceeded to follow Miro as he led them through the cavern. The sound of water dripping from stalactites punctuated every step they took. The water that did manage to splash in from the sea had coalesced into little pools, the smell of the ocean stagnant and overpowering. As they walked by, sea grasses that had been flung with the water retreated into their snipy cocoons. The pregnant quiet reminded Bronwyn of the cave beneath Porton. She had hoped that the path would lead up—toward the city—but instead, it led farther down.

*At what point will we hit the water level? Or maybe the tide will come in and drown us.* Miro and Issaroh seem oddly calm about the prospect. Only Clara appeared to share Bronwyn's misgivings.

The cavern alternated between wide chambers and narrow pathways. With each new cavern or pathway, the rock gave way to more and more sandstone. Trickles of sand from the desert above occasionally slipped through cracks in the cavern walls, the pitter patter of fine granules interrupting the all too quiet darkness. At the end of the third chamber, Miro finally stopped. He stood in front of a solid wall and began to run his hands over the cave. "Here," he said after a while, and thrust his torch forward to illuminate the faint hexagonal impression.

Bronwyn stepped up, looking back to Issaroh for confidence, and retrieved Laevin's seal. Aligning the item with the impression, she pressed it in. She expected to hear some type of click indicating she succeeded in aligning the token, but instead the grating of rock against ground assaulted her ears. The wall was pushed in like a double door, revealing more paths. They all stood awestruck waiting for something—anything—to happen.

# CHAPTER 23

*Corinth is one of the few nations with a formalized religion that still prays to their patron goddess, Kyrie. It is a theocracy with a high priest elected by other priests into the position. The high priest's judgment is absolute and above reproach. After the cataclysm Corinth destroyed Seketh and began to 'save' many of the cities of Mul'Tok by bringing them under their control.*

*—Issaroh, The History of Divinity, Part XXI*

At first, it was a small light. However, soon the fire snaked up the cave floor. The flame's path wound and looped back on itself several times. Then it flared into brightness, as a figure with two fiery-wings illuminated the darkness. A flamed circle rose above the head of the humanoid figure trapped within. The light reflected off the surface of the surrounding walls. Rather than sandstone like the caverns before, glass reflected the flames off the walls and ground.

"You have freed me," rumbled a low voice that echoed off the walls. "Where is my sister!" it yelled with ferocity.

Bronwyn froze at the sudden urgency of the voice. Issaroh and Miro were more prepared.

"Fria, goddess of death, ice, and fate, the Vigilant Eye, lend me your protection, Fragma Frios!" Miro chanted, erecting a thin wall between them and the figure. It was just in time, as the flame-encased whip came crashing against the structure, shattering it almost immediately.

"Fragma Lenos!" Issaroh called out, erecting a second barrier of stone to absorb the next three blows. The whip cut through the wall, turning the rock a bright orange in the process, causing it to ooze like lava.

Clara grabbed the axe from her back. "Lau'o'Penake, goddess of nature and rebirth, I call upon the courage of the earth, Petravolis!" Clara etched the runes into the air using her free hand. Loose rocks coalesced into a mass before her palm and she thrust a stone spike forward as soon as the wall had dissipated. The creature beat its wings forward, melting the projectile almost instantly.

Regaining her composure, Bronwyn drew her greatsword and began to rush the unknown foe. The flaming whip sailed forward and caught her sword in its grasp. She spun, freeing her weapon. The second lash fell closer to the hilt, and although she could bear the heat, when the humanoid whipped the fire-engulfed weapon back, she lost her grip of the sword. The blade clattered against the cave walls. She ducked as the third strike whizzed over her head and tumbled forward; the fourth strike hitting against the ground she previously occupied, but she was over the whip before it landed.

"Laevin, god of lightning and scrying, answer my plea, Bolta Levos," Miro chanted.

The runes illuminated the cavern and Bronwyn saw her assailant more clearly. He was only a man, with wings and a crown engulfed in flame, wielding a whip encased in fire. Miro's lightning arced forward, zigzagging through the air. The whip met the lightning and deflected the spell harmlessly against the wall.

Bronwyn took the opportunity to dash toward where her sword landed. She had to jump and duck against the whip twice more before she slid across the sand that had at some point in time melted into glass, reaching her weapon in a smooth, controlled slide.

"Yield and your death will be an easy one," the voice called out, and the wings buffeted the air once more. Bronwyn felt the heat radiating against her skin. She grabbed her greatsword and spun herself to the side as quickly as she could. She narrowly avoided the blanket of fire that erupted forth.

"Tremma!" Issaroh's voice called out as the ground began to rumble and shake.

Stalactites broke from the ceiling. *Great,* Bronwyn thought as she avoided them. Left, right, over the whip, under the whip. She brought her sword up to deflect the next blow before jumping backward, avoiding another falling stalactite.

"Retreat!" Issaroh called out.

The others were much farther back than Bronwyn was. She dashed toward them. The crack of the whip could be heard before it even made contact, and she spun around, wielding her blade against it. What little remained of her face-wrap erupted in flame as the fiery weapon grazed the edges. She flipped back, the second crack landing uselessly where she had been.

Her enemy fought like a human, its movements slow enough for her to avoid. At the next two cracks she brought her greatsword to bear catching the coils, then casting them off, allowing her comrades enough time to retreat. Once they exited the chamber, she followed suit. They turned to face their assailant after they regrouped in the next cavern.

"What the Chivas is that!" Bronwyn said, running past them.

"Defurge, god of fire and madness, answer my call, Inflagrata," Miro chanted.

The bright orange runes were pulled into the palm of Miro's hands and seemed to catch fire and coalesce until they formed a single ball.

Miro thrust both hands forward, engulfing the hallway Bronwyn had exited.

"You dare use my magic against me!" Defurge yelled, effortlessly blowing through the fire and entering their chamber.

"Is that … ?" Bronwyn asked, afraid of the answer.

"Is it Defurge?" Clara shouted.

"Geometric patterns!" Issaroh yelled. It must be some command or subject he had previously discussed with Clara and Miro because although Bronwyn didn't understand what Issaroh meant, Clara and Miro responded with a slight nod.

"Lau'o'Penake, goddess of nature and rebirth, grant me your protection …" Clara and Miro chanted in unison.

Bronwyn could see the sigils in their cast. she figured the casting time was similar to the ice wall. There was no way they would finish their spell before the whip bore down upon them. She sensed the impending attack before the lash even started to arc in their direction. She turned and rushed forward. The enemy's weapon gripped the base of her sword. They wrestled for control of it, until Defurge ripped it from her hands again. She watched as the red-hot blade slammed against the cave, wedging into the wall.

*Great, now I'll have to do it the hard way.*

"Fragma Lenos!" Miro, Clara, and Issaroh shouted almost in unison, forming a pyramid around their enemy—encasing him within. Bronwyn saw the stone begin to warp and glow. She ran up one side, jumped, and slid down the other before it turned to molten rock.

*I have the advantage,* she thought, unsure if she did; the whip would be much harder to wield in close quarters and she only had to avoid the deluges of flame from his wings. As the molten rock pooled, Bronwyn waited for the figure to turn his attention back to her. Instead, he focused on Miro, Clara, and Issaroh. The three of them dodged and deflected the whip strikes with more protective magic as Bronwyn waited in a defensive stance. Realizing that her enemy was unaware of her location, she rushed forward, slamming her elbow into the base of his skull. Despite grunting from the blow and staggering a step forward, Defurge remained conscious and slowly started to turn her direction. Bronwyn leaped back, spinning in the air, bringing her foot against the same spot she struck before. The figure fell against her second blow, and as it did, she saw the red gem from its necklace arc through the air. She didn't know why, but the necklace was important. She dove forward again to grab it.

"No!" Miro yelled, rushing forward.

As they both reached for the gem, their hands collided. She gripped the ruby jewel first, but his hands wrapped around hers.

Everything turned dark, and it was like Bronwyn was falling but had no sense of how long she fell. It seemed like the transportation magic, but Bronwyn did not feel sick as everything came back into focus. Everything was a soft crimson haze before it truly solidified. In front of them, a large horned beast wreathed in fire charged. Its upper torso was that of a brown skinned man, but its legs were hooved and furry and its head appeared to be that of a bull.

Bronwyn reached for her greatsword in its scabbard, then jumped back, suddenly remembering her weapon was stuck in the cave wall. However, the beast slammed against a barrier and raged, pounding its fists repeatedly at the red plane that separated them. The wall bent a little at its strikes but did not break. Despite the beast, she felt safe, as if the danger weren't present.

"Where are we?" she asked Miro, regaining her composure.

She glanced around. Flat surfaces intersecting in hard corners surrounded the room. Each wall housed a separate entity, and they all seemed to be advancing toward them or smashing against their respective barriers. It was strange. Their rooms seemed impractically small, and the occupants not like flesh and blood, but rather figures in a mirror. The way the planes intersected created an irregularly shaped room. The ceiling rose thirty feet high in some places, but then barely six in others. A soft red light illuminated the chamber.

"I think we're inside the gem," Miro said, looking at the bright red walls.

"Great, how do we get out?" Bronwyn asked, gazing around. She couldn't explain the unease she felt in this place.

"I don't think we can," Miro said, his voice lacking concern. "I wanted this Legendary Artifact to imprison something. Now we're in that prison."

"How did we get trapped inside a gem?" Bronwyn asked, annoyed by his calmness.

"I think when we touched it."

"Why didn't you tell me touching the gem would ensnare us?" Bronwyn shouted. "Don't you think that's important information? I knew this was a bad idea, but no, I wanted to trust you."

"I didn't know. Artifacts don't come with a detailed explanation. When you reached for it, I had this feeling, so I tried to grab it first."

Bronwyn wanted to force him to try to explain, but she knew that she had experienced the same impulse. "So, what? Now I'm stuck here, forever, with you?" she asked.

Miro turned to her. "Maybe? It could be worse."

"How? How could it be worse?"

"You could be trapped in here by yourself."

"I think I would rather be in here by myself."

"Hey," Miro called back defensively.

"Well, maybe you could find me a way out of this if you were still out there. Perhaps Issaroh can figure something out if he deduces where we went …"

Bronwyn scanned their surroundings. They stood on an opaque piece of red glass, surrounded by countless walls of a similar but transparent material. It didn't give or seem to be in danger of breaking. Each chamber housed another creature. Most of them were humanoid, but some of them weren't.

A beetle, consumed in fire, pushed a ball of flame using its back legs. A snake bared its fangs, causing molten lava to drip down them like strings of saliva. A woman engulfed in flames spun wildly around, dancing madly. Much like the entity they had fought, every creature was either enveloped in or brandishing a weapon coated in flame.

"Do you think we look the same way to them?" Bronwyn asked, approaching one of the panes.

"On fire?" Miro asked.

"No, like we're trapped in a picture?" Bronwyn touched the pane. It was smooth and solid and didn't budge when she pushed against it.

"Is that a … ?" Bronwyn pointed up to the ceiling.

Miro finished her sentence: "A dragon."

The red serpentine creature unfurled its wings and opened its mouth. They could no longer see the dragon, only the flames that bellowed forth from its open maw but were contained by the scaled creature's prison.

It made no sound. Nothing made any sound, making everything less intimidating, like they weren't real.

"The power of the gem may not be claimed by two," a woman's voice echoed through the chamber. "The power of the gem may not be claimed until the current bearer has died."

Bronwyn and Miro glanced at each other, then toward the panes, trying to find where the voice was coming from.

"Who are you?" Miro asked, his voice echoing off the chamber walls.

"I am the phoenix. I am Defurge," the unknown woman's voice answered back.

They scanned the panes again, looking for any type of bird.

"Are you a god?" Bronwyn called out this time.

"We are all Defurge. We are all gods."

It was impossible to tell where the voice was coming from. The room was irregular, making it difficult to scan each surface in any calculated way. "Where are you?" Bronwyn asked.

"Come forward," the disembodied voice replied.

Bronwyn spied an opening in the wall that hadn't been there before. It was large enough for them to pass through, making it unlikely she missed it in her first assessment of the room, but she hadn't seen it appear. She shrugged at Miro, and they walked forward. As Bronwyn passed through the opening, she looked up at the pane they were passing under. It was exceptionally thin. So thin that when she was looking at it directly it seemed to disappear. Once past the open pane, they turned around. She looked back on the chamber they had been in.

The chamber was the inside of a multi-faceted gem that resembled the one around Defurge's neck. It was suspended in the air, with nothing but blackness surrounding it. The massive gem was easily a hundred feet high. The curved structure appeared to be one-hundred-fifty-feet long at its thickest point, and Bronwyn was unsure whether the gem was bigger in this place, or she and Miro had shrunk to fit inside it. It would be impossible to figure out, and there was the very real possibility that neither was true. This space seemed to exist outside of the real world. Distance, light, sound, and everything else acted in weird ways.

A path extended forward, leading to a staircase. To the sides of the path, there was nothing except emptiness. Bronwyn wanted to go back inside the structure behind her, to see if the creature visible on one side of a pane also appeared on the other side. But the opening they had passed through was now closed off as well.

At the end of the current pathway, irregularly spaced stairs rose fifteen feet and met with a larger opaque surface. The walkway and stairs emanated the same soft, red light, but the area at the top of the stairs was still dark. As they approached, a hawk circled above. Its feathers blazed and left embers in its wake. As it descended, Bronwyn was amazed at the enormous size of the bird; its wingspan was easily fifty feet. Before it contacted the pane above the stairs, the phoenix turned to fire, engulfing the upper pane before disappearing.

Bronwyn started up the staircase. The closer to the top they got, the wider the stairs became. Finally, at the last stair, the upper pane illuminated. It was another of the opaque panes, but this one stretched twenty feet in every direction.

Across from them, a young, slender woman stood. She wasn't exceptionally tall, but her legs, arms, and neck were abnormally thin and long. Her hair was a deep crimson and descended to the small of her back. It was thick and billowed despite there being no breeze in this place. She wore a form-fitting, translucent red gown. The fabric burned with intensity. In front of her was a small stone table with three chairs and food set upon it.

In the middle of the platform to the right and left were two men, their legs crossed, hands folded across their chests, and eyes closed. The one on the left was completely bald. On the right, the man's hair was contained in a topknot. They wore white billowy pants and nothing else. Their bodies were covered in tattoos with ink that glowed red and flowed like lava over their exposed skin.

"Come, sit." The woman turned to them and motioned toward the chairs.

Bronwyn stared at Miro, who only shrugged and came forward. He took one seat and Bronwyn occupied the other. The woman sat across from them and picked an apple up from the table.

"They have no taste and no substance. I still like to look at them, to remember what it was like to eat." The phoenix turned her attention to them. "Why did you release us? The world was safe."

"I don't know where we are, or who you are," Bronwyn replied.

"Long ago, when the goddess Seraph tried to take her own life, a single drop of blood fell from the heavens and crystallized on its way to the earth. In that vessel was the immortality, rage, and grief of her unborn daughter. The first man to find the gem became the first incarnation of Defurge. He was driven mad by the power, like most were. When he was defeated, the next to possess the gem became the second incarnation. When they died, they came here, trapped for all eternity. Only we three were able to retain our sanity and attempt to keep the gem and its power from others." She extended her hands, pointing to the monks.

"They traveled to remote mountaintops and locked themselves in meditation to stave off madness, but they were found and slain." The phoenix squeezed the apple, and the fruit wasn't there anymore. "Our power is too great to remain hidden for long. I adapted well to the gem. I had already been reincarnated many times, and being composed entirely of fire, I was not subject to its maddening allure. I soared the skies, seeking to keep the artifact from others. Even I was eventually brought down."

The woman's eyes flared with intensity as she stared at them. "For four hundred years the gem was safely locked away, but you freed us. Do you desire power? Or do you hate the world so much you want to see it burn?"

"I came trying to find the Soul Gem, to trap a malevolent entity and prevent it from wreaking havoc on the world," Miro stammered.

"You came on a fool's errand," she chastised, her eyes burning with fire. "Yes, once one has perished, they will be trapped here forever, but first, they will inherit the flames and become the next incarnation of Defurge. The more powerful the foe, the more magic they would be able to command. You would only serve to destroy the world faster by delivering the gem to the one you seek to capture."

Bronwyn now understood. The Soul Gem they were seeking to trap Miro's monster was really the gem that gave Defurge's power. In a way the gem itself was a god. That didn't explain why none of this was recorded in any of the books Miro had reviewed, but then she pieced together the mystery. If this gem empowered one as a god, then it would be in the best interest to keep any mention of that fact away from mortals.

"I ... I didn't know," Miro said, still stammering.

"Mankind always seeks to harness without thought to the consequences," the phoenix lamented, the intensity in her eyes dissipating.

"Are we stuck here?" Bronwyn asked. "Forever?"

"I could liberate you. Return you to your mortal forms," the phoenix mused.

Bronwyn nodded quickly at the idea of being allowed free. The thought of remaining in a place like this—so devoid of noise and sunlight—made her feel untethered. She had no doubt she would be raving mad like the other inhabitants in a short period.

"However, I won't do that."

Bronwyn's hopes were dashed instantly.

"Unless you do something for me. You must bring Lau'o'Penake to the current incarnation. Convince her to rejoin with us, to temper our rage and grief."

"Lau'o'Penake is gone," Miro replied. "All the gods are. After the attack on Dalmarask, they decided they did the world more harm than good."

"So, we were so anathema to them, they would curse us to this eternal fate." The sadness in her voice was heartbreaking. "The world is doomed. Even if you could seal us back up, eventually another would come to claim the power and unleash the current incarnation or become the next. With no Laevin to stop us, the world will burn."

"Perhaps there's another way?" Miro offered.

The phoenix inclined her head, looking at him inquisitively.

"There is a hammer, used to forge the artifacts fashioned by the gods," Miro said. "It's supposed to be able to unmake anything the gods created. If we bring the hammer to bear on the gem, it could destroy it."

"You have this hammer?" the phoenix asked.

"No," Miro admitted. "We are looking for artifacts like it. We could reseal the current incarnation in this cavern, then return when we find the hammer."

"No, others would come seeking before you return, if you ever do," the phoenix said. "Only Laevin himself could reactivate the seal. You must take us with you, protect this vessel, ensure that no one can claim the gem. We can temper the madness of the current incarnation."

"Why didn't you do that all along?" Bronwyn asked, shocked.

"I only have enough strength to do it once," the phoenix said, addressing Bronwyn. "If this incarnation perished, I would become mad, like the other inhabitants, and there would be no hope. Can he do this? Recover the hammer?"

"I can," Miro replied confidently.

"Quiet—you're untrustworthy," the phoenix hissed at Miro. "I can sense the desire in your heart. It corrupts you. This one, she is pure. Her mind is unfettered."

"I think we can." Bronwyn tried to sound confident.

"If you fail, you must not hesitate to strike the current incarnation down and claim the gem for yourself." She laid her hand across Bronwyn's. "You might be able to resist and keep it from others like I once did."

"Why not have her harness the power now, and you can help her rather than the current incarnation?" Miro asked, and he flinched as the phoenix's eyes flared and stared him down. Bronwyn did not like the suggestion. The idea of being cursed to this fate if she were unable to destroy the gem or resist its temptation was abhorrent.

"You wish for her to risk her sanity when she might not have to?" The phoenix's voice seethed with anger. "The current incarnation will lose all sense of himself, of who he was and what he has done when I temper his insanity. Do you wish that fate upon her?"

"No," Miro replied quietly.

"Why do you keep such loathsome company?" the phoenix asked Bronwyn.

"He has agreed to keep my homeland safe," Bronwyn said, trying not to anger the phoenix. "If finding this hammer and destroying the gem will keep the world safe, I'll do it. He'll help me."

"Be careful when you make deals with a devil," the phoenix cautioned her.

Miro muttered, "I'm not—"

"Yes, you are!" The phoenix turned to him. Her hair rose into the air and turned to fire as she stood, pushing her chair back. "You are a loathsome pitiful creature. Your heart is full of pain, greed, and avarice. You are a snake, a worm." With each word, more of her body erupted into flame.

"No, no, no," Miro muttered and shook his head. He recoiled, squeezing his eyes shut and gripping his head in agony. Knocking his chair over, he stumbled backward. His body thrashed in pain, and he fell to his knees briefly. Bronwyn looked about for what could be causing it but saw nothing. Was the phoenix doing this? How?

"They're in my head. They're in my head," Miro muttered looking toward Bronwyn for help. First, a trickle of blood dripped from his nose, then began to pool at the corner of his eyes.

"You are evil, vile, despicable," the phoenix said, advancing toward Miro. "You are unfit to call yourself a man. We should destroy you here and save the world from you. If you took the gem, you would visit unspeakable horrors upon humanity!" As the phoenix screamed this her body became fully engulfed in flame.

"No, no," Miro muttered, trying to shake his head. He looked to the monks on the platform, then to Bronwyn. Pure terror was in his eyes; he closed them and raised his arms to the sky. The thunderous boom of lightning was deafening in this place, devoid of any sounds except for their own voices.

Bronwyn stared in shock as he reopened his eyes: they glowed a pale, sick blue. The monks began screaming in agony.

"You! Magic? Here?" The phoenix thrust her hand forward. "Begone!"

Bronwyn's body flew from the platform into the abyss. And then she felt the ground hard against her back. She opened her eyes. It was the cave. She remembered where her sword was. Bronwyn rose to her feet and ran toward the wall. Gripping the hilt of her weapon, she yanked it free from the sandstone. She dashed back to Miro's still-prone body and with both hands raised her greatsword into the air, ready to bring it down upon him in one swift motion. He had told her to run if he were to ever enter the trance again. There would be no running from him in this place. Even if they were to escape the cave, they would be caught while trying to flee up the cliff face. No, there was only one way to save everyone, to kill him now, like she once considered in Emestria.

"No," a surprised Issaroh yelled from somewhere behind her. His hurried feet slapped against the floor. But then he stumbled and fell. Clara rushed to help him back up.

Miro opened his eyes. They had returned to normal, but Bronwyn couldn't risk it. He gazed up at her, tears in his eyes.

"Do it," he said as they ran down his cheek. Although he didn't voice the word, she almost heard the inaudible "please" the look conveyed.

"I'm sorry," Bronwyn whispered as her tears started to blur her vision. She lifted the sword high, ready to thrust it into his heart, to make it quick, a mercy really. But as she prepared to bring the sword down, she hesitated, finding her muscles tense and refusing to move. She closed her eyes, hoping not having to look at him would make it easier, but still she found it impossible to bring the weapon down.

"Not like this," Bronwyn said. Shaking her head, she brought the greatsword to her side, holding it with her right hand, then with her left she leaned down and grabbed Miro by the shirt.

Miro looked stunned as she pulled him up, but his feet quickly reacted, helping him find purchase and stabilize himself. He looked at her and they both hesitated, then Bronwyn pushed him back and returned her two-hand grip to her sword. Everything seemed to slow around her and as she glanced back at Clara and Issaroh, they seemed to be frozen in fear or hope. Bronwyn readjusted into an offensive stance. "Fight me," she said to Miro.

His wide eyes seemed to indicate he didn't understand.

"If you want to die, fight me. I won't kill you while you lie defenseless against the ground."

Miro hung his head and replied, "I can't."

Bronwyn stepped forward and delivered a kick to his chest, pushing him back. "Fight me!" she yelled again. "If you truly want this then fight me!" The words of the general rang in the back of her mind over and over again, *If he should ever become a threat to Emestria, strike him down.* He would always be a threat, and with something as powerful as the gem in their midst, it wasn't him just being a magus that was a concern any longer.

"Laevin, god of lightning and…" Miro chanted but she had seen this spell before. She saw the runes he used, but these ones were wrong, unintelligible and not runes at all. He was chanting slowly and she knew if she waited the magic would fizzle into nothingness, resulting in no spell. He was giving her time to run him through. *Why do you want this so bad?* But the words of the general pushed her forward and her sword, aimed at his heart, finally seemed to be unfettered and dove forward with precision. Bronwyn squeezed her eyes shut, knowing she couldn't watch him die at the end of her sword, but knowing he had to.

"No!" three voices shouted in unison; Clara, Issaroh, and the phoenix? Then her sword stopped. A bright scarlet light caused Bronwyn to open her eyes. She expected to see Miro at the end of the blade, but instead the phoenix stood before her, both hands tightly holding the point of her weapon. The metal glowed red as it heated and in a matter of seconds the hilt grew too hot and Bronwyn was forced to let go, the sword dropping and clanging noisily to the ground. The sound reverberated and echoed off the walls.

Then Bronwyn felt her body untethered once again, like she was falling through a waterfall, unsupported but still feeling the resistance of the water. Then the soft crimson haze and she was back on the platform again with the phoenix and two monks.

"Why? Why stay my hand when you tried to do the same?" Bronwyn begged, stepping toward the phoenix. "Why stop me when I had the courage to finally act?"

"The monks probed his mind," the phoenix explained. "His mind was dulled and difficult to read; it obfuscated their vision, but they saw what tortures him so. A war, him trying to protect those he loved, risking his life, time and again for them. Getting them through the conflict, only to watch one fall from a cliff and the other corrupted by greed. His power is great; magic should not work in my realm. The monks scanned his future, to see his destiny. To see him learn to control it, to help others, to sacrifice himself to deliver us from our torment. I told you your heart was pure, but if you do this, it will be stained forever."

"Why? It's my duty," she replied, her fists clenching.

"If you stain your hands with his blood, your soul will be corrupted."

"And so I risk it? I risk the fate of the world and my homeland on the chance that Miro doesn't decide to take the gem? You said yourself he would use it to destroy the world."

The phoenix glanced away momentarily before saying, "We will not leave this incarnation of Defurge defenseless. I shall lend him my powers to protect him, as long as he journeys with you to recover the hammer."

"And will that be enough? Can you tell me with certainty that my people, this world, will be safe?"

"No, but it is the only choice," the phoenix said, stepping forward.

"Why…" Bronwyn's voice quieted, fearing the answer.

The phoenix' hand—hot and soft—caressed Bronwyn's cheek. "You care for him. You deny it, but we can sense it." The phoenix inclined her head in the direction of one of the monks. "It would have destroyed you if I did not stop your blade. You needed to have the strength to thrust the blade, but then the wisdom to take a step back and consider what your actions would cost you."

Then Bronwyn found herself in the dark void again, falling for what seemed like eternity. There was no sound, sight, or light to keep her mind from racing with thoughts. She wasn't sure if she was imagining the images, or if it were some product of this place. It seemed like a look at an alternate future, one in which the phoenix hadn't intervened. She saw what the phoenix said was true. She stared at Miro as his body slumped and slid forward along her blade. She let the blade drop, its steely-blue surface now tarnished with Miro's blood and held him as his body convulsed, his lungs struggling to pull in air to keep him alive. Wet, warm, dark-red blood stained her pristine breastplate, soaking into her clothes and pants. As she cradled his head, he choked, spilling more of his life-force down her shoulder, wetting the back of her clothes and running into her hair. Then, when he finally was dead, when the last spasms left his body, she turned around, to see Clara and Issaroh horrified. They did not pity her as the tears ran down her cheek and they hated her more that she had the gall to cry after doing what she needed to do. As mysteriously as the vision started, it faded to black.

Now back in the cave, in front of her, the phoenix was gone. Bronwyn looked about, seeing Clara had wrapped herself around a prone Miro and stared at Bronwyn with that same hate in her eyes. Issaroh similarly looked dismayed, and then Bronwyn saw *him*, what must be the current incarnation of Defurge, standing slightly off from the three others.

"He stays in the library with you," Bronwyn turned to Issaroh, pointing at him, "He researches the artifacts, but no more magic."

She picked up her sword, now cool again, and sheathed it. She ignored the collective sigh of relief. *Fine, I'm the villain.*

She half marched, half ran to the next cavern, away from Miro. Once she was out of eyesight and earshot, she fell to the ground, her heart thundering and her mind reeling. She wasn't sure if it was the feeling of moving to and from the gem twice in such a short length of time, or the images she imagined or witnessed.

After the initial panic passed, Bronwyn guzzled from her waterskin, trying to stifle her emotions by doing something ordinary. Then she sat, her knees tucked into her chest, and tried to process everything that had just happened. She wondered what was being said, of her, of the gem, of how they now had to babysit a god. Every now and then, she'd sip water trying to hold onto something real. By the time Issaroh appeared, the feeling had mostly dissipated, but the sand and seawater competed with each other as a reminder of where they were and what had happened.

Issaroh pointedly did not look at Bronwyn and sat on the other side of her. She turned to face him, ready for an admonishment or inquisition.

"Why am I suddenly the warden to gods and magi? All I wanted to do was save Emestria by finding these artifacts." Bronwyn tucked her hair behind her ears, looking at Issaroh. She had exhausted what little emotion remained in her body. She waited in silence, resting her head on her knees as she waited for an answer.

"I think he wanted you to do it," Issaroh said.

"I know he did," Bronwyn replied, unable to meet Issaroh's gaze.

"Miro told me about the place you were, about the prison for all the previous incarnations of the god. He told me what the phoenix said to him. That man, the one that I guess used to be the god, tried to explain more. I can't imagine what being in a place like that felt like."

"Did Miro tell you about how he fought back?" Bronwyn shuddered as she said it. "About the lightning, and his eyes."

"He said he remembered feeling voices in his head, being in excruciating pain, and woke up to see you standing above him." Issaroh's voice shook as he spoke. "He didn't know why, but when he saw your eyes, he thought he deserved it."

"I've seen it once before, in Emestria. He rose into the air, lightning gyrating off his body, almost killing Clara. Naani gave her life to stop him." She paused. "He told us if it ever happened again, we should run as far and as fast as we can. What is it?"

"The curse," Issaroh said, reconfirming Miro's earlier explanation. "You *should* run. When a magus tries to tap into the full energy of the Ywaigwai, they become a conduit for the raw power. They are a danger to everyone around them, and when the magic becomes too great, they are consumed by its essence. If Naani was able to stop him, he must not have entered the curse completely. But if he did, that would be his end."

"Why would someone do that to themselves?" Bronwyn asked after a minute.

"We can't control it. It's why I avoid combat, and why I think it unwise for him to continue this quest. He's too emotional, too fearful, too prone to entering the curse." Issaroh's voice was soft, which only made what he said sound more dire.

"He wanted me to kill him," Bronwyn said, tears forming in her eyes again. "Why? I should have believed you when you said he wanted to sacrifice himself. I thought it meant he would risk his life to kill the thing that destroyed Lynnfield, but this … Has he ever …?"

"I've never seen him act this way, but … he's lost Naani, his friends, and all he has left is us and his quest for the artifacts. Now the thing he has been hunting for years, to put things right, is not what he thought."

Bronwyn let the information sink in and debated what to say next, what to do next, how she was going to even accomplish her goal while trying to look out for Miro at the same time. "The phoenix said Miro craves power, that his heart is greedy. Is that why he became a magus? For power? He sold his soul just to become more powerful? The phoenix said he did things in the war to protect those he loved; does that mean he used the Ywaigwai's power to …"

A shiver ran down Bronwyn's spine. She gritted her teeth as she said what her heart had been warning her about for so long, and now she had to listen. "He caused the destruction of Lynnfield. I'm not sure how, but

I know he blames himself, and I can't help but think there is some truth in that. Maybe it was an accident, that he was trying to protect people and awoke the monster he blames, or maybe there is no monster. It's the only way I can explain his behavior."

Issaroh visibly winced. "I don't think that's true. You have to understand Miro. That's just not the person he is."

"Help me understand. Help me understand how I can continue to endanger others' lives when I may be travelling with someone that is partly responsible for the destruction of an entire region and tens of thousands of people."

Issaroh removed his glasses, pinched the bridge of his nose, and sighed. "If only you knew the man I mentored. He abhorred violence, but still, when he was forced into the academy, he tried to use it as an opportunity to change things. He thought if he fought with Prince Bryant, he could convince the prince of the folly of conflict—lead him to a better path. Miro was good and kind. Protected others. Gave what he didn't need to the people that had less than him.

"After the war, he changed. He became sullen and withdrawn. Forcing himself into exile only worsened it. He lived out in the cold so long, by himself, with no one to help soothe his guilt. I tried to be there for him, but I've been a horrible mentor. One mistake after another. I'm as much to blame for his state of mind as he is."

"He killed people," Bronwyn said with confidence. "I saw it in his eyes. I don't know whether by his hand—or if his actions led to others losing their lives—but I'm confident now. He tortures himself because he can't forgive the deaths he's caused. He wants to die." Bronwyn needed to move, but her body felt stuck to the floor.

"And you're to be his executioner to punish him for his sins?" Issaroh asked. "Why not fell me? Why not Clara? Why not yourself? We all have blood on our hands. Doesn't his inability to forgive himself make him better than us? Do you lose sleep over the lives you've taken or been responsible for?" His eyes pleaded with her.

She averted her gaze. "You said it yourself. He's too emotional, too prone to lashing out and hurting others—whether he means to or not. He's a danger to those around him." Bronwyn sounded less like she was trying to convince Issaroh. She was trying to convince herself.

"He's different around you." Issaroh's voice wavered more and more. "He doesn't listen to you; he believes in you. I'm confident that, given time, he can forgive himself, and help others. He wants to help. He wants to help you save Emestria. If he could only see himself through your eyes."

"I see him as a villain," she said with vitriol. "I'm not his savior."

Issaroh frowned. "Why don't you come back to the others with me. We can talk about this together. It's been an emotional day for all of us."

"I don't want to talk. I need to think. When the rest of you are ready to leave, I'll be here and follow you back to the library."

# CHAPTER 24

*Seketh was the smallest of the gods' territories, and their patron god was Chivas. Many nations hated Chivas for the role he played in the cataclysm, thus his name being used as a curse in the modern era. Corinth, the nation that was under the goddess Kyrie's protection, waged war against the nation of Seketh for many years until Seketh was decimated in 217 P.C.*

*—Issaroh, The History of Divinity, Part XIX*

As she walked through the ruined city of Dalmarask, Bronwyn fixed her icy blue eyes on the back of the Miro. When they first made this voyage, he held her arm as they traveled through the sand. Now in the moonlight he grasped Clara's instead of hers. Bronwyn could have easily overtaken them; they were keeping pace with Issaroh. Only Defurge kept Bronwyn company as they traveled under the night sky.

"Look around you, Defurge. This is what you did. This is what happens when men seek power," Bronwyn said, extending her hand toward the buildings.

Despite traveling with the former incarnation of the god of destruction, Bronwyn felt somehow at ease around him. Strangely, he reminded her of the first snowfall and how it quiets the land. He was handsome; his dark brown skin and long silvery locks were such a strong contrast they constantly drew the eye to him. Even the red of his irises seemed to demand attention. Defurge did not say one thing, then do the other.

Unlike Miro, who promised her he would help liberate her homeland. She gave Miro too much trust. They went after the artifact he wanted to, and now the world was in more peril than it was this morning.

The three in front stopped and Bronwyn slowed her gait. They did not move. The ley line had to be nearby. Bronwyn picked up her pace, anxious to be free of this desert and what it now represented. She glared at Miro as they gathered in a circle around Issaroh. His eyes focused on the ground. His brown shoulder length hair framed his face as he avoided Bronwyn's gaze. His face betrayed no emotion. No joy that he had tricked her. No sorrow that he had lied. No regret his mission failed as well.

"Ramun, god of time and space and traveler of this world, bless our journey, Summa," Issaroh chanted.

The circle appeared beneath their feet and glowed with a bright blue light. Bronwyn closed her eyes, knowing what came next. As the circle's light died down, Bronwyn ran to one of the bookcases. She doubled over, laid low once again by motion sickness. But she fought back the nausea, trying to show strength in this time of need. She did not feel Miro's hand on her back, trying to reassure her as she felt nauseous. Glancing out of the corner of her eye, she saw Clara was attending to Miro, likely trying to get him far away from Bronwyn, or somewhere to be alone with Clara. They all hated Bronwyn for what she almost did in the cave.

Once the nausea finally passed, Bronwyn walked past Defurge and headed for the baths. She ignored the others' chatter as she climbed the stairs. In front of her, one of the ten-foot golems that cared for the library barred her passage. She didn't even need to voice the word "move" for the automaton to step aside and allow her to continue her trek toward the bath. Once inside the bathhouse, she stripped her clothes off and laid them on the floor. After lifting one of the plates to supply hot water she lowered herself into its warm embrace. And the day just seemed to melt off her.

Everything in the library made her feel unnerved, but there was something about the bath. Only when she was within its waters did she truly feel at peace. This building was amazing, yet she always felt on edge. A feeling only she seemed to have.

She replayed the day through her head. She had worried Miro would betray her and run off with the soul gem once they found it. But he didn't. He followed her and did as she asked. He was probably scouring the library, searching for another artifact to go after. Maybe even one that would help her protect Emestria.

Why had she let the phoenix's warnings scare her so? Miro had always been upfront about his power. That he had no real control over it, that he might be dangerous. She had accepted that and come to her own conclusion that she could handle whatever threat he posed. If anything, their conflict in the cave proved that. He didn't even try and protect himself when she was about to run him through.

And why did she feel jealous about Clara? She had no feelings for Miro that Bronwyn knew of. They were friends at best. At worst, Clara thought him a bit of a buffoon. And it wasn't just jealousy; she felt shame and embarrassment as well. How could she be jealous of Clara? Even if she harbored some feeling for Miro, or just didn't want Bronwyn to be with him, why did it matter so much to her?

Bronwyn stayed in the bath for hours, ruminating on the oddity of the day, until she didn't hear voices outside or footsteps in the hall. She had no desire to see how they looked at her now. She exited the bath and looked at her clothes—well, not her clothes really. She had borrowed the outfit from the goddess Kyrie's wardrobe. When she wore them in the past, they made her feel strong, invincible, and untouchable. Now as she looked at them, a cold finger of dread traced her spine. A feeling she couldn't explain, something she had experienced all too often while in the library.

She opted for one of the robes hanging in the bathhouse and started heading for her bedroom, Seraph's bed chambers.

"Betrayal," a voice whispered.

Bronwyn looked around her. She did not recognize the voice. Probably a trick of frayed nerves and exhaustion. She flipped the switch down that interrupted the artificial light to the room and tiptoed to the bed. Sliding underneath her sheets, she found herself pulled immediately into the realm of dreams. More of a nightmare than a dream, one in which she found herself unable to distinguish between reality and fear, that gripped her so tightly she couldn't wake herself from it.

She was standing in this room. Two others were against the far wall. A man, with shoulder length brown hair and a slim frame. In his arms a woman that looked like her. Blue eyes and long blonde hair, but not her. As she cleared her throat they turned. It was Miro and, as much as she couldn't explain it, her. As she blinked, they weren't in the room anymore, but back in the Soul Gem.

After glancing around, when Bronwyn's eyes returned to Miro, he now had the phoenix's female form held in a passionate embrace against a red pane of glass. She tousled her hair and moaned as Miro's lips found purchase against the skin of her thin neck. Her arms were clasped tightly around him, red fingernails digging into the flesh of his back.

Bronwyn felt the anger burn as she charged forward. She didn't even know what she was doing until she had impaled them both on a spear. A spear she didn't remember holding until the wood haft was firmly thrust through Miro's body. She stepped away; scarlet blood staining her hands. She shook with the realization of what she had just done. Bronwyn reached to her side, for her dagger and thrust it under her neck, ready to slit her own throat. Blood ran down the blade until it pooled at the tip and dripped onto the floor.

"Daughter, Seraph, you musn't," A deep voice bellowed.

Bronwyn turned to see the man. A muscular wide frame with a short white beard. His hair equally white.

"Father, what have I done? I couldn't stop. I thought he loved me," Bronwyn begged for answers.

"It was not of his doing child. Chivas had tricked him. He thought that was you."

Bronwyn held the dagger closer to her throat.

"But you musn't," Laevin continued. "In your womb is your unborn daughter. The first god to be born in a millennia."

Bronwyn looked to her stomach. Underneath her red flowing silk dress she now felt the kicks of a child as her belly ballooned. She shook her head. *How is this possible? Am I the goddess Seraph? Am I supposed to be learning some lesson from this situation? That my jealousy or anger toward Miro would have made me like the goddess, dead in the eyes and unable to love again?*

"Betrayal."

Bronwyn woke with a start. Her eyes widened as she breathed heavily. It was some perverse amalgamation of the day's events and all the stories of the gods. She used the sheets to wipe some of the sweat from her neck and brow.

Around the room were the portraits of the goddess Seraph and all her lovers. The look in Seraph's eyes had always been forlorn, but now as Bronwyn stared at one of the pictures, the eyes turned sinister. This room was a curse. Bronwyn pulled the rest of the sheets free and hurried into the hallway. As she looked back at the doorway to the room, she heard the voice again.

"Betrayal."

*Is this a dream as well?* She walked down the hall, past the room of the goddess Lau'O'Penake and her husband Ramun.

"Death."

Then past the room of Laevin and his wife Kyrie.

"Vengeance."

And finally, she stood in front of the room of Fria, Goddess of ice, death, and fate, the Vigilant Eye, the patron goddess of Emestria.

"Duty."

Okay, Bronwyn could live with duty. She quickly ducked into the room. She had always avoided Fria's room. One is always safe avoiding anything to do with the goddess of death, but all the other options seemed worse. This room always felt colder than the others. Whether it actually was or it was just an illusion from the giant ice sculpture was impossible to say. Bronwyn hurried to the bed and went underneath the covers, pulling them up over her head.

# CHAPTER 25

*The first indication of the gods' absence became apparent after ten to fifteen years, when even the prayers of the most penitent of their followers went unanswered. Many believed the gods had abandoned them due to mortal greed. I argue that they instead left our realm to prevent their conflicts from destroying populations like they did in Dalmarask. The first skirmishes were minor, with nations believing the gods would intervene, but as it became clearer that humankind was left to their own devices, they quickly escalated into full-blown wars. Old rivalries and grievances resurfaced.*

*—Issaroh, The History of Divinity, Part XXV*

As Bronwyn shivered awake, she was surprised to find herself in the room of Fria, goddess of ice and death, but then last night slowly came back into focus. She remembered snippets of her obscure nightmare and felt a little embarrassed to not only admit that in the dream Miro was her lover but also that she was pregnant with, supposedly, his child. But then she remembered the words of who she was now sure was Laevin, God of lightning and scrying, and that it was the child of a god she was supposedly bearing. All of this was ridiculously absurd; she was not pregnant, and the gods were gone. She attributed the dream to the combination of stress and literally being surrounded by what the pantheon left behind when they departed the mortal world.

Oh right—then there was the fact that they left one god behind, Defurge the mad god, who was now supposedly going to help with their little adventure. With an audible groan, Bronwyn pulled the bedsheets tighter around her body, turned to her side, and took stock of the state of the room as she mentally prepared herself for who she'd have to talk to about the previous day, Defurge, Clara, Miro, and Issaroh, so just *every-body* was going to need an explanation of her behavior.

Fria's room was barren except for a small nightstand with a single mirror, a wardrobe, and bed. It reminded her more of the prison cell Miro had spent the night in than any of the other rooms. Every other room had decorations, ornamentation, and a bed located in the middle of the room. In this room however, it was a large translucent blue sculpture that dominated the space, and the bed, much smaller than any of the others, was tucked away into a corner. There were no carvings on the lone wardrobe, no portraits hung on the walls, and even the bed sheets were plain white linen as opposed to the silken ones in Seraph's room. *They aren't even that warm,* Bronwyn thought, trying to hold them tighter so the heat of her body last night would provide her some succor.

When that proved fruitless, Bronwyn threw off the sheet and realized she was still wearing the robe she had donned after her bath. Slightly too embarrassed to go walking about the library in such revealing attire, she walked to the other side of the room, side-stepping the sculpture, and opened the unadorned door of the wardrobe. It seemed that all of the gods clothing reflected their aspects and Fria's was completely inappropriate in the muggy swamp in which the library now lay submerged. However, Bronwyn wasn't looking to make a statement, rather to just find something temporarily as she made her way back to Seraph's room to retrieve her belongings.

Pulling a spotted white and black fur-lined robe from the wardrobe, Bronwyn noticed a small box at the bottom that was now revealed by the absence of the removed garment. She put the robe around her body then knelt to examine the box. Unlike the rest of the room, this box was intricately decorated with shards of mirror interlaced with silver, suspending the reflective surface and protecting the hands from the sharp edges that would have been between the shards. The clasp was a simple lever, and there was no locking mechanism.

Inside the box, the mirror motif continued, but felt-cushioned divisions in the inside separated several different items of jewelry. One in particular caught Bronwyn's eye: a silver necklace with a sapphire suspended in a pendant. She stared at that necklace for what seemed like hours but in reality was probably only a couple of minutes. She was strangely drawn to it. If Bronwyn were the type of woman to wear jewelry, it had a certain appeal to it, but then Bronwyn came to her senses, closed the box, and returned it to its location. She left the room, sparing a glance back at the sculpture, noticing again how ill-placed it was, requiring her to walk around it to get from one place to another in the room. For a practical god that would most likely have appreciated simplicity, it was a poor choice to prevent yourself from walking straight from bed to wardrobe, or from wardrobe to door.

Inside Seraph's room, Bronwyn found her gear, well-laid in the corner of the room, where she had left it last night. *No, had I left it last night in the room? Or did I leave it in the bath?* One of the homunculi had probably moved it, but how did she not remember something as simple as where she put her sword. She concluded that she must not have left it in the bath, because taking her sword into the room with the bath didn't make much sense either.

She would need to talk with Clara, Miro, Issaroh, and now Defurge, each in turn. Although talking with Issaroh would be the easiest of the conversations, she opted to do it last, so they could have it away from prying ears. Miro would be the most difficult to talk to and ideally, she would have preferred to do it last, but wanted to give him the credit of telling her anything she needed to know before she went to Issaroh to get the real answers. Clara it was.

As Bronwyn made her way to where Clara had been staying, Lau'O'Penake and Ramun's room. Bronwyn noticed that Miro was down in the stacks, book in hand, perusing it. She wondered if he were keeping to his word and now searching for an artifact to help Emestria, or if was he on another fool's errand to find something to trap the monster he blamed responsible for the catastrophe at Lynnfield.

A screech from Ferdinand caught Bronwyn unaware and startled her as she turned the corner into the bedroom. Clara was on the bed, reading her own book, and only spared a quick glance at Bronwyn before returning her attention to it. Bronwyn continued approaching until she was ten feet away from the side of the bed. It was a little awkward standing and trying to have a conversation while Clara was splayed on her stomach, but sitting down seemed even more embarrassing.

"I wanted to talk about what happened yesterday," Bronwyn said. "I think I might owe you an explanation, or …" But Bronwyn trailed off, not really sure of what she could say. Perhaps if she gave Clara the chance to ask some questions first, it would make it easier.

"You know, when I asked you if you'd cut me down in the swamp to save a thousand people, I didn't think you'd literally try and kill one of us with your sword."

Bronwyn winced. Apparently letting Clara talk wasn't going to make the conversation any easier. With a measured breath, Bronwyn squared her shoulders, determined not to contribute to any further fracturing of the group. "You never tried to electrocute any of us."

Clara closed her book, turned to her side, then sat up. With a pointed glare, Clara said, "He saved you in the woods, from the wolves, he probably saved us both."

"But he also told us that if something like that were to happen again, we should try and flee. When we were in the gem, he summoned the same type of lightning and I'm confident that if we had not been ejected by the gem he would have probably been in the same trance-like state."

"He said run, not run me through."

Bronwyn gritted her teeth, not wanting to show how the comment bit her pride. "It was a confusing fight, only made more confusing by being teleported in and out of the gem. I'll admit I was frazzled, a little scared, and my actions weren't a great response to what was happening. But there would have been no running from him in that place; it would be too hard to scale the cliffs and he'd catch us."

Clara picked her book back up and extricated herself from the bed, on the side opposite Bronwyn and closest to the bird. "I think I might take Ferdinand hunting for a bit. We don't really need to have this conversation. You've told Miro he's staying in the library from here on out, so it's not like we'll have any similar situations in the future."

Bronwyn clenched her jaw, but held fast to her resolve to keep this group together as best she could. "I need to know if you and I are still pursuing similar goals. You didn't sign up for this, and you definitely didn't agree to be watching over a god."

As Bronwyn spoke, Clara donned her leather glove and placed it beneath Ferdinand's talons until he stepped onto it. Clara didn't say anything till she was almost out of the room. Over her shoulder, she said,

"We're fine. I don't know what it was like being in and out of that gem. Miro tried to describe it, but it sounded like the type of thing you had to experience to understand. Your king is still paying, and I still have the falcon, so we're still stuck together." Clara turned her head and flashed a wry smile. "Just don't try and kill me."

With that simple gesture, Bronwyn's tension dissipated. If Clara were already trying to make light of the situation, then this would pass, eventually. There was more that Bronwyn wanted to say, but this resolution was probably the best she could hope for today. Maybe this boded well for her conversation with Miro.

As Bronwyn made her way from Clara's room, keeping a healthy distance so Clara wouldn't think Bronwyn was running after her, she spotted Miro again, still in roughly the same place. She was finally getting used to navigating the maze of bookshelves, but being among them still brought her considerable tension. Perhaps it was the homunculi constantly running to and fro and climbing on bookcases to replace books that didn't need replacing. When she finally found Miro, she also found three of the creatures.

The homunculi were not climbing up and down these bookcases, but rather standing around Miro, with beady eyes watching him as they disturbingly swayed in their stance. The strange spice-like odor was stronger here, and Bronwyn wondered if it were the homunculi she had been smelling all along. Every time Miro turned a page, they reacted with little flinches of their hands, probably waiting for Miro to finish the book so they could replace it. Why it would take three of them to do it, Bronwyn didn't know, but this library wasn't functioning as it should, something she would discuss with Issaroh.

Thinking back on it now, there usually was at least one homunculus around Miro when he was in the stacks. He didn't seem to notice them, and frankly Bronwyn had stopped as well. Perhaps it was the lack of movement that made these three stand out, or the way they watched him so intently.

Bronwyn cleared her throat before saying, "Miro."

Miro took his eyes off his book for a second and gave her a nod. With the homunculi standing around Miro in a semi-circle it made this conversation infinitely more awkward than the one with Clara.

Out of force of habit, Bronwyn folded her arms, which usually resulted in her chastising him, so she consciously unfolded them and continued, "I owe you an apology for the way I have been acting. But given how everything has turned out, I think you might agree that you not fighting might be in everyone's best interest."

"I don't blame you Bronwyn, I probably would have done the same thing in your situation." His voice lacked the gloom that he had exhibited in the cave when she told him he would be staying in the library from now on. His cavalier attitude also seemed to be a return to how he was acting in Emestria, and perhaps with sleep and the thought of the gem not being the solution he hoped it was, his behavior would be more level. "Besides, all I've got to do is read books and then send you out to do the hard work. You're getting the raw end of that deal."

Bronwyn forced a smile and Miro looked up from his book once again, trying to see if his attempt at levity was appreciated. "Still," Bronwyn said, "I think it would be best if you and Defurge gave each other a wide birth, especially since I'm not sure whether he can remove that gem or needs to keep it on his person."

"Is this about what the phoenix said?" Miro asked before continuing without giving Bronwyn a chance to answer. "Do you really think so little of me that you think I want power?"

"Well, no. I don't want to. But maybe if we knew more about each other, why we do what we do, then trust might be easier, or at least we could understand each other's motivations."

Miro sighed. "I never wanted power. And I'd never want that gem if I knew what it did. That thing is a curse, and I've already got one of those, which is one too many in my opinion."

He sounded genuine, so Bronwyn tried to take him at his word. "Is there anything you want to tell me? About your past, to explain why the phoenix thought you couldn't use magic in the gem? I was going to ask Issaroh—"

It was a quiet interruption, "Then ask Issaroh. I've told you as much as I know or care to. Maybe there is something he can tell you, or hearing it from him will convince you that I never wanted anything like that gem."

Miro replaced the book he had been reading and took down another, opening it as Bronwyn hesitated on what to say next. "I wanted to talk to you about the artifacts we're looking for, specifically those that would be easiest or most helpful to obtain."

"You originally wanted that one that was rumored to create food, so that's what I'm researching, while also keeping an eye out for where the Hammer of Unmaking might be. That's what you wanted, isn't it?"

Honestly, Bronwyn was pleasantly surprised that he would be pursuing those artifacts instead of others. "I know it's been a short time, but have you made any progress?"

"I always kept an eye out for it while doing my research for the gem, so I'm further along than you think, but nowhere near as much as I hoped. Colloquially, it was called the cornucopia, but it was originally gifted to one of the demigods, so finding out the name and origin of that demigod will probably be the best way to uncover its resting place. I was going to talk to Issaroh about it later. Maybe some stories about the demigods might narrow down the possibilities."

"Thanks," Bronwyn said, waiting for more, but when Miro didn't continue, she took her leave.

Like Miro, Issaroh had a habit of studying in the same place. Bronwyn was increasingly curious if this was a product of Issaroh as Miro's mentor, or if like living in isolation, it was a trait of being a magi. She had debated talking to Defurge next, but she had no idea where he was, and hadn't seen him yet, so she was glad to find Issaroh and Defurge talking. It sounded like Issaroh was catching Defurge up on what happened after the cataclysm and the next four hundred-some years. When Bronwyn entered Issaroh's study, that conversation ended as they looked at her expectantly.

"I'm glad to find you here, Defurge. I had some questions for you, and perhaps having Issaroh here might provide some insight, or give him a chance to answer something you may not know."

Defurge, who had been standing across from Issaroh, turned and sat down on Issaroh's desk, which groaned a little and shifted as he did. Issaroh's face blanked, but Bronwyn could tell the casual act wasn't something the old man appreciated.

"I will try and answer what I can," Defurge said, smirking at Issaroh's reaction.

"Now that the phoenix has cured your madness, do we run any risk of that happening again?" Bronwyn asked.

"Not until someone else takes the gem." Defurge held the gem aloft by the chain around his neck, and Bronwyn noticed the way Issaroh's eyes went wide and his gaze fixated on the red, shiny bauble. Issaroh blinked, and with a slight shake of his head stared down at the table instead.

"The phoenix said she would lend you her powers, so you could still wield fire in a somewhat similar way. Does that mean you can communicate with her, or the monks in any meaningful fashion?"

A frown passed Defurge's lips as he said, "Unfortunately no. I feel power in the gem, and sometimes I catch what I'd best describe as whispers from the gem that I think might be them trying to communicate with me, but nothing more than that. Perhaps with more time it might grow stronger, but I can't ask the phoenix questions, at least not yet, if that's what you were thinking."

"That is unfortunate. Having access to someone that may have been alive much longer ago could be helpful. You'll let me know if that changes?"

"I can."

"Were you conscious of anything that was happening in the gem while Miro and I were in there?"

"I was unconscious, and like I said, I can't really communicate with the gem, so it wouldn't make sense that I would know what was going on inside it."

"Hmm ... But when I was going to ... No, I mean before I was pulled back in the second time, I saw the phoenix again, so perhaps she can communicate with the outside world somehow."

"In the cave? I didn't see anyone other than you four," Defurge replied.

Bronwyn looked to Issaroh for a witness to what happened, but he shook his head before confirming, "There was no one else there."

"But I saw her," Bronwyn said. "Maybe she can appear to me or Miro because we saw her inside." But if the phoenix could appear, why hadn't she done so again? The phoenix had physically grabbed her sword. How had no one else seen that, or seen that it was red hot when Bronwyn let go? She wanted to see if the monks or phoenix could tell her more about how they saw the future or saw inside Miro's head, but that line of questioning had proven fruitless. Bronwyn stood in contemplation, trying to think of a question that might get her some answers, but was unable to think of anything.

"Was that all?" Defurge asked after a minute.

"For now, but I'd like to have a word with Issaroh in private. Do you mind leaving for a bit? I won't be long."

"Did you just tell a god what to do?" Defurge asked, his lip curling up and his brows wrinkling. Then he laughed pleasantly before adding, "Oh, you all are going to be fun."

With a kick of his legs, causing the desk to settle back to its natural position, not having to support Defurge's weight any longer, he turned and made a playful bow before retreating. Bronwyn gave Issaroh a concerned look, and after waiting to be sure Defurge was far enough away, she asked Issaroh, "Do you mind if we take a walk and talk?"

"A walk?" Issaroh asked as he cocked his head to the side.

"To have a private conversation," Bronwyn said. Issaroh nodded and donned a light linen robe over the clothes he was already wearing, Bronwyn exited the room, standing to the side of the door, waiting for Issaroh to join her. Once he exited as well, Bronwyn matched his step as the two of them proceeded out of the library, to the semi-revealed passage that didn't involve wading through waist-high muck.

"Did you know the soul gem wasn't what Miro was looking for?" Bronwyn asked when they were further through the library, far enough away from Miro so his interest wouldn't be piqued.

"No, if I had, I would have told him. I really thought it was what he was looking for. I certainly did not want to release Defurge upon the world again."

Bronwyn put both arms behind her back and clasped one of her wrists with her opposite hand. "What can you tell me about Defurge?"

"In my day, he was a powerful force to be reckoned with, feared by all. He was one of the only gods that didn't attract worshippers, except for those that had a tenuous grasp on morality or reality. Chivas was disliked, but he had *some* redeeming traits that drew worshippers to him. Defurge was destruction incarnate."

"Why was he defeated so easily, then?" Bronwyn asked.

"I don't know if I'd say that was exactly easy," Issaroh replied, earning him a suspicious glare from Bronwyn.

"He destroyed a whole town. We four beat what was essentially a god."

"He's not a god," Issaroh said. "But I have some theories. Perhaps the gem is similar to Ywaigwai in that it needs a new host occasionally. So, if the one host had it for hundreds of years, it could be significantly weakened."

"Hmm," Bronwyn contemplated. "A weakened body could be beneficial in case anything were to go wrong." *Like it almost did with Miro.* "But I do think we need to be cautious going forward."

After passing rows of stacks, they were upon the foyer of the library, which was capped by a large entryway, which, judging by the hinges, had probably held a set of doors. Why hadn't the golems repaired that?

Issaroh said, "Yes, caution would be advisable, but if what he says is true, that the phoenix wants the gem destroyed and any power he has is now reliant on her, I doubt he'd risk a fight without power. You did, after all, incapacitate him without the use of magic or a weapon really. The stakes for him are probably higher than they are for you or Clara. He knows his failure will result in eternal imprisonment."

The humid air pressed in on Bronwyn's lungs as they advanced through the short cavern, leading to the swamp proper. The temperature between the library and the surrounding swamp seemed to rise a degree with each step. Bronwyn glanced down at the ground, which was packed, dry mud. Issaroh shouldn't have much trouble navigating it. The ceiling was twelve feet high, large enough to accommodate the golems, and the inside appeared to be dug out rather than a natural formation. A sense of relief flooded over Bronwyn as she stepped outside the cave and her body relaxed in the morning sun.

Bronwyn said, "I don't know how much Miro told you of what happened in the gem, and he wasn't there the second time I went back in, but the phoenix said some concerning things to me." Issaroh turned to her, and she clarified, "About Miro."

"Oh …." Issaroh hung his head, staring at his feet as he navigated the mud and wet grass of the ground that surrounded the swamp.

"She said that magic wasn't supposed to work inside the gem, but Miro almost entered his curse. She actually sounded afraid of him when she cast us out the first time." Bronwyn stopped short of telling him of how the monks claimed to be able to look into the future, or how the phoenix said Miro would sacrifice him to destroy the gem. Issaroh didn't need to know those things. At least not yet.

"After the gods left, mortals began to command magic with a little more proficiency, so maybe magic wasn't strong enough when the phoenix and monks were imprisoned, but now it is. There were also no magi until after the gods left, so it could be Miro's status as a magus that allowed him to cast and startle the phoenix."

To Bronwyn, it sounded like Issaroh wanted to say more, and Bronwyn glanced over her shoulder, to make sure they were truly alone. "And what else?"

Issaroh sighed and his posture slumped a little, his back bowing. "You have to understand, I don't even think this is relevant, but Miro has always had an uncommon aptitude for magic. I lied when I said he was a competent sorcerer; he's by far the best healer I've ever met, and not only because he seems to learn magic easier than most, but because he will knowingly endanger his own life, leaving it up to luck to see who survives. It's what I think you don't understand about him."

"What do you mean?" They were approaching the area that Issaroh and Clara usually trained, and their manipulation of earth magic had scattered clods of dirt. Half-collapsed stone walls provided raised areas to sit.

"If I were to get sick, something serious like my heart failing, not that I was dead, but I was dying, Miro could try and heal me. He could use his magic to try and keep my heart beating, to keep my insides from eating themselves. Of course, this wouldn't cure the root problem, and his own magic would be constantly fighting my body, trying to heal it as my body killed more and more of itself, shutting down. Maybe Miro could buy me months of time, maybe years, but by doing that he would not only be incapacitated and be restricted to maintaining the magic, but he would risk his own life in doing so. If he tried to keep it up indefinitely, magus or not, we would both die."

Bronwyn nodded, then found a stone wall tall enough for both of them to sit comfortably. "Have you ever seen Miro do something like that?" Bronwyn sat down, then helped Issaroh sit next to her. She laid her hands on her thighs, thinking to herself how nice it felt to be out of the library.

"No, but I heard about it. Rumors of an orphanage that was lucky enough to have a healer work on their staff and donate their time. Sure, it was mostly patching up skinned knees and mending broken bones, but it was a service, one that most establishments like that didn't have access to. But one day an accident happened, a tree collapsed on the healer. She was unconscious, and without another healer nearby it was assumed she would die. So, a twelve-year-old boy walked up and started to treat her, not only mixing and applying a poultice to mend her broken ribs, but using magic to heal her internal injuries as well."

"I thought Miro became a noble after the orphanage. Who taught him magic? The healer?"

"No, he apparently taught it to himself. He had been healing skinned knees so that his friends wouldn't have to stop playing for two years. He was ten and taught himself runes just by watching someone else use magic." Issaroh leaned forward, putting his hands into his lap.

"Is it uncommon for someone so young to be able to cast?" Bronwyn asked.

"Not so uncommon; I've heard of children his age being able to use some magic, but they were taught rigorously from a young age and studied at an institution. They didn't just pick it up by watching someone else on a couple of occasions."

"But Clara learned how to cast a spell in one day."

"Simple things, not healing magic. Not enough to bring back someone dying. Of course, a twelve-year-old can't support the toll needed to heal that much damage, and Miro fell unconscious himself. He remained like that for an entire year. He was transferred between orphanages, since taking care of someone in that state was not only time consuming but costly. Eventually, one of the noble houses heard about the incident and adopted him, taking over his care. It took me years to find the origin of this story of the healing prodigy, and even more to track down where he was at the time."

"A pity that his moods make it less than ideal for him to be involved in combat. I didn't realize he was that proficient, but I also didn't know that healing magic was that hard on the body. But if he's here at the library, we can always return if we have your teleportation."

"I've told you I don't want to be fighting. I run the same risk as Miro if I become overwhelmed and enter the curse."

"You won't have to fight; it sounds like a lot of this is going to be about tracking down the artifacts. Which brings me to my next point, Miro is currently researching more artifacts and discovering their locations. He has some questions for you, but I don't know how much longer we can stay in the library with the way it's operating."

"What do you mean?" Issaroh asked, turning his body her direction and knitting his eyebrows.

"It's not working. And I think our presence is making things worse. I see more and more homunculi standing around doing nothing, just watching Miro. There are strange noises and there is just a feeling to the place."

"You're just adjusting to it. It can be a lot finding yourself in a place that foreign. The noises are either the homunculi or possibly from the electricity in the walls."

"Have you ever had strange dreams here? About the gods?" Bronwyn asked.

"Well, of course; you're surrounded by the gods. How could you not dream about them, wondering where they are, and what they're doing?"

Bronwyn sighed, seeing now that Issaroh probably wouldn't understand what she was saying. "I had a nightmare that I was Seraph when she slayed her lover. It felt so real, not like a dream, when it happened."

Issaroh put his hand over Bronwyn's and squeezed it. "You had a very difficult day yesterday. Maybe the others don't see it, but I do. A difficult decision, and then the regret that—although you knew you ultimately made the right choice—that you wavered before making it. Stress will manifest in odd ways."

"It's not just that. It's the feeling of unease in that place. It just seems to grow more with each passing day."

"Just give it some time." Issaroh let go of Bronwyn's hand, patted her forearm, and returned his own hand to his lap.

"Or I could fix it. You mentioned the library has been operating oddly for some time because of a missing artifact, the Eye of Sleepless Dreams."

"Yes, but that's been gone for over a hundred years. It's not like the library has gotten more dysfunctional with each year of its absence."

"We can always try returning it, then see what happens. Why do the people that took it even need it, or what guarantee is there that they still have it?"

"From time to time, the Shi'en will send some emissaries to visit. Their ancestral homeland used to grow the berries necessary for their coming-of-age ceremonies. They use the artifact as a replacement and are thankful for me not tracking them down and taking it back. They apparently think me some type of divine figure since I have not come seeking it."

"How do they use it?" Bronwyn asked.

"In the library, it serves as a way for the homunculi to see what is happening in the world so they can record the events. Since the homunculi don't need sleep, but still aren't really conscious, it constantly provides them with information, but it can still be used by a mortal. If you use it while asleep, it can give you visions to provide you answers to the questions you most want to know."

"Have you used it?"

"No, it is dangerous and the Shi'en have told me that some of the visions have driven men mad."

"Still, if it could return the library to its former glory, there might be a compromise we could reach. What if they return it to the library, but we allow them to use it for their rituals whenever they need—they just have to come here. You had said they were nomadic after all, and a pilgrimage to an unarguably holy site for a ritual seems appropriate."

Issaroh issued a throaty grumble. "We can talk to them. But since they're nomadic, I'll need to draw you a map of possible locations they might be. It could take some time, because although I've talked to them before, I never took maps on everywhere they said they'd resided."

"Please do." Issaroh rose from the stones, ready to quit their conversation, but Bronwyn had one more question, "What happened at the Battle of Lynnfield?"

Issaroh didn't turn around, but didn't walk away. "I don't know. I haven't asked him about the war, and I don't know if I want to know the answer."

Bronwyn had some time to think back about their conversation in the cave, and thought that if she presented her thoughts in a different way it might lead to more information. "Like I said before, I'm pretty sure Miro thinks he caused the catastrophe there. I don't know how legitimate his concerns are; he probably blames himself for a lot of things that happen, but the coincidence of him being a skilled sorcerer, becoming a magus around the same time, and his guilt lead me to believe that he might bear a sliver of blame. Perhaps he did something to enrage the monster that attacked, or he blames himself because he couldn't save the injured, or he could have imagined the whole thing and it was really a weapon that Rouke deployed. Heck, maybe he wasn't even there at the time and that's the only reason he's alive."

Issaroh crossed one arm across his chest, raised the other, and rested his forehead against his fist. "I think you're right, but I don't think he did it. Perhaps the thing he saw was the weapon Rouke deployed, and they lost control of it. Miro could have undergone his pact with the Ywaigwai trying to stop it, but was tricked just as I was. But just leave it be. The answer isn't important. It won't bring anyone back and it will just hurt Miro more."

"Thank you for being honest," Bronwyn said, not adding anything else and allowing Issaroh to walk back to the library. Bronwyn spent the rest of the day in idle relaxation, not wishing to return to the library until everyone had a chance to decompress without her there. She now had a plan, a concrete one, for how she would save Emestria.

Two weeks later, Miro uncovered the name of the demigod gifted with the cornucopia, Gwyndlyn Garanhir, a child of Marianna, Goddess of oceans, tides, and loyalty, but Miro was still searching for the final resting place of the artifact. And Bronwyn was still waiting on a map from Issaroh on where the Shi'en might be found this time of the year. However, time was running short, and the height of winter was in full swing in Emestria. Clara sent Ferdinand with a missive updating the king on their progress in researching the artifacts, and the one that came back with the bird reassured Bronwyn that the fight between Rouke and Emestria on the Iron Bridge was still a stalemate, but the worry over rations continued. The fact that Emestria had apparently started to let women fight in the war caused concern that King Bryant's words weren't a real indication of how dire things would be soon, but she still had time.

# EPILOGUE



*Two weeks after Defurge's release*

Fria waved her hand over the small, mirrored box she had brought with her, focusing on the image of a woman in steel full-plate armor bracing for a Roukian assault. The woman was at the head of an arrow-type formation, and large tower shields braced for an incoming charge of the Roukian cavalry. But the shields were not of any ordinary variety; the Emestrian steel was covered in a thick coating of ice, hardened by magic to the durability of diamond. The woman, with closely cropped hair obscured, wore a helmet that bore a striking resemblance to the skull of the former spirit guardian, Naani.

"For Emestria!" Jakul—the lieutenant that once served Captain Bronwyn Amyna—yelled as horses tried to break through the formation. Some did, but Emestrian soldiers with spears braced behind the defensive formation thrust their weapons forward, catching many of the horses and riders on gleaming, well-honed tips. Some of the advancing cavalry managed to break through, but for every shielded woman that fell, two more stepped in to replace their fallen comrade. After most of the riders had been incapacitated or slain, a litany of spells sailed toward the crystal shields. Fire, lightning, rocks, and razor-sharp ice rained down. Although some of the women fell, the majority of the spells were deflected by the shields.

"Advance!" Jakul, yelled as an answering volley of spells came from the Emestrian side. The Roukian Spellswords fell back, before a second division let loose their magic, preventing the Emestrians from advancing further. It was a war of attrition, but today was a good day; Emestria was gradually pushing their army across the Iron Bridge, toward southern Emestria. It would take weeks, maybe months until Rouke had to abandon the Iron Bridge entirely.

The Emestrian forces were aided by the narrow confines of the Iron Bridge, where the shield guard was protected on both sides, but once they crossed to the other side, the stalemate would continue. Emestria no longer had the manpower to secure their southern borders.

With a wave of her hand, Fria dismissed the image, instead calling up one of a woman with a large greatsword strapped to her back and long golden hair who sat upon a wall of stone. The quiet tears rolling down her cheek betrayed the strength Bronwyn tried to display, but that was why she was chosen. She could endure.

"It is done; Defurge is free," Fria said to Chivas, who was clad in an all-black uniform, his hair covering and framing his face like a helmet. They stood upon a grassy island in the sky. Trees bordered the clearing to the south and the land dropped off to the north, where the Library of Laevin once floated. The wind rustled the trees at the heart of the miniscule landmass. A light frozen mist travelled down Fria's gown to the grass below, rolling down the sloped surface and falling off the island like a waterfall.

Chivas frowned and asked, "That's what you wanted, right?"

"That's what we wanted," Fria replied. "There was always the possibility that the gem was destroyed while they were fighting."

"But there's still hope?"

Fria brought her right hand up to the ice encrusted socket that used to house her right eye—the Vigilant Eye that could see the fate of mortals. She had sacrificed it to put this plan into motion. "Last I looked, there were many paths that would lead to the destruction of the gem and the preservation of humanity."

Chivas crossed his arms over his chest. "And how many that lead to us having doomed them to death six-hundred years early?"

Fria scowled. "The time to be skeptical of this plan passed long ago. Remember, we agreed to do this, together."

"But so many dead at this point. Dalmarask, Lynnfield, Seketh, and possibly Emestria. Was this gamble really worth it? If we fail, they all die anyway. Think of all those lives we took prematurely because we are too headstrong to accept Laevin's will."

"No, we wanted them to have freedom, to not have their lives be subject to the will of the gods. How many times have you and I watched as nations declared war, and died just so the other gods could determine whose ideals were stronger."

"But Emestria still stands, while Seketh fell," Chivas lamented, clenching his jaw.

"I'm sorry, but one of us had to accept the blame."

"It's not your fault. I should have prepared my people better for the repercussions of our actions. We were the ones that started to put this whole plan into motion. Tricking Seraph to slay her lover so a new god would be born, releasing Raithe even though we knew he would sow destruction, and telling him how to survive absent our power, and be able to create magi. Perhaps if I made more demigods to enhance the number of my people that would be given increased strength like you, or size like

Marianna, Seketh would have survived. But did I deserve to protect my people or have worshippers when we had caused so much death?”

“What is done is done at this point.”

Chivas leaned over Fria’s shoulder to look at the mirrored box as Bronwyn Amyna wiped another stray tear from her cheek. “What chance do they have of success? Your champion is sitting by herself, alone, and weeping. Where is the strength you promised?”

“Strength is born of strife, conflict, and pain. She must be forged as any weapon would be.”

“She almost killed the magus; surely you saw that as part of your plan. And they came back to the library, another hiccup you failed to inform me of. Even I can see the library’s influence start to close around their souls; the magus is on the cusp of completely succumbing to its grasp. And his soul isn’t even being perverted into one of us. The homunculi have already started to feed him the herbs, making him into one of them, one of those things we used to make.”

“That won’t happen. My champion still resists the library’s influence.”

“And the mother, how much longer until she starts to succumb to the library’s influence? She’s staying in Lau’O’Penake’s old room. If she begins to take on the aspects of Lau’O’Penake, then who will she become? The young Lau’O’Penake that acts like a child, or the wise one that she is when she’s at the end of her life?”

“The mother isn’t important; she’s already served her purpose. She brought the magus and the champion together.”

“No, I think she is important. She’s the glue that holds all of them together. When the champion and magus start to drift, she’ll be the one that keeps them together.”

"Are you trying to say you know more about fate than me?" Fria asked, a wry smile on her face.

"And Defurge? He's already started lying and manipulating them."

"This incarnation will be useful; he'll help them when it really matters."

"I don't trust Defurge. I never have, and you shouldn't either. The only good thing about manipulating fate to create him is that it also created Lau'O'Penake, the only one of us that really understands the mortals, that fears death like they do. And Raithe; how could you ask me to create something that vile, and release it upon the world?"

"Raithe was necessary. His destruction was necessary, otherwise the magus wouldn't feel the need to sacrifice for the greater good."

"No, he always would have. His soul is born of too much of Seraph's love. And we're so cruel to him. Perhaps another Ywaigwai could have made him into a magus, one not bent on destruction."

Fria snapped her hand above the box abruptly, causing the image of Bronwyn Amyna to fade into a blue mist. "Why must you always be such a contrarian? We needed the strongest of the Ywaigwai."

"We all didn't have the ability to see and navigate the river of fate. An ability even you now lack. Each new hurdle is another deviation from a possibility you said was likely to happen."

Fria touched the empty socket where her eye once resided again, missing its presence and feeling blind to the future. "We can't intervene as echoes of our former selves. Even if we could, our intervention would be proving Laevin was ultimately right."

"How is this not intervening? How is our role any different at this point? You and I have both sat with the other gods and watched as nations pitted themselves against each other, betting on the eventual victor. We are no better than Laevin, or Kyrie, or any of them."

"Do not worry. I have made contingencies. The old man will surely see the change in his comrades, recognize that something is amiss, and pull them away from the library."

"If he has time," Chivas said, removing a pocket watch to see if he could tell the amount of time a mortal had left, but it spun uselessly, neither showing the decades, years, months, or days a mortal had before the soul departed the body.

Chivas turned away, but Fria touched his forearm and said, "Have faith, they will prevail. Trust in me, husband. Have my plans ever failed before?"

Chivas chuckled. "If they have, it was never around me. We should return. The other gods will get suspicious if we're gone too long." Chivas stepped forward and his body became a black mist that sunk to the ground and dissipated. Fria nodded and did the same, her own body disappearing in a soft-blue haze.

# Afterward

When I originally began this story, it was an idea for a RPG with all my favorite mechanics of old-school 16-bit games. After a significant episode during COVID, I decided to write the story as a novel and found it a much better format for the story I was trying to tell. Magi's Curse started out as a story just for me. After sharing it with others and getting positive reviews, I started considering publishing the work.

I knew that publishing a novel was more than just putting words on pages, but I had no idea what a big endeavor this book would become. I was introduced to the world of beta reading, query letters, developmental editors, copy editors, cover designers, and proof reading. In pursuing publishing, I was exposed to a world that I never knew existed. Throughout the experience, as daunting as it was, there were several voices that encouraged me to keep going.

I'd like to thank my family and friends, both past, present and future, for supporting me on this journey. Out of my beta readers, I'd like to thank Samara Saward, Desh, Maryanne Mare, Brandan R., Mikaela S., and many more I've lost track of over the last three years of editing. I would like to give a very special thanks to Emily Rappaport, my editor, for helping me see my potential as an author and for fostering my skills as a writer.

An even more special thanks goes out to Kelsey. When I started this writing journey, I never thought I would find my own blue-eyed warrior woman. Her strength and perseverance are inspirations to me every day. She is the steady voice encouraging me to keep my butt in the seat and keep working. I hope I can bring the same consistency, encouragement, and inspiration to her for the rest of our lives together.